SARAH'S HOME

BY
VICKY WHEDBEE

This is a work of fiction. The names, characters, and events are either the product of the author's imagination or are used fictitiously. All rights reserved in all media. No part of this book may be used or reproduced without written permission, except in the case of brief quotations embodied in critical articles and reviews.

In this book, there are words that are spelled incorrectly, in an effort to show the reader how they were spoken in the beautiful Smoky Mountain/Appalachian dialect. In addition, there are a few words used that are not well known in the context they were known for in the past.

TABLE OF CONTENTS

Dedication
Table Of Contents
CHAPTER 1 1
CHAPTER 2 13
CHAPTER 3 19
CHAPTER 4 25
CHAPTER 5 35
CHAPTER 6 43
CHAPTER 7 51
CHAPTER 8 57
CHAPTER 9 63
CHAPTER 10 69
CHAPTER 11 77
CHAPTER 12 85
CHAPTER 13 97
CHAPTER 14 105
CHAPTER 15 113
CHAPTER 16 123
CHAPTER 17 131
CHAPTER 18 139
CHAPTER 19 147
CHAPTER 20 155
CHAPTER 21 165
CHAPTER 22 177
CHAPTER 23 183
CHAPTER 24 189
CHAPTER 25 199
CHAPTER 26 209
CHAPTER 27 219
CHAPTER 28 229
CHAPTER 29 237
CHAPTER 30 245
CHAPTER 31 251
CHAPTER 32 259
CHAPTER 33 275
CHAPTER 34 283

DEDICATION

To Mom and Rodney here with me, and Dad in Heaven...

I love you.

CHAPTER 35..289
CHAPTER 36..299
CHAPTER 37..305
CHAPTER 38..313
CHAPTER 39..321
CHAPTER 40..331
CHAPTER 41..339
CHAPTER 42..347
CHAPTER 43..357
CHAPTER 44..371
CHAPTER 45..381
CHAPTER 46..389
CHAPTER 47..395
CHAPTER 48..407
CHAPTER 49..415
CHAPTER 50..421
CHAPTER 51..427
Acknowledgments
Other Books by Vicky Whedbee
Can I Ask A Favor?

CHAPTER 1

Hurricane Hollow, Union County, Tennessee
Summer/Fall, 1955 - Spring, 1956

Faith and Adohy's wedding night was a night of firsts. But not the *firsts* one would typically imagine for a girl at the tender age of fifteen years, and a boy/man barely eighteen. However, though young in years, the two of them had experienced more in their short lives than many souls much older.

In fact, most people lived their whole lives without enduring *any* of what Faith had. How many people could say that they had grown up thinking their mother was their sister? It had been kept a secret that Faith's mother, Sarah Jenkins, was brutally assaulted when she was only fourteen years old. The lack of nearby neighbors in Hurricane Hollow made it possible for Sarah and her parents, Carl and Rebecca Jenkins, to keep the resulting pregnancy under wraps, and then—with the help of the local country doctor—to take Sarah's baby, named Faith, to raise as their own. This selfless act of love for

1

their daughter instantly transitioned them from the role of Faith's grandparents to her parents, and in effect made Faith's mother, Sarah, her sister. It was their hopes that it would give Sarah a chance at a normal life, minus the shame that accompanied the title of unwed mother.

However, no one could have possibly anticipated that the rapist, Zeke Kufner, would return when Faith was only three months old to get his revenge. Intending to kill the entire family, he set the children's bedroom on fire, but his plan was thwarted when he was caught red handed by Carl, and during the fight that ensued, Carl's family were startled awake, enabling them to flee to safety. His wife Rebecca rushed back into the burning home to assist him though, and while the children watched and waited, safely huddled in the shadow of the cornstalks, the house burned to the ground.

After it became clear that their parents were not to be joining them, Sarah fled with the three children, Tommy, age seven, Aubry, age four, and Faith, age three months, through the cornfield to their Papaw Samuel's home, their late father's father.

In addition to coping with the loss of their parents, this tragic twist of fate thrust Sarah back into the roll of mother, not only to her birth daughter, Faith, but to Tommy and Aubry as well. She, Samuel, and the family doctor were now the only living souls who knew she actually *was* Faith's mother, and the plan was to take the secret to their graves. A few years later, the doctor did just that, leaving only Sarah and Samuel to harbor the secret.

But plans have a way of falling to the wayside when unexpected elements are added to the equation. This element came when Faith was fifteen years old in the form of Zeke Kufner. The rapist, arsonist, and murderer, presumed dead in the fire all those years ago, reappeared in Hurricane Hollow, alive and well, in 1955. No one ever really learned what his intentions in coming back were, perhaps to finish his failed attempt at annihilating the family, but when it was brought to Sarah's attention that an unknown older man was seen talking to Faith on more than one occasion, she took matters into her own hands in an effort to keep history from repeating itself.

The night she learned that the man had threatened Faith to "meet him *or else*", Sarah met him in Faith's place, having no idea it was Zeke she was going to encounter. It would prove to be the last attempt to protect her family she would ever make.

That was the night Adohy came out of hiding in Hurricane Hollow. His story, up to this point, was nearly as twisted and tragic as Faith's. At the age of five, he was found under the frozen bodies of his parents by a psychopathic murderer. He spent the next thirteen years of his life being beaten and abused by this man, until he finally escaped and stowed away in the back of a truck belonging to someone who had come to the man to purchase a pig. Unaware of the extra cargo they carried, Virgil and Millicent Thornton, neighbors of the Jenkins, inadvertently brought Adohy to their home in Hurricane Hollow.

Adohy hid out, foraging in their garden for food and sleeping in their barn at night, and in spite of his reprehensible upbringing, he somehow felt the need to repay his benefactors by making minor repairs he ran across that needed tending. When it became clear to the Thornton's that someone was carrying out random, bizarre reparations on their property,

3

they shared that information with the Jenkins—as Millicent and Sarah were best friends—and the quest was on to determine who this seemingly harmless, unknown guest was, that they now knew was sleeping in their barn. After a sighting that revealed he was a young Indian boy, it became a game of sorts, between the Thornton's and the boy, to prove their trust of each other and even more important to the Thornton's, to lure him out of hiding so they could learn of his plight.

During this time he caught sight of Faith and was entranced. He began watching her from afar on her daily visits to the Thornton's to work with the horses. This led to him seeing her safely home each trip, under cover, in the shadows of the forest lined dirt road. He, too, had seen the random visits between Faith and someone in a truck but had not been able to see the driver and assumed it was a neighbor. Faith was fleeing from one of these encounters when she accidentally met face to face with Adohy in the woods for a brief moment.

A few months into this game of cat and mouse with the Thornton's, and secretly escorting Faith to and from, Adohy happened upon the truck speeding away that fateful night, and followed it to the bluff overlooking Norris Lake, where he found a man brutally assaulting a female he feared was the girl he'd become infatuated with.

Flashes of being abused himself filled him with revulsion, and his first reaction was to protect her. He rushed the man from behind and a struggle ensued, taking them perilously close to the ledge, where the man lost his footing in the slick mud and slid over. In the blink of an eye, Adohy switched gears from fighting the man to trying valiantly to save him. As the man clawed at the ground to keep from falling, Adohy lunged forward and grasped his arms to pull

4

him back up to safety. When he looked down into the face of the man whose life he held in his hands, he had the shock of his life realizing it was the man he'd recently escaped from. Instinct almost made him recoil in fear, but despite the terror spreading through his body, he refused to let go. The sweat and the mud from the struggle, however, rendered it impossible for Adohy to maintain his hold, and the man slipped from his grip, falling down the face of the cliff to his death.

Staring in horror into the dark abyss, Adohy realized he had something clutched in his fist. A glance in the moonlight revealed the beaded Indian bracelet his mother had tied around his five year old wrist the night she had died so many years ago. Unbidden images of when the man had taken the bracelet from him invaded his thoughts, and he suppressed a shudder as he slipped the bracelet securely in his pocket, quickly turning his attention to the woman that was lying unconscious in the mud.

Seeing her face in the moonlight, the initial surge of relief that coursed through his veins was drowned when he recognized her not as the girl he'd been watching, but a family member of hers. He gently scooped the woman up and ran with her to her home. Rapping intently on the door to alert her family, Adohy placed her in the arms of the man that answered, then fled.

Tommy rushed inside with her, laying her unconscious body on the couch and the family gathered round her. A short time later she woke, but it was with her last breath that she asked Samuel to reveal the secret they had kept guarded for so many years, then she succumbed to her injuries.

All of this was more than any *normal* person would be expected to withstand over the course of an *entire* lifetime, but as unbelievable and astonishing as it was, it seemed as though all the forces of nature conspired to bring Adohy and Faith's young lives together in full circle. Because the man who fell to his death when Adohy was trying to save the woman, was not only the man who he'd recently escaped from, but Faith's father, Zeke Kufner. And the woman was Faith's mother, Sarah Jenkins.

A few times over the course of events above, Faith and Adohy's paths had crossed briefly, but it had only taken a second to make a lasting impression. The two of them connected immediately on a level of pure trust that few acquire even after *years* of intimacy.

In fact, after Sarah's death, Faith blamed herself and fell into a deep depression, to the point her *own* life was on the line. It was Adohy who inadvertently pulled her back from the abyss by letting her pull *him* from the sanctity of the forest, and they had been together ever since.

Virgil and Millicent Thornton soon after adopted Adohy legally, giving him a name and a new family, after searching in vain for his Cherokee relatives.

Faith and Adohy shared a bond unlike anything anyone had ever seen, but the night of their wedding brought them even closer. Though their wedding day had been magical, as it drew to a close, Adohy's nerves peaked and ebbed, threatening to make him sick to his stomach. Try as he might, he couldn't remember the last time he'd slept in a bed, never mind inside a house. The fear of feeling confined or trapped, sleeping indoors, was unsettling. Up to that day, the closest he'd come was a cot on Virgil and Millicent's front porch. He tried to put his mind at ease by recalling his first night on the cot and how he'd been astonished at the difference of it compared to the barn floor, and the pillow that was a luxury he'd not known what to do with.

Glancing at Faith, he remembered that now, unlike then, he was not alone, and gathering his courage, extinguished the lantern and disrobed. Lying down on the bed, he couldn't help but marvel anew at the softness of it, compared to the cot. As his eyes adjusted to the darkness of the room he could just make out Faith standing on her side of the bed, the glow of her white gauzy nightgown subtly illuminating the soft features of her face, and a peacefulness washed over him.

Faith was in awe of his dark silhouette and his sleek black hair fanning across the pillow, stark against the white sheets. If she was nervous she gave no indication as he held his hand out to her. She took it readily, and climbed in the bed to lie with her head on his shoulder. He pulled her closer, his lips pressing a soft kiss on her brow.

His heart pounded beneath her hand that lay splayed across his chest, and she wondered if he could detect hers, snuggled against his side. They were beating in sync until she slowly moved her hand down across his taut stomach causing his pulse to quicken, and she was amazed as hers sped up to match his again. They had learned to communicate quite well with words over the past few months, and when he rolled onto his side to face her, they found a whole new way to express their love for each other where no words were needed.

~~§~~

Months had passed since that night and now Adohy rarely thought about the cold lonely nights he'd spent sleeping outdoors or in barns. He had too much to look forward to, and wouldn't waste any time on bad memories. All he wanted now was to make new ones with Faith. Everything was bright and new with Faith by his side. Even the daily chores were more an adventure and fun, rather than like work.

Though their workday had lengthened with the building of Sarah's Home, they didn't grow tired of spending every moment together. If one had to be away from the other for even a few moments, it felt like a physical part of their self was missing. Fortunately, there was usually no need for them to be far away from each other for long.

Spring was just around the corner. In a week or so Sarah's Home would be done, and they would begin building their own little home. It had been their decision to wait, both feeling Sarah's Home was a priority. There were too many people that would benefit from it being finished as soon as possible, and it was a lot bigger than their home would be, therefore taking a lot more time, so once the property had been cleared, the construction started on it.

Building Sarah's Home had been a labor of love by the community funded by Millicent, as a tribute to Sarah. It was her desire to give those in need, whether child or adult, a place to go when they needed it. A safe haven from abuse, a foster home, or a place to convalesce.

Fred Murdock, Millicent's connection from the State Department of Indian Affairs during Adohy's adoption, had been a crucial link in getting through all of the bureaucratic red tape, which expedited things tremendously. As soon as the construction was complete and a final inspection done by the State of Tennessee, Sarah's Home would be open and ready for its new inhabitants.

It was during the adoption process that Fred came to learn of the help needed at the Beeler' s General Store and Mill, and needing a change of pace from the stress of the government job, accepted the job, sight unseen. Oppy Beeler owned and ran the store for years, until she took in a boy named Caleb, who had lost his parents. Caleb was a bit slow for his age but with her love and guidance, they discovered his ability not only to understand the Bible with ease but to retain the passages, and he grew from a bullied shy boy, into an ordained preacher and counselor for those in Hurricane Hollow. The years however caught up with Oppy, making it increasingly harder for Caleb to run the store, the mill, preach on Sunday, and tend to Oppy's every need. With the news that Fred Murdock was looking for a less emotionally challenging job, Caleb was happy to extend an offer of the job with room and board, which was graciously accepted.

No one was more surprised than Caleb to learn that "Fred" Murdock was not a man, as the name implied, when she arrived to begin her new life. With some adjusting to their living arrangements, Fred quickly proved to be a life saver at the store and helping with Oppy, but it was still too much to run the store, the mill, and the deliveries, so after much consideration, Oppy would become the first patient to move in to Sarah's Home. In just the short time since Fred had arrived,

Oppy's memory had deteriorated to the point that Faith was the only one she showed any sign of recognition with most days. No one was sure if she truly knew who Faith was or if there was just something about Faith that simply resonated with Oppy, but she was at peace around her and that was the important thing.

Oppy's room was almost complete and being decorated with items from her own room, so the transition would be as smooth as possible. The final items would be moved in on the day she was moved, to prevent her from noticing anything awry.

In the beginning, Millicent, Evelyn, and Faith would be the daytime staff, with help from Aubry limited, as she was still teaching, in spite of being due to have the baby at any time. Two other nurses had been hired to work overnight, until more occupants arrived.

Aubry had been grooming Evelyn to take over teaching for a few weeks after she had the baby, since Evelyn lived next door to the school. Then if everything went as planned, she would take the baby to school with her until the school year ended in only a handful of weeks.

~~§~~

On Saturday, March 3rd, 1956, Caleb finished the deliveries and closed the store early. It was time to take Oppy to Sarah's Home. Emotions threatened to overcome him as the time drew near, despite the days and weeks, *months* even, of preparation to make the move. Tears welled in his eyes, as he

10

approached her on the premise of going for a ride. She'd been at the store with Fred, while Tommy and Horace transferred the last contents of her bedroom to Sarah's Home. All that was left to make the transition complete was Oppy herself.

"Hey, Oppy!' Caleb said, approaching her, feigning excitement. "Watcha say we go fer a lil ride?"

It was a gamble that could go either way. At times she demanded to stay put, other times she lit up at the prospect of going for a spin. Caleb held his breathe as she pondered his request. It would make this so much more difficult if she refused. Much to his relief it was only a second before she understood what he'd asked her, and the light in her eyes as she looked at him gave him her answer! She attempted to stand on her own, but he stopped her, reminding her that she could stay as she was in her wheelchair and he could just roll her out to the car. She wasn't immobile, but the treks to the store from the house, and vice versa, were becoming problematic and took such a toll on her, they had gotten the chair to prevent any undue exhaustion and injury. Once they arrived at their destination, she was encouraged to walk around with supervision, to maintain the strength in her legs.

Fred held the front door open for Caleb to wheel Oppy through, closing and locking it behind them. She ran and opened the passenger door of her car just as they approached it. Caleb assisted Oppy inside, then folded her chair and placed it in the trunk, while Fred shut Oppy's door and climbed in the back. Once in the car, she glanced out the back window and her heart constricted when she saw Caleb wiping his eyes. She murmured a prayer to the Lord for him to give Caleb the strength and courage he needed to get through this difficult task, and watched as he finally took a deep breath and squared his shoulders. Then he walked around, slid in the driver's seat, and they were off.

Rather than driving straight to Sarah's Home, Caleb drove around the area in closer proximity to the store, not sure if or when she'd get the opportunity to see it again. He promised himself, that if she was able, he'd see to it that this wouldn't be her last time.

He glanced over at her. She seemed content, the edges of her mouth turned up in a slight smile. "Do you know where we are, Oppy?" he asked, gently.

Exasperation was evident when she answered, "Why shore!" Then, with a lilt in her voice, she proudly added, "We're where I growed up!"

Fred reached up from the back seat to pat her on the shoulder in congratulations. "That's right, Oppy!" she said. Clearly it was one of her better days.

Happy for her, a smile spread across Caleb's face, but it faded when he looked back at her and saw a tear run down her cheek.

CHAPTER 2

To say the move went off without a hitch would have been a stretch, considering when Caleb pulled up to Sarah's Home, Oppy decided she wasn't up for visiting. It took a bit of persuading to get her out of the vehicle and into her wheelchair, but by then Faith came out to greet them and her aversion was forgotten. She was preoccupied for a while taking a tour around and then inside the home, but suddenly she decided she was ready to go back to her own home. She put up a bit of a fuss again, when instead of being wheeled toward the front door she was taken in the other direction, but became happy as a lark when she was wheeled through the doorway and miraculously transported into her own bedroom. The machinations of the transition were lost on her.

In spite of the couple of hurdles, everyone agreed the move was a huge success! Sarah's Home's first occupant was official!

Caleb and Fred stayed with her for a few hours under the ruse of helping her get settled, but their reluctance to leave her was written all over their faces. In fact, she seemed to be more comfortable than they were, perfectly at ease in *her* room. While they fidgeted and fussed, pointing out to her where her things were, their nervousness palpable, she looked at them like *they'd* lost their minds. Of course she knew where her stuff was.

Since the progression of her illness she'd acquired a strange pastime that would keep her engrossed for hours. No one was quite sure what prompted her fascination with it, but if given multiples of any item, for instance a deck of cards, a jar of buttons, or a handful of coins, she would sit and count them over and over, sorting and stacking as she went. Then she would start over. At times it was hard to get her to stop to eat, bathe, or get some exercise.

Once Oppy was seated at the writing table in her room, immersed in counting and stacking her buttons, Faith took the opportunity to whisk Caleb and Fred out and put their minds at ease. Over a cup of coffee she gently reaffirmed all the reasons that this was the best decision they could make for Oppy's security and well-being.

Caleb and Fred remained dubious, until finally, at the mention of the twenty four hour care with nurses on site, their guilt ridden expressions began to wane, replaced with assurance.

With their duress temporarily allayed, they decided it was time to share some news they had kept under wraps from everyone.

It had been an answer to Caleb's prayers when Fred walked into the store. That wasn't news though. Everyone was aware of *that* blessing. What they didn't know was there was another unrequited yearning that Caleb had in his heart for years.

As he prepared to break the news, images of how it all came to pass flashed through his memory. He recalled how his knees had gone weak when he saw Fred for the first time, and how he couldn't believe the *she* was *the* Fred, coming to his aid with the store. That had been an unexpected blessing, but it also created a huge conflict in his principles. It had been agreed, prior to her acceptance and arrival, that as part of the compensation for working at the store, room and board was included in his and Oppy's home. But that was when he'd thought Fred was a *man*. With her a single woman, he could not in good conscience take a chance at putting her reputation at risk. She assured him that under the circumstances and with his standing in the community, surely there would be no defamation to either his, nor her, character, and while his head wanted to justify it, his heart simply could not.

He'd set up a cot in the back room of the store, and retired there each night after supper and seeing Oppy to bed. He went out of his way to share his sleeping arrangements to everyone he ran into, in an effort to spare any rumors or innuendo.

He and Fred were like soul mates from the beginning. She jumped right in, learning the procedure with ease and they worked together seamlessly. Though they learned a lot about each other during working hours, in the evenings during and after their meal, their time together was less disjointed and more conducive to carrying on complete conversations.

15

As Fred grew comfortable with Caleb and Oppy, she eventually confided in them that the reason she began to work with children in need was because she herself had been one. She'd been orphaned at the age of eight, when her parents had gotten killed in a car accident, and she'd had no other relatives able to take her in. Her voice quivered when she relayed how she'd lost everything that day. Her family, her childhood, and most of her belongings, including her cherished doll house that her parents had just given her the Christmas before they'd died. After telling them about her beloved parents, she tried to bring herself out of her depressing reverie, by describing to them her beautiful doll house.

As days turned into weeks, then into months, their rapport developed into a deep meaningful friendship, and eventually into love. Caleb's heart still skipped a beat at his good fortune when he thought of the day he asked her to be his wife.

It was Valentine's Day, just about a month prior, and also one of Oppy's good days. That morning, he'd presented both the women he loved, heart shaped boxes of chocolate and endearing greeting cards. Later that day, he left Oppy and Fred at the store to make his deliveries, however he slipped back to the house, to prepare a surprise for Fred.

That evening, they closed the store and they made their way to the house, Caleb wheeling Oppy in her chair. Once inside, as Fred lit a lamp in the kitchen to prepare supper, Caleb positioned Oppy at the kitchen table. When the room was illuminated, both women gasped in surprise at what they saw.

On the table stood a beautiful white Victorian doll house, complete with lattice work and flower boxes. It was two stories high and the back was completely open for ease in the placement of furnishings.

"Well, I lawd, aint it purty!" Oppy exclaimed, from her wheelchair situated between them.

"It's *gorgeous*!" Fred amended, looking at Caleb for explanation.

"It's fer you, Fred," he said softly in answer. After hearing about her dollhouse and how much it meant to her, he'd spent hours every night after he retired to the back room of the store, painstakingly recreating the house she'd described, from the handmade shingles on the roof to the polished hard wood planks on the floor.

Fred's brows rose in surprise, her eyes cutting from him to the house, then back to him. "For me?" she questioned in disbelief.

"Yes," Caleb confirmed, unable to tear his gaze from hers.

Oppy quietly listened to the exchange, her head swiveling back and forth at them on either side of her. After a moment she looked back to the dollhouse and said, "That shore is a funny lookin door knocker though."

Her remark got Fred's attention, and leaning in to get a closer look, she noticed the plaque over the front door that read Mr. & Mrs. Groaner, and the wedding ring in place of a knocker. Her lips parted slightly in stunned amazement, then slowing straightening, her questioning eyes found his again.

For the first time in his life he wasn't nervous and unsure. His love for her gave him courage. A confidence he'd never known. "Will you marry me, Fred?" he asked, confirming her suspicions.

A smile spread across her face. "Yes, I'll marry you, Caleb!"

They leaned to each other for a kiss.

Still seated between them in her wheelchair, Oppy said, "Kin we eat now?"

~~§~~

Forcing his thoughts from that day back to the present, Caleb nodded to Fred giving her the honor of making the announcement.

When everyone present was gathered around, she said, "Caleb and I got married!" While congratulations rang out, she proudly turned to Caleb for him to officially slip the ring on her finger. They explained that with everyone so busy trying to get Sarah's Home finished and ready to open, they'd just had a private ceremony with Preacher Loveday a few weeks earlier, but now they wanted to celebrate their union with everyone, and would make another announcement Sunday after church.

CHAPTER 3

Since it had been a while since the community had a good old fashioned covered dish supper after church, and they had good reason to celebrate with the barn raising of sorts completing Sarah's Home and now the marriage of Caleb and Fred, Millicent made the rounds inviting everyone to come to the Home that Sunday. The invitation was made under the guise for everyone to see the completed project, and Caleb and Fred could surprise them with their announcement then. Plus there was much more room in the yard for the community to celebrate, and that way the staff and the Home's occupants could also participate in the festivities.

The weather cooperated splendidly for the event. It was sunny, in the mid-sixties with puffy white clouds floating around like helium filled balloons. Some of the kids were stretching their imaginations envisioning shapes and images out of the ever shifting clouds, while others frolicked around as the women spread out the array of food, and the men put out chairs and warmed up their instruments to play.

Though the home had only been open a week, there were now two new occupants in addition to Oppy. With the arrival of the second resident, Millicent quickly realized she was going to have to carefully guard her heartstrings. It was a sweet blonde haired, blue eyed little girl named Tenley. Millicent felt her heart constrict at first glance. With the exception of Tenley's birth defect, the resemblance to the few pictures she'd seen of Sarah, at that age, was uncanny. Even Faith and Evelyn thought so, and had mentioned it to Tommy and Samuel, who had gotten to see for themselves today.

Tenley was four years old and had been born with a cleft lip and palate, which was more commonly known as hair lip. Few people knew how to care for a newborn with the debilitating deformity and as a result, some children didn't survive. Other factors such as ignorance, as well as superstition also came into play. The earliest documented history of cleft lip is based on a combination of religion, superstition, invention and charlatanism. While Greeks ignored their existence, Spartans and Romans would kill these children as they were considered to harbor evil spirits. Over the years, certain cultures still believed the deformity to be a sign the child was possessed. The latter superstition, for better or worse, ultimately began Tenley's journey to Sarah's Home. She was born in Kentucky to the parents of nine other children. Her parents hadn't given her a name, and by the time she was passed around, ending up at the hospital, no one knew even her surname, just that she was number ten of the children born to her parents. It was rumored that she was called Baby Ten by the staff for a while and from that the name Tenley was derived.

Neither the mother or father had any schooling which unfortunately had been passed down to all nine of their children. Perhaps it was due to their ignorance, or more likely, their ridiculous superstition, but the moment their baby was born and they saw her face, she was cast out like dirty dishwater. The mid-wife that had assisted in the birthing, had no choice but to take her away, but unable to care for another child herself, the baby was passed off from family to family. Though each family that took her in did so with good intentions, being unfamiliar with cleft palates, and the difficulty of feeding a baby with the deformity, they continued passing her off until, near death, she was taken to a doctor, who, realizing the gravity of the situation, took her to East Tennessee Children's Hospital in Knoxville. There, she was stabilized and nursed for the first year of her life, having surgery after surgery. She became a beloved fixture at the hospital and some say Tenley's parents' ignorance of her deformity had been a blessing, for had they not sent her away, she surely would have died.

After a year, she was moved to another facility, until a home was located that could tend to her continued medical needs. Due to the issues with feeding and many surgeries, she was much smaller and less advanced than most children her age. When she was a little over two years old the family that had been caring for her had another child of their own, and the extra care Tenley required was too much for them to continue with. So again, Tenley was sent from home to home, until it became apparent she was too fragile to be around even other children her own age, much less older, more physically active or aggressive children.

She was three years old, homeless, tiny, and barely walked or talked when word got around of the opening of Sarah's Home. The fact that the home was new with no other children in residence as yet, and the specialized care she would receive immediately, made it a perfect choice, and more correctly, the only option available.

Millicent couldn't believe that she and Virgil had gone so long yearning for a child, and now they not only had Adohy, but this little girl, who had been shuffled around for three years before finding her way to them. Sure, she realized that Tenley had been sent to the Home, not to her and Virgil, but the fact remained that she had no family, none that accepted her anyway, and if Millicent's heart had any say, she suspected Tenley would soon become the newest member of the Thornton family. Such was why she knew she would have to learn to control her maternal instincts. It wasn't feasible to think they could legally adopt every orphan that would grace their doorstep. And though Sarah's Home was created to help the helpless, and a loving tribute to Sarah, Millicent never dreamed until now that it was going to be a culmination of all of her and Virgil's thought to be unanswered prayers.

For now Tenley resided in Sarah's Home, as Faith and Adohy were still in Virgil and Millicent's guest room, not to mention the fact that Millicent had, as yet, to let Virgil in on where her heart was leading her.

The third new occupant was Chalmer. He was five years old and born to a young unwed girl who put him up for adoption in hopes of giving him a better life than she could. He was a little chunky, and when he smiled, dimples appeared on both cheeks. He had reddish brown hair with a sprinkling of freckles across his nose, and there was a little gap between his

22

front teeth. With times as hard as they were in rural Appalachia, he stayed in the orphanage until he was three, before a foster home took him in. But Chalmer was on the precocious side and a year later the foster parents threw in the towel when he slipped off one day and wasn't found for several nerve wracking hours until he came casually strolling back down a mountain side with a cork gun slung over his shoulder saying he'd been bear hunting. It had been the straw that broke the camel's back.

From there, he went from home to home until, out of options, he ended up at Sarah's Home. So far, he'd been a little rambunctious but between Virgil, Adohy, and Faith, they had managed to keep him occupied enough with the animals to keep him out of trouble. Their biggest concern was taking care to see that he and Tenley were kept separated, or closely monitored, when they were together. He was a little too rough and tumble for frail Tenley.

Chalmer was making the rounds now, thrilled to be meeting all the kids from the community. Out of the population of about one hundred fifty from Hurricane Hollow, or "Holler" as they called it, almost fifty percent were children under the age of eighteen. Narrowing that down to children between the ages of five to fifteen, made it approximately thirty kids. Reducing it even further to kids his age, give or take a year, left about fourteen boys and girls. Chalmer thought the possibilities of making some mischief today was endless and he couldn't wait to get started!

CHAPTER 4

When everything was set up, Caleb called for everyone to assemble so he could make his and Fred's announcement and say a blessing so they could eat.

"Ever'one! If I could get y'all's attention here fer just a minute, we'll get this here gatherin' underway!"

All the parents rounded their children up, and everyone drew nearer to hear Caleb. When they were ready, Caleb addressed them.

"I have a coupla things I wanna say, and then y'all kin eat!"

There was some laughter and a few kids clapped, ready to dig in! They'd been drooling over all the desserts just waiting to be eaten.

"First off, y'all shore done a good job on Sarah's Home. I, like most ever'one a y'all, knew Sarah well, an' I think she'd be plum tickled! I'm sure she's up there now, a-lookin' down over us with a big ole smile on her face. An' that smile is jes gonna keep on a-getting' bigger with ever' person that comes to call Sarah's Home *their* home."

There were nods of affirmation, and a few pats on the shoulder for Virgil and Millicent, who had Tenley in her arms and tears of happiness in her eyes.

Caleb asked, "Fred, can you join me here a minute?" She stepped up to his side, and he continued. "Y'all know Fred has been such a blessin' to me at the store and with Oppy," he stated, nodding toward Oppy. "But what most a ya *don't* know is somehow, some way, the good Lord decided to bless me even more by convincin' Fred to be my wife!" he exclaimed, holding Fred's hand up to show her wedding ring. Shout's of approval and jubilation rang out as the couple stood beaming at the croud.

A few of the younger kids were getting bored with all the talk. They just wanted to get it over with so the eating could begin. It was *possible* that Chalmer was instigating some of the unrest with a few of the kids. He'd pulled the pony tail of the girl standing on one side of him, and then retrieved a live earthworm from his pocket and dropped it down the shirt of the boy standing on his other side. The boy squirmed and fidgeted, trying to get the worm out, earning a stern look from his mother. But Chalmer stood straight-faced, seemingly hanging on to Caleb's every word. Samuel Jenkins knew better. He'd seen the whole thing, and was on to Chalmer's antics.

Samuel Jenkins was grandfather to the Home's namesake, Sarah, as well as her siblings, Tommy and Aubry, and great-grandfather to Faith. Having been a young boy himself and then raising his own son, Carl, and then, Tommy, he was pretty well versed in things little boys could get into. He decided to keep an eye on Chalmer. Something about him reminded Samuel of himself, and he smiled at the memories.

Caleb was through with the announcements now and ready to say the blessing. "Lord, we thank ya fer givin' us this beautiful day to get tagether with our family an' friends, and fer givin' us this glorious bounty to share in yer name! Amen!"

"Amen," resounded from everyone, most loudly from some of the more restless kids.

The children were tended to first. Once they had gotten plates of food and settled down to eat, the adult made the rounds. There was fried chicken; pot roast; sliced ham; pork chops; most any vegetable you could imagine, prepared in a variety of ways; cornbread; sliced white bread; rolls; and too many kinds of pies, cakes, cobblers, and cookies to count.

While it was true times were hard for most everyone, they all had something they'd grown, canned, raised, or baked that they could contribute when everyone came together. It all made for quite the spread. It wasn't often they each could have just about anything their hearts desired all in one meal.

Samuel was a bit perplexed with Chalmer. He watched the boy as they ate. He was plump, indicating he ate well before coming to be with them. But on the other hand, he seemed overwhelmed with the food, going so far as to steal tidbits off other kids' plates when they weren't looking. Perhaps it was just the number of *choices* he had today that he wasn't used to.

When everyone had eaten, those who brought instruments began warming up. Tommy and Horace helped

Virgil carry over a couple of sheets of new stuff, called plywood they had left over from building Sarah's Home. It was going to be used on Faith and Adohy's house, but in the meantime it could double as a dance floor. As soon as they got it laid down, a few men got up to buck dance. Then others joined in, and the celebration was in full swing.

With the excitement, Samuel lost track of Chalmer for a bit. Wondering what he was up to, Samuel searched him out, only to find him with a little magnifying glass, honing a ray of sunlight to a point on a little girl's frilly church dress. Without pausing to wonder where Chalmer had gotten a magnifying glass, he quickly made his way over to interrupt the process, and in the nick of time. There was already a little burnt pin spot visible on the fabric.

"Son!" Samuel called out, causing Chalmer to jump and drop the magnifying glass. He looked frightened, which made Samuel feel a little bad for startling him, but he needed to talk to the little feller. While some of his stunts were harmless and maybe even cute, he needed to realize that some of his actions could be very serious and have detrimental ramifications.

"How 'b-bout you an' me g-get ta know one anuther? My names S-Samuel. Whut's yers?" Samuel asked, gently but firmly.

It was something in Samuel's tone that made Chalmer decide that his first instinct to run may not be such a good idea. Instead, not sure whether he was in trouble or not, he timidly replied, not recognizing his own voice. "Chalmer." It sounded more like a question.

"Watcha say we g-go have a seat over there?"
Samuel asked, needing to sit down. He reached out to take
Chalmer's hand, and as they turned, he scooped up the
magnifying glass and dropped it in his pocket. He'd figure out
where it came from later.

Samuel led Chalmer back to where he'd been sitting.
The chair beside his was occupied now, so he pulled Chalmer
up onto his lap. The music was loud and everyone not dancing
was clapping and singing along, watching the people cut loose
on the makeshift dance floor. Chalmer glanced around
nervously, still not sure what to expect. If past experiences of
being caught doing something wrong were any indication, it
wouldn't be good. He might be packing his things up again.

Samuel was glad for all the merriment going on
around them. He could talk to Chalmer without drawing any
undue attention. "So, ya reckon we k-kin have us a talk, man ta
man?" Samuel asked in Chalmer's ear.

Chalmer responded by looking up at Samuel, still a
bit unsure, but intrigued by the idea of having a man-to-man
conversation. A timid smile tugged at the corners of his mouth.
Then he puffed up a bit and nodded.

Samuel took a deep breath and said, "Ya know, a
long t-time ago, I's just a b-boy 'bout yer age."

Chalmer's brows knit together doubtfully. "Ya was?"
he asked, clearly dubious.

Samuel pursed his lips trying to keep from smiling at
Chalmer's skepticism, and nodded his head in confirmation.
"Yep, shore was. Pert near same exact age, 'cept'n I d-didn't
have no other youngins around to p-play with." He glanced

29

around at the kids running and laughing nearby. "An' didn't have m-much in the way a t-toys neither."

Chalmer's brows rose now, imagining no kids *or* toys.

"So sometimes I'd p-pretend I's a lonesome ole p-prospector out ridin the range, looking fer gold—"

"Whut's a perspecter?" Chalmer interrupted, his nose wrinkled up.

"They's somebody that g-goes 'round lookin' fer g-gold. Ya know whut gold is?" Samuel asked.

Chalmer shook his head.

"It's a m-metal that's in the g-ground an' worth a lotta money, an ye k-kin make stuff outta it, like jewelry an' things." While Chalmer pondered his answer, Samuel went on. "Anyhow, I's walkin' round lookin' fer g-gold one day, pert near dark, an all of a sudden I seen this rabbit run inta a hole up in fronta me. I hadn't never seen a rabbit go in a hole afore, so I sneaked up real quiet like, an' sat down an' waited ta see if'n it'd come out again, if it thought I's gone—"

"Did it?" Chalmer interrupted again, too anxious to wait.

Samuel nodded. "It did, an' as I sat an' watched, four little b-baby b-bunnies come out too—"

"Did ya ketch 'em?" Chalmer cut in once more.

Samuel patiently continued his story, happy to have Chalmer's full attention. "Naw, I jes watched 'em fer a while, scamperin' round lookin' fer food."

Chalmer seemed disappointed that Samuel hadn't tried to catch the bunnies. "That's it?" he asked, wondering why Samuel would bother to tell him such a boring story. "So whut'd ya do then?"

"Well, I went b-back ever' day to watch 'em, and ever' day them babies'd get a little b-bigger and bigger. They was cute little fellers. Then one day I's sittin' there a-waitin' an' I had me a coupla match-sticks I'd took outta my mama's match holder. Well, I's jes messin' 'round with 'em, I didn't rightly know how to light 'em no way, an' accidently struck one up. It flared up an' scared me like, so I dropped it, and afore I knew it, it had took off to burnin' the grass. I took off a-runnin' cause I j-jes knew I's g-gonna get in a heap a trouble."

Chalmer looked enthralled and sympathetic at once. He knew the feeling well. "Did ya?"

"Get in trouble?" Samuel asked.

Chalmer nodded.

"Naw, I waited an' w-waited, 'bout got sick fer the w-worryin', but no one ever said nuthin' that whole night. Next day, soon as I could, I sneaked back over to where it'd happened." He paused, thinking back to that day.

Chalmer couldn't stand it. He *had* to know what happened. "Was it all burned up?" he asked breathlessly.

Samuel nodded his head. "Yeah, a b-big area was all burned up. Don't rightly know whut s-stopped it from a-burnin' the whole m-mountain up, but thank g-goodness it didn't."

When he didn't say anything for a few seconds, Chalmer again wondered what Samuel was telling him this for. For a minute he'd thought it was going to be exciting, but it wasn't turning out to be. After a beat he asked, "Is that it?" with a hint of disappointment in his tone.

"Naw, that ain't it," Samuel answered. "Ya see, I went b-back that evenin' ta see the bunnies, but they never come out. So I went the next d-day an' waited again, b-but they never showed."

"Maybe they come out when ya wasn't there?" Chalmer suggested.

"No, they come out 'bout the same time ever' night. I waited two more days, an' I ne'er did see 'em, so then next time I took me my mama's little spade—ya know what a spade is?" he stopped to ask Chalmer.

"Nope," Chalmer replied.

"It's a tool ya use ta d-dig in the ground with, like a shovel, but this'n was smaller. My mama used it in her g-garden. Anyhow, I took that spade and I started ta diggin' up that hole that the bunnies was in. I dug an' dug, but I finally got ta the end of the hole."

"Was the bunnies there?"

"Yeah, they was there. They were huddled up there with their m-mama, but they was all d-dead. All 'cause a me a-lightin that fire." Samuel said solemnly.

"They'd burned up?" Chalmer asked quietly.

"Naw, they wudn't b-burned up, they still looked as c-cute as they ever did. I don't rightly know if it was the heat from the f-fire or the smoke that killed 'em."

They were both quiet for a moment, contemplating.

Then Samuel said, "The reason I told ya that, son, was cause I wanted to show ya that there's consequences ta yer actions."

Chalmer wasn't sure what *son* meant. He'd called him that twice now. Come to think of it, he didn't know what conse. . .conse. . .that *other* word meant either, but before he could ask, Samuel went on.

"Ya see, I seen whatcha was a-doin with the magnifying glass over there. You pert near burnt a whole in that little girl's dress, and it coulda' started on fire. . ." He hesitated, to let those words sink in. He could see the wheels turning in Chalmer's mind. The boy may have been only five, but Samuel suspected that he was a little wiser than anyone realized. When the gravity of what could have happened set in, he looked up at Samuel with rounded eyes, speechless for the first time.

His point made, Samuel reached into his pocket and pulled out the magnifying glass, holding it out to Chalmer.

Chalmer looked at it, then up at Samuel, confused. "Yer givin it back ta me?" he asked in disbelief.

"I am," Samuel answered. "I trust ya with it. Ya know now it ain't fer b-burnin' stuff, only fer lookin' at stuff up close like."

Chalmer took it, turning it over and over in his palm, wondering if this was some kind of trick.

33

Samuel lifted Chalmer from his lap and set him back down on the ground. "Run along now an' make ya some friends ta play with!" he said.

Chalmer smiled and quickly started off before Samuel changed his mind.

Samuel hollered, "Hey, Chalmer?"

Chalmer stopped and looked back. Dang it! He'd just *known* it was a trick!

Samuel said, "They might like ya b-better if'n ya don't pull their hair or p-put worms down the back a-their shirts!"

Chalmer considered Samuel a moment, then a big grin spread from ear to ear, and he ran off!

CHAPTER 5

The festivities went on for several more hours. After working up appetites again playing music, dancing, and socializing, people went back for seconds and thirds until all the food was gone. Samuel considered his talk with Chalmer all afternoon and concluded that while he was confident that he'd gotten through to him the dangers of what he'd been doing, it was in his best interest to let Virgil and Millicent in on the situation.

Afterward, he was glad he did. They were able to put his mind to rest as to where Chalmer had gotten the magnifying glass in the first place. It turned out it was a prize from a box of Cracker Jacks. So the only thing still in question was how he'd known to use it in the manner he was, but Samuel hoped the issue would never arise again. They agreed that, given Chalmers history, maybe this approach, using positive reinforcement rather than taking the magnifying glass away and punishing him, would reap better results.

It seemed their theory was put to test the very next morning. Around four-thirty a.m. as Evelyn was cooking breakfast, Tommy and Samuel were sitting at the table having coffee, and they heard a thump that sounded as if it came from the front porch. Molly, the family's Beagle, lying on the floor between the two of them, raised her head at the noise, too. They exchanged questioning glances, but chalked it up to the wind.

Then they heard it again. Tommy decided to go investigate. Opening the front door he was surprised to find Chalmer standing there, barefoot, hands in his pockets. He looked over Chalmer's head out in the yard, expecting to see someone who had accompanied him, finding no one.

"Well, hey there lil buddy! Whut kin I do fer ya?" Tommy asked.

Peeking around Tommy inside the house, Chalmer said, "I's wunderin' if me an Samuel could have us anuther man-ta-man talk." He looked up to Tommy then, hopeful.

Suppressing a grin, Tommy answered, "I 'spect he's got time ta talk ta ya. Come on in an' let's see." He ushered Chalmer in the door glancing around once more for anyone else nearby.

Entering the kitchen, Samuel was surprised to see Chalmer coming back with Tommy.

Answering his questioning expression, Tommy announced, "Found this lil feller wantin' to have a man-ta-man with ya, Papaw."

Samuel looked past the two of them, and before he could ask, Tommy said, "It's jes him."

Molly's tail started wagging when she saw the little boy. She loved kids. But the effort was just too much for her to get up. She'd been just a puppy when Tommy picked her out of a litter of beagles when he was seven years old and she'd been their beloved pet since then, but her time was drawing near.

"Mornin', Chalmer!" Samuel said in acknowledgment, as though it wasn't unusual for him to be there. The fact that he was alone, pretty much told him that no one knew he was there, and to put him on the spot by asking would only give him the opening to tell a lie. He wanted to avoid that if possible.

"Ya had ya some breakfast yet?" he asked instead.

"Nope, not yet," Chalmer replied, glancing at Evelyn, licking his lips.

"Well, have a seat," Evelyn said, pulling out a chair, "and we'll fix ya right up. How do ya like your eggs?"

"Bloody," he stated, matter of fact.

She glanced back, brows knit, wondering if she'd misunderstood.

"I think he means runny yolks,' Samuel suggested, and Chalmer nodded.

"That's what I figured, I just never heard anyone call it that before," she said, her stomach turning a little at the reference.

She cooked them like he asked, and to go with the eggs he wanted sliced white bread with the crust pulled off. He ate several slices that he dunked in the egg yolk, sopping up every drop but refusing to eat the egg whites. Then he had a buttered biscuit with jelly, and a glass of sweet milk.

When they finished breakfast, Tommy headed out to work, but he mouthed that he would go let Virgil and Millicent know that Chalmer was there, so they wouldn't be worried. Samuel nodded.

"So, I hear ya needed ta have a talk with me?" Samuel asked, curious what was so important to bring him over before the sun was up.

Chalmer sat up a little straighter in his chair, man-ing up for his talk. His expression became serious. "Yeah, I got me a lil problem. Ya know them worms ya saw I had yesterdy?"

Samuel nodded.

"Well, I din't put none down nobody's shirt, like ya said..."

Evelyn sent Samuel a curious glance, but didn't interrupt.

"...an' so they's still in my pocket, but taday they's almost all dead."

Evelyn grimaced, hoping they weren't *still* in Chalmer's pocket, thinking she should have made him wash his hands before he ate.

"Well, that there *is* a p-problem," Samuel agreed, looking thoughtful. "Whut else ya reckon you'll be a needin' live worms f-fer, though?"

"Oh, I always keep me some worms cause ya jes never know when you'll be a-needin' em. Don't you?" he countered, catching Samuel off guard.

"Uh, well, shore, I mean I used ta, but I d-don't have much c-cause to carry worms in my pocket no m-more."

Chalmer looked crestfallen.

"*But*," Samuel added, piquing Chalmers hopes again, "I think mebbe we kin come up with a solution ta yer p-problem."

Chalmer lit up.

"Evelyn, ya gotcha one a them there containers that bakin' soder comes in? Ya know, the kind with a lid?"

"I do. I got a couple of them right here," she answered, taking one out of a cabinet and placing it on the table between them.

Samuel took out his pocket knife, noticing Chalmers interest. He took the plastic lid off the container and proceeded to cut small holes in it. Then he did the same with the can, taking care to keep the holes small so dirt wouldn't fall out.

"Now, this here ain't g-gonna last ferever, cause it's kindly like paper an' when it stays d-damp it's gonna come apart, but it'll last ya a g-good while, an' they'll be plenty more we k-kin make up when ya need em," Samuel explained, handing the can to Chalmer.

Chalmer took the can, turning it around in his hand, admiring it. "Wow! Thank ya! I bet I'm the onliest kid with they's own worm house!" he exclaimed. "Hey, kin I ask ya sumthin' else?" he asked, changing gears abruptly.

"Shore."

"How come ya t-talk light th-that?" he questioned innocently.

"Chalmer, I d-don't rightly know. It's jes the way the way I's b-born I reckon. D-does it bother ya?"

"Naw, I's jes wunderin. I ain't never heard no one talk like ya before," he explained.

"Well, I'm g-glad ya asked, cause ya jes might hear sumbody else one d-day, an' it c-could be embarrassin' if'n ya was ta say sumthin' about it to 'em. So j-jes remember, it ain't sumthin' a body k-kin help, it's jes the way they was born. 'Kay?"

"Kay," Chalmer readily agreed, accepting that explanation.

There was a knock at the door. Evelyn started to go answer it but Samuel stopped her. "I'll get it. B-be right b-back, Chalmer," wanting him to stay put. He figured it was someone coming to get him, since Tommy let them know where he was. He opened the front door. Virgil stood outside.

"Hey, Samuel," he said sheepishly, obviously embarrassed that a five year old had pulled one over on them, while in their care.

"Mornin', V-Virgil," Samuel answered, stepping out and pulling the door closed behind him. "Chalmer's jes finishin' up with breakfast," he informed him. Virgil started to apologize and Samuel put his hand up to stop him. "No need, it's no p-problem," he interjected, wanting to talk to Virgil about what to do before Chalmer realized he'd been caught. "Listen, g-goin' along with whut we a-talked 'bout yesterdy, I'm a thinkin' mebbe we jes let eem think he's got this one under his belt, an I'll send eem b-back home, keepin an eye on eem from here, an' you kin keep an eye on eem from there.

40

Least this here way, we know whut he's a-doin, an' where he's a-goin. If'n it gets outta control, we k-kin put a stop ta it then. Whut a ya think?"

Virgil thought about it a second. This was all new to him, whereas Samuel raised two fine men in his lifetime. Besides, being a boy once himself, it made sense. If they tried to lock Chalmer up, no telling where he might run to next time. "I think that's a good idea, Samuel."

"All right then, I reckon I'll g-go on ahead, an' send eem back home so's he k-kin get back in there afore y'all notice he's g-gone," he said with a wink.

"Thanks, Samuel," Virgil replied, reaching out to shake his friend's hand.

"Welcome, son," he answered, turning to go back inside.

Chalmer looked a bit surprised to see Samuel come back alone. For a minute, he was afraid he'd been caught. "Who wus at the door?" he couldn't help but ask.

"Ah, jes a neighbor a-lookin fer sumthin'," Samuel answered truthfully.

Chalmer looked relieved.

"Ya know, I's a-thinkin that mebbe ya oughtta get on b-back o'er there afore sumbody might be a-lookin' fer ya," Samuel suggested.

Chalmer pondered it for a second. He hadn't considered getting back *without* getting caught. He liked that idea a *lot*. "I reckon I do need ta be a gettin back. Thank ya fer my worm house!" he said, slipping out of the chair and grabbing the can off the table.

"Yer welcome. Now come on, I'll keep a-look on ya from the porch till ya get back there safe," Samuel said. "How'd ya get out without anyone a-seein' ya, anyhow?"

"Oh that's easy. I jes climbed outta the winder," he explained.

"Ya reckon ya kin get back in?" Samuel asked.

"Yep, shore kin," Chalmer replied.

Samuel figured he'd rather not know how Chalmer was so sure.

Chalmer called back over his shoulder to Evelyn, "Thank ya fer my bloody eggs!"

Evelyn grimaced again. "You're welcome!" she answered, swallowing hard.

Chalmer headed back off to Sarah's Home. He held onto his worm house with pride. He liked it a *lot*. And he was very happy to know he wasn't going to get into trouble. That made two times now that Samuel'd kept him from getting in trouble. He was beginning to like him a lot too!

CHAPTER 6

Samuel took a seat in his rocker on the porch and watched Chalmer make his way back to Sarah's Home. The moon, acting as Chalmer's personal escort, was shining brightly in the clear sky illuminating his path.

Chalmer went to his bedroom window, set his worm house on the window sill that was well over his head, hiked himself up and then inside, grabbed his can, then shut the window. Virgil—watching from the other side—and Samuel had both had their doubts as to Chalmers being able to make that leap up to the sill, and they were equally amazed and quite impressed at Chalmer's dexterity when he executed it with ease. Once he was inside safe and sound, Virgil gave Samuel a thumbs up signal, then went back inside himself.

Shaking his head, Samuel chuckled to himself. That was *some* boy there, he was thinking when he saw Aubry and Horace approaching.

As Aubry's due date had drawn near, Horace began accompanying her there every day, where she would have coffee with Evelyn and Samuel until it was time for the kids to start showing up for school. There was a longstanding plan in place everyone was aware of, that if she were to need assistance of any kind during school, she would just ring the bell. It could be heard easily and help could be there almost immediately. He was fine with that arrangement, but there was no bell at their home, nor on the way to the schoolhouse, and he wasn't taking any chances should something happen when she was alone. Once she was safely ensconced in Samuel and Evelyn's watchful care, he would join Tommy at the barn, and the two of them would head out into the fields.

Horace turned Aubry over to Samuel, who held his hand out to walk her inside. They both moved at about the same speed now, though she had more of a waddle than he did, and it was hard to tell who, exactly, was assisting who. Once they were seated at the kitchen table, coffee in hand, he and Evelyn recounted to her their early morning little visitor.

~~§~~

By the time breakfast was ready at the Home everyone had been apprised of Chalmer's extra curricular activities, so that extra care could be taken keeping an eye on him. The night nurses were to *inconspicuously* check his room every fifteen minutes to ensure he was in bed where he was supposed to be. If, or more probably, *when* they witnessed anything untoward, they were to notify Virgil straightaway.

Normally a hearty eater, they were all curious to see what excuse Chalmer would come up with for not being hungry since he'd already eaten at Samuel's. As it turned out, their curiosity was left unsatiated when he climbed up to the table and ate his normal breakfast fare without blinking an eye.

Evelyn was taken aback when she arrived to begin her part time day shift to see him sitting at the table with an empty plate before him but caught herself before she remarked. She cast a wide eyed glance at Millicent, who was sitting at the same table, feeding Tenley.

Millicent merely shrugged in reply. She was as amazed as everyone else and figured he'd have a belly ache soon, but she'd deal with that then.

Right now she was pleased as punch at the amount *Tenley* had eaten this morning! Maybe it was something in the air! Tenley had only been with them for about a week now, but Millicent could already see her little cheeks filling out!

As the morning progressed, she mulled over how she wanted to broach the subject with Virgil in regards to adding another official member to their family. She wasn't sure how much longer she could stand to leave Tenley at the Home at night, rather than having her in their home with them. Until Adohy and Faith's house was completed and the spare bedroom was available, Tenley could sleep on a cot in their room! She knew she was going to have to rein in her emotions when it came to other children that would be coming to the Home. They simply couldn't legally adopt them all. Her stomach clenched at the thought of Virgil having any objections to bringing Tenley into their family. What if he didn't think it was a good idea? Shaking off the negative thought, she made a promise to herself to talk to Virgil that very night. Surely he would—her mental conversation with herself was interrupted by the ringing of a bell.

The school bell? That meant Aubry needed assistance! Grabbing her bag, she called to Evelyn, who had heard it as well, and they rushed out the door, meeting Virgil in the yard. The three of them climbed into Virgil and Millicent's sedan, and within three to four minutes they were rushing in the door to the schoolhouse.

Aubry was seated at her desk, putting on a brave face for the children, not wanting to cause them any undue alarm. While she'd been standing at the chalkboard her water had broken, leaving a little trail of the fluid to her desk, the majority of which was now puddled beneath her seat. Fighting back a grimace as the first strong contraction wracked her, she'd asked one of the children to ring the school bell for her, telling her class she had a little surprise for them to mollify their curiosity.

Samuel was piddling in his little garden, that was situated between his home and the schoolhouse, when the bell rang out. Brushing the dirt off his hands, he grabbed his cane and had just made his way up the few steps to the entrance, when the others arrived. He and Evelyn distracted the children while Virgil and Millicent proceeded to assist Aubry out to the car, to be taken back to the Home for the delivery.

Out in the fields, rows apart, Tommy and Horace heard the tolling of the bell. Both their heads popped up above the chest high corn stalks at the same time, like toy versions of a Jack in the Box. After a second for reality to sink in, they hurried toward the sound, coming together at the end of the rows on the edge of the field. The weather was a replica of the previous day during the social, pleasantly warm and sunny with puffy white clouds floating intermittently in the sky. However, the sun proved to be a little more unforgiving when working in the fields, and with the tall plants effectively blocking any breeze, it boosted the temperature by several degrees. Tommy's brow was lined with beads of sweat and his face was flushed, but he noticed that, in spite of the heat, Horace's face was white as a sheet.

Anyone who knew Horace, knew he was a talker. Especially when he was nervous. Tommy recalled once, when they were kids, Horace's father calling him Chief Big Mouth. But as they made their way to the barn, and then to the truck to drive to the Home, Horace didn't say a word. It occurred to Tommy then that Horace wasn't nervous. He was scared.

They jumped in the truck and Tommy started the engine, put it in gear and accelerated, cutting the wheel to turn them in the direction of the Home less than a thousand feet away. He was worried about Horace. He'd never seen him this way. It made *him* nervous. And when he was nervous he had a tendency to tell really bad jokes. In an effort to get through to his best friend he said, "Hey! Buddy! This is a *good* thing! If she'd waited any *longer*, an' a-gotten any *bigger*, it'd taken her *two* trips ta haul ass!" He guffawed at himself, glancing at Horace, expecting to see his best friend laughing at his joke. Horace *always* laughed at his jokes. But Horace was staring straight ahead, silent.

They pulled in the yard at the Home and sprinted inside. Virgil met them as they entered and relayed that Millicent and another nurse were with Aubry and everything was fine so far. He had no sooner gotten those words out, when Aubry let out a blood curdling scream.

Tommy and Virgil exchanged a startled glance before rushing to catch Horace just seconds before he hit the floor.

They pulled a chair up under him and Virgil fetched a wet towel, while Tommy tried to rouse his friend. Sprawled in the chair with his arms dangling at his sides and his chin resting on his chest, Virgil wiped his face while Tommy gently shook him by the shoulders. Finally after a moment, he began to stir.

"Aubry?' he murmured groggily. "Aubry?" he said again, with a little more urgency. Then he bolted upright on the edge of the seat! "Aubry! Oh lawd, whut have I done, whut if I done went an kilt her, we dint hafta have no baby, we coulda jes stayed the two a us, I'da been happy jes the two a us, where's she at, how longs this gonna take, this is takin' too long, aint it..." he continued talking a mile a minute, waiting for no answers, as he stood and started pacing the room.

Tommy smiled at Virgil and breathed a sigh of relief. "He's back!" he said.

About then, Aubry let out another cry and Horace's knees buckled. They led him back to the chair, and made him sit down, just as his mother came in the door. She took over trying to calm him, and while the afternoon wore on, his father made it there, followed, one by one, by Evelyn, Samuel, Faith, Adohy, and others anxiously awaiting the new arrival.

With no idea how long it was going to be, the women went to the kitchen to help the staff prepare a meal to accommodate all the extra guests. It was almost dusk and the setting sun was casting long shadows of the furniture across the floor, when Millicent emerged from the darkened hallway bringing her from the recesses of the Home.

"It's a boy!" she announced.

Once again Horace fell silent as his grin lit up the room!

CHAPTER 7

The birthing went without any problems—other than Horace's incident—and everyone was healthy and well. The baby weighed six pounds seven ounces and was nineteen inches long. Horace and Aubry, or rather Horace, had long since decided on a name for a boy, Horace Franklin Stookesbury Junior. It would take a while for him to grow into his name, but Aubry wouldn't have it any other way after she saw the way Horace's eyes lit up when he'd said it.

He was led to the room to see her and the baby. He stopped in the doorway, shifting his weight from side to side, giving the illusion of walking but going nowhere. He could still hear Aubry's cries from the birthing and wasn't sure how he was going to be received since he was the one who had caused it. His look of contrition gave way to pure relief when Aubry commented.

"Well get on over here and see your baby boy!" she said with a smile, raising the crook of her arm up where Horace Junior's head rested.

The baby's face was still a little red and splotchy, his eyes shut, sleeping peacefully, as Horace approached the bed and gazed down at the two of them.

After a moment, Aubry said, "Do you want to hold him?" raising the bundled infant a bit.

Horace stepped back, eyes wide.

"Don't be silly, Horace!" Aubry giggled. "You aren't going to hurt him!" she promised. "At least come back closer and get used to him! You're going to have to hold him sooner or later!"

Horace moved close again. Gingerly his arm inched out and he caressed the baby's fist. The baby reacted by grabbing his finger, and Horace looked at Aubry, amazement shining in his eyes. A smile spread across his face and when he looked back at Horace Junior, the baby opened his eyes and mimicked his father's smile for the briefest of moments, leaving Horace to wonder if he'd actually seen what he thought he had.

Millicent entered the room. "So what do you think? Does he pass?" she asked Horace.

Horace broke his gaze away to smile at Millicent in answer, then looked back down at his son.

There it is, she thought. That look. No matter how many times she saw it there was just nothing that compared to a first time father's reaction to his child. "Well, I think since it's so late, it would be better for Aubry and Horace Jr. to go ahead and stay here tonight. You're welcome to stay too, Horace, if you want to. Supper's ready though, so you ought to go get something to eat," she suggested.

Again, Horace looked from his new baby to Millicent with a smile and a nod, then back to his son.

"Come on, I'll get you a plate," she offered, nudging Horace, as she looked at Aubry and winked. "There's a few more people that would like to get a peek at the baby if you're up to it, Aubry, then I'll bring you some supper too."

Aubry nodded. "Give me a kiss Horace and go on and get you some supper," she urged him. He gave her a kiss as directed, then leaned over to place a kiss on the baby's forehead. When he did, the baby let go of his finger and flailed his little fists around for a second then settled back to sleep. Horace was mesmerized by his every movement.

It warmed Aubry's heart to see the love and amazement on her husband's face. "Go on and get you some supper, now," she encouraged him gently. "We'll both be right here when you're done."

He finally took a few steps back, grinned one more time, then left the room.

It occurred to Aubry then, that it was the first time she could ever remember that he'd not said a single word!

§

Everyone waiting to see how Aubry and the baby were didn't have a chance to ask any questions.

They could hear him coming down the hallway and into the room…"Horace Franklin Stookesbury, Junior! He's one cute lil feller, smart too, y'all shoulda seen eem grab holt a my finger, an' strong? ya wouldn't believe how strong he is, he grabbed on an' didn't wanna let go, looked at me an' smiled, he's gonna be a heartbreaker, I kin tell ya that, cute lil feller, y'all are gonna love eem, he's a lil bitty thing but he shore is strong! did I tell ya how strong he is? an' cute? an' quiet? didn't make a peep, gonna be just like me! I kin tell already! y'all go on ahead an' go get a look at eem, yer gonna love eem, he's a chip off the ole block I tell ya! yes sirree—"

Millicent interrupted Horace's revelry calling him to the kitchen, and Tommy and Evelyn helped Samuel to the room to see his great grandchild. In reality, he'd been a great grandfather for quite some time, but it wasn't until Sarah's death that the secret had been revealed to everyone else that Faith was actually his first. This felt more real. He'd never allowed himself to think of Faith as his great grandchild to make sure he never let the secret slip. In the beginning it was never meant to come out in the open, but Sarah had changed her mind on her deathbed.

Samuel stood looking down at the baby. Yes, this felt more like his first great grandchild. He did resemble Horace like he'd said, but Samuel could detect Aubry and even hints of his son, Carl, and Rebecca, Aubry's parents, in this precious little boy. "You done went an' got yerself a fine little baby here, honey," he told Aubry.

"I know, Papaw," she agreed, smiling proudly.

"Aww," Evelyn murmured, making her way around the bed, with Tommy in tow. "Isn't he a cutie?" she cooed, nudging Tommy in the ribs, but he didn't respond. He wasn't sure how to react to this tiny version of his best friend. He'd never really thought about it before, but it seemed strange now that until just a few hours ago, this little person had been *inside* his sister.

Aubry carefully passed the baby to Evelyn and she turned to Tommy so he could see him up close. His previous unease faded as he marveled at the tiny figure. "Look at them lil bitty fingers, *an' them teeny nails!*" he exclaimed. He started to see the baby in a whole new light. "I ain't ne'er seen ears that small! An' that lil mouth is perfect! Wow!" he breathed, almost to himself. A second later he let out a chuckle, saying, "That mouth's gonna hafta do a whole lotta growin' ta keep up with his daddy!"

That reminded Aubry how quiet Horace had been. "Is he okay?" she asked. "He was awful quite when he was in here before—"

"Is he okay?" Tommy cut in. "He's on cloud nine! We couldn't a-none a-us get a word in edgeways when he come out! Ya shoulda heard eem! He's his good ole fast talkin' self!"

Evelyn and Samuel confirmed what Tommy said, putting Aubry's mind at ease, explaining further that Millicent was making him eat some supper.

§

After they left, Faith and Adohy went in to say a quick hello. They were a little more at ease than Horace and Tommy had been, having witnessed the birthing process so many times before with the animals, but it was no less fascinating to them to see a newborn little *person*. They made their visit short though, not only so Aubry and the baby could get some rest, but they knew Horace's parents were waiting on him to finish eating so they could see their first grandbaby.

§

After Millicent got Tenley and Chalmer tucked in for the night, at least she *hoped* in Chalmer's case, she crept back in to check on the new family, seeing to it that Aubry had eaten and they had everything they needed, including a cot for Horace, before heading back to her own house. It had been quite a day and she was tired, but she had something important she needed to discuss with Virgil that couldn't wait any longer.

CHAPTER 8

Nearly two weeks had passed since Aubry'd had the baby and she and Horace were in love with the little guy. In just the short time he'd been with them, they already couldn't imagine their life without him. Aubry had stayed home with him and Evelyn took over at the school as planned, but Aubry was ready to get back to work now. She loved that she could take Horace Junior with her for the few remaining weeks of school. She was confident it wouldn't be a problem, but they were making a trial run of it today in church, just to be sure.

Caleb still taught Sunday school and services every other Sunday on the off weeks that Preacher Loveday, the circuit preacher, didn't give sermons at the brush arbor by the general store. The school house was full to the brim today. There were rumors going around that Caleb had a pretty exciting announcement to make. Everyone was abuzz wondering what it could be, and no one wanted to miss it.

Millicent and Virgil had an announcement of their own. She'd talked to her husband the night Aubry'd had the baby as she'd promised herself. She'd wondered afterwards how she could have ever been worried about what Virgil's answer would be. Of course he'd said yes! He seemed nearly as excited as she was, and she didn't think his enthusiasm was just for her benefit. She'd waited for his admonition about getting too attached to the other children that would be coming, but he never said a word about it. As she thought about it, it dawned on her there could be several reasons why he'd not said anything. One, he could know in his heart that she was smart enough to realize that it wouldn't be possible to adopt them all. Two, he hadn't wanted to hamper their celebration with any negative thoughts. Or three...maybe he was leaving the discussion open...well, a girl could hope! In fact, Virgil had admitted to her that the same idea had crossed his mind with Chalmer, but he'd noticed how Faith and Adohy had taken the boy under their wings during the day. It had started in an effort just to keep him under a watchful eye and out of trouble, but he thought it may develop into something a little more permanent so, he'd held back, deciding to see how things progressed with the three of them before giving it any more consideration.

Since that talk, Faith and Adohy's house had been erected and the roof was on. It was coming along in leaps and bounds, due, in no little part, to the couple's seemingly unending energy. They worked side by side long after everyone else stopped for the day. They were probably anxious to finally start the next phase of their married life in their own home, and no one could blame them. They had been married over six months now. It was time.

§

Caleb waited until after the service to open the floor for the announcements. He figured if he did it before, everyone would be too excited to sit still. He knew at least most of the women were already squirming in their seats to get hold of Horace Junior!

As soon as they closed in prayer, he brought their waiting to an end.

"I had me a visit last week from a few representatives from the Tennessee Valley Authority. As y'all are aware, since the construction of the Norris Dam, they been expandin' electrical service to several of the surroundin' counties. Well, I got word that they was gonna be a workin' their way out State Route 33!"

Hoots and applause rang out and the room became animated with conversation and speculation, everyone voicing their thoughts and excitement.

Caleb held his hand up to get their attention back. "Now they didn't know how long it would be before it got ta us, or ta area's *off* of State Route 33, *but* when it does, we's gonna have electricity at the general store! That means we'll be able ta keep not only bigger quantities of perishable items, but have a better selection! An' then hopefully, it a jes be a matter a time afore they's electricity all up here too!"

He tried to answer questions as he could make them out, as the room echoed with all the excitement. Once it died down some, he asked if anyone else had anything to say.

Millicent raised her hand and, by prior arrangement, Samuel asked Chalmer if he could help him back to his house. Millicent & Virgil brought Tenley to the service with them today knowing they were going to tell everyone of their decision, and not wanting to leave Chalmer out, he'd come as well. However, though he was only five, he was wise beyond his years, and adopting Tenley was not something they would carelessly discuss in his presence.

Chalmer dutifully accepted Samuel's hand, rising to the challenge. Taking his assignment seriously, he held on to Samuel's free hand with both his hands, his eyes shifting from the floor in front of them with each step, back to Samuel, then back to the floor for the next step. It was precious watching the two of them, though perhaps Samuel was making it appear that he needed Chalmer's help just a *little* more than he really did. Once they were out of hearing range, Virgil and Millicent shared their news about adopting Tenley into their family. The paperwork would be finalized soon, and she would be Tenley Marie Thornton!

Back outside the church, Chalmer and Samuel made it to the little garden that Samuel had been tending to, albeit negligently. It was much smaller than the garden they normally grew, and even still it was more than he could keep up with. Everyone was so much busier and had more responsibilities than they'd had in the past, so no one had time to give him any help with it. Samuel refused to admit that he was growing older by the day and couldn't do the things he'd done all of his life anymore, but looking at the unkempt garden, it was becoming painfully obvious.

Chalmer was familiar with the garden at the Home. He'd been helping with it, and it was thriving. He paused now at the Jenkins' family garden. "How come y'all is lettin yer garden die?" he asked, unaware that his innocent query may strike a nerve with Samuel.

"Well, Chalmer, I t-tell ya, we ain't a *lettin'* it d-die on purpose. Ya see, its kindly b-been up ta me ta tend ta it, an' sometimes yer head thinks it kin do stuff yer body just c-cain't. Ya know, ya cain't plow a field a-t-turnin it over in yer mind," he explained.

A big crease formed between Chalmer's brows as he looked at Samuel.

Samuel chuckled when he saw the boy's expression and realized Chalmer had no idea what he was talking about. "See, they's a time I c-could do a wh-whole lot more then I kin now c-cause my body is a runnin' down. That's how c-come I needed ya ta help me ta walk b-back over here. Matter a fact, I need ya ta help me on the rest a-the way, an we'll sit on the p-porch a spell, whata ya think b-bout that?"

Chalmer resumed his careful assistance until Samuel was seated in a rocker on his porch.

"Thank ya, son," Samuel said. "Ya did g-good."

Chalmer nodded, backing up to the rocker beside Samuel's, but he seemed lost in thought.

Samuel chalked it up to him thinking about growing old someday. Church let out then and Virgil came to collect the little tyke. Samuel relayed what a fine job the young man had done, patting Chalmer on the back, and they went on their way, just as Charlie, a friend of Samuel's, stepped up on the porch for a visit.

"Howdie, Charlie!" Samuel greeted, reaching out to shake his hand. "Have a s-seat," he nodded, indicating the rocker Chalmer had just vacated.

"Samuel," Charlie acknowledged, gripping Samuel's hand, then taking the offered seat.

Tommy and Evelyn returned then, and after exchanging greetings with Charlie, Evelyn offered to fix them a cup of coffee, which they accepted.

"How's life been treatin ya," Charlie asked Samuel, after Tommy and Evelyn had gone indoors.

"Oh, fair to m-middlin, I reckon. You?"

"Bout the same, 'bout the same," Charlie nodded. "Hey, you know that feller I play with sometimes, o'er Maynardville way, Roy Acuff?" he asked. Charlie played the guitar really well, and played every chance he got.

"I do," Samuel answered. "I voted fer eem when he ran fer gov'ner, oh back in forty-eight, wudn't it?"

"Yep, he didn't make it," Charlie confirmed, then went on. "An' ya know, he done went ta Nashville once, an' a come back, then he went ta Hollywood, an' a-come back agin. Now he's a-wantin me ta pick up an' go back ta Nashville with em agin. Ya know what I told eem? I told eem "Roy ya gonna go ta Nashville an' come back broke. Yes sir, that's what I told eem."

They both chuckled, then fell silent, shaking their heads at the silliness of it, and continued on rocking, gazing out across the mountains on the peaceful spring day.

CHAPTER 9

The next morning after Tommy and Evelyn had gone, Samuel was sitting on the porch contemplating his discussion with Chalmer the previous morning. He'd absolutely hated admitting that he was getting old. The more he thought about it, the more he was determined not to go down without a fight.

He could either sit around and let Father Time have his way, or he could get out to that garden and show him that he wasn't a quitter. It was time he started practicing what he preached, and the best place to find a helping hand was at the end of his own arm. Yep, he'd been acting like he was a nickel short of a penny's worth of sense, and he needed to fix that right now. And that was exactly what he was going to do, just as soon as he finished his cup of coffee and had a nap.

§

He awoke feeling invigorated. Or, at least better. Invigorated was stretching it. He slipped his shoes on and grabbed his cane. He was going to go out there and show this garden who was boss. On the way, he couldn't help but think of Chalmer again. After all, it was Chalmer that was ultimately responsible for making him see that he needed to change his ways if he was expecting to hang around for any length of time.

He thought about the morning the boy had shown up in the dark to have a "man-to-man" talk with him. The memory brought a smile to his face. He was surprised he hadn't been back since then and thought perhaps it was due to the more watchful eyes he was under. He was such a cute little feller, he thought. His heart constricted then at the reality of the situation. He just didn't understand why nobody wanted the little guy. He was surprised too, that Virgil and Millicent hadn't considered Chalmer for adoption as well as Tenley. Yeah, she was a bit more fragile, and obviously needed more medical attention, and the fact that she looked like a mini Sarah certainly attributed to their decision, but she didn't need to be loved any more than Chalmer did, did she?

He wondered what the little feller's story was, and how he came to be there. And if there was something more he wasn't aware of, that kept Virgil and Millicent from adopting him as well. He couldn't ask them about anything as personal as that, it simply wasn't any of his business, but he didn't think they would object to telling him about where Chalmer'd come from. Maybe that in its self, would answer both questions. Maybe there was a chance his family would be back for him. He made a mental note to ask.

As he approached the small garden, he noticed right away a startling difference from the prior morning. Where before the row of wilted onions were bowing their final farewell, there was now a row of luscious green onions standing majestically proud, reaching for the sky. It couldn't be! Samuel was dumbstruck. "What in tarnation?" he mumbled to himself, walking down the row trying to figure out what had happened. He glanced across the rest of the garden, still as sad as droopy as it had been the day before. Had Tommy put some fertilizer on the onions and not mentioned it? No. That couldn't be it. Fertilizer wouldn't have helped those onions. Besides why wouldn't he have done the whole gar—he stopped when an image of Chalmer flashed through his mind. Then he recalled how pensive he'd seemed after they'd visited the garden yesterday.

He went to his truck and drove to the Thornton's. Virgil saw him pull up and went to see if everything was okay. It was unusual for Samuel to show up out of the blue.

Samuel was stepping out of the truck as Virgil approached.

"Samuel! Good to see you! Everything all right?" he asked, concern lacing his tone.

"Good, g-good," Samuel said right away, putting Virgil's mind at ease. "I's jes wondrin' if'n ya had a minute?"

"Why sure, Samuel, anytime, you know that," Virgil avowed, his curiosity rising.

Samuel nodded toward the garden that supplemented both the Thornton's and Sarah's Home's supper tables. "Ya recken we c-could take a g-gander at the garden over there?" he asked, giving Virgil no clue as to where this conversation was headed.

Virgil indicated they could, and they headed that direction.

Glancing around, Samuel asked nonchalantly, "Where's Chalmer?"

Thinking nothing of it at first, Virgil replied, "Oh, he's in the barn with Faith and Adohy, mucking the stalls." Then he began to wonder if this out of the ordinary social call had anything to do with Chalmer. "Did he come for breakfast again?" he asked, worried.

"Naw, I ain't *seen* eem since yesterdy after church," Samuel confirmed.

But there was something in the way he said it that left Virgil unconvinced that Chalmer hadn't been up to *something*.

They came up on the garden and a big smile lit up Samuel's face. Following his line of sight, Virgil looked to see what had made Samuel so happy.

"What the heck!" he exclaimed, looking at the partially missing row of onions.

"L-Let m-me explain," Samuel said.

§

After Samuel filled Virgil in, he asked, "Ya reckon, ifn I was ta c-come an' get eem an' a-bring eem b-back, that I could offer eem a j-job helpin' me ta work in the g-garden, an' mebbe pay eem a quarter a week?"

Virgil wondered how Faith and Adohy would feel about it. They were pretty close with Chalmer. "Well, let's go on over and let me see if the kids can get by without him, and if so, you can ask him yourself," he answered.

They could hear Chalmer as they drew near, but when they entered the barn he immediately went silent. He knew it was unusual for Samuel to be there, which could only mean something was up.

Virgil called Faith and Adohy aside and presented Samuel's request to them, surprised to see the look of relief on their faces. It turned out that keeping an eye on Chalmer was a full time job, and they were both grateful for *any* time during the day, no matter how small, that they could get twice as much accomplished, giving them more time to work on their house.

Samuel made small talk with an unnaturally timid version of Chalmer until he got a nod from Virgil. He recognized this version of the boy from before with the incident at the church social when he'd thought he was in trouble. The memory brought to Samuel's mind the magnifying glass, and he wondered if he'd done the right thing trusting Chalmer with it. He hoped so. He hadn't heard any more about it, and was pretty sure he would have, had anything occurred. Having Virgil's blessing now, he posed his offer to Chalmer.

Chalmer's demeanor changed instantly. "Ya mean it?" he asked, incredulous. "A whole quarter?"

"If'n ya work ever day, it works out ta be five cents a d-day. Ya reckon yer up ta it? It's a *man's* job."

"I sure am, kin we start now?"

"Well, I reckon ya done went an' d-did yer work there for taday," Samuel told him with a wink, and they both grinned like Chesire cats.

Vicky Whedbee

§

Tommy commented on the onions in the garden at supper, and Samuel filled them in on his eventful day. "Pert n-near brought t-tears ta my eyes," he confessed, eyes shining.

Tommy's heart swelled with the happiness emanating from his papaw. It had been a long time since he'd seen that look on his face, and he could actually _feel_ the sense of purpose that little boy had re-instilled in his grandfather. Who'd have thought that a mischievous little orphan boy could make such a change in a grown man, almost overnight. Yep, his papaw'd always told him there were _some_ things money just couldn't buy.

CHAPTER 10

At precisely four-thirty the next morning, there was a bold rap on the front door at the Jenkins' home. Tommy was still getting dressed, and Evelyn was cooking breakfast, so Samuel went to answer it. He had a sneaking suspicion who it just might be at that hour. He opened the solid wood door. Propping the screened door open with his body, stood a barefoot little boy named Chalmer.

"Ya ready ta git ta work? Ya cain't a plow a field turnin it over in yer mind," he blurted before Samuel could say a word.

It was all Samuel could do to suppress a face splitting grin, trying to take an *all business* approach instead. This boy just beat all! He looked out into the darkness, and said, "Ya got the right i-idear there son, but dontcha think we oughta l-let it git a lil lighter so's we kin see what we's a-doin'? Sides, ya probly ain't even a eat yet, have ya? A man c-cain't be expected ta work on a empty st-stomach, kin they?" As he spoke he looked out toward Sarah's Home to see Virgil come outside. Apparently he'd been alerted to Chalmer's absence. Samuel nonchalantly held a hand up to let him know all was well. He waved in return and disappeared back indoors. No one had, as yet, figured out how the little tyke had managed his outing to transplant the onions the previous day, and probably never would.

"Well, I reckon I could eat," Chalmer answered after a brief consideration.

"Come on in, then," Samuel said, stepping aside.

Evelyn had overheard the exchange and already had a place set for their guest.

Tommy, seated at the table now, watched as the two entered the kitchen and took their seats across from each other. His papaw had the lightest blue eyes he'd ever seen, though sadly, over the years the light had faded somewhat. But this morning he was taken aback to see a brightness that had been missing for quite some time.

"Chalmer here, jes informed me that ya cain't a-plow a field a turnin' it o'er in yer mind!" he told Tommy and Evelyn proudly.

That explained it! Tommy realized. He couldn't count how many times he'd heard his papaw tell him that before! He looked at Chalmer thoughtfully. Could it be possible that the adult needed the child more in this case, than the other way around? One thing was clear. It was a win-win. It made him feel a lot better knowing that the two of them would be spending time together during the day, when he was out in the fields.

§

Normally after breakfast Samuel leisurely enjoyed a second cup of coffee in his rocker on the porch, but Chalmer was chomping at the bit to get to work. Samuel had a notion that maybe he'd bit off more than he could chew with this little firecracker, but it was fleeting. It tickled him that not only had Chalmer remembered what he'd said the day before, but figured out what it meant! He was going to have to be careful what he said around his little sponge like brain!

Drawing nigh to the row of onions standing tall like proud soldiers, Samuel exclaimed, "Well, lan sakes! Would ya looky here!" He glanced at Chalmer curious to see what his expression would reveal. "Ya reckon they know'd ya was a c-comin' taday an' decided they'd best straighten up an' grow right?"

Chalmer looked at him with a crooked grin, squaring his shoulders back. "Yeah, it was probly *somethin'* like that," he boasted, without anymore explanation. "Where we startin'?" he asked, effectively changing the subject.

"Well, when yer f-figgerin' on which job ta do first, always do the hardest one. That way ya save yer gravy til last."

He could see the wheels turning in Chalmers head, and reminded himself that the boy was only five years old. Even if he understood this figure of speech, he still wouldn't know what would be the hardest job to do first. "I reckon we need ta g-git them there weeds outta here. They's a chokin' the vegetables out," Samuel suggested.

"Yeah, that's what I's gonna say," Chalmer nodded, a picture of seriousness, and they both got down to work.

71

Neither of the two of them noticed that Samuel's stuttering had diminished substantially.

§

Samuel had an inverted bucket to sit on as he worked so he was able to hang on longer than usual, and between that and Chalmer's robust energy, they made good headway in just a few hours. But the morning sun was getting up there now, and the temperature was rising.

"Ya reckon we could git us a drank a water?" Chalmer finally suggested, wiping his brow.

Relieved, Samuel thought he'd never ask. "I reckon it is 'bout break time," he answered, looking up at the sun. "Brush the dust off'n yer b-britches legs, an' we'll go an sit us a spell."

After they got their fill of water, they headed out to the porch to rest. On the way, Samuel stopped at the sewing basket and selected a section of an old cotton sheet and some string. Outside he took a seat in his rocker. "Ya wanta go pick me outta rock 'bout so big?" he asked Chalmer, indicating the size with his fingers.

He nodded. "Whatcha makin'?" he asked, going down the steps.

"You'll see here in jes a m-minute," Samuel replied.

Chalmer came bounding back up on the porch. "How's this'n?"

"Perfect," Samuel said, reaching for the rock. He proceeded to use his pocket knife to poke a hole in the four corners of the twelve inch square of fabric. Running string through the holes, then around the rock, he tied it off and pulled it tight with his teeth. He wound the thread loosely around the rock including the fabric, then he handed the bundle to Chalmer.

"Now, take it and go ta the edge a-the porch and toss it kindly up in the air an see what happens."

Chalmer looked dubious, but did as he was told.

As planned, the rock dropped, the string unwinding and the fabric billowing out catching the air on its way down, gently floating the rest of the way to the ground.

Chalmer's eyes lit up and he grinned from ear to ear looking back at Samuel in amazement, before running down the steps to retrieve the rock. He wound it up like he'd watched Samuel do, and threw it again. And like before, it unwound and drifted, swaying to and fro, before making landfall in the yard. He repeated this process over and over until Samuel was ready to fall asleep watching him, his heart happy. After a few more throws and trips off and on the porch, it didn't take much coaxing to get Chalmer to settle down for a nap, too.

~~§~~

On the other side of the ridge a few miles away, two twelve year old boys were playing hooky from school. They had heard of a huge wild strawberry patch someone had recently found, and they wanted to get to it before all the luscious fruit was picked. The person that had found it was being stingy with the specific location, but they knew the general vicinity and were confident they could search it out.

The problem was, that it was near the old long since abandoned house in the overgrown back section of Mr. Hutchinson's property. Everyone around there knew the house had belonged to his parents, and the kids figured it had to be a couple hundred years ago since he was about a hundred years old himself. *And* everyone knew it was haunted. They'd been warned and warned all their lives not to go near the old Hutchinson house.

Not too long ago though, some kids had ventured too close and got so scared they'd ran back home not even considering the fact that they were going to be caught red handed skipping school. Or maybe they did, but were too scared to care. Anyway, the next day in school they were telling everyone the house was, indeed, haunted and swore they heard strange noises coming from inside to prove it!

Today, on their trek, the boy's were nearing what they considered to be a point of no return from the house. It was hard to make it out from this distance, with the brush, trees and kudzu overgrown around it, but they could see the chimney breaking out above the foliage, glaring at them as if daring them to come any closer.

They'd still not found the strawberry patch. But as they stood silently staring at the house, the patch slowly came into focus, growing on a mound that stood higher than the grass, about thirty feet from where they stood. *Closer* to the house.

They looked at each other, neither of them willing to admit they didn't want to go any closer. Looking back at the patch, they could see the bright red strawberries from there, and they seemed to be calling their names! Their mouths were watering now, and not wanting to be the one to chicken out, they agreed it was worth the risk.

Gingerly, they crept through the tall wheat grass, inching closer and closer to the forbidden fruit. After what seemed like forever, they were upon the outer edge of the patch and they each plucked a juicy strawberry, popping it in their mouths without even brushing it off. It was the sweetest strawberry they'd ever tasted, and they readily grabbed another. Then another. Lost in the pleasure of their rewards, they filled their mouths forgetting about the haunted house watching them.

Until they heard the snap of a twig.

It came from the other side of the mound of strawberries, between them and the house. They both froze, nearly choking on the juicy fruit they were devouring, unsure of what they'd heard. Then the unmistakable crunch of a footstep on the dry debris covering the ground echoed in the air around them. Sure they weren't alone now, fear tingled down their spines as they crouched low, ducking below the top of the mound, thankful for its solid protection.

It didn't take them long to realize whatever they'd heard could easily traverse *over* the mound, unmindful of the crushed strawberries in its wake, and the next crisp footfall sent them running. Before they'd gone very far, one of them tripped and called out to the other as he fell. His friend reluctantly stopped and turned back to help him. As the boy leaned down to grasp his buddies arm, he raised his eyes in the direction they'd run from, just in time to see a blur of something huge disappear into the overgrowth surrounding the haunted house. After that, neither one of them slowed down until they were home.

CHAPTER 11

The number of patients at Sarah's Home had grown to ten over that past few weeks. Fortunately, at least for Millicent's sake, none of them were alone in the world. They all had families, but were either elderly and in their final stages of care, or younger in need of rehabilitation after surgeries or debilitating injuries.

Tenley was no longer at the home, having made the transition to Virgil and Millicent's, however she still accompanied Millicent there during the day, where she spent time in the playroom, watched over by everyone. Chalmer was still spending the days with Samuel and loving every minute of it. Virgil had, however, put an end to him slipping out his bedroom window in the mornings, barefoot, and instead accompanied him for a distance before Chalmer would take off to Samuel, who was waiting for him on the porch.

The garden had been transformed under their care and vegetables were getting ripe for the picking. The sunshine, exercise and special company had put a bounce in Samuel's step. He'd always started his morning upon awakening by greeting Sarah whose photograph was the first thing he saw in a frame standing on his dresser. As he dressed he would talk to her, generally recounting his new aches and pains, before relaying how much he missed her every day. Just a few days ago though, he realized he'd not had one new complaint. In fact, all he'd been telling her about was his days with Chalmer! He held her picture up closer to his lantern to get a better look. He could swear her smile was bigger and brighter than ever. It didn't make him miss her any less, but it sure eased a little bit of the hurt from losing her.

It wasn't lost on Samuel that school would be letting out for the summer soon, and in the fall Chalmer would be starting, but he refused to dwell on it. He just knew he had to make the most of the time that he had. He already missed the boy something fierce on the weekends. He had a good mind to ask if he could start joining them when the family got together every Sunday for supper. Matter of fact, that's exactly what he was going to do. He'd run it by Tommy and Evelyn this morning, then go talk to Virgil and Millicent when he took Chalmer back this evening. He'd already been staying for supper during the week, one more on Sunday shouldn't be no problem.

Evelyn mentioned it to Millicent went she got to the Home that morning. "I tell you, you wouldn't believe the difference in Samuel since Chalmer's been coming there!" she said.

"I know, it's been good for Chalmer, too. And Faith and Adohy have gotten so much more done on their house without Chalmer in tow. Lord knows, it would be good to have extra eyes on him on Sunday, at least! Did you hear what he did last weekend?" Millicent asked.

Evelyn could sense Millicent's exasperation and she felt a defensive little tug on her heart strings. She shook her head. "No. What did he do now?" she asked, with a chuckle, not sure if she wanted to know or not!

"Well, the kids were out of the habit of watching him so closely and they got busy, and you know that bright red, brand new pedal car Virgil got for him, right after he came here?"

Evelyn nodded, waiting with raised brows.

"Well, it's blue now," she said, dryly.

Evelyn's hand shot to her mouth to hide her laughter.

"Yeah, he found some of the kid's paint for the house, and when they weren't looking he painted his car," she stated. She was straight faced but her eyes were twinkling. Even she couldn't be mad at the little guy long.

One of the nurses came out then and asked for assistance with Oppy. She was refusing to eat again. When this happened in the past, the only thing that she responded to was Faith. While Evelyn went to find her, Millicent followed the nurse back to Oppy's room.

~~§~~

Over the ridge, between Big Ridge State Park and Norton Cemetery, word was traveling like wildfire throughout the community about the recent chain of events with some of the youngsters and the old haunted Hutchinson house. It seemed that once the two stories got out about the kid's playing hooky, and what they'd seen and heard, it suddenly became the dare of the century. They'd all gotten in trouble for skipping school and going to the area they'd all been warned to stay away from, but they thought it had been worth it, as they were heroes of sorts now.

Over and over they were asked to recant their events, which were embellished a little each time until the tales became as tall as *they* were. At that point, kids not brave enough to go themselves began to dare others that were too hardheaded to back down. That wasn't the worst of it though. It wasn't enough just to go out to the haunted house during school hours, where they took the risk of getting caught. They had to go at night.

This led to multiple injuries, from sprained ankles, to stitches, to broken arms. The more seriously you were hurt, the bigger the accolades. Unable to put an end to this craze, and fearing the worst, the parent's of some of the injured kids called a meeting to alert other parents of the dangers their kids faced if they were taunted into accepting the challenge. It was determined that they needed to assess the situation firsthand. The next morning a chosen few assembled to inspect the area, and possibly contact old Mr. Hutchinson in regards to knocking the house down to prevent any more fascination with it, before, heaven forbid, there were any more injuries, or worse, because of it.

At daybreak, they set out on foot. It had been years since any of the land in this area had been cultivated making it impossible to get there by any other means. If demolition was deemed necessary they could plow through the brush with a tractor, but unless and until they came to that conclusion, they didn't want to make it any easier for the kids to go there by clearing a straight path. In truth, a trail would have possibly prevented some of the wounds, but that wasn't their goal. The solution lie in getting rid of the source of the madness.

There were five men, carrying a variety of tools, including machetes, sickles, hammers, and pry bars. They had no idea what awaited them at the old homestead, but if the stories they'd heard were any indication, it would take some work to get up to the actual house. After nearly forty-five minutes of trudging up the slightly inclined rugged terrain one of the men finally spotted the chimney in the distance. True to the accounts, it stood stoically above the house, beckoning them.

Glad to have what was, hopefully, the hardest part of the mission behind them, they ambled around the structure, evaluating the situation. Had it not been for the chimney, it would have been impossible to tell a home was there. Tall weeds and even small trees had sprouted haphazardly around the building and the entirety of it, trees and all, were completely enshrouded with thick layers of kudzu.

There was no way to tell what condition the homestead was in, unless they hacked their way in to it. Deciding to take a breather before tackling the task at hand, they used their machetes to clear a place to sit. None of the men had ever seen the house in its day and had no idea where, under the blanket of kudzu, the front door stood. They began to ruminate about when the rumors had first started about the property and surrounding area being haunted, then laughed at the ridiculousness of it.

Their laughter abruptly halted when a very distinct thud reverberated from under the mass of greenery beside them. Silent, with confusion mirroring on their faces and their eyes asking one another if they'd heard the same thing, another thump rumbled in their ears.

The hair stood on the back of their necks momentarily until one them voiced that some sort of critter must have burrowed in and made it his home. Chagrin flooded the features of the other four men as they hastily searched out their tools to start to work, not making eye contact with each other lest their embarrassment show.

They each picked an area and began slicing and chopping their way to the *not* haunted house. After several minutes one of the men called out, "I think I gotta door over here!"

The others converged to the same area and carefully avoiding each other, widened the opening. Above the door there was what appeared to be a metal roof extended out a few feet, but no indication of a porch or steps that had apparently rotted away over the years and melded with the earth beneath their feet. The bottom of the door was a couple of feet off the ground, the door handle above their heads. The handle turned, indicating it wasn't locked, but the door didn't budge.

After butting it several times with their shoulders to no avail, they resorted to their hammers and pry bars. Tapping the end of the bar between the jamb and the door with the hammer, they were able to pry it back until the door busted around and away from the handle. Without the surrounding door to hold it in place anymore, the handle relinquished its duties and fell to the ground.

With a push the door swung inside unimpeded and the men were immediately met with an atrocious stench that had them backing away, gagging. After a few minutes to recuperate, one of the men pulled his shirt up over his nose and mouth and retrieved his hammer. Holding his breath, but keeping his nose and mouth covered with his hand and shirt for good measure, he approached the opening and leaned inside, tapping forcefully on the floor with his hammer, testing its strength before staggering back to take in a gulp of air.

"It seems fairly solid," he choked, pulling in another breath.

Two of the others decided to give it a go. One tied a bandanna over his nose, the other took a handkerchief out of his back pocket, quartered it, and held it in place over his face. One after the other they held onto the door jamb and hopped inside. It took a moment for their eyes to adjust to the darkness. The kudzu nearly blocked out all of the light. Blinking, they shuffled a few steps forward, carefully testing the floor before putting all their weight on it. Looking around the small room, one of them men tapped the other on the upper arm and motioned to what appeared to be a sofa or bench on the other side of the room, piled high with blankets.

They inched their way toward it, taking short breaths in through their mouth but keeping their covers pressed tightly over their noses. As the first man reached the couch he began pulling back the blankets one by one. The second man stepped up beside him and they glanced at each other and shrugged. It just appeared to be layer after layer of blankets and quilts.

Curiosity began to overtake the other three men and they were at the door preparing to crawl inside, when the first man pulled back the final blanket.

Both men reared back in horror and revulsion, as a partially mummified skull leered at them with an evil grin, and they proceeded to empty the contents of their stomachs onto the floor.

CHAPTER 12

The men were still doubled over, heaving, when a furious growl pierced the air, a split second before what felt like a brick wall crashed into them. The pile of blankets on top of the corpse softened their landing, but the weight of the wall was still pressing on them heavily. It took a moment for it to register that the wall was clawing at them and screaming like a banshee.

Neither man understood what was happening, but fearing for their lives they struggled to get free, wishing, too late, that they'd heeded all the warnings of the haunting.

The other three men had witnessed the fracas and they rushed to the aid of the first two men. It took all three of them to wrestle the wild attacker off long enough for the first two men to regain their footing and get a look at what they were dealing with. A quick glimpse was all they got before it became clear it was going to take *all* of them to gain control and they joined in, hoping that the five of them was *all* it took.

One of the men broke away, took a knife out of his pocket and grabbed one of the blankets, slicing off a long strip. It cut easily and he prayed it was because his knife was that sharp, and not that the material was dry rotted. Grabbing an end of the strip of fabric in each hand, he tugged on it, testing it for its strength. It withstood the tension and would hopefully suffice until he could cut more and double it up.

The other four men had wrangled their opponent to the floor and were trying to grab any of the flailing limbs they could, to tie together, but the writhing, blood, sweat and vomit was not making it an easy feat. Several grueling minutes passed before their attacker was hog tied successfully, at least they hoped, and they fell back against the surrounding walls, gasping for breath. The putrid smell had now permeated their nostrils and was no longer registering in their exhausted brains.

Finally able to get a good look, they were amazed to see that the assailant, an enraged, violent, out of control giant just moments ago, had been reduced to a weeping and apparently *frightened* man. A *really big* man. His hair was long, greasy, and disheveled, no doubt due, at least in part, to the struggle, and his face was covered with scraggly hair. His fingernails were jagged, which had most definitely played a part in some of the gouges and scratches all the men now sported. His clothes were filthy and tattered, and he had one old scuffed work boot on, but not tied.

Between the big bear/man's muffled sobs, it sounded like he was saying something. Listening carefully, the men could make out a word that sounded like…"mama". Yes! That was it. He was calling out to his mama! Baffled, the men exchanged glances, wondering why a grown man would be calling out for his mother. From there, it wasn't a big leap to surmise that that's whose body was under the blankets.

Now that the pieces of the puzzle were falling into place, the men were feeling a little less threatened and discussing a plan of action, when one of them noticed a boot, clearly exposed after the altercation shifted the blankets. It was eerily similar to the one the tied up man on the floor was wearing. A *man's* boot.

Alerting the other men, they began to doubt their previous assumption that it was the man's "mama" under the covers. And if that wasn't "mama", who was it? And where, exactly, was "mama"? Reluctantly, they decided to look a little closer at the cadaver under the blankets. As they began to slowly get to their feet, their stirring caused the bound man to react by curling up into a fetal position, shying away from them, his crying reduced to a whimper.

While the others looked on, one of the men guardedly made his way around him, even though he appeared incapacitated now, and stepped up to the covered body. With his nerve threatening to evaporate, in one swift move he gripped the bottom blanket and yanked it back, revealing the head and torso of the unknown individual.

As repulsion washed over them anew and they grimaced and dry heaved, swallowing back the bile in their throats, the man on the floor began to speak again.

"S'no use, Daddy won't eat," he informed them mournfully. "I tried an' tried, but he jes won't eat." His voice rose in despair, and still on his side, he began a rocking movement, as if trying to comfort himself. He repeated, "Daddy jes won't eat, Daddy jes won't eat..."

All eyes went back to the body and they noticed then, not only the sparse facial hair and the man's shirt, but strawberries, some fairly fresh and others older and reduced to mush, lying all around the skull.

More of the mystery was unraveling. Apparently the corpse was the bear/man's father and the bear/man/son was not right in the head. Though the cause of death was unclear, the remorse from the dead man's alleged son and his obvious effort to feed his father, conveyed to them that he'd loved him, and therefore, *hopefully* hadn't contributed to his death. They looked at the distraught bear/man in a more sympathetic light.

While determining that the two men who had originally been attacked would go for help and the other three would stay and stand guard in case anything transpired, one of them moved toward the doorway the bear/man had emerged from and he became very agitated again.

"Caint go there!" he yelled, twisting and pulling on his restraints. "Mama ate! Mama ate!" he cried out. His vexation increased exponentially with every step closer the men got to the next room. "No! Cain't go there," he screamed louder, jerking violently on the ties binding his hands.

Realizing there may be another body in the house, the closest man went through the opening. About fifteen seconds later he ran back into the room. "Uh, they's somebody in there! It's a woman!"

His announcement didn't really surprise the other men. From what their prisoner was saying and the way he was thrashing about again, they figured his *mama's* body must be in there. It was the next revelation that surprised them!

"She's alive!" he exclaimed.

The bear/man's rants made sense now. *"Mama ate! Mama ate!"*

"But she don't look real good," the man added, stepping aside so the others could see for themselves. The two that they had decided would go for help exited the room with a renewed urgency in their step. They hurried to the front door, hopped down to the ground and rushed off.

The two men that were still in the room with the woman weren't sure what to do. There were two separate piles of filthy looking blankets on the floor that appeared to be where they'd been sleeping, but she was on the floor in the far corner of the room. She was wearing a threadbare nightgown, and she was so thin she looked almost as bad as the skeleton in the other room. It was hard to tell if the discoloration on her arms and legs was bruises or dirt. Her wrists and ankles were bound, and the skin around the ties looked red and scarred. Her face was gaunt with dark circles around her eyes, and her hair was so matted and dirty it was hard to tell what color it was.

She had her knees drawn up to her chest and was trying to hide her face behind her twig like upper arms. She lowered her arms a fraction to peek out, checking if they were still there, and seeing they were, she struggled to get closer into the corner, clearly terrified.

Pity weighed heavily on the men, and they tried to assure her they weren't going to hurt her.

"It...It's okay ma'am," one of them stammered. "We're a-gettin' ya some help," he promised. Realizing it didn't ring true, since they were still there, he offered in explanation, "Well, a couple of *other* feller's went fer help."

She didn't seem to understand, and when they made any movement she cowered even closer into the corner, so they backed off, telling her help would be there soon and they wouldn't leave her. On their way out, they took in the perimeter of the room. They saw what looked to be a pile of carelessly discarded empty mason jars and lids. Apparently, the remnants of their food source. They also noticed then, the strawberries in varying degrees of decay on one of the bed of blankets, just like what was around the head of the corpse in the other room. They presumed this was what the bear/man had been feeding his "mama". But what didn't make sense was why her arms and legs were bound. Actually, there wasn't much that made sense here. They backed just outside the doorway keeping an eye on her from afar.

Joining the other man, the three of them stood in the small area between the two rooms with a vantage point to both the woman and the bear/man, quietly considering what the story was behind this crazy situation.

It was over three hours before the rescue team made it back to the house. They'd had determine how they could bring the two of them back and once that was decided, they had to get the necessary equipment to make it happen. They would need to raze a pathway with a tractor in order for a truck to be driven up to the house. That was fairly easy. But then they had to round up a doctor that could evaluate the condition of the two of them, and probably sedate at least the bear/man, possibly the woman, too.

Once they had all they needed, they began the trip back. The tractor mowed down a swath wide enough for the truck to follow behind. It wasn't a smooth ride but it was the best they could do. The two men and the doctor rode horses back, cantering along behind the truck, and leading horses for the other three men that were keeping guard at the house. That way if the woman wasn't physically able to ride in the front of the truck, there would be plenty of room on the back for both of them to lie, sedated.

The men at the house heard the tractors rumbling motor and blades clearing the way to them and breathed a sigh of relief. Both the woman and the bear/man had been no trouble. The woman was still pressed into the corner, but had let her arms drop to her sides, with her head and body leaning against the wall. They were pretty sure the bear/man had fallen asleep but didn't want to go close enough to check and possibly wake him up. As the noise from the tractor drew nearer though, the sound roused him, and he reacted bolting upright, his eyes wide in panic.

As the fog from his sleep dissipated, he looked with confusion at his bound wrists and feet. You could see as his mind unfolded the events from earlier, and upon seeing that the men were still there, he scrambled away until the wall stopped his retreat, and cowered in that position much like the woman in the other room had done.

The doctor pulled himself up inside the house and blinked, letting his eyes adjust to the dim lighting. He didn't react to the odor. Either it had aired out some or he was familiar with it. He did a quick visual assessment of the two patients. The woman was definitely malnourished, but didn't appear to be in any medical distress. He turned his attention

91

back to the bear/man. He would clearly need to be sedated in order to be removed from the house. Giving him the injection was going to be the trick. He decided to try the straight up approach.

"Hello, young man," he said from the middle of the room.

The bear/man watched him warily, but didn't react. The other men thought that was promising. The doctor took a small step closer.

"Your father wouldn't eat?" he asked.

The bear/man shook his head.

"But your mama ate?"

This time he nodded.

The doctor was pleased. He'd wanted to ensure the bear/man that they didn't think he'd done anything wrong. Next he wanted to try to find out who they were.

"Can you tell me your name?" he asked in a soft soothing tone.

"Benny," he said proudly.

This was good. He was relaxing some and the doctor recognized Benny's desire to be acknowledged.

"Benny. That's a nice name. Do you have another name?" he prompted, hoping to be able to identify the family and track down any relatives.

"Benny," he said again, matter of fact.

Disappointed, the doctor realized it could take a while to learn their identity from Benny, possibly never, but he could try again with Benny's mother. For now he needed to get Benny to trust them and convey that they weren't going to hurt him, and he was sincerely hoping that *no one* got hurt.

"Benny, you can call me Doc, okay?" he told him, trying to establish a rapport. "Would you like for me to help your father?" he asked.

A vigorous nod.

"Is it okay if I check on him?"

Another vigorous nod.

Without making any sudden movements, the doctor went and looked over the corpse. He was able to detect, by this point, that Benny had some mental issues. The extent of those issues, were yet to be determined. This could possibly help the situation if things went the right way. He proceeded to examine the corpse, and then asked the corpse if it was okay to give him some medicine. As if the corpse gave their blessing, he enacted giving it a shot. He then asked if he should give some of the same medicine to Benny as well. Acting as though the answer was yes, he turned to Benny.

"Your father would like for you to have some medicine too, okay?" he asked him.

Benny looked like he wanted to refuse and he glanced at the corpse.

"It's okay, your dad wants you to," the doctor assured him.

Benny's eyes cut from the doctor to the corpse then back to the doctor. Fear reflected in them. It was hard to tell which one he was more afraid of, his father or the doctor.

The doctor hated to take advantage of it, but Benny's fear of either angering or letting his father down would work in their favor. The doctor advanced closer to him slowly, repeating that his father would be very happy if he got his medicine.

Benny started to whimper but kept glancing back to the corpse, and though he clearly wanted to get away, he didn't try to.

When the doctor was close enough, he knelt down, face to face, with Benny. "Okay, I just need to get to your arm like I did with your dad. Can I do that?" He reached toward him but Benny flinched.

"Daddy?" he cried out.

"It's okay," Doc interjected quickly before Benny panicked. "Daddy wants you to take your medicine. You don't want Daddy to be upset do you?"

Benny shook his head vehemently.

"It will only take a second. Your daddy will be so proud of you!" Doc pulled back the shoulder of the coat Benny had on, in spite of the warm weather. Under that was another coat, and then another, and another. It turned out that the bear/man was actually quite thin himself. The bulk was from the many layers of coats.

The men watching from behind glanced at each other, chagrined now, that it had taken five of them to take down an underweight boy that was touched.

94

Once Benny's shoulder was exposed, Doc was able to give him the injection with no resistance. It was sad really. Benny was probably harmless under the right care, he thought, watching as Benny's eyes slowly closed as the sedative took effect.

Once Benny was out, he stood and gave the men waiting the go ahead to relocate Benny to the truck, and he went to examine the woman.

She was extremely wary of him but didn't put up much of a fight, possibly because she didn't have any strength left. With no layers of coats to contend with it was easy to give her the injection. She wasn't a danger, but she was going to have to be carried out and he felt that she would be less traumatized if she were sedated, like Benny. He only gave her a cursory examination, more concerned with getting them to a facility prepared to treat them, before they awoke.

CHAPTER 13

It had been a long day for Tommy and Horace, particularly Horace. But with them working together all day it was bound to affect Tommy too. It started with Horace arriving for work thirty minutes later than usual, causing both of them to get out in the field behind schedule. It all went downhill from there. They got caught in a downpour out there and decided to wait it out, trying to make up for lost time, thinking it would pass quickly. It didn't. Eventually they packed up and headed in, getting nearly out of the field when the sun came back out. They turned and went back to work.

During a break, Horace explained part of the problem with his mood. "I tell ya, I ain't got no sleep fer like four nights, now."

"How come?" Tommy asked.

Horace sighed. "Oh, Horace Junior. I reckon he's got his days an' nights mixed up, ya know, he sleeps all day at school with Aubry, even with all the racket from the youngens, but then soon as its dark an' time ta go ta bed, here he goes, don't matter what I do, or what Aubry does, he jes won't stop cryin', he won't let us lay eem down, he cries if we hold eem, he cries if we walk eem, he cries if we don't walk eem, he cries with a wet diaper, an he cries with a dry un, he cries with a bottle, an' he cries without a bottle, its cry, cry, cry all night long, Aubry tries ta take care of eem, so's I kin get some sleep, but then I feel bad cause she needs ta get some sleep too, and I cain't get ta sleep no way with eem a-cryin', so we both ain't getting' no sleep, she's tired as I am, I reckon, cry, cry, cry, all night long, I tell ya I ain't ne'er heared so much comin' outta one person non-stop."

Horace's last sentence left Tommy wanting to say "seriously?", but he didn't, happy that Horace had gotten it out of his system.

But Horace wasn't done. "Then soon as it's 'bout time to get up, bam he's asleep, he don't make a peep all the way ta the school, all day durin' school, 'cept ta eat, then he's back out, Aubry's tried ta keep eem awake durin' the day but he ain't havin' no part of it, I'm so..."

He went on...and on...until all Tommy was hearing was "blah, blah, blah".

After break, they went back to work hoping for a fresh start, but things continued to go wrong. Trying to figure out how to turn things around, Tommy recalled one particularly bad day he'd had a while back. Figuring it was worth a shot, he told Horace he had an idea and for him to follow his lead. They headed in from the field, stopped to put things away at the barn, then without letting anyone know they were back, headed down the road. Tommy reasoned that no one else needed to know they'd stopped early, it was for a good cause, besides, Aubry and the kids were still in school, and Samuel and Chalmer were probably taking their afternoon nap.

Much to Tommy's surprise Horace didn't ask any questions. He was too busy talking about diapers and bottles and crying and sleeping and not sleeping.

When they arrived at the lake, Horace looked around as if he was just realizing where they were and wondering why.

As Tommy had hoped, there was no one else there because the water was still like ice, much too cold for swimming. Without explanation, he pulled the little boat they kept hidden, out of the brush and instructed Horace to get in while he pushed them off, then hopped in himself. Once seated, he told Horace to take the oars and row them out a ways.

Horace did as instructed, but began to question what Tommy was up to.

"Whut are ya tryin' ta do, wear me out more?" he asked.

"Quit yer moanin'," Tommy laughed. "Yer gonna see here in jes a minute," he said, sure that it was a really good idea.

Once they were a respectable distance away from the shore, Tommy asked Horace for the oars. He took them and flung the first one as hard as he could toward the shore.

"Whut the heck are ya—"

Before Horace could finish his sentence, Tommy slung the second oar toward shore, knowing Horace would argue with him otherwise, and his lesson would fail. Neither oar quite made it to land, but they were floating, so Tommy wasn't concerned. Mission accomplished, he looked at Horace and remembering his papaw Samuel's words, he said, "Now, row us back with them *other* oars." He looked at Horace smugly, feeling pretty good about things going perfectly, so far.

Sure that Tommy had lost his mind, Horace said, "*Whut* other oars?!"

The smugness on Tommy's face morphed into dread. He quickly scanned the boat, realizing the old broken down oars his papaw had made him use to row back with before, weren't in the boat anymore. Someone had apparently finally laid them to rest, and he'd neglected to check first.

Reluctantly making eye contact with Horace, they both turned to gaze longingly at the new oars floating about as far away from them as they could get.

Their eyes met again, Horace's speaking volumes that Tommy didn't want to hear, and Tommy's were twinkling with mirth. He let out a nervous chuckle, waiting for Horace's response.

"I ain't a-getting in that water," Horace stated, straight-faced, failing to see the humor in their situation.

"Aw, ya ain't gotta get in the water," Tommy said, spreading his arms wide to paddle with his hands. But the width of the boat prevented him from reaching the water.

Scooting to one side he used both hands to paddle, effectively turning them in a few circles, but getting no closer to shore.

Horace watched, still not amused.

Tommy moved to the other side and paddled a bit, then switched back, finally going forward, albeit in a zigzag pattern, but at least headed in the right direction.

Horace shook his head. Taking pity on Tommy, he leaned over and began rowing on the opposite side and it straightened their course toward shore. Tommy glanced back over his shoulder at him appreciatively.

"Yer such a goof," Horace told him.

On the way back they picked up the oars, pulled the boat out of the water and put it away, shaking the numbness from their hands caused by the frigid water.

"Ya gonna tell me whut that was all about?" Horace asked, as they headed home.

Tommy told him about Samuel's lesson with the old oars, and how sometimes you have to row with the oars you've got.

"Uh huh..." Horace murmured thoughtfully, his brow creased. "And whut 'xactly's that gotta do with sleepin'?"

Tommy thought about it for a second. It had made sense earlier, but now he was at a loss for words.

Horace gave him a playful shove as they walked along. He kind of got what Tommy had been aiming for but he wasn't going to admit it.

As they neared the house, they noticed the activity over at Sarah's Home. Samuel, Chalmer, Aubry and Horace Junior were on the front porch, watching also.

There were several vehicles, as well as numerous people milling about. They could see that at least two of the vehicles were patrol cars, and saw uniformed officers. Their first thoughts were Adohy, remembering his last encounter with the authorities. They hoped it had nothing to do with him, and each prayed he was okay.

It was at least thirty minutes before Evelyn came home from her shift and they were filled in on what was happening, and she also confirmed that Adohy was fine. It had nothing to do with him.

"I only caught bits and pieces of the story, and the police officer's are still trying to get to the bottom of everything, but it seems that they found this man and a woman he says is his mama, in an old *supposedly* haunted house over the ridge near Norton Cemetery," she explained.

"Oh, I heard a-that place, o'er by Big Ridge State Park an that cemetery with the sunken grave!" Tommy recalled.

Samuel and Horace nodded in recollection, too.

"Well, anyway," Evelyn went on, not sure about all the haunted stuff, "the man, they say, is not mentally stable and that's why they brought him here, and not only that, but there was a dead body of a man, supposedly his daddy, and his mama was bound hand and foot and severely malnourished. They brought her, too."

"Sounds like mebbe the man oughtta b-be in jail," Samuel offered.

Tommy agreed and added, "And I ain't real thrilled with you a bein' 'round somebody dangerous."

Hoping to put his mind at ease, Evelyn explained, "Both of them are sedated right now and I heard one of the officer's say that they couldn't keep him because of him not being right and needing medical attention. Plus they don't know the whole story or if he even did anything wrong. So he's got to be held here until it's determined what his condition is, mentally and physically."

"What about the woman?" Aubry inquired.

Sympathy washed over Evelyn's face. "Oh gosh, I only got a glimpse of her, but what a mess," she answered. "I'll find out more tomorrow, when I go back to work.

§

At the Home, Faith and Adohy, taking a break from the final finishing touches of their house, had just taken Oppy outside for some fresh air, when the vehicles transporting the patients and the authorities arrived. Faith noticed Adohy stiffened visibly at the sight of the officers but she touched his arm gently, interrupting his fearful reverie, bringing him back to the present and safety.

He looked at her gratefully, love and a hint of embarrassment evident in his eyes.

Reassuringly squeezing the hard bicep of his arm, she smiled at him with adoration.

Only a short distance away, they turned Oppy's wheelchair so she could watch the activity as well, while the patients were loaded onto stretchers and wheeled into the Home.

As they were rolled by, Oppy became a bit animated, and her eyes lit up. "Red!" she called out, pointing in their direction. "Red?" she questioned, nudging Faith, still pointing ahead.

Faith wasn't sure what to make of it. She scoured that area looking for the color red. Some clothing, or a blanket, anything to explain what Oppy was referring to, finding nothing.

As soon as the crowd dispersed Oppy's enthusiasm faded away, and Faith and Adohy exchanged a puzzled glance. Unable to determine the target of Oppy's interest, they shrugged their shoulders and continued the stroll pushing her along, until some of the commotion settled down inside and they could take her back for her supper.

CHAPTER 14

After consulting with the Doctor that transported the patients, it was determined it was in everyone's best interests, *particularly* the patient's, to keep them sedated until more thorough examinations could be made. That would also enable the staff to give them sponge baths safely, and hook up IV's for their dehydration and some much needed nutrients, without fear of them yanking them out.

After a day or two, when they had received enough sustenance to be out of danger, they could be weaned out of their drug induced coma and mental evaluations could be conducted. If they were cooperative and able to eat by mouth, great. If not, they would have to be restrained and continue to be fed and medicated intravenously.

The Doctor stayed on to give his medical opinion and consultation with Millicent. Partly because he was already on site, and partly because he was vested in their cases now. They began with the woman.

She appeared to be in her late fifties, but given her circumstances he said she may actually be a few years younger. There were no distinguishing marks on her for the sake of identification. But her wrists and ankles were scarred deeply, indicating at the very least, prolonged binding, probably years. Most of the discoloration on her body appeared to be dirt and grime build up, again from possible months of not bathing. Her hair was matted and mostly gray but based on her pubic hair it appeared that it may have been brown or auburn at one time.

A further vaginal examination showed no signs of assault, at least, not in the recent past. She had both ovaries and her uterus, indicating she'd had no hysterectomy or overt medical issues there, though she'd most certainly been through menopause, based on her age.

Her resting heart rate was seventy eight beats per minute, perfectly in range, and her circulation felt strong in her extremities. Her breathing was unimpeded.

It seemed there were no broken bones at present, but without x-rays the doctor couldn't say with certainty. Her temperature was normal, her eyes were green and reacted as expected to light, and her reflexes responded to stimulation. Her teeth weren't in the best of conditions, but again, given her apparent lack of a nutritious diet and amenities, that was not unusual.

Her nails were short, jagged, and brittle, also a side effect of a poor diet. Her inner ears looked normal, but they would have to assess her hearing after she was awake.

After the doctor completed her physical, he gave the go ahead for her to be bathed, and an IV to be administered.

He would complete his other examination and return to check on her afterward.

Millicent escorted him to Benny's room. His layers of clothing had been removed, and he was much less intimidating inert and covered with a sheet. His examination revealed much the same as the woman's, no physical abnormalities other than the obvious poor diet, or in Benny's case, apparent lack of diet altogether. His skin was loose and sagging, a clear indicator of having lost a great deal of weight very quickly. Given his height of approximately six feet four inches, and the extent of flabby skin on his body, he had indeed recently had quite an intimidating stature.

After an oral exam disclosing that Benny had wisdom teeth just coming in, contradicting the doctor's previous assumption of him to be in his thirties, he corrected his estimate to the much younger age range of early twenties. And based on their short interaction before he was sedated, he estimated that he had the mentality of someone even younger, possibly preteen. That would be determined later.

Benny's other stat's were all in the normal range. The Doctor gave his assent for him to be bathed and shaved, and hooked up to an IV as well, and he would return to check him again before he left.

He accompanied Millicent to her office to discuss what he was aware of that had transpired prior to their arrival. Any more information would have to be obtained from the authorities after they completed their investigation.

He was able to tell her where they were found, the condition of their dwelling, the empty mason jars that had apparently been their source of food at one time, and the only evidence of recent sustenance was strawberries, noting there was a large wild strawberry patch nearby.

There was no furniture of any kind, other than the ragged couch the corpse was resting on. The only clothing they'd seen was what they each had on, but there was an astonishing number of blankets, both covering the body and as pallets to sleep on. He imagined it was due to being their only way to stay warm throughout the winter, and even then it seemed impossible they'd survived. He speculated perhaps that was the cause of death for the man's body that was there.

Giving her all the information he had, they returned to the woman's room to see what progress had been made. They were taken aback at the transformation. Her hair had been far too matted to salvage, and they'd had to cut it off fairly close to her scalp. But it had been washed and dried and looked much better. With all the grime washed away, you could see the fairness of her skin. She was milky white, indicating a lack of exposure to the sun, the only other color on her face and arms were from freckles. Her IV was in place and she appeared to be resting comfortably.

They checked in on Benny, and again, were amazed. He was unrecognizable from his former appearance, bathed and clean shaven. His hair had been cut as well, making him look more his estimated age.

They discussed an appropriate treatment plan for the two of them, and the Doctor asked Millicent if she would be opposed to him checking back in on them in a few days. She made it clear that she not only had no problem with it, but welcomed it, since he was the only one, thus far, that had seen them conscious. He agreed to come back in two days to monitor their mental state as they weaned them from the sedative, and make a comparison from earlier today.

After Millicent walked him out, she was met with the officers that had evaluated the scene. She led them back to her office for privacy, and they exchanged contact information, before relating their findings. Or lack thereof, really. They had the body sent to the county morgue for an autopsy and hopeful determination of cause of death. The house was searched, with no information found that could lead to their identities.

It appeared they had been there at least several months, based on the amount of empty mason jars in the room the woman had been held in, though that could vary depending on how much they ate in a day. They'd found a cellar of sorts, or more accurately, a crawl space, two steps underground, below what had been the kitchen at one time. There was a short access door and once you ducked through that and went down the two steps, there were shelves lining the sides of the six by six by three foot space. They'd found a few broken mason jars with rotted remnants of fillings, and that led them to believe it was where they'd acquired most of their meals.

Prior to the men clearing a path to the front door, there was no visible way to get in or out of the house until they located a tunnel that had been wallowed out, they presumed by Benny when their canned food was exhausted. It lead from a window and continued under the brush and kudzu, low to the ground. He would have had to crawl in and out on his stomach, probably in search of food. It was fortunate for them there was a large wild strawberry patch not far from the house. There was no water source, other than a bucket with rain water that was located just outside the man-made tunnel. The dipper in the bucket was what led them to that assumption.

They also found several pots with lids, apparently retrieved from the kitchen, that had been used for relieving themselves, but found nothing else. After the search, they contacted the very elderly owner of the property, who was unaware that the house was still standing, much less inhabited.

Unless the body could be identified, or until the two patients were awake and could tell them who they were, their investigation was at a standstill.

Millicent made them aware of the course of treatment, and subsequent plan to slowly let them regain consciousness in two days, under the doctor's supervision. It was agreed they would return then also, but asked if anything transpired prior to that time, that Millicent please get word to them. She assured them she would.

§

Faith and Adohy were through working for the day and walking through their house, checking their progress and admiring what had been completed, when they realized it was done. Finished! There was nothing left to do! The icebox, wood stove, and furniture had been moved in. Some furniture was new, some handmade, some handed down, but it was all theirs now. The curtains were in place over the windows, pictures were hung, pots, pans, plates and utensils were in the kitchen.

The house was perfect. Nowhere as fancy as Virgil and Millicent's or as large as Sarah's Home, as theirs was only four rooms at present, a living room, kitchen and two bedrooms, but it was exactly what they wanted.

Faith's heart skipped a beat as they looked at each other, smiles playing on both their faces. It was hard to believe they finally had their own home! Just the two of them! Faith envisioned cooking breakfast and supper for just herself and her gorgeous husband. It was almost like they were just getting married all over again! Thinking back it occurred to her that not once in their married life had they eaten a meal without other people. The thoughts of it being just the two of them made even eating sound intimate! Then she realized they didn't have any food yet, but that could be remedied easily enough. They just needed to go visit Caleb and Fred at the store and stock their cabinets.

When the thoughts of something as mundane as food shopping together sounded as exciting to her as it did, she wondered what else they'd been missing for so long! Evidently, Adohy was considering the same thing.

"Come here," he murmured, his voice thick with emotion.

She walked into his arms and they kissed passionately, until it began to build to a tempest and they made themselves back off. Taking a step away, Adohy asked "How long before we can move in here?"

Faith grinned. "Just as soon as we can make a grocery list!" she replied, grabbing his hand and tugging him along to find a pen and paper.

CHAPTER 15

The aroma of meatloaf, Adohy's favorite, wafted through the air as Faith prepared their first meal in their new home. Their first meal alone. Halfway through mashing the potatoes she realized her hands were shaking. Trying to laugh it off, nothing usually rattled her cage, she finally had to admit she was behaving like a Nervous Nellie!

She'd been fine all day throughout the shopping and putting things away, then making strawberry shortcake for dessert, but as the evening drew near, the nerves crept up on her. She had no idea why! She took a deep breath, trying to calm herself. For crying out loud, she wasn't this nervous on her wedding night, she thought!

She planned to finish supper, then had promised to go make sure Oppy had her meal and by then Adohy would be done with his work. The fact that she'd not cooked a whole meal entirely alone before either was lost on her until she was doing it. Maybe it was a combination of so many first's that had her feeling out of sorts.

§

It wasn't until the next morning that she realized she'd been shaking with excitement not nerves! The night had been perfect from start to end! The entire meal was delicious, and the rest of the night was even better. Yes indeed, she was one lucky girl, and she knew it! Even all the activity going on at Sarah's Home today couldn't compete with her bliss.

The authority's had already arrived by the time she went over, and the IV's had been removed. It was just a matter of time before the patients were awake. Everyone was on high alert, waiting anxiously for their reactions when they came to, and ready to subdue them, if necessary.

Faith took advantage of the calm before the unknown to get Oppy fed and ready for her day. Oppy was fine most everyday with the other staff for everything, except for when it came to eating. That was reserved for Faith only, and it was okay. Faith was just glad she lived right next door!

Both doctor's, Dr. Wright, the one on call for Sarah's Home, and Dr. Martin, the one who had brought the patients there, were on site and monitoring the weaning process. Benny had already started stirring, and he was the one they were most concerned with, given his reaction when he'd been confronted before.

When he finally opened his eyes, the last person he'd seen before he'd lost consciousness was the first person he saw. The doctor had asked the others to stay back in the hopes that he wouldn't be frightened and over-react.

"Hi Benny," Doctor Martin said softly. "You've done very well! I'm very happy about that!" he encouraged.

Benny's eyes darted around the room, no doubt trying to place where he was, but the doctor kept speaking in a soothing tone to keep him calm.

"Yes, you did a very good job! I bet you must be hungry! Are you hungry, Benny? Would you like something to eat?"

Benny nodded his head, still checking around the room.

The doctor gave a slight nod for food to be brought in. "We have some food for you right here. They are going to bring it in for you, okay?"

Benny looked toward the orderly standing in the doorway with a tray of food and tensed up a bit.

"It's okay, Benny," the Doctor assured him. "It's just your food. Scrambled eggs and bacon! Doesn't that sound good?"

It must have appealed to him, as he nodded and licked his lips.

With another nod from the doctor, the orderly entered slowly and placed the food on the bedside table. Taking care not to make sudden movements, the doctor pulled the tray closer and holding out his hand to assist, asked Benny if he could sit up in the side of the bed. With the food in sight, Benny took the doctor's hand and pulled himself up. As soon as he was upright, he grabbed a spoon and began shoveling food in his mouth as fast as he could.

115

"You don't have to rush," the doctor explained. "And there is more if you want it."

Benny nodded his head, even though there was still more on his plate.

He ate two plates full of eggs and bacon with two biscuits before he showed signs of slowing down. Once he was done eating, he drank a full glass of sweet milk.

After he emptied his cup, he suddenly got a startled look on his face. "Mama! Gotta feed mama!" he cried out, trying to stand.

"It's okay, Benny!" the doctor said, placing his hand gently on his shoulder to keep him from standing. "It's okay! Mama already ate," he lied. "She's fine! She just wants you to rest. Okay? Can you do that for her?"

Benny seemed confused and unsure what to do. The doctor changed the subject.

"Can you tell me your whole name?" he asked.

"Benny," he answered.

"Do you know when your birthday is?" Dr. Martin tried.

"I ain't got no birthday," Benny said sadly.

Noting that tactic clearly wasn't going to work, but not wanting to broach the subject of "mama" again just yet, the doctor asked, "Do you have any brothers or sisters?"

Benny shrugged.

This was an unexpected answer. Did he not know if he did or not?

Benny started rocking back and forth. Something about the question made him nervous. The Doctor decided to change topics again, his main focus to keep Benny calm until he was secure in his surroundings and with his new caregivers. Once that was managed, they could broach these subjects again. They still had the woman to question as well, and she may be more forthcoming, making all of this unnecessary.

Benny had noticed his reflection in the window across the room. Seeing Benny's fascination with the person he saw in the window, the doctor asked if anyone had a mirror. A small hand mirror was obtained within moments.

"Would you like to see how you look, now that you've been cleaned up?" he asked.

"Cleaned up?" Benny asked, his brow creased, eyes clouded with confusion.

"Yes, you had a nice bath and a shave. You look very nice. Would you like to see?" The Doctor held the mirror up. Keeping hold of it, he positioned it so Benny could see his reflection.

Benny flinched away at first but kept his eyes on the mirror. Realizing his movements were matched in the mirror, he looked closer. His hand reached up to his chin to feel the smoothness without the facial hair. A slight smile emerged under the bafflement. He looked at the doctor as if he were being tricked, then back to the mirror. He leaned in close again and turned his head from side to side. A full smile spread across his face. He ran his hand over his short hair.

"You had a haircut too! It looks nice don't you think?"

117

Benny nodded, still smiling at his reflection.

The doctor started to move the mirror and Benny pulled his hand back up, continuing to preen.

"Okay, I have to put the mirror away now," the doctor started, but Benny wasn't done. Dr. Martin let him admire himself a few more moments and an idea came to mind.

"Do you like to play any games?" he asked, trying to get Benny to move on to another topic.

That did it! Benny eyes lit up and he dropped his hand from the mirror.

"CandyLand!" he shouted and clapped.

The doctor looked at the staff in the doorway hoping he hadn't opened a Pandora's Box. Would they possibly have a CandyLand game? A few seconds later he was presented with one. Of course. It *was* supposed to be a children's home, after all!

He invited a few of the staff inside under the ruse of playing CandyLand with Benny and he was all for it. No issues with the unknown people, no violence, no cares in the world once the game was brought out. He even forgot about the mirror! He appeared to be just a young boy in a grown man's body. A young boy looking for love and acceptance.

Now, on to the woman.

As they approached her room a nurse advised Millicent and the doctors that she'd just opened her eyes. They watched her for a moment from the doorway, but there was no movement, she merely stared at the wall across the room. Perhaps she wasn't completely conscious, yet.

They entered slowly, nearing the bed with caution, both for their safety and so as not to startle her. Dr. Martin held up his hand to have the others hold back, while he took a few steps more, so that she could see him.

"Hello?" he said softly.

No response. Not even a flinch.

"Can you tell me your name?" he asked.

Nothing.

He leaned down to look into her eyes. They appeared clear but empty. He waved his hand in front of them but it was as though he wasn't there. She continued to stare through him, blankly. He checked her eyes with light and her pupils reacted normally, so the problem wasn't there.

"Do you mind if I help you sit up?" When she didn't answer, he gently pulled back the sheet covering her. Glancing over his shoulder for help, Dr. Wright stepped up, and each placing a hand under her arms, they pulled her to a sitting position and placed her feet on the floor.

She made no resistance, and stayed where they'd placed her, sitting upright on her own.

Leaning down to eye level again, Dr. Martin asked, "Are you hungry? Would you like something to eat?"

She simply stared ahead.

He asked for a plate of food to be brought in. While they complied, he conferred with Dr. Wright, explaining that her temperament was much different than his last encounter with her, describing her fear and reaction to other people's presence. They surmised that perhaps she was having lingering affects from the medication.

Within a moment, plate in hand, Dr. Martin held it in front of her face.

No recognition.

He took the spoon, scooped up some scrambled eggs and held it to her lips.

No response.

They decided to lay her back down and give it a little more time. In the meantime they would check back in on Benny.

He and the two staff members were immersed in the game. Benny appeared to be having a great time. No threat to anyone.

They discussed a plan of action, deciding to see how the day progressed without any more questioning. Let him adjust to his surroundings, the staff, his room, without any stress. They would give him a mild sedative to help him sleep overnight. If all went well, they would try again tomorrow.

Millicent and the doctors spoke to the officers who had arrived, to see if they had been able to determine who the duo was. Explaining that it wasn't looking very optimistic yet but there was still a slight possibility they would be able to get through to the woman, the officers said they would come back the next day.

Returning to the woman's room, they found her as they had left her. The attendant relayed that she hadn't moved. They helped her to sit and tried once again to entice her to eat, to no avail.

Doctor Wright recalled a case he'd read about, and proposed that as a coping mechanism she may have retreated deeply inside herself to block out reality. Without knowing what she'd been subjected to it was hard to say. They were also now considering the possibility that she'd had an adverse reaction to the medication. If she did not become more reactive, and eat or allow herself to be fed, she would have to go back on the IV.

Millicent suggested letting Faith have a go at getting her to eat.

The doctors were agreeable.

After Faith was summoned, she stopped to grab a long sleeved smock. She'd had no problems feeding Oppy, but didn't know what to expect from this patient and had no desire to be wearing any food today.

Once in the room, she was apprised of the situation. She took the plate and carefully sidled up to the woman, taking a seat beside her on the bed. She shifted the plate to her left hand and placed her right hand on the woman's shoulder, gently.

The others stood quietly, watching.

Faith slowly began to move her hand across the woman's upper back in a slow caressing massage. During this, she began to hum so softly the others could barely detect it.

When she stopped humming, in a slow motion, she picked up the spoon and brought it to the woman's mouth.

The others gasped audibly when the woman opened her mouth and took the spoonful of eggs. Faith allowed her a moment to chew and swallow and offered another bite, which she took. After a few bites, Faith took a slice of bacon and nonchalantly held it out to her, but she didn't take it. While she continued to stare ahead, Faith broke a piece of the bacon off and brought it to the woman's lips. She opened her mouth, letting Faith place it inside, then chewed and swallowed. She showed no interest *or* aversion to the food.

Faith attempted once more to get her to respond by holding a cup of milk to her, but she refused to fall for it. She would, however, allow Faith to hold it to her mouth while she drank.

The doctors considered it a win. They were amazed at Faith's ability.

When she was through, they asked her what she had been humming.

She smiled and said simply, "Sarah's song."

CHAPTER 16

The rest of the day passed in much the same fashion, with no change to note in the woman's condition. She continued to allow Faith to feed her dinner around noon and supper in the evening, and had enough of her faculties to use a bedpan when encouraged, but showed no other signs of being aware of her surroundings. She would not answer any questions, or focus her eyes on anyone or anything. She was like a life-size version of a marionette.

Benny was easily kept occupied with games, and had no problem eating on his own. If he continued eating at the rate he did the first day, he would regain his weight in no time. He appeared to be happy and got along well with anyone who came to his room, his previous fear of people and duties to feed his mama, apparently forgotten.

After a few more days of the same, Benny was dressed and allowed to come out of his room to the common area. Any patients who were able to, were wheeled or walked there on their own and could go and visit with family or other patients.

Benny was as taken with his new clothes as he had been with his haircut and shave. His excitement was contagious as he modeled them for everyone who cared to look. It was like watching a boy on Christmas morning.

He had no problem coaxing some of the other patients into playing games with him, and was actually quite uplifting for a few that had been feeling a bit lonely.

A few days later, when Benny had graduated to going out doors for a while each day, it was with one of these melancholy patients that Millicent witnessed a most moving incident. She had been sitting at a table doing some paperwork while overlooking the patients in the common area. Tenley was sitting at a child size table having a snack of milk and cookies. She had her new little red wagon parked closely at her side.

For some reason after Tenley finished a cookie, she carefully took her cup of untouched milk and her other two cookies, placed them in her wagon, then picked up the handle and slowly pulled the wagon across the room. Curious as to what she was doing, Millicent watched discreetly as Tenley approached an elderly woman named Irma, who had been feeling poorly. She'd been sitting idly, trying to hide her aches and pains, but still, a tear had escaped and ran down her cheek. Tenley took her napkin with her cookies in one hand and the tiny cup of milk in the other hand and held them out to Irma, in offering.

Tenley's back was to Millicent now, so she couldn't see her face, but she could see Irma's eyes light up behind her unshed tears. Her aged and gnarled hand reached out to cup Tenley's little cheek, then she gratefully accepted the cookies and milk. As they conversed back and forth, inaudibly, Millicent's heart swelled at the change in Irma from her daughter's little act of compassion.

When Irma was finished with the cookies and milk, Tenley placed the empty cup back in her wagon, and left with a wave, pulling her wagon back to her child size table. As the little wheels turned on the wagon, so did the wheels in Millicent's head. She called Tenley to her and told her how proud she was over the act of kindness, adding the idea it had given her.

That became the start of the two of them baking cookies every day, and her escorting Tenley to deliver them in her wagon to the patients who were able, spreading her sweet innocence to those in need of a smile. It was a brilliant success. Tenley loved doing it every day and learned every ingredient and quantity, using little dosage cups to cut out the bite size cookies. She became the princess of Sarah's Home and the highlight of the patient's day.

~~§~~

In light of the persistent state of unresponsive wakefulness of the woman thought to be Benny's mother, she was dubbed Jane Doe for identification purposes until such time as she was identified. There had been no word on the identity of the corpse, as yet either, and though the case was still open the authorities had ceased coming daily to the Home for updates. Millicent was to contact them upon any breakthrough.

Physical therapy had begun on Jane in an attempt to prevent and reverse signs of muscle atrophy. She had gained some weight and was able to stand, assisted, for short periods of time, long enough to make the transition from the bed to a chair, but there was no change in her ability to focus on objects nor had she made any attempt to speak when questioned or otherwise. She continued to eat as prompted, but only if Faith was doing the prompting.

Dr. Martin had reduced his visits to Mondays and Fridays, just to stay in touch and abreast of any improvements. Consulting with Dr. Wright, they decided to try showing her to herself in the mirror as they had done with Benny, hoping for a positive reaction, or the very least, to spark some sign of recognition, but her eyes remained blank and unfocused.

It was the consensus of both doctors that contact with Benny could possibly be detrimental not only to Jane, but Benny as well, so they were going to continue with the current course of action.

The lack of change in Jane was just the opposite with Benny. He was growing both in size and relations. He had no compulsions about talking to anyone he came into contact with, or asking them to play CandyLand with him. If they preferred not to play that game, any game would do. In spite of his age, they'd determined that he couldn't read or write, but Evelyn had begun to do some work with him in those areas, and he showed promise of being able to retain the lessons. He'd also been learning to help in the garden and feeding the animals and did as asked, without complaint. He took great pride in positive encouragement, thriving on the accolades. They had as yet to find anything he wouldn't eat. He was a lot like Chalmer in that aspect.

The two of them hadn't been acquainted yet, due to Chalmer spending his days at the Jenkins' house with Samuel, but Chalmer's sixth birthday was over the upcoming weekend and Millicent was considering having a little birthday party for him at the Home. She thought it would be a nice activity for some of the patients to look forward to.

~~§~~

Friday arrived with a little summer shower, but it passed quickly leaving it a bit humid and warm. Samuel could deal with that, he was just relieved the rain hadn't lasted long. As a surprise for Chalmer's birthday, he'd planned to take him fishing. It was the last day of school and from then on out the lake would be teeming with kids and adults alike, fishing, or swimming to get cooled off.

Chalmer's birthday was Saturday, and they were planning a party at the Home, but this was part of Samuel's birthday present to him. He'd gotten a new little cane pole just for Chalmer, and truth be told, he'd forgotten how much he'd missed fishing, himself. If they were lucky, the two them just might be able to fry up a mess of fish for supper before Tommy and Evelyn came home, and surprise everyone.

After breakfast Samuel presented Chalmer with his fishing pole.

They were on the porch, watching the sun come up like they always did. When the rain stopped and the sky lightened up, promising the end of the showers, Samuel decided it would be okay to go ahead with his plan. The last thing he wanted to do was give him a fishing pole, then tell him they couldn't go fishing because of the rain.

"Ya know, Chalmer, I heared ya had a birthday a-comin' up," Samuel stated.

"Yep! Tomorrow! I's gonna be six whole years old!" he answered, stretching himself a little taller.

"Six? Well I reckon it's time then..." Samuel said thoughtfully, his voice trailing off. He continued rocking, contemplating.

"Time fer whut?" Chalmer asked cautiously, not sure if it was time or not.

"Well if yer g-gonna be six whole years old," he stood and opened the screen door, Chalmer watching his every move, "then it's high time ya got yer own fishin' pole!" he announced, pulling the pole from behind the wood door and holding it out to Chalmer.

Chalmers eyes got big as saucers. "No kiddin'?" he asked, before making a move.

"No kiddin'!" Samuel chuckled, as Chalmer jumped down from the rocker. But he had to swallow back the lump in his throat when Chalmer ran past the outstretched pole and wrapped his arms around Samuel's thighs, hugging him with all his might.

He reached down and petted Chalmers head, swallowing hard. Feeling himself getting choked up and before he reached the point of no return, he said, "Don'cha wanna take a look at it?"

Chalmer let go of Samuel's legs and turned to take hold of the pole. "This here is one fine lookin' fishin pole, ain't it, Samuel?" he said proudly, examining it.

"It shore is, yes sir. Ya reckon we oughtta go check it out an' make sure it works right?"

"Ya mean it? We's gonna go fishin'?" Chalmer asked, hopeful.

Samuel pursed his lips and nodded. "I reckon we should."

"Oh boy! This day's jes gettin better an' better!"

Chalmer already had his worm house. He carried that with him everywhere he could get away with it. They got the rest of their gear together and took the truck down to the lake. Once there, they transferred their stuff to the boat, and Samuel rowed them to an area that he'd had luck at before. He cautioned Chalmer on how to behave in the boat, then helped him get baited up and his hook in the water. Chalmer took pride in choosing the perfect worm suitable for the job, and didn't flinch sticking it on the hook. It was *finally* fulfilling its chosen duty.

By the time they got back home, they not only had enough fish to fry for supper, but had enough to invite Horace and Aubry to stay as well. Tommy and Horace picked a head of cabbage, a few carrots and some onions from the garden, and the girls made coleslaw and fried potato wedges to go with Chalmer and Samuel's mess of fish, along with some mouth watering hush puppies.

Chalmer went back to Sarah's Home and to bed that night, thinking that things couldn't get any better.

Tommy and Evelyn sat in the swing on the porch, after Samuel called it a night, talking.

"Ya noticed since Chalmer's been comin' here ever'day that Papaw ain't been a-hardly stutterin' at all?" Tommy asked.

"Mm hmm," Evelyn murmured. "They've been so good for each other, all the way around. Samuel's been so much more active, he looks better, he's practically stopped stuttering. He's done that all his life, hasn't he?"

"All *my* life, anyways," Tommy confirmed.

They continued to swing in silence, both lost in their thoughts.

CHAPTER 17

Saturday evening rolled around just in time, before Chalmer busted a gut with excitement. It never occurred to him that he'd be getting any other gifts, he was just anxious to tell everyone about his new fishing pole and all the fish they'd caught the day before. That, and of course, the cake and ice cream.

They'd already begun churning with two churns, everyone taking turns to earn their bowl full. They were making one vanilla and one with some of the last of the strawberries from the season.

Caleb and Fred came up to celebrate and visit with Oppy, bringing with them another gift that Samuel had ordered for Chalmer. They updated everyone that the electrical lines were getting ever closer to the store. They hoped in a month or two to have power, and in the meantime he and Fred had been running wiring in the store for outlets. It was another cause to celebrate.

When the ice cream was ready, they dished it out and lit the birthday candles, singing Happy Birthday to Chalmer, who was eating up the attention. He helped pass out the bowls of ice cream letting the guests choose their favorite, vanilla or strawberry. Benny opted for the pink one, putting a big spoon full in his mouth. After one taste, he got up and handed the bowl to Millicent. She took it, surprised that he didn't want it.

"You don't like it?" she asked him.

He shook his head.

Then she remembered being told that he and Jane had apparently *existed* on strawberries alone for a while before they'd come there. She chose a bowl of vanilla and offered it to him.

He looked at it hesitantly.

"It's okay. I think you'll like this one," she told him, extending the bowl a little closer to him.

He took it and she waited while he sampled a tiny taste of it.

He smiled. "Good!" he said, sitting back down to eat it.

Millicent continued on around the room, checking that everyone had their own helping.

The strawberry seemed to be the flavor of choice, and Faith took a bowl to Oppy. She really seemed to enjoy it, so when Faith was through feeding her, she decided to slip out for a moment and take a little bit to Jane. She had a soft spot in her heart for Jane. There was just something about the way she would only react to her that was touching. Before the strawberry ice cream ran out she got a few spoon fulls and went to Jane's room. Relieved to see she was still sitting in the bedside chair, not having been put to bed yet, Faith said hello, as she entered the room.

She sat down on the bed. "I brought a special treat to you!" she told Jane. Taking a bit onto the spoon she held it to Jane's mouth.

Jane's arm shot out knocking the spoon out of Faith's hand, ice cream splattering down the front of her shirt. Caught off guard by the sudden movement, she examined Jane's face and eyes for any change, finding none. Naturally she'd not worn the smock, she thought dismally, grabbing a tissue to wipe the ice cream off. Assuming it was an uncontrollable muscle spasm, she put another spoonful to Jane's mouth, and thankfully didn't end up wearing it, but Jane's lips were clinched tightly.

Baffled, she tried one more time but Jane wouldn't open her mouth. She gave up, told Jane good night and left the room. Back in the common area, she searched out Millicent and filled her in about the incident. Millicent shared with her Benny's dislike of the strawberry ice cream too and her best guess as to the reason why, which in turn raised their hopes by the negative reaction from Jane. Maybe she *was* still in there somewhere. They just had to figure out how to get to her!

Chalmer couldn't have been more elated when he found out he was getting more presents. There were toy trucks with wheels that turned, and one that looked like a circus wagon that you pulled with a string and it played a tune. He was fascinated with that one. *Until* it came to the gift that Samuel had gotten him.

When Samuel handed it to him, Chalmer looked up in surprise. "Anuther one? But ya already got me a fishin' pole, ya aint a-takin' it back are ya?"

"Naw, that there's yer pole. It ain't a-goin' nowheres. This present's from me an' Tommy an Evelyn," he explained.

"Oh! 'Kay then!" he said, relieved, tearing open the package. It was a transistor radio. He'd seen a few of the kids after school with the boxes that played music, and had asked Samuel about it. Looking up at Samuel, he asked, "Is this whut I think it is?"

"Shore is," Samuel confirmed.

"With a real live battry an' everthin'? It's gonna play music?"

"Well, turn it on an' check an' see if'n we kin pick up anythin'," Samuel suggested.

Chalmer turned the wheel and with a click, static rang out. He jumped at the sudden noise, then laughed at his reaction. He turned the tuning wheel and got a faint voice fading in and out. Continuing on, he passed a loud sound, then backed the wheel up to tune it in. Music filled the room and his face lit up! Everyone clapped as the song *Love Sick Blues* by Hank Williams played, loud and clear.

Tommy pulled Evelyn up to dance, and a few others swayed to the music. Some patients clapped or tapped their toe in time. It had turned into a real party. Virgil picked up Tenley and went to Millicent, giving his girls a turn, but halfway through the second turn, Millicent stopped and looked back to Benny who'd caught her eye on her way around.

He was sitting in the corner with tears streaming down his face. Virgil followed her line of sight and nodded as she told him she'd be right back. Millicent wondered what could be wrong. He'd seemed fine before, after the strawberry ice cream, but maybe it had triggered some bad memories.

She went to him and asked softly, "Benny? What's wrong?"

He shuddered, and pulled in a breath. "I ain't got no birthday," he sobbed.

Millicent's heart shattered. It had never occurred to her that this birthday party would affect Benny in a bad way. To see a seemingly grown man distraught like this, was too much.

She looked back at Virgil, not sure what to do. Seeing her distress, Virgil handed Tenley to Faith and Adohy and went to see if there was anything he could do to help.

She whispered to him the issue and between the two of them they decided on the spot to announce that the following Saturday was thereby declared Benny's birthday and everyone was invited back next week at the same time to have another party. She hoped she was doing the right thing but couldn't imagine what in the world it could possibly hurt. Counting the date off in her head she told Benny that his birthday was going to be June sixteenth, one week from that day. She didn't know if he understood exactly but it seemed to appease him and he stopped crying, and she offered him another piece of cake that he accepted enthusiastically.

With the crisis averted, she went back to finish her dance with her husband and daughter.

Chalmer was picking up a station on the radio out of Knoxville and a show by Cas Walker, *The Farm and Home Hour*, had come on now. It was to promote a line of grocery stores that Cas Walker owned. Few of the people in the room had been even been to Knoxville much less seen such a store as Cas Walker's. While they gathered around listening, Cas Walker announced the first performance of a little girl named Dolly Parton. She began to sing and Chalmer was enchanted. When the song was over and Chalmer heard that she was ten years old, he announced then and there that he was going to marry her one day. Everyone cheered at his lofty expectations.

After the show and the evening was drawing to a close, Chalmer went around thanking everyone for his gifts. It didn't take a rocket scientist to figure out what his most prized present was. In fact, everyone had enjoyed the opportunity to listen to the Cas Walker Show. It was a rare treat for them down in the Holler to pick up the station in Knoxville, even for the few of them that did have transistor radios.

Evelyn was helping clean up, when she noticed Chalmer gathering up his gifts to take to his room. The radio had been turned off to preserve the battery, but he was still singing away, doing his rendition of *Love Sick Blues*. It was adorable. *Out of tune*, but adorable. It was the song that had been playing when he'd first turned on his new radio. She was amazed that he'd not only remembered what song was playing but retained some of the words, albeit *not* so much of the tune! She watched him for a moment while the others were saying their goodbyes. She chuckled to herself remembering his vow to marry the little girl, Dolly, on the radio. Maybe he thought he had the love sick blues over her!

She walked over to him. "Hey Chalmer, do you know what love is?" she asked.

He scrunched up his face, thinking. "I reckon I don't know fer shore," he answered.

She rubbed her hand over his chest and tummy and said, "Love makes you feel real good in here."

Enlightened, he exclaimed, "Then I reckon I must love pinto beans an' cornbread!"

She laughed. "Well, what about Samuel? Do you love *him*?"

Nodding, he confirmed, "I shore do! I love him *and* bloody eggs!"

Ugh. She swallowed. *I have got to get him to call them something else!* she thought to herself. "Can you think of anything else you might love?" she asked, expecting him to say Dolly.

"Well," he said, considering, "I reckon I love lots a things!" Then he added, "I love *you!*"

You could have knocked Evelyn over with a feather. Her knees went weak, then her heart melted.

CHAPTER 18

Down at the General Store toward the end of the following week, Caleb and Fred were putting away an order that had come in, which included another transistor radio. Millicent and Virgil were going to give it to Benny on Saturday for his birthday, after seeing how taken Chalmer had been with his.

As they were stocking the shelves, Eunice Small came in. Her name fit her well. She was a little elderly lady, barely five feet tall, who had lived walking distance from the store her whole life, with her mother, father, and sister. When her parents passed away, she and her sister Bernice, neither of whom had ever married, lived together until Bernice's passing a few months prior.

The two women made ends meet making and selling simple hand sewn dresses, or mending items for others. Since Bernice passed, Eunice had been having a hard go of it, but Caleb and Fred had been looking out for her, as best they could. They let her charge things she needed, leaving items off here and there, but making sure she didn't notice. She was determined to take care of herself, and they didn't want to break her spirit. It was about all she had left.

She'd just finished her shopping, and Fred was totaling it up when the bell jingled on the door and a distinguished looking man stepped in.

With Fred busy assisting Eunice, Caleb offered to help when the man approached the counter.

"Howdy!" Caleb greeted. "Kin I help ya?"

The gentleman relayed he'd just stopped in for a couple of cold drinks for him and his wife, who was out in the car.

"Well, I got some cool ones, but they ain't *ice* cold cause the ice man ain't come yet. We're a-waitin' on the electric lines to come through here, but *they* ain't made it here yet, either. These'll wet yer whistle though if ya still want a couple."

While Caleb was explaining this, the man couldn't help over hearing the conversation between Eunice and Fred, even though Eunice was speaking quietly.

"Fred, I know I already owe ya a lot, but once I get me some fabric an' get some more dresses made an' sold, I kin get ya all caught up. It won't be long," she promised.

Before answering Caleb's question about the cold drinks, the man pulled him aside. "I don't mean to pry, but how much does the woman owe?"

Caleb hesitated, not sure if he should say or not, but was curious why the man wanted to know. "Well, I think it was bout twelve dollars and change before this order. She lives by herself now that her sister passed," then caught himself before saying anymore. He still didn't know why the man was asking.

The man said, "I'll take them two cold drinks and..." he reached into his pocket and retrieved his billfold. Flipping it open, he pulled out a twenty dollar bill, "...put the rest on her tab."

Caleb took the offered bill, and glanced at Eunice. He wasn't sure how she was going to react to the gesture, so while he thought about how to handle it, he went to get the cold drinks. When he returned, Eunice had already gone out the door. Well that decided that. He'd go to her house and tell her about it later so she wouldn't be fretting over her bill when she needed something else.

He thanked the man on Eunice's behalf, and asked if he was from around there.

"No," the man shook his head, then realizing he hadn't introduced himself, said, "I'm sorry." He extended his hand to shake. "My name's Herschel Brock, my wife Ella is out in the car. We're on our way to Baptist Hospital in Knoxville to see a specialist. She's been very sick for a while now and we're hoping they can help her."

"I'm sorry ta hear that, but it's nice ta meet ya. I'm Caleb, an' this here is my wife Fred," he told him, canting his head toward Fred.

She stepped over to shake the man's hand, noticing his perplexed expression. "Winifred," she explained, while they shook.

He smiled and nodded in understanding, looking a bit sheepish that she'd caught his puzzlement.

"Happens all the time," she said, brushing it off.

"Well, I'd better get going. My wife is already very tired from the drive."

"We'll keep ya both in our prayers. That was very kind a ya ta take care of Eunice's bill. It will be such a blessin' fer her," Caleb informed him.

"It was my pleasure, and thank you! We need all the prayers we can get!" he said earnestly, waving goodbye.

§

There were two new arrivals that day at Sarah's Home. Orphaned brothers, Jubal and Enos Wentz, fifteen and sixteen years old, respectively. They'd run away from their last foster homes because neither home could take them both. Truth be told, they'd both been in so much trouble, they'd been lucky to get taken in at foster homes at all, but their age played a big part in that. They were cheap labor.

As it was, they'd been caught in Maynardville, trying to break into a store. Millicent could only hope it was because they were hungry and looking for food, and not from meanness. Since they'd not actually broken in yet, and with nowhere else to take them, they were brought there. They were advised that if they were to get into any more trouble they were going to end up in juvenile detention, where they'd stay until they turned eighteen.

They both proved to have quite the attitude with the authorities and the staff. It was clear to see they were going to have their hands full with these two boys. Millicent prayed they were up to the task and could get through to them, before it was too late.

They'd only just arrived and she was already concerned about them interacting with the other patients, especially Benny. Thankfully, Chalmer was rarely there anyway, and with luck she could keep them apart when he was. Both Benny and Chalmer had been doing too good to be influenced by these boys bad behavior.

Wanting to get them occupied right away before they could cause any chaos, Millicent thought that possibly Virgil could put them to work with the horses. While the boys were being shown to the room they were going to share, Millicent sought Virgil out, filled him in on the situation, and asked his opinion.

He considered it a moment and decided he could try to use them training with the horses. Maybe between being able to work together and the responsibility of learning about the horses, it would appeal to them enough to keep them out of trouble. He shrugged, and said it was worth a try. Millicent hugged him and went to get the boys.

They were sprawled across their beds laughing about something, but when she entered they both clammed up. She didn't take it personally, boys will be boys, she thought.

The oldest boy, Enos, looked her up and down with a leer, and said "Maybe it ain't gonna be too bad here after all."

Jubal snickered at the remark, but stopped when Millicent gave him a no nonsense glare.

She said a silent prayer that this didn't turn into a disaster, and for the Lord to give her the strength and the wisdom to deal with these two. It seemed like Jubal looked up to his older brother, so if she could keep Enos in line, things just might work out fine. Counting on appealing to his desire to show off for his younger brother, she laid it on thick.

"You know, Enos, there's something here we could really use someone who's strong and reliable on, I mean, *if* you and Jubal think you're up to it." She waited to see if he would take the bait.

He glanced at Jubal, who was watching for his response. Enos sat up on the bed, and bent his head from side to side to loosen his shoulders and flexed his arms a bit. With a sniff, and trying to look uninterested, he said, "Depends. What is it?"

Jeez. This kid could give James Dean a run for his money, she thought. "Well if you think you two can handle it, come with me." She turned and left the room without looking back. She walked down the corridor, willing them to be following behind her. At the door she stopped and finally turned to check. Thankfully, they were standing there.

She led them out toward the barn to Virgil, and announced, "I know you've been needing a couple of good, strong, young men that you can depend on, and I thought these two might fit the bill." She winked at Virgil to give him a heads up on the ruse.

"Uh, yeah, yeah...that's exactly what I need. You boys know anything about horses?" he asked, turning his attention to them.

They glanced at each other before Enos answered. "Yeah, they got four legs an' ya ride 'em?" he smirked, then laughed out loud, looking at Jubal expecting him to be laughing too.

But Jubal stood straight faced, timidly awaiting Virgil's response.

Enos stopped mid chuckle and looked at Virgil, too.

Millicent bit her lip. This wasn't going as she'd hoped.

Virgil wasn't amused. "Yeah, that's exactly right, but Millicent must have been mistaken here, cause ya see, I don't need no wise guys," he said, and started to turn and walk away.

Before Millicent could say anything, Enos blurted, "Okay!"

Virgil stopped.

"Okay," Enos relented with a sigh, his eyes cast at the ground. "It was just a joke."

Virgil turned back. "Well, out here there's no time for jokes. That's how people get hurt," he warned. "There's a time and a place for joking, and this ain't it. Now if you think you can remember that, then we'll get along just fine."

The boy's looked at each other again. Jubal nodded slightly, a yearning plea in his eyes. This place didn't seem too bad, and they were finally together again. He didn't want that to end.

"We can remember," Enos told Virgil.

"Well, let's get to work then. I'm Virgil," he said and reached out to shake each of their hands.

They told him their names and Virgil stepped aside extending the palm of his hand to lead them ahead. As they walked past him, he winked back at Millicent with a knowing grin.

Relieved that he had everything under control, she went back to Sarah's Home, desperately in need of a break. It had been an eventful day so far and it was only half over.

The mail had come and she sat down to go through it. One particular envelope caught her attention. It was addressed to her and Virgil and was from one Lewis J. Pendergriff, II, Esquire. She took the letter opener and tore the envelope open. As she scanned the paper inside, her hands started to shake and she felt the blood drain from her face.

§

Caleb and Fred looked up as the bell jingled on the door, surprised to see it was Millicent in the middle of the day, but their smiles died on their lips when they took in her stricken expression.

CHAPTER 19

For a moment, Fred and Caleb both feared that something had happened with Oppy but noticing the papers in Millicent's hands, quickly realized that though she would have been deeply affected had it regarded Oppy, she would have been more tactful breaking the news to them. Fred dropped what she was doing and called over her shoulder, asking Caleb to grab a chair. She rushed to Millicent's side.

"Millicent, honey, what is it?" she asked.

"This came...today..." she choked out. "What does...it mean?" she cried, thrusting the papers toward Fred.

Caleb arrived with a chair and had Millicent sit down, while Fred perused the letter. They waited expectantly, with Caleb's hand on Millicent's shoulder for moral support.

As Fred scanned the document, her free hand crept up, covering her mouth. The letter read,

To whom it may concern,

In the matter regarding the Native American individual, of unknown age, also known as Adohy White Horn Thornton, the subject of an adoption proceeding dated August, 10, 1955, please be advised the proper civil procedure was not adhered to by law, thereby effectively rendering the aforementioned adoption process incomplete and unlawful.

As such, any and all legal matters entered into by said aforementioned individual, also known as Adohy White Horn Thornton, a false identity, of unknown age, a Native American are also to be considered unlawful, up to and including a marriage to one Faith Anne Jenkins, a minor Caucasian female. As of receipt of this correspondence please be advised such marriage to be considered legally null and void.

Furthermore, until such time as aforementioned individual, also known as Adohy White Horn Thornton, a false identity, of unknown age, a Native American, can prove otherwise, he is hereby ordered to cease and desist the use of the illegally obtained surname of Thornton, and also is hereby remanded to the Qualla Boundary, the Reservation for Native American individuals located in Asheville, North Carolina, effective immediately.

Any variance in the aforementioned orders set forth in this correspondence, or failure to relocate to the Qualla Boundary, a Reservation for Native American's, located in Ashville, North Carolina, could result in the arrest and imprisonment of the aforementioned individual also known as Adohy White Horn Thornton, a false identity, of unknown age, a Native American, with criminal charges including

but not limited to, obstruction of justice,
false identity, fraud, forgery, and
pertaining to the aforementioned individual
Faith Anne Jenkins, a minor Caucasian
female, aiding and abetting in the
delinquency of a minor, and statutory
rape.

Receipt of this correspondence serves as
documentation that the aforementioned
individual, Adohy White Horn Thornton, a
false identity, of unknown age, a Native
American, has been truly and legally
informed.

Sincerely,

Lewis J. Pendergriff II, Esquire

She re-read it out loud, both to make sure she hadn't
missed anything and so Caleb would know what was going on.
When she finished, she leaned down to address Millicent.
"Honey, this has got to be a mistake. You wait right here and
let me get my purse. We'll go to Maynardville right now to get
this straightened out, okay?"

Millicent nodded, unable to speak through her tears.

Fred stood, making eye contact with Caleb, a silent
question in her eyes.

He nodded, "Yeah, shore, I got this here. Y'all go on
and git this taken care of." He massaged Millicent's shoulders
softly. "I'll be a-prayin' fer ya," he was promising her when
Fred returned with her purse and car keys.

On the drive, Millicent tried to compose herself. "I'm
sorry," she told Fred. "I just didn't know who else to bring this
to. I didn't even tell Virgil I was leaving," she worried.

"Honey, you don't have anything to apologize for. We'll get this figured out. There has to be a mistake," she said reassuringly.

But it had the opposite effect.

"That's what I'm afraid of!" Millicent wailed, starting to cry again. "What if he's not really ours, what if they're not legally married!" her voice rose, as she broke down.

Biting her tongue, Fred assured her. "We'll get if fixed honey, whatever it is, we'll get it fixed."

It was nearing three o'clock when they arrived, and the City Hall closed at four. Hurrying inside they went to the family division and waited for the next available clerk. When their turn came, they showed the clerk the letter, waiting while she looked it over.

Once done, Fred asked, "What does this mean? How could this happen? The adoption was finalized here. What could be wrong?"

The clerk turned and asked another clerk to pull the family court file on Adohy and the Thornton's. Turning back, she said, "I don't know, but this does sound serious. Do you have legal counsel?"

They both shook their heads.

"Well, you may want to get one. The child that you adopted was Native American?

She was addressing Millicent, but they both nodded.

"I can't say for sure, but maybe there's an issue because of that. We don't get too many adoptions through here involving Native American's."

The clerk returned with the file and handed it to the young lady helping them.

She looked through the paperwork, checking forms and signatures, shaking her head, baffled. "I don't know. Everything appears to be in order, but in light of this letter, if I were you I'd get an attorney that has experience with matters concerning Native Americans. That's the only thing I can think of that could be a problem."

"Don't let them take Adohy away from us!" Millicent begged, becoming distraught again.

Fred stepped in. "Do you know anyone? Can you recommend someone?" she asked.

The girl grimaced apologetically. "I don't. I'm sorry." Feeling helpless, she added, "Maybe someone in the legal aid department can? It's right across the hall if you want to slip over there and ask. They should still be there," she said, glancing at the clock on the wall.

Fred nodded, and grabbed Millicent's hand to hurry to the legal aid department. They obtained the name of someone who may be able to help them, and they asked to borrow the phone to call his office, but he couldn't see them until the following afternoon at one o'clock.

Millicent was beside herself on the ride back. "I don't know what to do. Should I tell Adohy and Faith what's going on, or wait till we know more tomorrow?"

"Honey, I don't know. My instinct is to wait. There's no sense getting them all upset over what could be a simple misunderstanding. On the other hand, if it were me, I think I'd want to know right away..." she trailed off, then added reluctantly, "just in case."

Millicent looked at her, tormented.

"If you want, I'll go with you, and you can fill Virgil in on everything. Then if you decide to tell them, I'll be there for support. Honey, I really think everything will be fine. We did hundreds of these adoptions while I worked for the State Department of Indian Affairs. I'll go with you to the attorney tomorrow too and make some calls while we're there. Okay?"

"Thank you," Millicent said, her gratefulness shining through her tears.

They stopped by the store to get Millicent's vehicle and let Caleb know the latest, then headed to Hurricane Hollow.

Virgil reacted much the way Millicent had, but without the tears. He had question after question. Worry lined his brow.

After much deliberation, considering it was five p.m. now and the appointment was at one o'clock the next day, they decided to not upset Adohy and Faith until they knew more. The idea that Adohy could be incarcerated could cause them both to panic and that was the last thing they wanted.

To make sure there was no undue alarm, Virgil agreed to let Fred accompany Millicent to the attorney and he would stay there to keep Enos and Jubal out of trouble. They

would tell everyone Millicent was helping Fred with a
personal matter.

It was the longest night of Virgil and Millicent's life.

CHAPTER 20

Fred and Millicent arrived early at the attorney's office, hoping to put an end to the nightmare, but he'd been held up in court and the secretary offered to reschedule them. That was not an option for Millicent, so they had no choice but to wait. On the bright side, while they waited the secretary was kind enough to allow Fred to use their phone to make a few calls as long as they were quick.

The attorney arrived at two-thirty, introduced himself as Harold Barnfield, and apologized profusely, asking them to follow him into his office straightaway. He was a short, heavyset man, and looked to be in his mid to late fifties. As he laid aside his briefcase and took off his suit coat, draping it over the back of his chair, he asked, "Can you give me a brief rundown of the history of your relationship with the...Native American in question?"

Millicent did as asked and then handed him the letter. "Please, just tell me, can they take Adohy from us?" she pleaded.

"Let's see what we have here," he replied without answering her question, while he looked over the letter.

Millicent sat wringing her hands, and when she looked at Fred, the fear in her eyes was palpable.

Mr. Barnfield called to his secretary. When she appeared in the doorway, he asked, "I need you to send for copies of the adoption papers from City Hall."

"Yes sir," she answered, and left.

Addressing Millicent, he said."I am not familiar with Mr. Pendergriff, but I will give his office a call, and see if we can get to the bottom of this. In the meantime, I will look over the paperwork from the adoption proceeding and make sure it's all in order—"

"Can they make Adohy go to the Reservation?" Millicent cut in. She couldn't stand it any longer. She had to know.

He hesitated, considering how best to answer. He sighed. "There have been some folks, *activists*, trying to stir up controversy against Native Americans, against letting them reside outside of the reservation, against being adopted by non Native American families, etc., and I'm not going to mislead you, this is mostly uncharted territory. I am not especially well versed on situations such as this." He could see the tears welling up in Millicent's eyes. "Now, having said that, in light of the fact that Adohy has not been officially recognized by the Cherokee Nation, and you have documentation of the adoption

by the State of Tennessee, at least for now, unless it is over
turned, or proved to be in error, the law as I see it would be on
your side."

Millicent sighed audibly, and sank back into her
chair.

"At least for now," he put out there again. "But I
assure you, I will reach out to the Department of Indian
Affairs, and anyone else necessary to get to the bottom of this.
As far as I know there have not been any new laws enacted
regarding non Native Americans adopting Native Americans.
So for the time being, I don't believe he can be forced to
relocate to the Reservation. If we can confirm that the
paperwork regarding his birth and age is in order, and he is in
fact legally considered to be an adult, I don't believe that he
would have to go back there, regardless of the adoption
outcome."

Fred spoke up now. "I helped with the paperwork in
this case and—"

He interrupted, "I'm sorry, I didn't get your name."

"Oh, it's Fr—er Winifred Groaner. I formerly
worked for the State Department of Indian Affairs, and
assisted in several adoptions to non Native American families
and there has never been an issue that I'm aware of. We
followed the same procedure in this case."

"Well, that's good to know. As I said it may all be a
simple misunderstanding, or it may have to do with the
controversy stirring over such adoptions that have called this
into question. Whatever the case may be, we'll get to the
bottom of it. Now, I must tell you, there is a chance that if the

adoption is somehow found to be incomplete, that *would* also make any other legal matters entered into, such as the marriage, null and void."

"Oh no..." Millicent murmured, raising her hands to cover her face.

"But let's not get ahead of ourselves," Mr. Barnfield reassured her. "I just want you to be fully informed and aware of the possibility."

She took a deep breath and nodded. "I, I mean *we*, my husband and I, haven't told him about this yet. Should we?"

"I would apprise him of the situation, certainly. It would be best for him to be prepared for whatever outcome." He waited, giving them a moment to consider everything they'd discussed. After a bit, he asked, "Do you have any other questions?"

Fred and Millicent looked at each other, then shook their heads.

Fred offered, "Your secretary was very helpful and allowed me make a few phone calls to the State Department briefly, but no one there could tell me of any changes they were aware of in the procedure regarding adoptions."

"I can assure you that we will do some research, make some calls, and do our utmost to get this matter resolved as quickly as possible," he promised. "Feel free to call or stop in whenever you are able for any updates, and I will certainly notify you immediately as soon as I know more."

"Thank you," Millicent said, with her best attempt at a smile as she stood to shake his hand.

§

The distance from his office back home seemed to have doubled. Thankfully Fred was driving. Millicent rode along with a heavy heart trying to imagine breaking the news to the kids. Adohy and Faith had been so happy, how could she shatter their lives with this crazy mess? Especially when she had no answers, no reassurances that everything they thought they knew to be true and real in their lives could be snatched away in an instant? *One* mistake, *one* oversight in the adoption proceedings could wipe out the validity of everything from then on. The only good thing she could think of to lighten the load was that they didn't *think* anyone had the right to force him to move to the reservation.

She thought back to all the correspondence, research, and even a trip to the Reservation itself, and the lack of interest in getting anyone to assist them at all because Adohy couldn't prove he was part of their tribe. Now that he'd moved on with someone who took him into their family willingly, someone was trying to tear that apart.

She sighed, and Fred reached over and gave her hand a squeeze.

"I just can't believe this is happening, Fred," she cried.

"I know, me either," Fred commiserated, wishing she could say more to put Millicent's mind at ease. The problem was, until they made sure everything was followed by the book, and they determined that the adoption was deemed legal, everything could unravel. "I'll be right there with you tonight and every step of the way, and if it's okay I'll bring Caleb tonight, too, for moral support and counsel."

"Thank you. That would be nice if he could come and pray over the kids," she admitted.

"Absolutely."

§

Millicent arrived back at her home, just as Virgil and the boys, Enos and Jubal, were finishing for the day. Virgil sent them along back to Sarah's Home while he went to see how Millicent had fared with the attorney.

"How did it go," he asked, opening the car door for her.

She responded by stepping out of the car and collapsing into his arms in tears.

"Hey, hey, what's this? What did he tell you?" he asked, a knot forming in the pit of his stomach.

He walked her the few steps to their porch and up to have a seat. "Here, just tell me what he said, honey."

She walked him through the whole meeting, leaving off with the news that they needed to tell the kids what was going on.

Thinking out loud, he said, "I wish we knew more. I hate to upset their lives unnecessarily." Then to Millicent he said, "You *do* know that we will fight to make everything right, don't you?"

She nodded, love and gratefulness pushing through the misery on her face.

§

After supper, Fred and Caleb accompanied them to Adohy and Faith's new house. It went about as well as they had feared. It took a while to get them both to understand that no one could just force Adohy to go to the Reservation. That seemed to be their biggest fear. That and the threat of him being incarcerated. All of them prayed together, and then Caleb talked to just the two of them for a while, before they left them to themselves for the night.

§

Spent, and terrified for what was to come, Faith and Adohy went to bed and held each other as if would be the last time. For hours, neither let go, both lost in the different scenarios that could play out before them in the days to come, until they both fell into a restless sleep.

§

The next day was Benny's newly appointed birthday, and the party was scheduled for that evening. He was so excited he could barely contain himself. He told everyone he saw over and over that it was his birthday and made sure they were coming to his party. At breakfast he'd invited Enos and Jubal, who just looked at each other unsure what to say, taken aback with his demeanor. It was their first encounter face to face with Benny.

So far, they'd done okay working with the horses under Virgil's tutelage. He'd had to get onto them a couple of times due to their language and some crude remarks regarding some of the animals mating, but other than that it was going better than he'd anticipated.

Since they'd been invited firsthand from Benny to his party, Millicent had no choice but to let them attend. Which also meant that Chalmer, the rest of the Jenkins family, and everyone else would be exposed to them and their antics. She crossed her fingers that they behaved.

After everyone arrived, they began to get the ice cream churned, and all pitched in as before including Enos and Jubal, who had not one complaint. Millicent began to relax a little. When the ice cream was ready, the candles were lit on the cake and they sang the birthday song.

Benny clapped in time to the song, then burst out in applause when it was done. "It's my birthday! It's my birthday!" he sang out.

It was quite the sight considering his age, and would have been very heartwarming were it not for the pall that hung over the room for those that had been privy to the letter that week. It was then that she noticed Enos elbow Jubal and say something under his breath, and they both laughed hysterically.

They caught her eyeing them and stopped, but it didn't put her at ease. She couldn't help but stay on edge the rest of the night, glancing at them every chance she got.

Benny opened his gifts, and as happy as he was with all the new games, as predicted the transistor radio was the most favored. He unwrapped it and tuned it in to some music and it should have been as festive as the week before, but it fell short. No one felt quite like dancing.

Unfortunately, the loud music stopped abruptly, and everyone over heard Enos saying "I don't know what's more lame, this party or Benny!"

All eyes shifted to him.

There was silence until Chalmer said, "Whut's *lame* mean?"

Tommy and Evelyn pulled Chalmer aside, while Millicent went to escort the two boys from the lame party.

Virgil helped Benny get the music playing again, trying to salvage the evening. A slow song was playing and Adohy stood, pulling Faith up and close to sway to the music. It was either an attempt to help Virgil get the party going again for Benny, or an excuse to hold his wife as close as possible while he could. Maybe both.

Tommy wasn't sure how he felt about Benny. He didn't know him very well, but he did have to admit it made him nervous for him to be around Chalmer. Even so, he didn't take kindly to anyone making fun of him, either. He would have liked to have a minute or two with them two boys. See how they liked being made fun of. His not being comfortable with Chalmer around Benny was compounded exponentially now, with those boys in the picture, too.

Chalmer was still asking him and Evelyn what lame meant.

Trying to change the subject, Evelyn asked, "Hey, you had another payday, didn't you?"

Chalmer nodded, grinning, remembering his cache of coins.

"So how much ya got now?" Tommy asked.

Chalmer's brow creased. "I don't rightly know cause I cain't count yet." But his little mind just wouldn't let his previous question go unanswered. "What does la—"

"So, what are ya gonna buy with yer money ya got saved up?"Tommy interrupted, determined to get him to forget about the incident.

Chalmer didn't have to think about this question. He already knew the answer. "I'm gonna get me a pair a overalls, *just like* Samuel's!"

Tommy and Evelyn's eyes met over Chalmer's head. It was the last thing either of them had expected to hear come out of his mouth.

CHAPTER 21

A week passed. Millicent was both somewhat relieved that there wasn't another letter, and no one had shown up to take Adohy away, but at the same time worried sick that it could still happen any moment, without warning. She forced herself to stay as busy as she could and keep her mind occupied.

She and Tenley were making their daily batch of cookies, and she realized as they were ready to be baked that it was a good thing Tenley knew the recipe by heart. Millicent didn't remember a thing about mixing the batch up that morning. She could only hope Tenley had measured the ingredients out right. Time would tell, she thought, as she put them in the oven.

Feeling bad for not paying attention during their mother/daughter ritual, she pulled Tenley close and gave her a big hug. She vowed to herself to do better. Every day with Tenley was a day she couldn't get back, an opportunity to make new memories, and she wanted to do just that. She also promised herself that if there was no news today, she was going to see Mr. Barnfield Monday morning. Surely he'd been able to find *something* out by now.

She cleaned up the kitchen, and put the ingredients away, then checked the cookies. They were done. While they were cooling, it occurred to her, too late, she should have waited to see how these came out before she cleaned and put everything away. She took a spatula and slid it under one of the cookies, then broke a piece off and blew on it to help the cooling process. Tenley stood by, waiting patiently, as Millicent popped the piece in her mouth and chewed. A smile spread on her face. It may have been her imagination, but she would have sworn they were the best sugar cookies they'd made yet. Or rather that Tenley had made all by herself. She handed the rest of the cookie to Tenley, for her approval. She took a bite and mirrored Millicent's smile.

They divided them into their individual bags, loaded the cups of milk in the wagon, and started on their rounds. Those that were able had started gathering in the common area, their encounter with Tenley delivering the treats was the highlight of their day. Tenley took her time with each one, always happy to extend a hug along with the cookies.

Once everyone in the common area had their goodies, they continued on to the other patients that couldn't leave their rooms. Millicent hesitated at Jane Doe's door. She'd not bothered to let Tenley deliver to her room before, because Jane was still in what they called in a wakeful coma, only responding to Faith at meal time. In spite of that, for some reason, Millicent decided to give it a try. Jane was sitting in the bedside chair. Millicent stepped in the room first and said hello, then explained that Tenley had a little surprise for her. Jane, as expected, didn't respond. Tenley pulled her wagon in, and Millicent watched carefully for any reaction from Jane.

Nothing.

Tenley held the bag out to Jane for a moment, then, when she didn't take it, Millicent explained to Tenley that Jane wasn't hungry and they would just have to go on to the next person. She helped Tenley turn her wagon around and they left the room.

Had either of them looked back, they would have seen Jane's hand slowly reach out to them, as a barely audible "Ssss..." sound escaped between her lips.

But they didn't.

~~§~~

Sunday was an off day for church services in Hurricane Hollow, because Caleb still held services at the brush arbor by the store every other Sunday, especially since Preacher Loveday had to stop making the circuit.

With a day off, having no plans whatsoever, other than the family supper that night, Tommy had every intention of sleeping in for a change. There was nothing that needed to be fixed, no chores other than gathering the eggs and milking the cow, and he found himself looking forward to being lazy all day.

When the sun set, Samuel took Chalmer back to Sarah's Home for the night, all the while thinking how he hated this part a-the day. He jes couldn't help worryin about the lil feller. He'd taken to walking him to his room and helping him get ready for bed each time, but tonight they walked in just as Benny was trying to round up players for the new games he'd gotten for his birthday.

"Ya wanna play, Chalmer?" Benny asked, as they entered.

"Kin I stay up n play fer a lil while, Samuel, pleeaasse?" Chalmer begged.

Samuel wasn't real sure about this. He looked around the room, trying to think of a good reason to say no, but when he met the orderlies on duty with the worry in his eyes, they nodded their heads that it would be okay. "You'll be watchin over the game?" he questioned. They replied they would. "And you'll see that Chalmer gets to bed soon?" he stalled.

"Yes, sir, everything will be fine," they assured him.

Against his better judgment, he gave in. He hugged Chalmer goodnight, and left feeling uneasy.

Benny needed four players for his game and it looked like the two orderlies were going to have to fill in, until Jubal and Enos entered the room. Benny automatically asked them to be the other two players, unaware of Millicent's request to try to keep them separated.

"That's okay, Benny, we'll play with you," one of the orderlies cut in, not expecting the other two boys to want to play anyway, and hoping to nip the situation in the bud. Much to her surprise, Jubal said, "Naw, we'd kinda like ta play, wouldn't we, Enos?" he said, nudging him.

Enos didn't much want to, but relented for Jubal's sake. "Yeah, why not," he muttered.

The orderlies looked at each other, unsure what to do. It could get ugly if they told them they couldn't play, and the two of them had been doing okay recently...they decided it could be the lesser of two evils if they just let them play and kept a close eye on everything.

The boys set the game up and began to play after the orderlies read them the rules. Wonder of wonders, the game not only went well, but Enos won, fair and square, and actually seemed to enjoy it. The orderlies breathed a sigh of relief as they sent Enos and Jubal to their rooms for the night and then one orderly each escorted Benny and Chalmer to their rooms, as promised.

§

At five-thirty Sunday morning, there was a pounding on the Jenkins' door. Tommy startled out of a deep sleep, pulled on his dungarees and hurried to see what the commotion was. Samuel was close on his heels. Evelyn joined them, pulling on her robe, as Tommy opened the door. Chalmer stood on the other side of the screen door, in his pajamas and barefoot, tears streaming down his face.

"Chalmer, buddy, whut's wrong?" Tommy asked, prompting Chalmer to step back as he slowly pushed the screen door open.

Samuel's felt his blood pressure spike as he thought back to the night before and his gut feeling about leaving

Chalmer there to play that game with people he had no business being around. He followed Tommy out and they both knelt down to Chalmer.

"Whut happened, Chalmer?" Tommy asked.

"Did somebody hurt you?" Samuel ground out through clenched teeth.

"Somebody tooked my radio," Chalmer sobbed.

Somewhat relieved that it wasn't anything worse, Samuel and Tommy both took a deep breath, but their ire was piqued that anyone dared to mess with Chalmer.

Samuel started to stand. "I got me a good mind as ta who it was, too. That Benny feller," he growled, getting to his feet.

"But Benny's my *friend*," Chalmer cried.

"Maybe not fer long he ain't," Samuel said, heading off the porch, forgetting he was as barefoot as Chalmer was.

"Naw, Papaw, I got this," Tommy assured him, standing to catch his shoulder to stop him.

Samuel looked at him, undecided.

"I *got* this," he reaffirmed, "y'all jes go on inside an' I'll be right back."

Evelyn held the screen door open for Samuel to usher Chalmer inside. "Tommy at least put on your shirt and shoes," she urged, hoping it would give him time to cool down.

He glanced down at his bare chest and followed the other two inside, to do as she asked.

170

§

Over at the Home, they were just changing shifts when Tommy arrived. After he explained what had transpired, the orderly that had put Chalmer to bed, overheard him on her way out. She filled Tommy in on the game, stating that Enos and Jubal had played as well, and that the orderly that had taken Benny to his room had already left for the day.

Upon hearing that the two trouble makers had been involved, Tommy immediately switched gears over where the radio had gone and who was responsible. The orderly, not big fans of the boys either, agreed to let Tommy go and ask them about the incident but only as long as she went with him. She had to show him to their room anyway.

The sun had come up enough that they could see both boys asleep in the room when they entered. Chalmer's tear stricken face flashed before Tommy, and his anger flared again. "Okay which one a-ya stole Chalmer's radio," he yelled, causing both boys to sit upright, as he walked over and snatched back the covers on Enos's bed.

Automatically defensive, Enos spit out, "I dunno whut yer talkin' bout!"

Tommy looked at Jubal, who shook his head in agreement with Enos.

"Yeah, well, we'll jes see 'bout that," Tommy replied, turning objects over and looking under items in their room.

"Whut are ya doin?" Jubal cried out. "We done tol' ya we dunno nuthin' 'bout it."

171

Tommy kept looking and when a search failed to turn up anything, he warned them. "Y'all better hope I don't find out ya took that little boy's radio, an' ya best be a-stayin' away from eem from now on!" He turned and left, leaving Jubal and Enos looking at each other, shaking their heads.

"Jerk," Enos muttered.

"Ya didn't take Chalmer's radio, did ya, Enos?" Jubal asked.

Enos looked at him in disgust. "Naw, I didn't take no stupid radio," he spit out. They both laid back down on their beds, wondering what happened to it.

On their way down the hall, Tommy asked about Benny. The orderly was reluctant to let him go there, after seeing how he went after Jubal and Enos.

Figuring she was already going to be in trouble for letting Chalmer slip off again unnoticed, she decided she'd better take the lead on this one. "You wait here, and I'll go check his room. But he'd have no reason to take Chalmer's radio when he's got one of his own," she reasoned, before going to check.

Benny was awake when she got to his room. He was sitting on the edge of his bed sorting cards out in one of his games.

"Good morning, Benny," she said.

"Mornin'! Wanna play a game?" he asked.

"No, I can't right now," she answered. "But I was just wondering, do you still have your radio?"

"Yep, it's right here," Benny said, turning to his other side and flipping his pillow back. His action revealed two transistor radios. "Hey! How'd I get two of 'em?" he exclaimed.

"Benny!" the orderly said, disheartened. She really hadn't expected it to be him. "Why did you take Chalmer's radio?" she asked, as she stepped to pick them both up, examining them.

Benny brows knit together. "How'd I get two of 'em?" he asked again, scratching his head.

"One of these is Chalmer's, and you're going to be in trouble for taking it," she reprimanded him. There was no difference between the two so she chose one, and tossed the other back on the bed.

Benny's confusion morphed into fear. "I'm in trouble?" he whimpered, looking toward the door. He pulled his feet up on the bed and backed up against the wall, his knees pulled up to his chest, watching the door.

Back down the hallway, the orderly handed the radio to Tommy, shamefaced. "Benny had it," she confirmed.

Tommy shook his head. Papaw was right, he thought, his confrontation with Jubal and Enos weighing on his mind now. As he considered what he should do, he heard his papaw's voice echoing… "*Ya cain't shake hands with a clenched fist, son*". Dang it! He was right again. He took a deep breath and said, "I reckon I need ta go tell 'em boys we found the radio." He started that way then turned back, "Kin ya get me some clothes fer Chalmer?" he asked. "He's still in his pj's. Oh, an' he needs his shoes, too."

The orderly said she would, and they headed in their different directions.

It was a long walk back to the boy's room. Much longer than the first time. He stopped in their doorway, and when they saw him they both bolted upright in their beds again, looking past him for a referee, seeing no one.

Tommy sighed. "I jes come ta tell y'all we found the radio." He hesitated. "An' I'm sorry," he added, turning away. There! He did it, and it was a bitter pill to swallow.

Enos and Jubal looked at each other, each finally daring to take a breath, and collapsed back on their beds.

§

Evelyn had breakfast ready when Tommy returned. Chalmer was ecstatic to have his radio back. They ate, and then Evelyn went to help Chalmer get dressed while Tommy filled Samuel in on what had occurred.

"I knew it!" Samuel said. "I'm tellin ya, that boy ain't got no business being round *any* a them other'ns," he maintained, even though Jubal and Enos hadn't been the culprits.

"I know," Tommy agreed.

Chalmer and Evelyn returned then, and Samuel, addressing Chalmer, said, "Whatcha say we go an' see if'n we kin find any blackberries that's ready ta be picked yet?"

"Oh boy! Kin I bring my radio?" he asked, not ready to let it out of his sight just yet.

"Why shore," Samuel told him, and they headed out.

He said not a word.

Tommy slid down in his chair, exhausted. So much for sleeping in and no stress today, he thought.

Evelyn poured them both another cup of coffee and sat back down to hear what she'd missed while getting Chalmer dressed.

When he finished, they were both silent a while, reflecting.

About ten minutes passed without either of them saying a word. Then simultaneously they said, "I think we should adopt Chalmer."

CHAPTER 22

Fascinated that they'd both arrived at the same conclusion at the same time they asked, simultaneously again, "When did you come up with that?"

They laughed.

Evelyn shrugged. "I've been thinking about it for a while now," she admitted.

"Me too," Tommy said.

"It just seems like the next logical step," she said. "I've fallen in love with the little guy..."

"Me too," Tommy nodded. "An' him and Papaw are practically inseparable. An' it'll be even more so after this."

"Yeah, and I'm not real thrilled about him going back over there at all, now, not without one of us anyway, especially over night."

Tommy shook his head. "I don't think that's gonna happen. I ain't sayin that Millicent don't run a tight ship, but she ain't there all day an all night, an' there ain't no one else there that young."

"And when he told us he was saving up his money for a pair of overall's like Samuel's?"

"I Know! That bout did it fer me!" Tommy told her. "An' we got the room. He can pick either Faith's or Sarah's old room."

"I know they're doing the best they can but I don't like him running over here in the dark, even if no one else bothered him, there's bears and stuff..."

Tommy looked at her dubiously.

"Well, I know we haven't *seen* one," she said sheepishly, "but that don't mean they aren't out there!"

"Yer right, yer right," he soothed. It *was* a good point," he thought, adding it to his mental list of pros.

"So are we going to talk to Samuel about it when they get back?" she asked, fingers crossed.

"Yep," Tommy answered, knowing it was as good as a done deal.

§

Samuel and Chalmer came home a short while later, blackberry-less. They'd found a bunch of them, but none quite ready for picking yet.

Giving Tommy the signal, Evelyn asked Chalmer if he could help her for a moment, allowing Tommy the

178

opportunity to speak to Samuel in private. Tommy asked Samuel if he could talk to him on the front porch.

They went out and took seats in the side by side rockers.

"Papaw, me an Evelyn was a-talkin' while y'all was gone and we got ta thinkin' that maybe we oughtta keep Chalmer over here. I mean full time like. Like maybe we oughtta adopt eem."

Samuel was quiet a moment, pursing his lips as he stared out over the yard and Sarah's Home in the distance. Tommy was beginning to think Samuel was going to say it wasn't a good idea, when Samuel looked at him, his eyes swimming in tears.

"Ya mean it?" he asked, his chin quivering.

Tommy let out a relieved chuckle. "Yeah, I mean it!" he said, reaching over to hug Samuel's neck.

When they parted, Samuel said, "I jes couldn't stand the thought a havin' ta take eem an' leave eem there alone agin tonight," he said, talking and smiling at the same time, even while a tear ran down his cheek.

"Well, it's settled then," Tommy said, blinking back his own tears. "He aint goin' back. We'll go an' talk ta Millicent later an' let her know. Ya wanna tell Chalmer, now?"

"Let's do it!" Samuel said, taking his handkerchief out of his pocket and wiping his eyes.

"Evelyn! Kin you an' Chalmer come here?" Tommy called out.

When she got to the door, they exchanged a look, and Tommy nodded his head. Evelyn grinned.

"Hey, Chalmer?" Tommy began, picking Chalmer up and sitting him in the rocker he'd just vacated. "Do ya know what being adopted means?"

For some reason, Chalmer's expression became melancholy. "Well, I reckon I heared other kids a-sayin that's when ya gotta go live with someone else," he said, his eyes downcast.

Tommy glanced up at Samuel and Evelyn. Chalmer's expression made sense now. He thought he was going to be taken away.

"Well, yeah, it means that, but it also means you'll have a mama an' a daddy, an' you'd be part of a family!"

"I reckon," Chalmer said sadly.

"So, what if I told ya that me an' Evelyn wanna be yer mama an' daddy? What'd ya say 'bout that?" Tommy asked softly, as Evelyn went and knelt beside him.

It took a second for Tommy's words to register with Chalmer. Slowly his head raised. He looked at Tommy and then Evelyn. "Ya mean it?" he asked quietly, with no change in his expression yet.

They both nodded their heads, smiling.

"Ya really mean it?" he asked again loudly, his voice ringing with excitement.

They kept nodding their heads as Chalmer sailed out of the rocking chair knocking them both over backwards. They all fell to the porch laughing.

Samuel quickly pulled his handkerchief out and wiped his eyes again before anyone could see.

Pulling themselves into a sitting position, Tommy held Chalmer back and said, "Ya know what else it means?"

Chalmer shook his head.

"It means that my papaw, Samuel, is gonna be yer papaw, too!"

Chalmer's eyes grew even larger and he turned and leaped into Samuel's arms.

This time Samuel's handkerchief made the rounds, and no one tried to hide it.

Chalmer released Samuel's neck and leaned back. "Does this mean I kin start a-callin' ya Papaw Samuel now?"

"It shore does!" Samuel nodded.

Chalmer turned around and sat in Samuel's lap. He looked at Tommy and Evelyn and asked, "An' I kin start callin' ya mama an' daddy?"

Evelyn just reached for Samuel's handkerchief again, and Tommy told him yes.

"We'll go over an' tell Millicent directly and then go ta Sarah's Home an' git yer stuff," he was explaining to Chalmer, when Samuel said, "Here she comes now," nodding his head in that direction.

Tommy and Evelyn turned to see the Thornton's pull into the yard.

Millicent jumped out and ran up onto the porch, while Virgil extracted Tenley from the car.

"I was just told about what happened! Is everyone okay?" she asked, clearly concerned.

As she spoke, she noticed everyone's smiling faces. Not what she'd expected after the morning's incident. Confused, she asked, "Am I missing something here?"

Chalmer piped up. "I'm getting' 'dopted!" he announced. Even more confused now, she looked from Chalmer to Samuel then over to Tommy and Evelyn, who all still sat with smiling faces.

Virgil stepped on the porch with Tenley, ready to make his apologies, and he stopped short, joining Millicent in her confusion, when he noticed the grinning faces all around.

"You mean it?" she finally asked. It seemed to be the question of the day, and Tommy, Evelyn, and Samuel busted out laughing.

"Yes!" they all shouted.

"Mean what?" Virgil inquired.

"They're adopting Chalmer!" Millicent squealed, hugging him and Tenley, nearly knocking them over in the process.

As they hugged, Tommy kissed Evelyn.

And while Tommy kissed Evelyn, Samuel leaned forward and nibbled on Chalmer's ear. He squirmed, dissolving into a fit of giggles.

CHAPTER 23

Chalmer was officially moved that afternoon, having chosen Faith's old bedroom because it was directly across the hall from Samuel's. Since Millicent was going to see the attorney regarding Adohy's case in the morning, she said she would see if he could oversee Chalmer's adoption too, if not, she would go to the attorney that handled Tenley's adoption. It should be open and shut, like Tenley's had been.

The rest of that day and into the next, Benny was afraid to leave his room. He couldn't play his games for being unable to take his eyes of the door to his room. Even eating was not a priority, which was definitely out of the ordinary for him since he'd been there. No one was quite sure what had triggered this change in his demeanor, but attributed it to him being caught with Chalmer's radio. It wasn't until Millicent had been able to question the two orderlies that had been on duty the morning the strange behavior had begun, that she was able to get to the bottom of it.

In fact, it brought to light not only what she believed to be behind Benny's behavior, but the real story behind how the radio came to be in his room. According to the orderlies, after the game between the four boys on Saturday night, one of them helped Benny pack up his games and seeing the radio, she assumed it was Benny's and placed it on top of his stack of games. She then accompanied Benny to his room, while the other orderly accompanied Chalmer.

The orderly remembered Benny sitting his games down after arriving in his room, then picking up the radio and slipping it under his pillow where he'd been keeping it since he got it. She had no reason to believe it wasn't his, and believed that it was an honest misunderstanding, that no one realized Benny's radio was already under his pillow until the next morning when he pulled his pillow back. Which explained his confusion over there being two radios.

What happened next was what Millicent thought triggered his behavior since that incident. Upon finding him in possession of both radios the other orderly recalled telling him that he would be in trouble, and his fearful reaction of cowering against the wall on his bed.

Millicent felt that it was a fear that stemmed from prior to his arrival, and was why he kept watching his door, awaiting the person that was going to exact that punishment, the person that he referred to as his father, presumably, the unidentified corpse. With this new information, she went straight to Benny's room.

He saw her as soon as she walked into his doorway as his eyes were glued to it. As expected he was pressed against the wall as far away from the door as he could get.

"Benny? What's wrong?" Millicent asked, as she entered slowly.

"I'm in trouble," he said, his bottom lip trembling.

"No, Benny. You're not in trouble." She approached the bed cautiously. She knew that people tended to overreact out of fear, and had no desire for things to get out of hand. "There was a misunderstanding. We know you didn't take Chalmer's radio. It was an accident."

"A' accident?" he asked, some of the tension in his posture visibly easing.

"Yes, it was an accident, and you are *not* in trouble. Okay?"

He looked at the door one more time, just to make sure. "Okay! Wanna play a game?"

Millicent smiled at his resilience, but it concerned her that he hadn't been able to forget to be afraid as quickly. His father must have been really bad. "I have an appointment, but how about we find someone else that can?"

He nodded, sliding to the edge of his bed.

"Are you hungry," Millicent asked, remembering his poor appetite the past few days.

"Yep!"

"Pick out a game, and let's go get you something to eat," she told him.

§

Once that was settled, she headed to Maynardville to see the attorney, hoping he was in his office this morning. She needed to hurry to get back in time for her and Tenley to make their cookies.

It was her good fortune that he was, and agreed to see her.

After exchanging greetings, he offered her a seat."I'm glad you stopped in. I'm afraid we haven't made much progress." Seeing her disappointment, he hurried on. "We've tried to contact Mr. Pendergriff numerous times daily to no avail, which is curious, so we've mailed a response to his summons. I have also sent an investigator to North Carolina to check him out."

"Have you—"

"Heard from the investigator?"

She nodded.

"Not yet. He was just sent this morning."

Her face fell again.

Hating to make matters worse for her, he reluctantly said, "I'm afraid I have more bad news. Since his first letter, he has filed a motion for the court to overturn the adoption, which means that even if the adoption was completed correctly, and according to all the paperwork I've reviewed, it was, but there would now be a hearing for him to give cause. Without being able to confer with him, I am not aware of what grounds he is alleging. You will probably be receiving the letter of dispute and motion to overturn in the mail today."

"So what does that all mean?" she asked, her hands trembling.

"It means he's asking the court to set a date to have a hearing to overturn the adoption," he stated, flatly.

"Oh no," she whispered, her hands covering her face.

He gave her a moment to compose herself.

"Are you sure that you have never had any dealings with this attorney in the past?" he asked.

Millicent looked up, her eyes clouded with confusion. "No, I don't think so, why?"

"Well, I could be wrong, but this seems to ring of something personal. Your husband hasn't had any business dealings with him, or *anyone* that there was a problem with?" he probed.

"No, we've never had any disgruntled clients," she shook her head.

He thought over what she said. "Well, maybe my investigator can come up with something before there's a date set for a hearing. It is peculiar that no one is answering the phone at his office. Let's hope for some answers in the next day or so."

"Okay," Millicent agreed, standing to go. She wished now she'd asked Fred to come along with her, but she'd been so sure there was going to be good news.

§

She brought Virgil up to date when she returned, careful not to let Faith and Adohy see that anything was wrong. She'd decided to wait to tell the kids until the investigator had a chance to look into the situation, and Virgil agreed. They had been trying to put it out of their minds until

187

they heard otherwise, and seemed to be doing as well as could be expected. There was no need to upset that tenuous balance with nothing more than she had now.

As Mr. Barnfield had predicted, there was a copy of the motion that Mr. Pendergriff had filed with the court to have Adohy's adoption overturned, in the mail.

With her heart hurting, she put on a happy face, and went to keep her standing appointment with her daughter and sugar cookies. It went without incident, and lifted her spirits as much as anything could today.

On their rounds, she was surprised to see that even Oppy was starting to respond to Tenley's visits. She considered trying Jane Doe again, but decided not to spend the extra time. As soon as they finished, she wanted to go let Samuel know what she'd found out about Benny and the radio fiasco, as well as fill him in on what she'd learned at the attorney's that morning, in confidence, since it affected their family as well.

It wasn't until she saw Chalmer and Samuel's smiling faces that she realized after the news she'd gotten at the attorney's office, she'd completely forgotten to ask him about handling Chalmers adoption for the Jenkins'.

She apologized profusely, and promised to see what she could find out the following day.

Samuel assured her that it was understandable, and not a problem. They were truly thankful for her help.

CHAPTER 24

Tuesday morning, Millicent made the trip back to Maynardville. She went alone since the trip was mainly in regards to Chalmer's adoption, but she wasn't kidding herself, she had her fingers crossed there had been some news from the investigator yesterday, after she'd left the attorney's office. As luck would have it, he was there again and took her directly back to his office.

She apologized for another unscheduled interruption, and forcing herself not to ask about Adohy's case, at least not first, she explained the main reason for her return so soon.

He replied, "I'll be happy to handle the adoption proceedings."

Which led her up to what she was chomping at the bit to ask about. "It won't interfere with your time on Adohy's case?" she asked.

He smiled at her bluntness. "I can assure you that won't be an issue."

She went ahead and gave him Chalmer's information, along with the Jenkins' and he said they would be notified with a date and time to come to his office and go over the paperwork.

She nodded, but hesitated, and he was sure by her expression she really had something else on her mind.

"Did you, by chance, hear from your investigator?" she finally asked.

Bingo! He kept a straight face. "As a matter of fact, I *did* hear from him shortly before we closed yesterday. It's not much to tell you, but it seems that the address on his correspondence, his office, has been closed for quite some time. We haven't had time to determine the reason, if he's moved to another location, and if so why his stationary hasn't been updated, or if he doesn't have an office at all anymore and is just still using his old stationary. All of the above is highly suspect. My secretary is also confirming that his license is current and if he is, in fact, even licensed to practice law in Tennessee, since he is apparently residing in North Carolina."

"I don't understand," Millicent struggled, shaking her head.

"I don't either, Mrs. Thornton—"

"Please, Millicent's fine," she interrupted.

"Millicent," he nodded, "I don't understand what it all implies either, but hope to receive more news today that will shed some light on this Mr. Pendergriff."

There was a moment's silence, then he asked, "Is there anyone you know that has a phone that you could borrow to call the office, rather than make the drive?"

"No," she sighed, "No one. Hopefully they will have one at the General Store soon, where Fred-er Winifred is, but not yet."

"I see, well, you're welcome to stop in any time, as I said before. I can't guarantee that I will be here each time, but in the event of my absence, I will give my secretary instructions to fill you in with any news we may have acquired. In addition, if I uncover anything of any relevance to the case, I will come to you with the news at the earliest possible opportunity."

Relieved that he didn't seem to feel she was being a nuisance and was trying to do everything he could to keep her in the loop, she thanked him and let him get back to work.

The truth of the matter was, he was as confounded by this Pendergriff guy and what all this was really about and wanted to get to the bottom of it nearly as much as she did.

§

Faith saw when Millicent arrived back at Sarah's Home and caught up to her. She'd noticed all the comings and goings and had a feeling there was more happening than what they'd been told.

"Millicent!" she called.

Millicent stopped. Darn it! She bit her lip, trying to decide what she should reveal. She hated lying, but she just knew Faith was going to ask. She put a smile on her face and turned.

"Hi, Faith! Is everything okay?" she asked, as Faith approached.

"Yes, or at least I hope so, that's what I was going to ask you."

Shoot! "Well as far as I know," she answered, winging it. "I went to see about Chalmer's adoption this morning." She was trying to sound as lighthearted as she could.

"And?"

"And Mr. Barnfield is going to handle it, and set up an appointment for the paperwork to be gone over," she said, brightly.

"Did...you...find out anything else?" About Adohy, I mean?" Faith asked, hesitantly.

Millicent swallowed. "Well, all I found out today was that the office for Mr. Pendergriff has been closed for a while."

With raised brows, Faith asked, "Closed?"

Millicent detected the hopeful lilt in her voice. "Yes, but it's possible he's just moved to a new office and hasn't gotten new stationary, yet."

"Oh..."

"*But* Mr. Barnfield said he would personally come and let us know the second he found out anything relevant to the case," she promised. It was a *slight* exaggeration, but well intended. "I'm sorry, honey. I know how hard this is," she said, pulling Faith in to hug her.

"I know you do," Faith told her, her voice muffled by Millicent's shoulder.

They released each other, and Faith went back the way she'd come, wishing there had been better news.

Millicent watched her as she walked away, hoping she'd done the right thing by trying not to lie, even though she knew that was basically what it boiled down to anyway. Lying by omission. She went inside to seek out the orderly caring for Tenley, so the two of them could bake cookies, but more than that, she *needed* Tenley for the emotional boost that she always provided.

§

Some days Benny worked outside with whoever could use him, but since Virgil was working with Enos and Jubal, that meant Adohy and Faith would have to be in charge of Benny, and in light of what they were dealing with, Millicent had encouraged Benny to stay inside as much as possible and play his games. He was happy with that arrangement, loving the interaction with other patients and especially the mid afternoon cookies and milk.

He'd been happy as a lark since she'd made it clear he wasn't in trouble, and she made sure that the staff were aware if there was any problem pertaining to him doing anything wrong in the future, to consult her before they made any remarks as to his guilt or innocence. Something in his past had left him deeply, emotionally scarred. She looked forward to the day they knew his story.

The patients had started to gather in the common area, and Benny was keeping three of them entertained with one his games when they entered with the freshly baked cookies. It had become such a special moment for some of them, they got visibly excited. Which may have been what led to Oppy attempting to stand on her own from her wheelchair, which she *could* do, but only if she was assisted. Millicent wasn't sure if Benny had picked up on this from prior example, or if he just saw before anyone else that Oppy was in trouble. It happened so fast.

All she knew was that one second Benny was absorbed in his game and the next second he'd jumped up from his seat so quickly that the chair slammed over backwards, hitting with a bang, as he sprinted to Oppy and caught her before she hit the floor. Millicent and the other orderlies rushed to Oppy's side as he carefully sat her back in her wheelchair. He stepped back then, as everyone checked her over to see she was unscathed.

When everyone turned their eyes to Benny in amazement, for a moment he looked like a deer caught in the headlights.

Oppy broke the spell by saying, "Thank you," as she looked up at him gratefully.

Then everyone else joined in.

"Yes, Benny! Thank you!"

"You did great!"

"Good job! You saved Oppy from being hurt!" they said, patting him on the back.

Benny beamed!

"Whut's his name?" Oppy asked. She was told, knowing she'd never remember.

Benny was a hero for the day. He got two servings of cookies and milk. That day was the beginning to a step forward in them knowing what made Benny tick. He thrived on positive attention. It was suspected that the two servings of cookies had something to with it too, when he became ever attentive to the other patients and trying to help them as much as he could, but when he continued to do so without the extra reward, that theory was disregarded. The patient's "thank you" seemed to be reward enough for him.

Over the next days, and out of earshot, some of the staff began referring to him as the Gentle Giant.

And over the same few days, much to everyone's surprise, Oppy and Benny became fast friends.

By the time Sunday arrived and Caleb and Fred came to visit Oppy after church, she and Benny were thick as thieves. Caleb was astounded and he and Fred were both tickled to see Oppy playing games with Benny. Benny was as patient as he could be with her, teaching her how to play the same game over again, everyday. She was smiling and appeared to be having the time of her life. Had they not seen it firsthand for themselves, they admitted they may have been a little unjustly concerned about the interaction with Benny. When they were informed of Benny's heroic act earlier in the week, saving Oppy from probable physical harm, Benny earned a place in *their* hearts, as well as Oppy's.

Benny had no problem with Caleb interrupting the game to shake his hand, and when Oppy recognized him too, for the first time in ages, Caleb's heart was near to bursting. He asked Benny if it was okay for him to say a quick prayer of thanks and Benny agreed, even though he didn't have any idea what a prayer was.

Closing the prayer, Caleb said, "Amen."

"Amen!" Benny echoed. "Aaammennn!"

Caleb had no idea what he'd started.

§

Before Caleb left that day, Millicent had a special prayer request for him. In a few weeks, Tenley was scheduled to have what Millicent hoped to be the last cosmetic surgery to correct the deformity of her upper lip. She asked that he and Fred pray for that, as well as for Adohy and his case, and that it all be deemed a misunderstanding and cleared up and over with before Tenley's surgery.

Caleb began with a prayer on the spot. When he was finished and the three of them said, "Amen," they heard Benny across the room shout "Amen!" after them. It warranted a laugh between them all.

§

Millicent and Tenley had taken to baking two batches of cookies on Saturday, so that only if Tenley insisted she wanted to make the deliveries on Sunday, they could slip over and do it, otherwise the staff could hand them out. So far, she'd not passed up the opportunity. Millicent knew the patients would be disappointed when Tenley had her surgery and wouldn't be there to hand them out, but it should only be for a few days and she was afraid Tenley would be more let down than everyone.

They loaded up her wagon, and began the rounds. As they approached Jane Doe's room Millicent decided to let Tenley try once more to reach out to Jane, but looking in her room, she saw that Jane was getting her physical therapy, so she continued on. Behind her, Tenley paused in the doorway.

The nurse saw her, and said, "Hey, Tenley!"

"Hi," Tenley replied with a wave, before disappearing to catch up with Millicent.

Had the nurse been looking, she would have seen Jane's eyes focus briefly to search out Tenley, too.

But she wasn't.

CHAPTER 25

That Wednesday was the Fourth of July. Sadly, for most folks in Hurricane Holler it was just another day, not able to afford to take a day off in the middle of the week. The best they could do was let their kids go swimming or fishing when their chores were done.

At Sarah's Home, they celebrated by putting red, white, and blue sprinkles on the cookies.

Samuel and Chalmer went blackberry picking, and this time the berries were ripe and juicy. They'd found a big patch a few weeks earlier and were happy to see no one else had. They began to fill their buckets with relative ease until Chalmer noticed some beyond his and Samuel's reach. Determined to get to them, he pushed in a little farther than he'd been told to and got hung up on the thorns.

"Uh...Papaw?" he said. He'd gotten used to calling Samuel, Papaw, and apparently really liked the sound of it. He

199

put it at the beginning or end of every single thing he said to Samuel. And Samuel didn't mind. It was music to his ears.

Samuel was busy picking berries and answered, "Yep," without looking.

"Ya reckon ya could git me unstuck, Papaw?" Chalmer asked, calmly.

He looked to find Chalmer surrounded by clinging blackberry brush that had latched onto his shirt and britches, making it impossible to back out without getting scratched up.

Going to his aid, Samuel tried to keep a straight face. "Son, what have ya gone an' done? Didn't I tell ya ya'd have ta be careful not ta get up in 'em like this?"

"Yeah, Papaw, but them there's the best lookin' ones I seen," he explained, nodding toward the berries in front of him, still just out of reach.

Samuel eyed the berries, and looked around, after carefully extracting Chalmer from the thorns.

"Well looky here," Samuel said. He found a space between the berry patch that made it possible to step a little way up the slope of the mountain and approach the same patch from the other side. "Now jes be careful and don't fall atop of 'em, but now they ain't outta yore reach."

Chalmer grinned and reached to pluck the big berries with no problem.

"Sometimes, it's a-easier to plow 'round the stump," Samuel said, chuckling to himself. He expected Chalmer to ask what he meant, but Chalmer didn't say anything, too busy getting his prized berries. Samuel figured he just didn't hear him.

When they filled all they could carry they headed home but stopped by Aubry's to see her and Horace Junior and give her some of their yield. She was happy for the offering, but had an idea.

"Well, how about we come on back to the house with you, and we'll put all these berries together, and I'll make us a cobbler, and fix dinner, too? That way Evelyn won't have to cook when she gets off work, and it'll give us some time to visit."

"Mm hmm!" Chalmer exclaimed.

"That'd be right nice, hunny," Samuel told her.

It turned out that Tommy and Horace had to call it a day, early. They'd had a problem with the plow. Tommy was telling Samuel about it when they came in. "It came from outta nowhere. Bam! Hit that rock and that was all it took," he said, shaking his head, aggravated.

Chalmer piped up with his two cents worth. "Dontcha know sumtimes it's a-easier ta plow 'round the stump?"

With a dour look, Tommy cut his eyes to Samuel.

Samuel raised his brows. "Boy's right," he said, soberly. Inside, his heart was singing.

Down at the General Store, Fred and Millicent were pleasantly surprised to see Herschel Brock come in the door. He was the gentleman who had paid off Eunice Small's tab on his last visit.

She'd been reduced to tears when Caleb had gone to tell her the kind act the man had done. He'd been worried she may have been a little offended, seeing it as charity, but she was ever so grateful. It had taken a world of weight off her shoulders.

"Hey there, Herschel! Good ta see ya! How's yer wife?" Caleb greeted him, looking past him out the store window for Ella, Mr. Brock's wife.

"Caleb," he nodded, "Fred," he addressed, with a smile, remembering his last faux pas with her name. Answering Caleb's question, he said somberly, "I'm afraid Ella passed away."

"Oh no!" Caleb and Fred both replied, regretfully.

Fred wiped her hands and came around the counter to give him a hug in condolence. "I'm so sorry," she said with sincerity.

"We both are," Caleb added.

"Well, that's what brought me here, actually."

Fred and Caleb were perplexed, but waited for him to elaborate.

"You see, Ella had been in a lot of pain for a very long time. We knew the end was coming and I think that she was actually looking for *anything* to take away her suffering, even if it was death. That said, I know she was afraid of dying.

I didn't know what to do to help her. The day I was here, I remember that Eunice had already left before I told you about Ella's health and where we were going, and Ella said she didn't mention it either. But while I was in here talking with you, Eunice stopped to talk to her. She said she had something for her. Ella was surprised, but played along thinking that Eunice was just confused. Then Eunice pulled this out of her purse and handed it to Ella." He held up a well worn sheet of paper filled with words, written with a shaky hand. It read:

Psalms 23:4 Even though I walk through the darkest
valley, I will fear no evil, for you are with me,
Your rod and your staff, they comfort me.

Deuteronomy 31:8 The Lord himself goes before you.
And will be with you, he will never leave you,
nor forsake you. Do not be afraid,
Do not be discouraged.

1 Corinthians 2:9 What no eye has seen, nor ear heard,
nor the heart of man imagined,
what God has prepared for those who love him.

When Caleb and Fred finished perusing the handwritten note, Caleb offered in explanation, "She lost her parents an' recently her sister. Maybe she carried this for consolation."

"Yes, I recalled you telling me that. My question was how did she know that my wife needed to hear these words of comfort? By the time I returned to the car that day, there was a marked change in my wife. She wasn't afraid of what was to come. She spent her last weeks in peace, and dare I say, happy. When I told her that Eunice was a seamstress too, she made me promise to bring her something. I'm here to fulfill her final wishes. I have it out in the car. By the way, she carried that paper with her till the end," he told them.

Fred offered, "Would you like me to go get Eunice? She doesn't live far."

He looked grateful. "Would you mind? I was hoping to be able to thank her in person," he said.

"Absolutely," she said to him, then to Caleb, "I'll be right back."

While she was gone to pick up Eunice, Caleb and Herschel unloaded the car. Caleb was speechless.

It was only a few minutes before Eunice and Fred returned.

"Eunice!" Herschel welcomed. "I'm sorry to have interrupted your day," he said.

"Don't be silly! It ain't often someone comes jes ta see little ole me!" she replied. "I'm happy ta see ya. Cept, Fred

204

here, tol me that yer wife went ta be with the Lord. I'm sorry fer yer loss, but she's in a better place. Nothin but glory by the Lord's side fer her now," she attempted to comfort him.

"I believe that, and it gives me peace. But it was your kindness and this," he held up the note, "that brought her peace in her final days."

"Oh, that tweren't me," she batted her hand at him. "That was him," she corrected, pointing to the heavens.

"That may be true, but you were the messenger. You helped her through the hardest time in her life, and I am forever grateful to you."

"I'd tell ya thank ya, but I cain't take credit fer that," she hedged.

"Well, she was a seamstress, like you, and it was her final wish for me to make sure that you got this," he said, stepping aside to reveal bolt after bolt of beautiful different fabrics, in floral, plaid and solid prints. There was a huge box filled with buttons, spools of thread in an array of colors, reels of lace and trims, and every kind of sewing notion you could imagine. As she took it all in, he moved the box to reveal a state of the art electric sewing machine.

"Lan sakes alive! I cain't take all a-this fer sumthin I didn't even do!" she exclaimed.

"Eunice, if you hadn't been here that day and stopped to talk to her, she would have spent her last days in pain and fear. Now maybe the Lord is ultimately responsible, but he chose you to deliver his message, and for that, my wife, Ella, wanted you to have this. Now, you wouldn't want me not to fulfill her last wishes, would you?"

She took a deep breath. "Well, since ya put it thataway, you stinker," she said looking at him like he'd pulled fast one on her. "There's just one problem. I ain't got no electric fer that there machine."

Fred looked at Caleb with a silent question, canting her head toward the little back room he'd used to sleep in when she'd first come to town. He knew exactly where she was going and nodded.

"Um, Eunice, I think I may have the answer..." before anyone could say anything, Fred suggested, "You know the electric is going to be here soon, and there's a room right back here that would be perfect for you to set up shop, plenty of room for all the fabric, you'll have electric for the machine, and best of all, everything you make can hang right out here for sale! What do you think?"

Everyone waited for Eunices's reply.

"What do I think?" she paused. "I think, PRAISE THE LORD!" she shouted, with her hands held in the air!

Herschel forgot himself and gave her a big hug! When he realized it, he pulled back. "I hope that was okay?" he asked.

"Why you!" she said, pulling him back down for another one!

Caleb said, quoting, "And let steadfastness have its full effect, that you may be perfect and complete, lacking in nothing, James 1:2-4."

"Amen!" they all agreed.

"Now, there's one more thing," Herschel said, and Eunice began shaking her head, overwhelmed. Herschel laughed, "I'm not going to ply you with more stuff," he promised, and she sighed in relief. "On my way here I noticed that there was a nice looking diner open in Maynardville, even though it's the Fourth of July, and I would be honored if you all would join me for supper there and keep me from having to eat alone on a holiday!"

Eunice said, "All this, *an'* a night out on the town? Mercy, what's a girl ta do?" She looked at Caleb and Fred, awaiting their response.

Caleb announced, "Well, it *is* a holiday, I don't think it will hurt ta close up shop a little early!"

207

CHAPTER 26

On Friday morning, Dr. Wright and Dr. Martin were both scheduled to come do assessments on Benny and Jane Doe. Dr. Martin had reduced his visits to once a week, since Benny had been progressing so well and there had been no change in Jane.

After Millicent updated them on Benny's heroic act with Oppy, and the subsequent newfound will to help others, she wanted their medical expertise on an idea she had. It had only occurred to her this week, since Benny and Oppy had become close.

In her office, she ran it by them. "Initially, it was thought to be in both Benny and Jane's best interest to keep them separated, but in light of such promising progress with Benny, and with no change whatsoever in Jane, I wanted your opinion on how to proceed. Do you think it would be detrimental to Benny's progress to see Jane, and if not, do you think there could be any benefit for Jane to see Benny?"

Dr. Martin asked, "Is it possible for Benny to be allowed to observe Jane without her being aware?"

Millicent thought for a moment. "Well, I had been seriously considering having her taken outside for a few minutes each day. I thought the fresh air and sunshine could be good for her. If you agree, it's possible that we could set it up where he could see her through a window, without her being able to see him."

Both doctors considered this.

"It's *possible* it could be a setback for Benny, but he seems very resilient, and overcame his attachment to her quickly when he first arrived here with all the other distractions he was afforded," Dr. Martin suggested, looking to Dr. Wright for his thoughts.

"Yes, I agree," Dr. Wright said. "In fact, I would like to be present. Is it possible this can be arranged while we are here this morning?"

"Absolutely, I can go get it underway now," she told them, standing. "I'll be just a just a few minutes."

She had to get an orderly to get Benny to go to his room under the pretense of getting a different game, while another got Jane into a wheelchair, and outside near a window. Once they were in that position, she retrieved the doctors and had them waiting in the common area when Benny re-entered the room.

Benny was familiar with both doctors now, after their many visits, and they both made sure to give him accolades on his quick response to Oppy, the prior week. This, as planned, bolstered his spirits substantially, before they put their test in motion. With a nod, they gave Millicent the signal to proceed.

"Benny, can you do me favor?" she asked, relying on his desire to please.

"Yes!" he answered, as she'd expected.

"Can you look out the window here and tell me who you see?"

He walked over and leaned down to look through the screen. "That's Brenda!" he said, calling out, "Hi, Brenda," through the screen.

Brenda heard him and waved, turning Jane so that she wouldn't see Benny. She hoped that Benny had been able to see Jane before he'd called out.

"She's nice," Benny said, straightening.

"Yes she is," Millicent agreed. "Do you see anyone else you know?"

Benny looked out again, this time pressing his face against the glass, peering through the double panes of the raised window.

"Nope," he said, matter of fact.

Millicent and the doctors exchanged glances.

"Okay Benny! Thank you! That was very helpful!" Millicent praised him, playing it up a bit. "You're going to play a game now?"

"Yes!" he said, when she reminded him. "Are y'all gonna play?"

211

"Maybe later, okay? We have to check on some other patients, now," she explained.

"Okay, bye bye," he told her and the doctors, going to the table where his games were.

When Benny was out of range, Dr. Martin suggested, "It's possible he doesn't recognize Jane in her current condition. She does look remarkably different."

Dr. Wright added, "Yes, it makes one wonder if he was around Jane *prior* to her being in the condition she was when they were rescued."

They watched Benny unpacking his game, while they mulled over what to do next.

Millicent sent an orderly to tell Brenda to bring Jane back to her room through the rear entrance, until they decided.

Millicent told the doctors, "To the best of my knowledge, Jane has shown no signs of being alert to anything going on around her, unless Brenda noticed any change with her while they were outside. I'm afraid it's highly unlikely she would even look at Benny, and *if* she did, there's a big chance that she'd not recognize him either."

"That's true," the doctor's agreed.

Dr. Wright went on to say, "However, at this juncture, I think it would be worth a try. At the very least, it would eliminate the need to keep them separated."

"I concur," Dr. Martin said.

Millicent asked, "How do you want to go about this? Escort him to her room, or bring her out here?"

Dr. Martin suggested, "I think it would be best to have her in her room, where she is familiar with her surroundings."

"Yes, we need to keep the conditions as controlled as possible, so that if there *is* a change we can determine the exact cause," Dr. Wright said. "First, I'd like to find out from Brenda if she had any reaction to being out of her room, before we proceed."

"Yes, of course. I'll go speak to Brenda, and see that Jane is settled back in her room," Millicent told them.

It was nearing lunch time and Millicent noticed Faith coming in the door to prepare to feed Jane. She asked her to hold off a bit, until the doctors were through. She looked at her watch. It was Friday and she hadn't heard anything since the Jenkins' had gotten the letter confirming their appointment regarding Chalmer's adoption, and she had hoped to go to Maynardville and check on any news. Realizing the day was slipping away, a thought occurred to her. "Faith, since you're already here, would you mind helping Tenley get started with today's batch of cookies?"

"You don't have to twist *my* arm! I'd love to!" she replied.

"Great! Thanks so much! I'll send her to the kitchen," Millicent called over her shoulder, hurrying on to Jane's room.

Brenda relayed that she had watched as best she could for any response from Jane, but being behind her to push the wheelchair, she couldn't say definitively that she was sure there was no reactions at all. She could, however, confirm that since she'd been back in her room, there had been no change.

After giving the doctors Brenda's update, they decided to go ahead with their test.

Millicent approached Benny and asked if he could help her with one more favor, and again he was happy to oblige.

He accompanied them to Jane's room. At the door they stopped and asked Benny if he could go in and say hello to Jane, but to do it carefully so as not to frighten her. He assured them he could.

They gathered in the doorway as he stepped into the room. Jane sat in her bedside chair, staring into space. She didn't appear to notice that anyone had entered.

Surprisingly, exactly like they'd asked, Benny walked slowly up to her, and in a soft voice he said, "Hello, Jane."

There was slight twitch of her brows.

Benny apparently thought she hadn't heard him. He leaned down in front of her face, and said it again.

The three onlookers in the doorway held their breath as Benny got so close to Jane's face. But this time there was no response.

"I don't think she's here," Benny turned and said to them, with his amazingly accurate diagnosis.

Millicent motioned him to come out, as Dr. Martin murmured, "Out of the mouths of babes," still astounded at Benny's remark.

Asking Brenda to continue to monitor Jane, Millicent told her she would send Faith in to relieve her and feed Jane her lunch. The doctors went along to her office while she went to collect Faith. She and Tenley had just gotten the batch of cookies on the baking sheets ready to go in the oven. Checking her watch again, Millicent thought she could still make it to Maynardville if the doctors were almost finished.

Picking up on Millicent's tension, Martha, the head of the kitchen staff, offered to watch over Tenley and help her start her deliveries to help save time. Martha was like the grandmother of the Home, a sweet, heavyset woman, very short with an ample bosom, and Millicent trusted her implicitly. She accepted her offer and thanked her, ever so grateful.

Faith retrieved Jane's tray and headed to her room. Just outside her door she realized she'd forgotten her smock but brushed it off, figuring Jane would be really hungry since her lunch was late today. She went in and set the tray on the bedside table, pushed Adohy's mother's bracelet up her arm out of the way, and told Brenda she could go on her break.

In Millicent's office they were discussing the slight movement of Jane's brows.

Dr. Wright asked, "Has anyone else addressed her as Jane, prior to today?"

"No," she replied. "I was concerned it could cause her to be confused as to her identity. I was emphatic with the staff."

"It certainly looked briefly as though she may have been exactly *that*, confused over being addressed by that name, which would indicate that on some level, she knows, at least, that Jane is not her name," Dr. Martin postulated.

"Or it could have been something as inconsequential as a muscle tic, given the lack of response the second time he said it," Dr. Wright countered.

"Precisely," Dr. Martin agreed.

"Which brings us back to square one, with the exception that it doesn't seem to be necessary to keep them from seeing each other," Millicent summed up.

During this discussion, Faith had begun to feed Jane. As she suspected, Jane appeared to be hungry, accepting every bite without hesitation.

Faith was just raising a bite of food to Jane's mouth when Tenley and Martha paused in the doorway. With the spoon hovering in front of Jane's mouth, Faith looked over her shoulder and said, "Hey! She's just eating now, can you come back later?"

"Kay," Tenley said, moving on down the hall.

As Faith watched her pull her wagon out of sight, there was a sudden terrified earsplitting scream, and before Faith could react, her hand holding the spoon was flung back, and in the blink of an eye Jane raked the tray of food to the floor, overturned the chair she'd been sitting in, and was crouched in the corner of the room, sobbing.

The crash and piercing scream echoed throughout the Home.

Both doctors and Millicent rushed out of her office toward the sound of the melee. Finding Martha holding a very frightened Tenley to her chest in the hallway, Martha indicated the disturbance was in Jane's room.

Inside, they took in the scene, as Faith was attempting to get around the chair to Jane. When Jane screamed again in terror, Faith was called away, and by that time Brenda had arrived. Doctor Martin barked an order for a sedative, and she hastily complied.

Retreating to the hallway, Faith recounted the events leading up to Jane's outburst. Brenda returned with the syringe, and Dr. Martin took it, slipping back into Jane's room. Similar to the first time he'd seen Jane, he was able to approach her without incident, giving her just enough of the shot to calm her.

After a few moments, they were able to get her back to her bed, and she was sedate enough for the room to be cleaned and straightened.

Faith left to change clothes and catch her breath, vowing to never forget her smock again. Every time she did, it was like she was just asking to wear someone's food.

Baffled as to the reason behind Jane's emotional state, wondering if it was a delayed reaction to Benny, the doctors decided to let Faith have a go at feeding Jane again, since she was the only one who could.

Faith was a little reluctant, but agreed, her heart going out to Jane. She knew she had to still be hungry. But Jane refused to eat.

They decided to give her some time, and left Brenda to monitor her.

One hour later, they attempted it again. She wouldn't open her mouth after repeated attempts. Faith even tried singing Sarah's song again, which had gotten through to her the first time, but there was no change.

As it was late in the day, the doctors left with the orders if she refused to eat by the following afternoon, they would have no alternative but to sedate her completely and put her back on IV's for sustenance. They both agreed to return Monday morning.

It was too late, by this time, for Millicent to go to Maynardville. It was just as well, she thought. She didn't think she could deal with any more upheavals that day.

By five o'clock Saturday, there was no change in Jane. Not even when Tenley came to her room. Her eyes were blank. Like Benny had predicted earlier, she wasn't there.

She was sedated and the IV's were hooked back up.

CHAPTER 27

Monday morning, as scheduled, Dr. Martin and Dr. Wright returned to assess Jane. Millicent had withheld her sedative so that they could see how she reacted when she awoke. She'd not had whole food since her breakfast on Friday morning.

When she regained consciousness and had time to become alert, she was assisted into her bedside chair.

The upheaval of said chair during the incident on Friday was not lost on the doctors. It was not a light chair, such as one would find at a supper table, made of only wood, or light metal. This was a padded and upholstered chair, consisting of considerable weight, purposely so that patients were not able to move them around easily. Granted, they presumed there was a great deal of adrenaline due to her extreme fear, but they were still amazed that she possessed as much strength as she did.

They felt that her need to be assisted was more from lack of will, rather than lack of ability. So that would be addressed in the coming days. Her physical therapy continued, even while she was sedated, so regardless of what was determined today, she shouldn't suffer any setbacks physically.

After sufficient time for her to adjust, Faith was asked to attempt a feeding. Donned in her smock—that she vowed never to forget again—she talked, pleaded, cajoled, sang, caressed, but nothing she did was reaching Jane. Whatever it was that triggered the terror in Jane had caused her to regress possibly farther than she had before.

Disappointed, both doctors agreed to let Faith have another go in a few hours, but if she didn't eat, she would have to have the IV's once more, and in order to keep her from attempting to rip the IV's out she would again be sedated. If it came to that, it would be a huge setback.

They couldn't help but be inclined to think the incident stemmed from a delayed reaction from her meeting with Benny, but it just didn't add up. When Faith tried again, it yielded the same results. Nothing. Jane was back to the state of a wakeful coma.

Perplexed, they asked to be notified if there were any problems over the next two days. They were both going to contact associates more educated with cases such as Jane's, in hopes that they could possibly offer any suggestions on how to proceed. They would return on Wednesday for another attempt to reach her.

When the doctors left for the day, Millicent and Tenley did their cookie delivery, and then she headed for Maynardville, with her fingers crossed.

To her dismay, Mr. Barnfield was in court, and wasn't expected back that afternoon, until late. Per his instructions, however, his secretary filled her in on what she knew to date.

"I'm sure this is very frustrating for you, Mrs. Thornton," his secretary began.

"Please, Millicent's fine," Millicent told her.

"Thank you, and I'm Polly," she said, with a smile. "This whole situation has been as intriguing as it's been confusing. We've been able to confirm that Mr. Pendergriff's license is current, and surprisingly, he *is,* in fact, licensed to practice in both North Carolina and Tennessee."

Millicent was dismayed to hear this, but had prepared herself for *some* bad news. "Okay," she said with a sigh, "so were you able to find out anything else?"

"Well, as we already knew, his office has been closed for quite some time. We've not been able to determine, *so far,* if he has a new office. There's no indication of it, as yet. That would lead us to believe that he's working out of his home, however, we've not been able to determine where that is, as yet, either."

When Millicent's brows knit in confusion, Polly tried to explain.

"Let me back up a bit, I can see you're confused."

"Yes, please," Millicent nodded, grateful.

"Okay, during our investigation we were able to ascertain that he is, or at least *was,* a very highly regarded attorney, the only child from a very influential family, and resided in the family home, or *mansion*, really."

Millicent's heart was sinking as Polly went on.

"*However*, there have been conflicting reports from people that we've spoken to, as to his present situation. His parents have both passed, and the mansion was sold several years back. We have not been able to locate his current residence, *or* where he is operating from." She paused, letting Millicent take the information in, and to see if she had any questions.

"Doesn't that seem strange?" Millicent asked.

"Yes, very," Polly agreed. "It's—"

"Intriguing," Millicent finished for her, understanding now what she'd meant earlier.

"Yes," Polly said.

"So, anything else?" Millicent asked, wanting at least a *shred* of good news.

The apologetic expression that flashed across Polly's face said it all.

"I'm afraid so," she said, hesitantly. "We just received a court date this morning, and it doesn't look like there's anything we can do to stop it. At least, not yet. The best we could hope for at this point, is to delay it."

Any expectations Millicent had for good news were dashed. Almost afraid to ask, she said, "What's the date?"

"It's for Monday, August the sixth," Polly informed her.

Millicent's mind was spinning. *At least it's a few weeks away, and after Tenley's surgery. But it's so soon!* She wasn't sure whether to be relieved, or upset. But it felt like upset was winning.

"Did Mr. Barnfield say what he was going to do?" Millicent finally asked.

"He said that we needed to get to the bottom of what's behind Mr. Perdergriff as soon as possible, so that we will know what our next move should be."

Millicent took a deep breath. She'd suddenly gotten a splitting headache, and her shoulders were very tense, which was, no doubt, fueling the headache. "Would you, by chance, have any aspirin?"

"I do!" Polly answered, happy to help. She pulled open her desk drawer, and retrieved the bottle, setting it across her desk in front of Millicent, then went to get her a cup of water.

"Thank you," Millicent said when she returned, accepting the cup. She took two aspirin, then thanked Polly again. During this exchange, Millicent, worried about so many different things, the trial, and Tenley's surgery topping the list, made a decision. There was no way she was going to Knoxville for the surgery and worrying the whole time about someone coming after Adohy, while they were gone. She was going to talk to Virgil, but knew he would agree. They would send Adohy and Faith on a mini honeymoon somewhere during that time. Somewhere no one would find them. They'd worked hard and deserved it, and it would ensure their safety until she and Virgil were back home with Tenley.

Before she left she inquired about Chalmer's adoption and was told that the Jenkins' had come in for their appointment, that everything was in order, and that it was scheduled for the twentieth of that month. Millicent did the math in her head. That would be the Friday after the surgery. They would be home by then, and Faith and Adohy would be back in time, too. With that settled, she left. Her headache was already better.

§

At the Jenkins' home Samuel and Chalmer were finishing up in the garden for the day, and headed in for a snack before they took their nap. On their way, in they stopped to pet Molly, who didn't raise her head but greeted them with a wagging tail. She had taken to sleeping in the hall between Chalmer's and Samuel's rooms at night, apparently torn between the two of them.

It was becoming an effort for her to make it from there to the front porch, only going off the porch to do her business.

After Chalmer and Samuel had their naps, they went to their rockers on the porch to await the mailman. They weren't expecting anything, it was just part of their ritual.

"Ya reckon I kin give Molly a lil piece a that ham we have, Papaw?" Chalmer asked, before they went out.

"I think she'd like that, son" Samuel told him.

Chalmer got a piece and took it out with them. Molly was waiting where she'd been when they went inside, between the two rockers they always sat in.

She took the ham from Chalmer, and he giggled when Molly licked his fingers afterward. "She shore loves ham, don't she, Papaw?" he said. He slid her bowl of water over to her and she lapped up some, then laid her head back down.

"Yep, she does," Samuel agreed with a chuckle, reaching down to pet her head.

Chalmer climbed up on his rocker, and they talked a little, but mostly just rocked, watching for the mailman.

He came before long and stayed to visit a few minutes, then went along to finish his route. The only thing he had to deliver to them was the weekly newspaper that Samuel got.

Samuel started to look the paper over, when Chalmer commented that Molly slept through the whole visit from the mailman. "She must be really tired, huh Papaw?" It was more an observation, than a question.

Samuel lowered the newspaper and looked down at Molly between them. "You okay, Molly girl?" he said to her. She would normally, at the very least, wag her tail when he talked to her. But she didn't. He reached down to pet her again, but she didn't move.

He laid his paper aside and got down on his knees in front of her. "Molly?" he said, sliding his hand under her chin to raise her head.

"She's really sleepin', ain't she, Papaw?"

225

Samuel didn't answer right away. He turned and sat on the porch, straightening his legs before him and pulled Molly over onto his lap. She lay limp with her head laying off the side of his leg, while he ran his hand from her head to her tail, in a loving caress. Tears ran down his cheeks.

"Papaw?" Chalmer asked quietly. "Why cain't ya wake her up?"

"Well, son," Samuel said, his voice cracking, trying to figure out how to explain it to Chalmer. "Molly went ta check on Sarah."

Chalmer looked at Molly, clearly there with them, confused. "Sarah?" he asked.

Samuel gently moved Molly off his lap and using the rocker to lean on, pushed himself up off the porch. "Come with me an' I'll interduce ya ta Sarah," he told Chalmer.

Chalmer followed him to his bedroom. Inside he took the framed picture of Sarah off his dresser and sat on the edge of his bed, pulling Chalmer up beside him. He showed the picture to him. "This here is Sarah. She was Tommy's, yer daddy's" he corrected, "sister. That means she was yer aunt."

"Where's she at?" Chalmer asked.

"She went ta be with the Lord," Samuel said. "In heaven," he added, so that Chalmer might understand. "Ya remember Jesus, that ya learn about in church, an' that I read ta ya 'bout?"

"Yeah, in the Good Book, that ya call it?" he asked.

"Yep, that one. Ya remember 'bout God, an' Heaven?"

Chalmer nodded.

"Well, Heaven's a place, if'n yer good, like Sarah and Molly was, then that's where ya go when yer time here is done, *if'n* ya asked God ta fergive ya a-yer sins or anythin' ya done wrong," he clarified, figuring Chalmer wouldn't know what sin was.

Chalmer was quiet a moment, then asked, "Like me a-burnin' that girl's dress an' ya lighten' that fire that killed them bunnies?"

"Yep, jes like that. If ya believe in God an ask eem ta fergive ya, he will, an' then when it's yer time, ya get ta go an' live in Heaven. An' their ain't no sickness, ner pain, ner nuthin' bad in Heaven. Ya know how Molly couldn'tna hardly walk no more? Well she's a-runnin' 'round in Heaven now with Sarah. She don't hurt no more, an' won't never hurt agin. She'll be like she was when she was a puppy, ferever."

"But she's out on the porch," Chalmer said, not quite understanding.

"That's only her body she used here on earth. What was inside, the part of her that was Molly, went ta heaven an' got a brand new body that won't never git old," he explained.

"So she's a-runnin' an' playin', now?" Chalmer grasped.

"Yep, she shore is. We'll miss her a bunch, but we jes gotta remember that she's as happy as she kin be now."

"Ya reckon she'll miss us?"

"Well, we jes gotta be good, an' one day we kin go an' find out, okay?"

227

"Okay," Chalmer agreed.

When they were finished with their talk, they went back out to the porch. Tommy and Horace were just coming in from work. They told them about Molly going to Heaven, and the four of them put her in her final resting place just to the side of the porch, where she would be near, with a handmade cross to mark her place.

CHAPTER 28

Enos and Jubal had a bit of an attitude problem, understandably so, after being falsely accused in the transistor radio debacle, but in the weeks since, had appeared to have put it behind them. Virgil had been extremely pleased with their progression with the horses. It seemed they just needed something challenging to keep them occupied, which was rewarding in itself.

Due to their hard work, the pride they had begun to take in their responsibilities and their dedication to doing well, Virgil asked them to accompany him on his monthly check of the fencing around the perimeter of their property. He loved this ritual, the peace and quiet and time to think, but there may come a time that he would need someone else other than just Adohy or himself, to do, not only the inspection, but the work required to mend the fence should it become necessary, so he decided to add this to their list of responsibilities.

"Enos, Jubal, can you saddle up three horses? Mine, and one for each of you," Virgil told them that morning, out of the blue. They reacted with doubt that they'd heard him correctly.

"One fer both a *us*?" Jubal questioned.

"Yes, I appreciate your hard work and dedication, and you've proven you can handle the responsibilities so far, so I want you to come with me to check the perimeter of the property today. We'll need to take some supplies, like an ax, in case there's any small tree limbs in our way, and a hammer and some nails for any minor repairs to the fencing. If there's any kind of major damage anywhere, then we'll just assess it and go back with the necessary supplies. I don't foresee any major problems, there haven't been any bad storms since I last went, but tree limbs can fall without warning, so you never know." He went back to what he was doing which effectively signaled the end of his explanation, so the boys went to do as they were told.

As they walked away, they glanced at each other with big smiles. It was the first time for either of them to be told they were doing something right, much less be rewarded. They stood a little taller for it.

With the horses saddled, they began the trek. There was a fairly accessible trail along the interior of the fence line, but there was some new growth that impeded the space and Virgil, leading the way, hacked it back with a machete as they went along. It was a sunny day, and for the most part they were sheltered from the sun's burning rays by the towering trees looming above them, but at times there were open spaces with no tree's or brush.

The sudden change in the light as they went through these areas made them squint from the brightness. They had just sauntered into an area like this when, without warning, Virgil's horse reared up in fright, causing him to crash to the ground with a thud. As he was struggling to get his bearings, a shot rang out, startling him but getting his attention instantly.

Still lying on the ground, he turned to see Enos standing with a rifle pointed right at him! It was his own rifle that he always carried for safety, that must have fallen to the ground when he did. His heart was pounding, as he watched Enos slowly lower the rifle. It took a moment before he realized that Enos's eyes were fixed on something just beyond where he was laying, and following Enos's line of sight, he saw the remains of a very large moccasin with a bloody stump where its head had been. A relieved sigh escaped his lips as the situation was becoming clear. He looked back at Enos in amazement, and then on to Jubal holding the reins to Enos's horse. How had Enos dismounted that quickly and shot the snake before he'd been bit? Even with plenty of time it wouldn't have been an easy shot to make!

Jubal dismounted then and wrapped the reins to both horses around the fence post, hurrying to his side, while Enos picked up his cane that had also fallen a few feet out of his reach.

Jubal was the first to speak. "Uh, Enos, we got a lil problem here," he said, looking down at Virgil's leg.

As Enos approached, Virgil looked at what Jubal was, to see his dungarees soaked in blood around his knee. It was then he began to feel the burn from the wound, and the warm blood running from it. Judging by the amount of blood, it must have been pretty bad. Confused as to how he'd been shot when there was only one round fired and the moccasin was clearly the recipient, the sun began to blind him to the point of darkness.

When Virgil collapsed it spurred the boys into action. Without thinking, Enos pulled his belt off and between the two of them they were able to tie it around Virgil's thigh tight enough, they hoped, to at least slow down the bleeding.

"Grab my horse, Jubal, an' take the saddle off, then bring her over here. We're gonna have to git Virgil across her back."

Jubal did that, while Enos grabbed the rifle and Virgil's cane and tied them to Jubal's saddle.

It was a struggle, but they managed to get Virgil across the horse's back. Jubal asked, "How're we gonna keep eem from slidin' off?"

"I'm gonna ride with eem," Enos stated, hopping onto the horses back and taking the reins. When he did, he saw the machete lying on the ground that had been under Virgil. Now Virgil's injury made sense. Jubal grabbed the machete, mounted his horse and they hurried as fast as they could back to Sarah's Home.

It took about twenty minutes for them to get there, and that was at nearly a full run. Jubal dismounted and ran inside to get help, while Enos hopped down and checked on Virgil. A nurse ran outside with an orderly close on her heels. One look at Virgil draped over the horse had her sending the orderly back inside for a stretcher.

It was Wednesday and Millicent was in her office with Dr. Wright and Dr. Martin, when she was alerted to the emergency. They arrived outside as the orderly returned with the stretcher and assisted with the transfer of Virgil from the horse to the bed. Once there, one doctor began checking Virgil's vitals, while the other located the wound.

"We need to get him inside before we can determine if he's severed an artery or a vein. Do you have a room we can operate in?" Dr. Martin asked.

"Yes," Dr. Wright replied, nodding to the orderlies to take Virgil there. "I'll lead the way." Addressing Millicent, who was asking Enos and Jubal what had happened, he said, "We'll do everything we can."

"Is he gonna be okay," Enos asked Millicent, as they followed everyone inside.

"I don't know yet. But if he is, it will be thanks to you two for getting a tourniquet on him, and getting him here quickly. How in the world did he cut his leg with the machete?" she asked, as they rushed along.

Jubal said, "When he fell off a-his horse, before Enos shot the snake."

Millicent stopped, and turned to look at them. "What?!"

Enos answered this time. "A snake spooked his horse, and when it reared up, Virgil fell off. He was clearin' the trail with the machete, an' I reckon must a cut his leg when he fell."

"How did you shoot the snake?" she asked, incredulous.

233

This time it was Jubal who spoke up. "Ya shoulda seen eem, Millacent! He was fast as lightenin'! I didn't even know what was happenin' before BOOM, he'd done jumped off a-his horse, grabbed up that rifle an' shot the head off a that snake. Shot eem dead, before he could bite Virgil!"

Millicent's bewildered expression faded and gratitude was shining in her eyes when she looked back at Enos.

"His horse ran off, an' the saddle off my horse is still out there. Ya want us ta go an' get it?" Enos asked, trying to change the subject and get the attention off him.

Faith and Adohy rushed in then, and Millicent asked Adohy to help the boys find Virgil's horse, while Faith went with her.

Faith waited outside the room where the doctors were taking care of Virgil, while Millicent went in to see if there was anything she could do.

By the time the doctors had done everything they could, Adohy and the boys were just coming back inside. They'd retrieved the saddle and located Virgil's horse.

They saw Millicent heading to them but were unable to ascertain from her expression if it was good news or bad news.

Millicent walked straight to Enos and wrapped her arms around him, before she allowed herself to break down.

Fearing the worst, his hopes deflated before she leaned back and said, "You saved his life!" between her sobs. Then she pulled Jubal into the embrace. "You *both* saved his life!"

234

There was a collective sigh of relief from everyone. Adohy hugged Faith, after Millicent relayed Virgil's condition.

"He lost a lot of blood, but if you two hadn't been there, he would have surely bled to death. Because you put the tourniquet on him and got him here so quickly, you stopped that from happening." She hugged them again, then asked, "How did you know to do that?"

Enos shrugged. "It jes seemed like the thing ta do," he answered, not really sure himself.

She didn't see the need to tell them that Virgil had severed his Great Suphenous vein that carries blood back to your heart and he would have lost less blood had the tourniquet been *below* the cut rather than above, because the end result was the same. The tourniquet staunched the flow of blood, and they'd gotten him back before the loss of circulation caused any problems.

She told them, "The doctors were able to cauterize the vein, and Virgil should be just fine once he's all healed up. It was the leg that had been so badly damaged from the plane crash during the war and was the cause for him needing the cane, so he should be as good as he was before this. He'll be weak for a while until his body can replenish all the blood he lost, though."

"We kin take care of everthin' with the horses til he's better," Jubal offered, and Enos nodded in agreement, adding, "Adohy said he'd help, too, with whatever was needed."

"Thank you! I have no doubt that the three of you can handle everything just fine," she said. "Now, I'm going to go check on him!" she told them, before giving them all one more hug.

Faith offered, "I'll go help Tenley with the cookies!" as Millicent was hugging her.

"Thank you! I forgot all about the cookies!" Millicent said, hugging her again before leaving the room.

CHAPTER 29

Millicent considered changing the date for Tenley's surgery to give Virgil time to recuperate, but he insisted that she leave it. What better way to recuperate then sitting in a hospital room with Tenley, or relaxing in a hotel room? Realizing he had a point, she decided to leave it as it was. He had also agreed with her that, for everyone's sanity, Faith and Adohy have a little honeymoon while they were gone, too. That would be one less thing to worry about.

That meant Jubal and Enos would be in charge of the yard, the horses, and everything else outside at the Home, and Evelyn would be in charge inside. Virgil and Millicent were confident that they could all handle it just fine for the few days, though it would definitely be a test for Jubal and Enos.

Should any problems arise, Samuel, Tommy and Horace, were nearby, and Caleb had offered to come back on that Tuesday, just to check on everything for good measure. Millicent suspected that Caleb was a little concerned about

Oppy while Faith was going to be gone, but they were one step
ahead of him. Faith had already been thinking about what they
could do if she were to get sick or be away for some reason, so
she had an idea to have Oppy take her meals in the common
area with Benny. Oppy loved it. Then to test her theory, during
a meal she pretended like she had to go out for a moment. She
asked Benny if he could take over feeding Oppy until she
returned. She and Millicent had watched from afar, and it
played out like a carefully written script. Oppy happily let
Benny feed her with no qualms.

It was a win/win situation because, of course, Benny
was on cloud nine for having been of help, and when he was
praised for a job well done, he wanted to continue to feed
Oppy every day. And so it was. A week had passed with no
problems whatsoever. Even though Faith had been worried
about there being a problem if she were ever unavailable for
whatever reason, when Benny took over so easily, at first she
felt a little remiss that someone had been able to take her
place. It had been a little flattering that she was the only one
that Oppy would eat for. In the end, she was grateful that it
was so rewarding for Oppy and Benny to be there for each
other, and she wondered if Benny would have the same effect
on feeding Jane. She thought it could be worth the chance,
since Jane was still having to be sedated. Both Dr. Wright and
Dr. Martin were due to come in today, so she took her idea to
Millicent.

Millicent's only hesitation was that they had never
been able to determine if Benny's last visit with Jane was what
had caused her setback. She had her doubt's, and so did both
doctors, but Jane was the only person who knew the answer to

that for certain. Millicent agreed to consult the doctors when they arrived.

An hour later, as they were seated in her office, she recounted their breakthrough with Oppy and Benny, and presented Faith's idea to let Benny try feeding Jane. Since neither doctor had been able to come up with any alternatives, they felt it was worth the try, as long as Benny was willing.

Benny's only reluctance was leaving Oppy long enough to make the attempt, but when Millicent explained how important it was, he happily complied.

As before, Jane was allowed ample time to come out from under the sedation, and when she had, she was moved from her bed to the chair, with the chair situated so they could observe from the doorway without being a possible distraction. Then the tray of food was brought in by Brenda, and Benny was allowed to enter, under the instructions not to make sudden movements or noises that could frighten Jane in any way.

His ability to understand and follow instructions fascinated everyone, but most of all the doctors. He slowly advanced on Jane, remembering not to call her by name.

"Hello," he said softly, like he'd heard Brenda speak to her. "Are ya hungry? It's real good taday," he said, as he spooned up a bite. He held it to her mouth. Everyone clamored closer in the doorway to see if there would be any response. Benny held the food there a few seconds, but she didn't react. He waited a few seconds more, then said, "Ya oughta try it. *Oppy* liked it. *Oppy* ate all a-hers up," he cajoled, like one trying to coerce a baby to eat.

The seconds ticked by and as everyone's spirits fell, Jane finally opened her mouth and accepted the food. Bewildered expressions were met with bewildered expressions as they looked at each other, careful to remain quiet. Benny continued to talk softly to Jane as directed, and she ate everything on the plate.

It was another huge success, and it was all due to Benny! When he was done and left the room, they took him down the hall before showering him with praise, so not to startle Jane with any loud voices. They didn't even have to ask him about the next feeding. He volunteered!

Millicent said, joking, "If he keeps this up, I'm going to have to put him on the payroll!"

After a while, giving her meal time to settle, the doctors and Millicent went back in to see Jane, but there were to be no more breakthroughs at this visit. She remained unfocused, staring into space, showing no sign that she was aware they were there. They knew she had to be cognizant to some extent, otherwise she wouldn't have allowed Benny to feed her, but just *how* cognizant remained to be seen.

Being Friday, they had several feedings before Millicent would be going away Sunday evening. The doctors instructed them to continue as they had this morning unless there were any complications, or Jane refused to eat. If that became the case, she was to be sedated, and fed through IV's until they returned on Monday. They would reevaluate then and leave further instructions until all returned on Wednesday.

Faith was so relieved that Jane had begun to allow herself to be fed again. Benny was becoming her hero, too. She hadn't realized how concerned she'd been about Jane,

240

especially since she and Adohy were going away, until she started eating. After this breakthrough, the reality that they were actually going to go away for a few days was beginning to set in, and the excitement began to rise. There *was* a little voice in the back of her mind wondering if she was losing her touch though.

After much debate, Tenley finally agreed to *teach* Martha how to make the cookies so that she could take over for her during her surgery, and she went over it step by step, down to how to load them in her wagon. Martha played along brilliantly. When they were done, Tenley was confident Martha could get through the few days, til she returned.

While they were doing this, Millicent made another trip to Maynardville. She hadn't heard anything from the attorney all week, and couldn't leave Sunday without some kind of update, besides she reasoned, she needed to leave a number she could receive messages at while they were in Knoxville. Having access to a phone was one of the only comforting things about this trip.

On the way there it occurred to her that it was Friday the thirteenth, but she brushed the thought away. She wasn't superstitious, in fact, she was *confiden*t there would be some kind of news today. As if to reinforce her hopes, she reminded herself of the huge breakthrough with Jane, despite the date.

When she arrived she found that Mr. Barnfield was not in the office, but again, that was okay, she told herself, Polly could fill her in on any new developments.

After she and Polly exchanged pleasantries, Millicent told her, "In addition to hoping for some new information, I wanted to leave you the name of the hotel we will be at in

Knoxville, during our daughter's surgery." She gave Polly the number. "The surgery is scheduled for Monday morning, and if all goes as expected, we should be back home by Wednesday, but *please,* if you learn of anything, please leave us a message. I will check at the front desk several times a day."

"I certainly will, Millicent," Polly assured her.

There was a moments silence and Millicent got a sinking feeling in her gut. Swallowing it back, she asked hesitantly, "Do you have any new information?"

Polly looked away and fidgeted with a few things on her desk, stalling, then finally said, "We're still following leads on Mr. Pendergriff, but we were able, through the court, to ascertain the reason for his motion to reverse the adoption." She looked up at Millicent then, who was still standing in front of her desk.

Polly's regretful expression prompted Millicent to sit. "And?" she asked.

"Well, in cases of adoption involving Native American children, their tribe must be notified prior to the adoption. Mr. Pendergriff is alleging that there was no such notification made. In our search of the records, we have been unable to find any such document either," she explained, her voice getting softer as she spoke, as though to soften the blow of her words.

It didn't quite have the desired effect though, as the news landed like a left hook to Millicent. "But, I don't understand. Mr. Barnfield said everything was in order."

Polly nodded. "It's a slippery slope, and we are still hoping to be able to prove that since," she paused, trying to remember Adohy's name, "Ado..."

"Adohy?" Millicent provided.

"Yes," Polly said gratefully, "I'm sorry, I wasn't sure how to pronounce it. We're still hoping to prove that since Adohy had a Registration of a Foundling done, according to the law, *that* nullified the necessity to have a record of the tribe being notified."

"And if it doesn't?"

Polly didn't have to answer. Her face said it all.

Millicent left wondering if there was something to Friday the thirteenth after all, but she quickly put that out of her mind and focused on the positive. They had tried to prove that Adohy was part of the Cherokee tribe for months, to no avail. They had done everything the court had required them to do. But just to make sure, she stopped by the General Store to see Fred on her way home.

§

An hour later, armed with Fred's assurances that they had done everything by the book, Millicent went home, determined to stay positive. And there was no way she was putting this new information on Adohy and Faith's shoulders before their mini honeymoon.

CHAPTER 30

Sunday afternoon, Adohy and Faith followed Virgil, Millicent and Tenley to Knoxville, where they had dinner before Tenley had to be checked in at the hospital. Afterward, following Virgil's directions, Adohy and Faith left for Gatlinburg. It was a quaint little town where there was an arts and crafts community, and it was near the Smoky Mountain National Park, where they could lay low and explore.

It was nearly dark when they arrived, and being a Sunday, most places had long since been closed. They checked in to a motel and spent the first night of their honeymoon, in a room with electric lights, and indoor plumbing. It was a very inexpensive motel, but they felt like it was the best thing money could buy. It was like magic to flip a switch and have the lights turn on and off. The next morning they awoke early despite having planned to sleep in. They dressed and went in search of breakfast, and then to see what the town had to offer.

Faith was taken with the shops that displayed beautiful colorful chenille bedspreads outside, blowing in the breeze, the likes she'd never seen before. She promised herself she would get at least two of them before they went home, one for them, and one for Virgil and Millicent. If she had enough money, she would get one for Aubry and Evelyn, too.

They spent the day strolling hand in hand through the art and craft community, picking up little handmade gifts to take back with them, then had dinner before going back to their motel.

At the office, they checked to find that Millicent had left a message. Tenley's surgery had gone well, she was recovering beautifully, and barring any complications, would be discharged Wednesday morning as scheduled. This meant they had one more day for their mini honeymoon. Since they had seen pretty much everything there was to see in Gatlinburg, they decided to go off the beaten path the next day. Asking for suggestions in the office, they learned there were waterfalls they could hike to, nearby.

Early Tuesday morning they dressed in shorts and shoes suitable for hiking, then went to get breakfast. At the diner, they were greeted and treated like family and when they explained they were on their honeymoon and going to see the nearby waterfalls today, the owner of the restaurant, a plump older woman named Nellie, offered to pack a picnic lunch to take with them!

They were given directions for a few different options, and after talking it over, they chose the most difficult waterfall to access, for a couple of reasons. One, the degree of difficulty would mean less people they would encounter, and two, the benefit of the rewards to be seen, once the hike was accomplished, was the greatest.

The day was sunny with cotton candy clouds floating on the horizon, and after getting their packed lunch they began the drive to the point that the trail started to Ramsey Cascades. The temperature was pushing ninety degrees, and it was going to be a bit of a hike, not only in distance but in difficulty, on the 2200 foot elevation gain.

Adohy followed the instructions that Faith read off.

"We need to go east on 321 out of Gatlinburg, for six miles," she instructed. "Then we make a right turn into Greenbriar." After a short distance on this gravel road they came to a sign that said Smoky Mountain National Park. They looked at each other and grinned. Though the park was opened in nineteen-forty, the same year Faith had been born, neither of them had been there before, and it was a very meaningful moment for both of them.

"After about three miles, we'll come to a fork in the road." When they reached the fork, she told him, "We need to go left and cross the bridge, then go another mile and a half! That's where the trail starts."

As they'd hoped, there were no vehicles in the parking area, so maybe they would have the day to themselves. They grabbed their picnic lunch and embarked on their journey to the waterfall.

One of the locals in the diner at breakfast, named Earl, and elderly man who had lived in the area his whole life, filled them in on some of the sites they would encounter on the trek. He told them he'd been a park ranger for a while, before his retirement, and gave them a lesson on why the park had been created in the first place.

"It was ta stop the destruction of the ancient forest. Them loggers was a-tearin' down everthin' in their path. The section over by Ramsey Cascades is one a-the onliest unscathed areas in the Park," he relayed proudly.

"Really?" Adohy and Faith asked, genuinely interested.

"Yes siree," he acknowledged. "Yer gonna see the some a-the largest trees in the whole park on this trail. There's the third tallest maple, at one hundred-forty-one feet—"

Adohy and Faith expressed awe at the height he mentioned.

"—an' the second tallest white oak at one hundred-twenty-three feet, an' the tallest black cherry tree in the park, at one hundred-forty-six feet!" he ended triumphantly.

"How will we know where they are?" Faith asked.

"Oh, they's marked with placards, ya cain't miss 'em," he assured her.

Faith and Adohy didn't realize just how impressed they were going to be, until they actually saw them firsthand. They were magnificent! Trying to see to their tops was dizzying.

This part of the trail followed the Ramsey Prong of the Little Pigeon River, and they had passed several little waterfalls and rapids, interrupted here and there by cool clear pools of water. Under the canopy of the trees, it was shaded and cooler, with lush greenery all around, wild flowers, and moss covering rocks in, and near, the stream.

Around two miles into the hike they came to a very long and narrow foot bridge that spanned about twenty feet high over the creek, which they crossed with ease. It was after this that the trail began to become more rugged and strenuous. Adohy climbed steep rock steps, carefully navigating through roots, rocks, and boulders, leading the way, testing the trail for safety before waiting and giving Faith the okay to follow. Fortunately their age and physical condition made it a relatively simple feat.

After nearly four miles of climbing and hiking overall, they came to the cascades. It was every bit worth the work. It was the tallest waterfall in the park, and judging by what they were looking at, it had to be the most spectacular. Water gushed over several tiers, dropping one hundred feet into pools at the bottom. Adohy pulled Faith close in a hug as they just stood and took in the site, speechless.

After several minutes of soaking in the beauty and serenity, they found a spot to sit and have their picnic, grateful to be the only people in sight.

Nellie, from the diner, had outdone herself, and they enjoyed the delicious ham sandwiches that were still cool from the chilled grapes and nectarines she had packed. Sated, Adohy leaned back against a tree, and pulled Faith over to lean back against his chest, where they were mesmerized by the endless flow of water crashing over the edge in its earnest quest to dance gracefully over and around the rocks that waited below.

Though neither of them had mentioned the real reason they were on this mini honeymoon, it had been lurking in the back of their minds, and Adohy finally addressed it.

"Everything here reminds me of you," he began.

When Faith started to sit up, he tightened his hold around her to keep her leaning back into him, and continued.

"See how fast the water is pouring over the side?"

She nodded.

"That's how my love feels pouring from my heart when I look at you. Your hair is like the sun shining down, and your eyes are like the pools of water that I could drown in. Your arms surround me like these trees, and your love is the air that I breathe." He nudged her to turn and look at him now. When she was looking into his eyes, he said, "No one can take that from me. No matter what they do, or where I am, I will have you around me."

Faith shook her head and started to say something, but he put his finger over her lips to stop her.

"No matter what happens, as long as you love me, I can endure anything, and I will always find my way back to you," he promised her, looking deeply into her eyes.

Faith tenderly placed her hand on the side of his face, love radiating from the core of her. She told him, "Then you will always find me, because there is *nothing* that could *ever* make me stop loving you." Her conviction drove her words home, before she kissed him as if it would be their last kiss.

CHAPTER 31

Things had gone well while Virgil and Millicent were away. There had been no problems whatsoever! Enos and Jubal had outdone themselves, and Virgil couldn't have been more proud, though he had to admit, a little relieved, too. He'd had faith in them, but one just never knew until they'd proven themselves. And they did, with flying colors. It was comforting to know they had taken such pride in their duties. What a difference a little bit of trust and confidence had instilled in them. It was already hard to remember the attitudes they'd had when they'd first come to Sarah's Home.

Oppy was blossoming under Benny's attentions, and Jane was looking healthier than ever. Unfortunately, there was no change in Jane's demeanor otherwise. She was still in what they considered a wakeful coma, in that she showed no interaction with anyone, or anything, other than simply allowing herself to be fed, and put through her physical therapy. Her hair was growing, and there was discussion as to whether they ought to keep it short, or let it grow and risk

Benny recognizing her and making the connection to their previous relationship. It was determined they would keep it trimmed for now.

Tenley's surgery was healing well, as was Virgil's wound. It seemed the trip was a blessing in disguise for everyone it affected. The surgeons had done a wonderful job with Tenley's deformity and they hoped, in time, no one would be able to tell she'd ever had a cleft palate. The rest Virgil got while they were away acted as an accelerant to his healing, an answer to Millicent's prayers, and he was going to be fine.

To top things off, there were four new colorful Chenille bedspreads in Hurricane Holler, and Faith and Adohy were closer than ever.

It was Friday morning now, the day of Chalmer's adoption. He awoke before anyone else.

"Is it time? Is it time?" he yelled out, running first to Samuel's room, then to Tommy and Evelyn's, even though it was still dark outside. After being startled awake, they couldn't help but be touched over his excitement. It was a big day for them all. Seeing it was nearly four a.m. they realized they would be getting an earlier start than they had imagined.

Evelyn and Tommy had a little surprise for Chalmer and Samuel but decided to give it to them after breakfast. No one but Samuel knew that he had a surprise for them as well, but he wanted to wait to tell them about it after the proceedings, when they were on their way home.

Fixing Chalmer's favorite, bloody eggs and sliced bread with the crust cut off, Evelyn thought back to the day that Chalmer stole her heart, and all the incident's leading up to the final shot from Cupid's bow. It was one of those incidents that inspired the surprise they had for Chalmer and Samuel. It probably wouldn't be that big of a deal for Samuel, but she knew that Chalmer would be thrilled with it.

When she was younger, adopting a child had never occurred to her, but it simply couldn't feel more right! Sure, she wanted them to have biological children of their own one day, but for now their family was perfect, she thought, as she looked around the table.

After the breakfast dishes were done, she brought their packages out.

"It's a special day, so we wanted to get a little surprise for the two of you," she said, as she placed the gifts in front of Chalmer and Samuel on the table.

Chalmer eyed the unexpected gift with wonder. "We get a present, too?" he asked, in amazement. "Even though it ain't our birthday, ner nothin'?"

Everyone laughed, and Evelyn explained that it was *sort* of like a birthday since he was officially going to be family after today. That was a good enough reason for him, and he and Samuel went about opening their packages at Evelyn's prompting.

They pulled the paper back to reveal brand new denim overalls and crisp white dress shirts. It was identical to what Samuel wore to church on Sunday and what Chalmer had been saving his earnings for. They were exactly alike, just several sizes different.

"Wow! Look Papaw! It's jes like yers!" he exclaimed, pulling the clothes out to hold up.

Samuel chuckled at his exuberance. "It shore is!" he agreed.

"Kin we wear 'em taday, Mama? Daddy?" Chalmer asked, looking at each of them in turn.

Evelyn's heart skipped a beat. It was the first time he'd called them that. She looked at Tommy, who looked back at her, and she could see it had done the same thing to his heart.

"You sure can! That's why we got them for you! Now you can s—" she was going to say he could save his money for something else, but Chalmer had already run off to change into his overalls.

"Is it okay with you, Samuel?" Evelyn asked.

Samuel could only nod, not making eye contact. Evelyn saw his chin quiver as he stood to go change, too.

§

The proceedings only took a few moments in the judge's chambers. All preliminary paperwork and meetings had already been executed, and once the last of it was finalized, the judge, seeing Samuel and Chalmer, dressed identically in new overalls and white shirts, standing hand in hand, knowing the answer before he voiced it, asked Chalmer, "Are you happy, son?"

Chalmer hesitated and took a deep breath, then looked at the judge with furrowed brows. Tommy and Evelyn glanced at each other, concern evident in their eyes. Did

Chalmer not understand what the judge had asked him, they wondered, getting knots in the pits of their stomachs.

When Chalmer didn't answer right away, Virgil and Millicent exchanged a confused glimpse between themselves, too. During the hesitation, Faith grabbed Adohy's hand, squeezing hard, nervous about what he was going to say. Horace and Aubry had already stepped out because Horace Junior was getting pretty vocal, and Aubry didn't want it to upset the judge, so they were spared the anxiety of the moment.

Finally, Chalmer said, "Well, ya see, I'm jes a kid. I only jes turned six years old. Fer a long time nobody wanted ta keep me 'round. But after taday, now I got me *two* birthdays, an' I got me a papaw, *an'* a mama an' daddy that wants me. I reckon a kid cain't get no happier than that!"

You could hear the tears drop in the silence.

§

All Samuel had to say to Tommy on the way home was for him to take them to Clyde Wilkens' place and Tommy knew what the surprise was. He didn't say anything to spoil it for Chalmer and Evelyn, though, and his excitement level rose the closer they got, remembering the day this had happened for him years ago.

Chalmer didn't know there was another surprise coming. They pulled into the Wilkens' yard and got out of the vehicle. Clyde had been expecting them and came out to greet them.

"Howdy Samuel," he said, reaching to shake Samuel's hand. "That's a might fine looking boy ya got ya there!"

"Yes sir. This here's Chalmer. Chalmer *Jenkins*, as of taday, an' fine as they come," Samuel stated, clear as a bell.

Clyde had known Samuel all of his life, and had never known him to not stutter. He glanced at Tommy in surprise, and Tommy just raised his brows and nodded in answer.

"Well, he shore looks like a chip off the old block!" Clyde said in reference to their matching outfits. "Yer lookin good, too! Looks like y'all is a blessin fer each another!"

"Ya like my overalls?" Chalmer asked Clyde. "They's jes like my papaw's," he pointed out proudly.

"I shore do! Them there's some fine lookin' overalls!" Clyde told him. He looked at Samuel then. "Ready fer me ta call 'em?" he asked.

Samuel nodded, and Clyde let out a loud whistle. A few seconds passed and then seven of the cutest beagle puppies they had ever seen came running from the back side of a barn. Their long ears were floating up and down in the air as they bounced toward them.

Chalmers eyes got big as saucers as the little fur balls headed for them. He dropped to his knees and within seconds was covered in flopping ears and wagging tails, and slobbery kisses. You could hear him giggling under the pile of puppies.

Tommy and Evelyn joined Chalmer in the fray, while Samuel and Clyde looked on.

Clyde said, "I meant what I said about ya lookin' good, Samuel."

Samuel nodded. "I feel good, Clyde. That boy has breathed life inta me I didn't know I had left," he confessed.

"I kin see that," Clyde acknowledged.

Samuel called out to the three of them on the ground with the puppies, "Y'all go on an' pick out one, now."

Chalmer squealed, "We kin keep one! We get ta keep one!"

It took several rounds of elimination, before they narrowed it down to *the* one. Chalmer was tickled that they had all chosen the same puppy. "That's funny we all picked this'n," he said, holding the puppy in his arms. He shrugged, "Guess it was meant ta be."

Tommy froze and was gazing at Chalmer, stunned speechless.

Evelyn saw Tommy's expression and asked what was wrong.

Tommy stood up, watching Chalmer frolic with the puppy. He smiled. "Nothin's wrong," he said vaguely, lost in thought.

"Why did you get that look on your face when Chalmer said it was meant to be?"

"Because, when Papaw brought us here to get Molly when she was a puppy, I prayed the whole way here, for him to still have a puppy left for us. Sarah said, if it was meant ta be, the puppy would still be here. So I prayed, "Please let it be meant ta be" over and over till we got here! And he still had it!

257

It *was* meant ta be! It jes floored me when Chalmer said that exact same thing!" he explained, before joining Chalmer again.

Evelyn watched the two of them wrestle with the puppy. She couldn't believe *just* how meant to be that it was, or how it filled her heart.

With the choice made, they thanked Mr Wilkens and loaded up to go back by the general store to thank Caleb and Fred for setting up the beagle arrangement. When they were on their way, Chalmer asked, "Kin we go back and see the judge fer a minute?"

"What for?" Evelyn asked.

"Well, ya know how he asked me if'n I was happy? An' I said I reckon I couldn't get no happier?"

"Yes?" she answered.

"I jes wanted ta tell eem I was wrong," he said. "An', kin we name the puppy Happy?"

Like anyone could say no.

CHAPTER 32

Aubry and Horace had gone ahead, back to the Jenkins' house to start supper for everyone. She was fixing Chalmer's favorite, chicken and dumplings, and brought a birthday cake from her house that she'd made the day before, for the celebration.

Horace tended to the baby on the front porch, waiting for the others, while she got everything going. She was so happy that things had gone smoothly at the adoption proceeding. The problems concerning Adohy's adoption had everyone on edge, and rightly so. Chalmer had been such a blessing for everyone, she'd been praying there would be no issues.

It was only a little over a week before Adohy's case went to court, unless Millicent found out something today from the attorney. She was anxious for them to get there so she could find out. When she heard someone coming in, she hurried into the living room to find it was Faith and Adohy, but they told her that Millicent and Virgil were right behind them. Aubry wasn't sure how much Millicent and Virgil had shared with Faith and Adohy at this point, so she didn't mention it to them.

True to their word, Millicent and Virgil arrived a few minutes later, and Aubry could tell by Millicent's ashen pallor that the news wasn't good. She hoped they would get a chance to talk privately, soon. Millicent and Faith pitched in on helping with supper, while Virgil and Adohy waited with Horace and the baby on the porch. About an hour later, the others arrived with the new puppy in tow. By the time he was introduced to everyone and shown his new home, supper was ready and they sat down to eat, while he waited nearby, patiently.

For all intents and purposes Millicent seemed as jovial as everyone else, but one had only to look into her eyes to see the worry. It wasn't until after supper and the cake, when Faith went out with the others to play with Happy, that Millicent was able to fill Aubry and Evelyn in on what the attorney had told them.

Over a cup of coffee, and with a heavy heart, Millicent asked them to pray that something changed over the next week. The attorney's investigators had still been unable to locate Mr. Pendergriff, though he was still communicating with the court using his previous address and stationary. Mr. Barnfield had said there was a lead they were pursuing that they hoped would shed some light on the case, but they had no way of knowing whether it would pan out or not, especially in time to be of use in court. She finished the update by telling them that she and Virgil were going to have to bring Faith and Adohy up to date on the circumstances, and planned to do so that evening after the celebration. After that, all they could do was wait and pray.

§

Every member of the family and beyond, did just that, prayed and prayed some more, bringing them to the morning of the hearing.

Everyone was asked to wait in a room next door to the courtroom until they were ready to begin. Much to their surprise the courtroom was standing room only, with the exception of the first rows behind the attorney's tables. The attorneys were already in place in the front of the room, and as they filed in murmurs arose in the crowd when Adohy entered. He looked regal, standing tall and proud in his suit, his long, black hair, shiny and streaming past his shoulders.

They were taken aback at the amount of people present and wondered if they were there for other cases, but were advised by council that that wasn't the case. Somehow word had spread about Adohy's plight, and the people were there either to show their support, or lack thereof. It would remain to be seen. Possibly they were just there to see if he came in dressed in a loin cloth and feathered head dress. It was rare for people in these parts to see Indians at all, as they mostly stayed at or near the Qualla Reservation. Most would have been surprised to know they dressed just like everyone else.

Mr. Pendergriff was at the table for the state, his presence proof that he actually existed. His disheveled appearance gave question to how *well* he existed, however. He wore a three piece suit that was wrinkled and had seen better days. He was short and portly, his round face scarred with pock marks. The back side of his balding head held the remnants of what hair he had left, albeit sparse and oily.

Millicent knew better than to judge a book by its cover, but taking in his appearance, she couldn't help but be just a little less worried. As they approached to be seated, however, he looked at them with such open derision, his leer becoming clearly hateful when it landed on Adohy. Millicent felt her concern rise and surpass her earlier trepidation.

Adohy was seated at the table beside Mr Barnfield and his assistant, and when everyone was in place, a bailiff entered the courtroom through a side door and announced, "All rise! Court is now in session. The Honorable Judge Price Clayton presiding."

Everyone stood as the judge entered in his black robe and stepped onto the bench, taking his seat. He he was a tall and dignified looking man, with silver hair.

"You may be seated," the bailiff told the courtroom.

The courtroom clerk, seated at a desk off center and in front of the judges bench in the lower level, stood and recited, "This is case number 67C01-0656-CV-00284, in the matter of Adohy White Horn Thornton. Present in the court are the defendant and his attorney, Mr. Barnfield, and the plaintiff, Mr. Pendergriff."

"Are we ready to begin, counsel?" Judge Clayton addressed the attorneys.

"We are, Your Honor," they both replied.

"Very well." Canting his head toward the plaintiff, he said, "Mr. Pendergriff, you may present your case."

"Thank you, Your Honor," Mr. Pendergriff said, as he stood and cleared his throat. "Your Honor, the State intends to prove that the defendants are in violation of following the proper procedure of adoption, as set forth by the State of Tennessee, and the Department of Indian Affairs regarding a Native American, and furthermore as a result is now using an improper alias, and as such has entered into an illegal union with an underage female. We ask the court to render the adoption null and void, instruct the defendant to cease and desist the use of the improper alias, to annul the illegal union, and to order the defendant to the Qualla Reservation where he belongs."

"Objection!" Mr. Barnfield shouted, standing abruptly. "It has yet to be determined where the defendant *belongs,* Your Honor."

"Sustained,' the Judge said. "You will refrain from sharing your unfounded opinions, Mr. Pendergriff," he instructed.

"Yes, Your Honor," the attorney agreed, taking his seat.

"Counsel?" the Judge prompted, looking at Mr Barnfield.

"Your Honor, we intend to prove that the adoption process was adhered to, to the letter of the law, that the defendant has the legal use of his name, the marriage contract is valid, and he has the right to live where he pleases. We have reason to believe Mr. Pendergriff has ulterior motives for this flagrant abuse of the courts time."

"Very well, let's begin," Judge Clayton directed.

Mr. Pendergriff rose and began going over the arduous rules and procedures for adoption, submitting paperwork as exhibits to the court. Then he delved into the additional rules and procedures regarding Native American adoptions, and noted the lack of required paperwork that would have been necessary to have completed the process according to the law.

As Mr. Pendergriff was presenting his case, Mr. Barnfield kept glancing back toward the entrance to the courtroom as though he was expecting someone. As time passed, his glances became more frequent, and his agitation seemed to increase. Millicent hoped they would take a break soon so that she could talk to him.

Finally, after nearly an hour, Mr. Pendergriff came to a close. "So, you see, Your Honor, I believe we have sufficiently proven that the process in the adoption by the Thornton's of one, Adohy White Horn, is incomplete, and any and all agreements entered into beyond that are null and void."

Mr. Barnfield glanced once more at the double doors to the courtroom, when the judge addressed him.

"Your Honor, If I may, I would like to request we take a short break before I begin?" Mr. Barnfield asked.

Judge Clayton looked at the clock and said, "We'll take a short recess until eleven o'clock."

"All rise," the bailiff called as the Judge stepped down from his bench and exited through the side door to his chambers.

Once his door was closed the conversation level rose in the courtroom as people stood and moved about.

Millicent approached Mr. Barnfield. He was speaking to his assistant, who was nodding her head at his instructions, and when he was done, she hurried out of the room. He turned to Millicent then.

"What do you think? It seemed like you were waiting for someone?" she asked.

"Yes, we are still waiting to hear from our investigator. A big part of our case hinges on the lead we've been working on, and it's crucial he get here soon or it will be for naught," he explained, before turning his attention to the stacks of papers on the table.

Millicent could see he was distracted and didn't want to interfere. She stepped away to give him space to concentrate on the case.

They all stepped out of the room to get a drink of water, and stretch their legs, until it was time to go back in. They felt everyone's eyes on them, and saw people hiding their whispers behind their hands. It was impossible to read their expressions, so it was unclear whose side they were on.

At precisely eleven o'clock, the bailiff announced, "All rise."

Once everyone was in place, court was called to order, and the Judge asked Mr. Barnfield to begin.

"Your Honor, I believe Mr. Pendergriff has shown the court that the proper procedure for the adoption was followed, up to the requirements for Native Americans. This is an exceptional case, and where the correct procedure becomes less black and white, right or wrong. I can cite several, *hundreds* even, of previous cases of adoptions involving

Native Americans as case in point examples that show everything required was done according to the law. However the issue here is that Adohy White Horn had no record of birth. In fact, he had no record of his full name, and after extensive searches and much research, there were no records proving he was a part of the Cherokee tribe." He paused and glanced over his shoulder at the door, before continuing.

"Due to the inability to locate any family, it was necessary to file for a Certificate of a Foundling in order to provide him with a record of birth, which I have here," he handed a copy to the clerk of court, who entered it as an exhibit. "On this certificate, his place of birth was listed as the first place he could remember being, and what was believed to be his birth date was obtained from a piece of jewelry that was gifted to him by his birth mother prior to her death." Again he paused and glanced at the door. As if willing it to open, it did, and his assistant hurried in quietly. On her way up to the council's table she met his eyes with a brief shake of her head. He sighed visibly before continuing.

Trying to regain his train of thought, he said, "Your Honor, the sur name White Horn was also obtained from this same piece of jewelry. Even with the information said jewelry provided, it was not an acceptable means of proof by the tribe, nor did it lead to any other possible family members within the tribe.

Faith toyed with the bracelet on her wrist that Mr. Barnfield referred to, as she listened.

"Therefore, all attempts to attach him to the tribe were exhausted. Your Honor, Adohy's last memory of his family was of his mother and father, in Anderson County, when he was five years old, where they froze to death protecting him from the elements, and where he consequently was held captive and abused, until his escape some thirteen years later."

There were audible gasps from the galley of the courtroom.

A stern look from the judge silenced the outburst.

"Objection, Your Honor. While I'm sure there's a sad story indeed, that's not what we are here for," Mr. Pendergriff said, sounding bored.

Mr. Barnfield reacted by saying, "Your Honor, if you could allow us a little leniency, we are trying to provide the history of how the Certificate of a Foundling came about."

"Overruled," Judge Clayton said to Mr. Pendergriff, who tossed his pen on the table and leaned back in his chair, exasperated. "Make it brief," the judge instructed Mr. Barnfield.

"Yes, Your Honor," Mr. Barnfield agreed.

The door to the courtroom opened again, and a man slipped in. Mr. Barnfield looked back, and the man nodded to him, before squeezing into the end of an already overfilled bench.

"Your Honor, during our investigation of this case, we've uncovered a witness that we believe can shine a light on, not only this case, but other cases Mr. Pendergriff is actively trying."

Mr. Pendergriff's attention was at once recaptured and he sat up and looked around behind him, his brows knit in confusion.

"We believe that this proceeding is the result of a witch hunt brought about by Mr. Pendergriff who has a personal ax to grind, regarding not just Adohy White Horn—"

Murmurs in the room resounded.

"— but each and every adoption involving a Native American!" Mr. Barnfield announced, his voice rising to be heard over the audience.

"Objection!" Mr. Pendergriff shouted, jumping to his feet.

"Order!" the judge demanded, pounding his gavel on his desk.

The courtroom was quickly silenced.

After initially reviewing the case files, Judge Clayton felt like there was something amiss in this case. Then he'd heard that there were other similar cases being pursued by Mr. Pendergriff, all regarding Native American adoptions, and nothing riled him more than a waste of the courts time and resources. Maybe it would be possible to put an end to it, once and for all. Besides, he was actually curious to find what could be behind this fiasco.

"Overruled," he ordered.

Mr. Pendergriff cut in, "Your Honor—"

"Overruled!" Judge Clayton said again, loudly.

Mr. Pendergriff dropped back down into his seat, looking around behind him again, wondering who was going to be called.

"Proceed," the judge told Mr. Barnfield.

"We would like to call Thadeus Running Bear Pendergriff to the stand, Your Honor," he said, but the last of his words were drowned out by the commotion.

"Objection!" Mr Pendergriff jumped up and shouted, his voice almost a squeal, hardly heard over the audiences stunned verbal reactions. His face was blood red.

Bang! Bang! Bang! The judge's gavel rang out! "Order! Order!"

The room slowly quieted as Thadeus Running Bear Pendergriff came through the door. He was a striking looking man, about six feet tall, dressed in a suit, with long shiny black hair, similar to Adohy's. He came to the front of the court and was sworn in by the clerk of court, before taking a seat in the witness chair, next to the judge.

Adohy eyed the man respectfully, feeling a little less conspicuous now that there was someone else there that looked similar to him. Millicent and Virgil glanced at each other hopefully, then shared an optimistic look with the rest of the family and friends seated down the row.

Judge Clayton nodded at Mr. Barnfield to proceed.

Addressing the witness in the box, Mr. Barnfield asked, "Can you tell the court your nationality?"

"I am full blooded Cherokee Indian," he stated.

Murmurs in the audience were silenced with a look from the judge.

"Yet your name is Thadeus Running Bear Pendergriff?"

"Yes."

"Can you tell the court how that came about?" he prompted.

"I was adopted when I was nine years old by Lewis and Beulah Pendergriff."

The audience sounded out again. One strike of the gavel brought about silence. Attorney Pendergriff's head was downcast, his hand scrubbing at his brow.

Mr. Barnfield glanced at Attorney Pendergriff as if he was surprised to hear this. Knowing the answer to his next question, he asked, "So, can you tell the court your association with opposing counsel?" He gestured toward the attorney, who had yet to look up.

"He's my brother, by adoption," Thadeus answered.

The noise rose and the judge banged his gavel. It was becoming routine. Question, answer, noise, gavel, repeat.

"Are you close with your brother?"

Thadeus looked solemnly at the man sitting, slumped, at the table. "No," he stated. Then added, "But not by choice."

"Can you expound on your answer?" Mr. Barnfield asked.

Thadeus looked down at his lap, trying to decide where to start. "Lewis, uh, Mr. Pendergriff," he canted his head at his brother, "was an only child before I was adopted. He was eleven. I was nine. I think he resented the attention from our parents my being there took away from him."

When Thadeus said "our parents" Attorney Pendergriff looked up and his eyes were shooting daggers. He noticed the Judge witnessing his display of emotion, and hung his head again.

"So, were you ever able to have any kind of relationship with him?" Mr. Barnfield asked.

"Regretfully, no. After our parents died and left their estate to us, split equally, he made it clear he wanted nothing to do with me, and never wanted to see me again, unless it was at my funeral."

There was a collective gasp from the crowd.

Thadeus continued. "He's made it his life mission to try to see that there are no more integrated adoptions, and trying to have as many as he can overturned. He's squandered his half of our family's fortune in attempt after attempt to keep Native American children corralled on the Reservation, and not intermingling with white people. He was a successful attorney until our mother passed and her will split everything fifty/fifty, then he became obsessed. He's lost everything he had, his substantial inheritance, his home, his practice, to the point that he can't even pay the rent on his motel room. In spite of this, I still love him and would like nothing more than to be a fami—"

"Family?" Attorney Pendergriff jumped up, shouting! "There IS no family! You destroyed the family!"

Bang! Bang! "Order!"

"We will never be family—!"

Bang! "Order in the court! Mr Pendergriff! Sit down!" the judge ordered.

"You and your kind aren't fit to walk the same ground as white people! You are all trash!"

"Order!" Bang bang bang! The judge shouted, but it fell on deaf ears.

"YOU ARE SCUM!" Attorney Pendergriff bellowed. "YOU ARE NOT MY FAMILY!" he spit out, before charging toward Thadeus. The bailiff intercepted him before he reached the bench.

The judge stood, slamming his gavel on his desk, shouting, "You are in contempt of court!"

It was chaos. The bailiff and Attorney Pendergriff were wrestling on the floor, with him still shouting obscenities at the top of his lungs. His eyes were wild. He'd clearly lost his grip on reality. Another bailiff rushed in to help and between them they were finally able to subdue Attorney Pendergriff. He was handcuffed and carried out, kicking and screaming.

After a moment, the Judge called the court to order once more, and there was instant silence.

"Case dismissed," he said, throwing down his gavel in exasperation, and retreating to his chambers, closing the door with finality.

The room erupted with applause.

CHAPTER 33

It was over! The nightmare had ended! Everyone had been standing during the melee, watching as Mr. Pendergriff went ballistic, the room pulsating with adrenaline and tumult. The abrupt end left Adohy weak in the knees and he sank down into his chair, the gravity of the situation only now fully revealing itself. There had been fear these months leading up to this, of course, but he'd been so sure, rather naively he thought now, that he could and would persevere. And though the outcome had proven just that, it was greatly due to his Attorney and Thadeus Running Bear Pendergriff, he realized, as he was being besieged from behind with hugs and congratulations by various family and friends.

Finding his strength, he stood and met Mr Barnfield's eyes. A simple handshake couldn't convey the sincere appreciation he had for everything this man had done. He wrapped his arms around him and gave him a hearty hug. When he pulled back, he thanked him from the bottom of his heart, and then asked if he could be introduced to Thadeus, who was making his way from the witness box.

Mr. Barnfield intercepted Thadeus and brought him face to face with Adohy. The courtroom quieted, watching the exchange between the two of them. In spite of the wide opinion that they were considered a minority by many, those present could see the pride in these two men as they stood tall with squared shoulders, their long black hair the last vestiges of a symbol of their heritage, they refused to depart from.

Mr. Barnfield made the introductions.

Adohy, nearly as tall as Thadeus, stood before this man who had traveled to this courtroom and bared his soul to save Adohy, a person he had never met, from the wrongful actions of not just another stranger, but of a member of his own adopted family. He was searching for the words from his limited vocabulary, as he extended his hand, when Thadeus took his hand and pulled him into a warm embrace. Words were not needed. Thadeus had been witness to his brothers repeated grievances over the years and seen the toll it had on numerous families. He just hoped that it was finally over, even though he wished it had come about from a reunion with his brother, and not the way it had.

The two men promised to keep in touch before going their separate ways. Adohy would always be grateful to him.

As it turned out, no matter what the crowd in the courtroom had harbored toward Adohy, or Indians in general, prior to the trial, after the hearing they were moved to show their support and happiness at the result.

The celebration was long lived.

~~§~~

The summer progressed with relative ease, enough drama from the previous months to last most of them a lifetime. Life at Sarah's Home resumed to normal, with Benny still amazing everyone and proving his worth, daily. He thrived on taking care of anyone he could and continued to treat Oppy as his number one priority. He had become a trusted and dear member of the Home, and had a special place in Caleb and Fred's hearts. Oppy had good days and bad days remembering the people in her life, but always seemed to know Benny. Perhaps because he was usually nearby.

He and Faith alternated the meal times with Jane, and she was doing well, but still hadn't made any new advances in her recovery. Dr. Martin had stopped coming three times a week, reducing his visits to once a month. Dr. Wright continued to monitor her care on his rounds.

Today during his consultation with Millicent regarding Jane, they decided to make some changes in her daily routine, by seeing how she reacted to short outdoor excursions, as well as brief visits to the common area among other patients. If there were no detrimental effects, the lengths of her activities could be extended as she acclimated to the change, both mentally and physically.

Millicent was happy to have a new course of action for Jane. She prayed that it had some positive results. She planned to put it in effect right away.

They would start with short jaunts with her being wheeled around outside in the mornings and evenings when the heat was less intense, for her to become used to the activity, and if all went well she would graduate to being subjected to more people in the common area. Millicent had some orderlies prepare Jane for her first outside visit in several months.

The test went without incident and continued twice a day throughout the week. The following week they implemented phase II of the plan. After her breakfast she was wheeled into the common area. There were only a few others in the room at this time of day, as most had already eaten and were either back in their rooms for naps, therapy, or baths, et cetera. However, a few of the more able patients remained sitting in easy chairs reading, or visiting with others. Jane's first encounter with other patients yielded no results or changes in her consciousness.

The same continued for three weeks until they decided to move her to the common area for her meals. Benny was otherwise engaged with Oppy, so Faith tended to Jane. Again the trial progressed smoothly, with Jane eating, as usual, without incident, but with no perceptible change otherwise.

After Benny finished feeding Oppy, they prepared to play a game. While he was setting it up, Oppy glanced around to see Jane seated in her wheelchair, being fed at a nearby table by Faith.

"Red!" Oppy said, waving toward Jane.

Faith heard her and looked around to see who Oppy could be referring to, but there was no one else around. She continued to feed Jane, while Oppy and Benny went about their game, but something kept nagging at Faith, until a vague memory came to mind. She concentrated, trying to place it, and finally recalled it was the day that Jane and Benny had first been brought to the Home. She and Adohy had been taking Oppy for a walk, and Oppy had kept saying the word red after seeing them taken inside. There had been no indication of anything "red" around, and Faith had thought that Oppy was just confused.

Now all these months later, Oppy was seeing Jane for what Faith supposed was the first time since then, and she was saying "red" again. It could be coincidence, but what were the odds? As soon as Jane finished eating, Faith was going to tell Millicent about it.

§

Faith tracked down Millicent and recanted the occurrence from months ago, and what had transpired this morning. She agreed it warranted looking into, and would talk to Dr. Wright as soon as he was through with his current patient.

Under his advisement, they brought Oppy to Jane's room to see what, if anything, happened.

Jane was sitting in her bedside chair, staring into space. Immediately upon being wheeled into Jane's room and seeing her, Oppy addressed her.

"Hi, Red," she called out.

It wasn't the color red she meant! She was using it as a name, or more likely, a nickname. It made sense, looking at Jane's hair. It definitely had an auburn hue visible with the gray.

279

Could it be there was finally some hope to finding out Jane's real identity? Looks of surprise and optimism circulated between the doctor, Millicent, Faith, and other staff.

They watched from afar for a moment more to see how Jane responded to the reference, but when she didn't, Millicent approached Oppy.

"Oppy? Do you know her?" she asked gently, gesturing to Jane.

Oppy nodded her head. "She's my friend," she said, matter of fact.

Millicent glanced at the others in the doorway, fingers crossed. "Is that her name? Red?" she asked.

"Yep. She's my friend," Oppy said again.

"Can you tell me the rest of her name?" Millicent queried.

Oppy thought for a second before replying, "Jes Red," but confusion was beginning to cloud her face.

Millicent was mindful not to pressure her, but longing for a helpful answer, asked one more question. "Do you know where she lives?"

Again, Oppy was thoughtful, then said, "Why shore, silly! She lives here!"

Everyone's hopes were dashed.

But at least they had something to work with. If Oppy knew her, chances are it was through the General Store, which meant Caleb may possibly know of a friend of Oppy's, named

Red. It was too important to put off. She left right away to go and ask him.

He was out making deliveries when she got there, so she visited with Fred and Eunice Small, who was there setting up her sewing room, getting prepared for the electric to be connected any day now. The lines had been strung down the road, they were just waiting for the extensions to be brought from the main lines to the individual homes and buildings. It was going to be a memorable year!

Fred could think of no one by that name that she recalled seeing in any of the receipts from the store, but felt sure that Caleb would remember, if he knew her. Millicent prayed that Fred was right. They would know soon.

Within an hour Caleb returned, and Millicent was to be let down once more. He'd never known of anyone that Oppy had ever referred to as Red. But Millicent refused to give up that easily. She had a thought.

"How would you feel about coming up to the Home tonight for supper? You can visit with Oppy and meet Jane. Maybe you will recognize her!"

Caleb and Fred consented, and with renewed optimism, Millicent went back to the Home to prepare for supper. Word spread of the chance that Caleb would recognize Jane, and everyone was anxiously waiting.

It only took a moment for Caleb to take a look at Jane and reveal that, to the best of his knowledge, he had never seen her before in his life.

CHAPTER 34

Another dead end. How could it be that Oppy could be so sure that she knew Jane, yet Caleb not know who she was, and no one had reported anyone missing in the area in the past several years? Did Jane just remind Oppy of someone she used to know? Was Oppy simply confused? Given her state of mind, and her inability to not even recognize her own family on any given day, her reliability wasn't the most sound, but the fact that both times she'd seen Jane she'd addressed her by "Red" was just too much to ignore.

Jane's method of treatment continued with her daily outings and meals with other patients, and Oppy continued to call her Red whenever she saw her, but by the time September rolled around, Millicent had gotten no further as to her true identity.

September meant that school was starting back, and that would bring about some changes at the Home. Jubal and Enos were required to attend school at least until their level of academics was determined. Jubal had turned sixteen in August, and Enos would be seventeen in November. If Enos graded high enough, he could be graduated, and continue to work at the Home rather than attend school. That was the agreement, and both boys were content with it.

Even though the two boys resided at the Home, Virgil and Millicent felt and treated them as family, and they were both indebted to the boys for saving Virgil's life. They simply couldn't put a price on that. It was remarkable, the change in the two of them since their arrival, and it was all due to some discipline, structure, care, and positive reinforcement. So, in light of all of that, Virgil and Millicent had a plan. They hadn't presented it to the boys yet, it would be determined by how they did in school. They would proceed from there.

Tenley could have started school too, and if it weren't for her very small stature and recent surgery, Millicent may have let her try it, but she and Virgil decided to keep her home one more year and help her to be more prepared to start the next year. It just wasn't worth the risk of her getting hurt being around so many other children, especially with most of them older and bigger.

School starting was bittersweet at the Jenkins' home. Aubry was happy to get back to work, though she *had* enjoyed spending the summer with Horace Junior. He was almost six months old now, and his grandmother, Horace's mother, would be keeping him during the school day, giving them a chance to bond. It would be the longest Aubry had been without him at one time, but she knew it would be good for all of them. She'd made her peace with it.

Samuel, on the other hand, was struggling. Chalmer had become such a big part of his day that he was going to miss him greatly. It was different now, than when the other kids went to school. Then, he was active and still working hard every day. He didn't have all that work to occupy his hours anymore. Imagining the days without Chalmer there keeping him active without realizing it, and making him laugh time after time, oh yes, it was daunting. All this time he'd felt like he'd been the caregiver, but he was beginning to wonder if it hadn't been Chalmer all along.

Chalmer had mixed emotions about school now. Part of him was excited to see what it was all about, and especially being with other kids he otherwise rarely saw. But he really looked forward to every single day with Papaw, and now there was Happy who needed him, too. It made him sad to think about being away from both of them most of each day. He just hoped this school thing was all he'd always hoped it would be.

Over the summer more children had arrived at Sarah's Home but none of them were physically able to attend school. There was a little eight year old girl that had been severely burned and scarred from tripping and falling into a bonfire, leaving her blind in both eyes. She had a long road of recovery to make and then physical therapy to help her learn to adapt to a life without her sight.

There was a boy, twelve, who had gotten bad infections in both of his ears that damaged his hearing. He was going through surgeries to try to correct it, but so far they hadn't been successful. On top of that issue, he was having mental, as well as behavioral problems coping with his diminished and nearly non-existent hearing.

There was another girl that reminded Millicent of Tenley, in that she was as sweet as she could be, but had a condition that caused her bones to break very easily. Due to that, her family, which consisted of a mother, father, and four brothers, two younger and two older than her nine years, had no choice but to give her up to Sarah's Home, where she would have less chance of injury and care that they could not afford.

With the other new patients in addition to these children, Millicent had hired two more nurses and more orderlies, and work had begun on their first expansion. She marveled at how her proposal, that hadn't even been *imagined* at the beginning of the prior year, was an incredible success.

Tenley had taken back over her cookie making and deliveries, and even though her workload had nearly doubled, she refused to give it up. Millicent was so proud of her determination and work ethic even at her young age. She decided to let her continue as long as she wanted to. Anyway, she treasured the time it gave them together doing the baking, and if circumstances allowed, making the deliveries. There had been times that she'd had to have someone stand in for her, but only if absolutely necessary.

It turned out this was to be one of those days.

They were just entering the common area for Tenley to deliver the cookies when Brenda, one of the nurses, cried out for help. "Millicent! Faith! I need some help here!" She was bent over the slumped figure of an elderly patient.

Millicent left Tenley in the care of Sandi, one of the new orderlies, and ran to assist.

The patient, eighty eight year old Ingrid Baxter, was in life threatening distress. Millicent was there in just a few seconds.

"What's wrong?" she asked Brenda.

"I think she's choking on something!" she explained, trying to pull Ingrid up.

Millicent helped get Ingrid sitting up and while Brenda held her, checked her airway. There was nothing she could feel with her fingers in Ingrid's throat, so using the heel of her palm she struck Ingrid in the center of her back with a little force. It didn't help. She tried once more, with a little more intensity and the impact caused Ingrid to cough up a thimble she'd been using to sew.

Once her airway was cleared, she began to cough and gasp for air.

"How in the world did she get choked on *that*?" Brenda wondered out loud, not expecting anyone to answer.

"I don't know, but let's get a wheelchair and get her back to her room, so we can check her and make sure she's okay," Millicent instructed.

Ingrid was the oldest member of Sarah's Home, but also the most mobile and lucid for her age. In defiance of growing old and the fact that her eyesight was diminishing, she still insisted on doing her embroidery. And she was very good at it. One of the best Millicent had ever seen. No one had any reason to believe there was a danger to her having her little sewing kit, with thread, thimble, and tiny scissors, which she understood had to be kept out of the hands of other patients. And there had never been a problem, until today.

As they were getting her into the wheelchair the orderly brought to them, Ingrid had recuperated to the point that she could speak.

Millicent asked, "How in the world did you get choked on your thimble, Ingrid?"

"Oh, I pulled the dab blamed thing off a my finger with my teeth jes fer a second till I got a-holt of my needle, then afore I could get it back on my finger, I went ta sneezin' and sucked the dab blamed thing down my throat!" she explained with annoyance.

"My goodness, Ingrid! You nearly died!" Millicent admonished.

"You think I don't know it?" Ingrid bit back. "I reckon I won't be a-doin' *that* no more!" she declared, then seemed to think it was funny, and chuckled.

"I should hope not! Otherwise, we'll have to take it away," Millicent warned gently. Ingrid had some gumption, that was for sure, she thought. If she wasn't so sound of mind she *would* have taken it away, but she trusted that Ingrid wouldn't do anything so silly again. She believed it was just a bizarre accident. Ingrid's sewing was her lifeline. The irony was, that it had nearly killed her, too.

They began to leave the common area with Ingrid, and with the crisis averted, Tenley began passing out her prized cookies. It was a welcome distraction, as all eyes in the room were still on Ingrid. All eyes except Jane's. Her eyes were on Tenley.

CHAPTER 35

Sandi helped Tenley pass out the cookies and milk, and before long most everyone had gone back to what they were doing, with Ingrid out of sight and out of mind. Millicent normally didn't bother letting Tenley try to give Jane any cookies because she was still in the wakeful coma, but Sandi, being new, wasn't familiar with Jane's diagnosis and she had seen Jane watching the little girl. She seemed to be looking forward to her cookie, so she reminded Tenley to not pass her up.

However, when Tenley held the cookie out to Jane she merely looked at her, making no effort to take what was offered.

"Well, I guess she doesn't want one today after all, Tenley," Sandi said, surprised. "Let's just get everyone else served." They finished handing the treat out to the rest of the patients in the room.

Jane's eyes followed Tenley as she made the rounds, but no one else noticed.

It was to be several weeks before Tenley and Jane were in the same room again.

~~§~~

School had been in session for over six weeks, and Enos was testing off the charts. It was determined that he could be graduated and go back to work with Virgil, if he so desired. Virgil and Millicent discussed the idea they'd had again and decided it was time to present their offer to Enos.

"Enos, you know that I –er *we* will be eternally grateful for what you did, and you too Jubal," Virgil said, including him, "for saving my life, out riding the perimeter. I've been told I would have surely bled to death, if not for your quick thinking."

Enos and Jubal nodded their heads, listening intently. Both Virgil and Millicent had thanked them numerous times already, so they were a little concerned about why they had called this meeting. There had to be something wrong.

Virgil went on. "Millicent and I couldn't be more proud of you boys, and consider you both part of the family now."

Jubal and Enos glanced at each other, pleased to hear what Virgil had said, but were more confused than ever.

Millicent interjected, "We could never repay you for Virgil's life. We simply can't put a price on it."

Virgil took over again. "So this is what we have to offer—"

Enos interrupted, worried about where this was going. They didn't want anything to change. They were the happiest they'd been in a long time. "Ya don't need to offer us nuthin'," he said. "Things is jes fine the way they are." He looked at Jubal for confirmation, and Jubal nodded.

"Yep, things is jes fine," he agreed.

Virgil chuckled. "Well, we *are* happy to hear that, but we want to do something more. Enos, you have passed every test with flying colors, enabling you to be graduated from high school."

Jubal punched Enos lightly on the arm, razzing him. "Tol' ya!" he said, happy to hear his brother had done so well.

"In light of your quick thinking the day of the accident, and how you instinctively knew what to do, Millicent thinks you could be a natural in the medical field. So, we're prepared to pay for you to go to college and get your degree."

Enos and Jubal didn't respond right away. They were processing what Virgil had said, and wondering where the joke came in.

"Now, it doesn't have to be the medical field, it can be whatever field you choose, but if it *is* the medical field, we ask that you come back here to Sarah's Home to practice. If you go so far as becoming a Doctor, we will build you an office here next door to the Home so you won't have to travel far. Jubal, you still have another year of schooling to get through, but if you decide to, the offer stands for you when the time comes, too."

There was silence for a while, and when it became clear that Virgil was serious, Enos finally reacted.

"Ya ain't kiddin'?" he asked quietly, in disbelief.

"No, we are one hundred percent serious!" Virgil told him.

"We're serious!" Millicent reiterated.

Enos looked at Jubal, at a loss as to what to do.

"What are ya lookin at me fer? Say yes!" Jubal told him, pride evident on his face.

Enos still took a moment to let the offer take hold. College? He'd never considered going to college in his life! And what about Jubal? They would be separated again.

As if sensing the reason for Enos's hesitation, Jubal added, "Don'cha worry none 'bout me! I'll be fine here! Ya gotta think bout yerself now!" he encouraged.

They looked into each others eyes, and when Enos could see that Jubal was sincere, he turned back to Virgil and Millicent.

"Okay!" he said, still not believing it himself.

They celebrated and began making plans. Enos didn't want to go too far away, so Millicent told him she would check into him going to the University of Tennessee, and promised to find out when he could start, in the meantime, he would come back to work with Virgil.

~~§~~

By October, Enos was officially signed up to start at the University of Tennessee in January, at the beginning of the second semester. It was agreed they would find him housing prior to that date, with all expenses covered so long as he kept his grades up.

Enos couldn't believe his good fortune. When he thought about the road he'd been going down, and in hindsight taking Jubal with him before they got sent to Sarah's Home, it made his stomach constrict. There was simply no one like Virgil and Millicent. They were the best people he had ever met. He would see to it that they weren't disappointed, if it was the last thing he did.

~~§~~

Chalmer had adjusted to school with little trouble. He was doing well, thanks to everything he'd learned from his new family helping to get him prepared. The school day could be a little shorter for his liking, but it went by pretty quick, still leaving time to spend with Papaw and Happy, so he reckoned he'd survive. He had something he wanted to ask for, since he'd been going to school every day and doing so good, but was waiting for the right time to ask.

After dinner that night, he decided it was time. "Ya know how I's been doin' real good at school an everthin'?" he started.

"How *I've* been doing," Evelyn corrected.

293

Chalmer looked at her a second. "No, how *I've* been doin', not you! You don't go ta school!" he said, laughing.

They all shook their heads. That boy!

"That's what I meant," Evelyn tried to explain. "You said I's."

Chalmers brows wrinkled. "I din't say nuthin 'bout my eyes," he rebuked, confused.

Evelyn looked at Tommy and Samuel for help, exasperated. When neither of them jumped in, she said, "Never mind, what's this about you doing good at school?"

"Well, ya know how I go ever'day, *all* day long, an' don't complain ner nuthin'?"

"Yes," she said, wondering if they were ever going to see where this was going.

"So, ya know how Halloween is a-comin' up?"

She took a deep breath. "Yes."

"Ya see, I been hearin' on my radio, that they's got a Halloween display at that there Cas Walker place, an' I's wonderin' if'n maybe we could go an' see it?"

Evelyn started to correct him again, but decided to talk to him later about it. She looked again to Tommy and Samuel, who exchanged questioning glances.

Tommy offered, "Let's jes see how good ya do in school 'tween now and then, an' we'll see. How's that?"

It wasn't exactly what Chalmer wanted to hear but it wasn't a "no" either, so it would have to do. "Okay," he relented. That meant he was going to have to be real good for a little while.

~~§~~

The next day while Horace and Tommy were working, Horace said, "Ya know, I heard tell that little girl that was singin' on the Cas Walker show that Chalmer liked so much, Dolly sumthin', was gonna be on there again the end a this month. I was thinkin' maybe we could all go and take Chalmer ta see her. Whatcha think?"

Tommy answered, "He was jes askin' last night at supper 'bout goin' ta see the Halloween display at the Cas Walker store. Let me talk ta Evelyn 'bout it. Sounds like it'd be fun."

~~§~~

The next day, Evelyn made a run down to the General Store. Caleb and Fred had gotten the electric hooked up about a month before, and shortly after that, they got a phone line. Fred kept a log for anyone that placed long distance calls, and she would add the charges to their account when the bill came in.

Evelyn made a call and was able to find out that the Saturday before Halloween, the little girl, Dolly Parton, was going to be performing again on the *Cas Walker Farm and*

Home Hour in Knoxville and if they got there early enough they could watch her in the little radio auditorium.

When she got off the phone, she told Fred what she'd found out, and invited them to come along.

"Well, that sure does sound like fun! Maybe we could work things out so we could close a little early that day. It would sure be nice to get out and do something! I'll talk to Caleb about when he gets back," she said, a lilt in her voice at the prospect.

While Evelyn was there, she couldn't help but notice the cute little dresses that Eunice had made. They were so colorful and pretty, she fawned over the fabrics. The attention to the added little details were exceptional. She couldn't help but buy one for herself for the outing to Knoxville.

After seeing her selection, Fred said, "Oh, this one is so pretty! I've had my eye on that pink one over there with the roses on it! I think I may treat myself to it if we get to go, too!" she admitted.

Evelyn turned her attention to Eunice, who had stepped out of her sewing room. "Miss Eunice, you are the best seamstress I've ever seen!" Evelyn told her. "Why, these are better made than any dresses I've had, and *way* better than I could do, any day!!"

Eunice blushed and waved the compliment off. "Well, go on now. If you had one a-these here fancy sewin' machines, you could do it jes as good, I bet."

"She's being modest," Fred said. "I saw her dresses *before* she got that fancy sewing machine, and they were every bit as good as these!"

Evelyn remarked, "Well, the sewing machine didn't pick out the fabric, the design, the buttons, or the trim, so I think I know who should get the credit! And I'm going to tell everyone I see about these beauties!" she promised Eunice.

"Well, thank ya, honey. That's might sweet of ya!" she said gratefully.

§

By the time Evelyn spread the word about the outing, keeping it a secret from Chalmer, of course, Samuel decided to accompany her and Tommy and Horace and Aubry, along with Virgil, Millicent, Faith, and Adohy. The next few weeks passed quickly, as they looked forward to the date.

CHAPTER 36

When the Saturday before Halloween arrived, the excitement level was high. Mid-afternoon everyone loaded up and headed down to the store to make sure Caleb and Fred were going to be able to join them. They were just finishing wrapping things up for the day. Caleb had let customers know, with plenty of advance notice they would be closing early today. All he had to do was hang the closed sign in the window, and they were off. It was hard to say which one of the bunch was looking forward to the outing the most.

Evelyn and Fred were wearing their new dresses, and when they'd told Aubry and Faith about them, they'd bought one for themselves, too. Faith hadn't had a dress on since she'd gotten married, but decided to change that, at least for today. Judging by the look on Adohy's face when he saw her, she thought she might just do it more often.

The days were still warm but the evenings cooled off quite a bit so the girls brought light cardigans with them, in case they needed them. The guys all wore dungarees, except for Samuel and Chalmer. They had on their new overalls.

Horace and Aubry invited Fred and Caleb to ride with them, making a caravan of three vehicles on the road to Knoxville. Ten minutes into the drive, Chalmer started.

"Are we there yet?" he asked, even though there was nothing surrounding them but pasture.

They explained that it was going to take about forty-five minutes before they even got to Knoxville.

Fifteen minutes later, he asked, "Has it been forty-five minutes yet?"

He was told to start watching for buildings and that would mean they were getting close. The plan was to go to the Cas Walker store first to see the Halloween display. Chalmer still didn't know about going to see his little heartthrob sing afterward.

He was beside himself when they got to the outskirts of town, and bewildered when they actually made it to the city. The buildings and cars and people were beyond anything he had imagined. They located the Cas Walker store and sure enough, they had a big display set up in the front. There were bins and bins of Halloween candy to choose from, to buy, surrounding a somewhat eerie cemetery scene. In the midst of the cemetery was a tall, creepy, skeletal looking man.

Chalmer's excitement turned to trepidation as they approached the display. He stopped walking and looked on, taking it in before going too near.

"Are ya shore ya wanna see it?" Tommy asked.

300

Chalmer became pensive, thinking about what the other kids would say if they heard he got to come all this way and didn't go up close. When he saw the man in the cemetery give some other kids, who didn't seem scared at all, some candy, he made up his mind. "Yep," he said, decisively, but his footsteps forward were slow and short.

As they neared, they could see the man held a shovel and appeared to be digging a grave. Then he let out a frightening laugh and announced, "I'm Digger O'Dell, an' I'll be the last one ta let ya down!" and he laughed again. Chalmer's eyes were as big as saucers but he stood his ground, and when Digger offered the candy, he reached out and took it. Once he had his candy and realized he would live to tell about it, he puffed up a bit at his bravery. Oh the stories he could tell now.

Evelyn drew the line at letting him go see the man that was buried alive in the parking lot. It was a stunt that Cas Walker did to promote the grocery store, and the man was only supposed to stay down there one or two nights, but business spiked so much, Cas Walker left him down there another day or two. The guy had a light down in the hole with him and people could look down a pipe and see him. The men went to check it out, while the women sidetracked Chalmer with candy.

After the guys had a look, they all grabbed a quick bite to eat before Chalmer filled up on candy, and so they could get to the radio station in time to get inside for the show.

During supper Chalmer insisted he wasn't the least bit frightened seeing the display, and it seemed to not have any lingering affects. When they parked at the WIVK radio station, the questions started again.

"Where we a-goin' now? Ta see more Halloween stuff?" he asked, on the way inside.

"No, we're going to listen to some people sing," Evelyn explained, without revealing the surprise.

"Oh," Chalmer said, not very enthused.

They were led to the auditorium, and got seats right up front. Chalmer looked around, fidgeting, not the least interested in the singers, until Dolly was introduced.

Everyone watched as the surprise registered on Chalmer's face. He was mesmerized as Dolly sang her heart out. His eyes never left the stage, and followed her after she was done, until she was out of sight. After that he sat back in his chair in a trance, thinking, no doubt, about Dolly. It was precious to watch.

They were told that after the show, sometimes some of the performers came out to sign autographs. Evelyn hoped beyond hope that Dolly would be one of them. They milled around nonchalantly, not wanting to give Chalmer false hope, and much to her delight, before long, Dolly and her Uncle, Bill Owens, joined the people who had come to see the show.

It turned out that someone that Evelyn had told about Chalmer's infatuation with Dolly relayed the information to Dolly's uncle, who had her come and greet her biggest fan. They even knew his name! Chalmer saw her the moment she came back in the room. He froze, looking much like he had at Digger O'Dell, watching as she and her uncle headed straight for him.

Evelyn and the girls were giddy behind him, nudging each other, watching the scene unfold.

Dolly walked right up to Chalmer, standing a few inches taller, being a few years older, and said, "Chalmer?"

Chalmer swallowed hard and nodded.

"I jes wanted ta come an' thank ya fer comin' ta see the show! Did ya like it?" she asked him, not a shy bone evident in her body.

Again, Chalmer could only nod.

The adults made introductions and shook hands during the exchange between Dolly and Chalmer. As Chalmer stood silent, Dolly's uncle told her she should go say hello to some of the other people there. She waved to them all and turned to go, when Chalmer called out.

"Dolly?"

She stopped and looked back. "Yes?"

"I'll always love you," Chalmer said, never more serious in his life.

Surprise washed over the adults listening. They fell silent, waiting to see what Dolly would do. A second passed and a big grin spread across her face. She ran back to him and gave him a quick peck on the cheek, before running off to catch up to her uncle.

It looked like Digger O'Dell had just been out done.

§

Back at the Home, Sandi was on duty again, and in charge of watching Tenley until Millicent returned. They had

303

already made the cookie deliveries that day, but at supper time, Sandi noticed Jane watching Tenley again, long after Benny had finished feeding both she and Oppy. Realizing that Jane's room wasn't on the list who they'd delivered to earlier, she decided to see if Tenley wanted to take her a cookie now. The poor lady couldn't take her eyes off Tenley.

There was already plenty made for the Sunday treat, so they went and got a few to give to Jane. She watched as Tenley approached and held out the cookies.

Jane would only look at Tenley's face. Then Tenley raised her hands, putting the cookies between their faces, at eye level. Jane's focus went to the cookies briefly, then her right hand twitched. While Tenley waited patiently, Jane turned the same hand over in her lap. It seemed to take great effort, but Tenley noticed and placed the cookies in her palm.

When Jane didn't begin to eat her snack, Tenley asked sweetly, "Aren't ya gonna eat yer cookie?"

Jane blinked.

Sandi and Tenley waited a few seconds more, but when Jane made no attempt to eat or answer them, they started to leave.

Then they heard a barely audible, "Ssaarraahh?" It sounded almost like whisp of air.

"I think she thinks your name is Sarah," Sandi said to Tenley. "Wonder why she would think that?" Turning her attention back to Jane, Sandi corrected, "No, her name's Tenley."

Tenley waved goodbye, and the two of them left Jane with her cookies.

CHAPTER 37

When Millicent got back from their outing, she went to the Home to get Tenley, and check on things. Brenda, the night nurse on duty, met her when she came in the back door.

"Hi! How was your night?" she asked.

"It was so much fun! I'm so glad we went! How was everything here?"

"Everything was fine. There was *one* thing I wanted to tell you about, though. When I came to get Jane, to take her back to her room after supper, she was holding two of Tenley's cookies."

"*Jane* was holding the cookies?" Millicent asked, thinking Brenda said the wrong name.

"Yes," Brenda confirmed. "*Jane.* That's why I wanted to make sure you knew about it. When I tried to take them from her she clutched onto them. I wasn't sure what to do, and didn't want to break them up to get them from her or upset her."

"Did she seem alert or anything?"

"No, she was the same as usual, just grasping the cookies. I was going to ask Sandi and Tenley if they gave them to her, but then I got sidetracked with Mrs. Pierce getting her meds, and haven't had a chance to find them and ask," she explained.

Millicent nodded, understanding. "That's okay. I'll find them and look into it. What about Jane? She should be in bed by now. Did she do anything with the cookies?"

"Last I checked she *was* in bed, but she still had the cookies in her hand," Sandi told her.

"That is so bizarre. I'll go check on her, then find Sandi and Tenley. Thank you, Brenda," Millicent said, heading down the hall to Jane's room.

Jane was in bed asleep, and sure enough, the cookies were in her hand. Millicent gently pulled them free, and placed them on the nightstand, hoping if she awoke looking for them, she would see them. Then she went to find Tenley and Sandi.

They were in the common area sitting on one of the couches where Sandi had been reading to Tenley, before Tenley drifted off to sleep, her head propped against Sandi's arm. Sandi was just trying to maneuver her way out without waking Tenley, when Millicent found them.

"Hi, Sandi," she whispered.

"Hi," Sandi answered. "She just went to sleep," she said, slipping the rest of the way out from under the little girl,

easing her down on the couch. She stood and smiled at
Millicent. "How was your night?"

"It was great! But I need to ask you about something
that happened here tonight," Millicent said.

Sandi's smile morphed into concern. "Is everything
okay?" she asked.

"Yes, yes, everything is fine. I'm just a little
confused. Do you know the patient Jane?" Millicent asked.

Sandi thought for a second, but hadn't met and
learned every patient's name, since her schedule was usually at
night when they were sleeping. When she struggled trying to
place her, Millicent described Jane.

"Oh, yes! I remember her! Is something wrong with
her?"

"No, I don't think so. Did Tenley give her cookies
today?" Millicent asked.

"Well, not during the regular delivery, but after
supper. Jane?" she asked making sure she had the name right.

Millicent nodded.

"Jane was watching Tenley like she really wanted a
cookie, so—"

"Wait, what do you mean she was *watching* Tenley?"
Millicent interrupted.

"Well the last time I helped Tenley deliver, I noticed
her watching her, but when Tenley tried to give her one, she
wouldn't take it. Then tonight, I noticed she kept watching her

again, and she wasn't out here when we delivered earlier, so we got two from tomorrow's batch and took them to her."

"You said you saw her watching Tenley the *last* time? When was *that*?"

"Oh, let's see...Oh! Remember when the lady got choked on the thimble?" Sandi recalled.

"Yes, that was weeks ago," Millicent said.

Sandi nodded. "That was the last time I saw her, until tonight. And she looked like she really wanted a cookie, so we gave her two."

"So, you put them in her hand." It was a statement, not a question.

"Not really. I mean, at first it looked like she wasn't going to take them again, like the last time, but then she turned her hand over in her lap, and Tenley put them in her palm. Oh! And Jane thought Tenley's name was Sarah! I thought it was strange at first but then I realized she probably thinks Tenley lives, here, and it's Sarah's Home, so I guess she was putting two and two together. I told her that wasn't Tenley's name, though."

Millicent closed her eyes trying to piece together how Sandi thought that Jane thought Tenley's name was Sarah. "Okay, I'm a little confused here. Tell me again, how you know Jane thought Tenley's name was Sarah?"

"She called her that," Sandi stated.

Okay, Millicent thought. They must be talking about two different patients. That was the only thing that made sense. She glanced down at Tenley, sound asleep on the couch, and looked to see who was nearby. Seeing another orderly, she asked them to stay with Tenley for a few minutes until she came back.

Then she told Sandi, "Come let me show you Jane. I think we're talking about two different people, because Jane doesn't talk. She's in a wakeful coma."

Sandi's face fell. "Oh, okay. I'm sorry, I'm not sure what her name is, then."

"It's not a problem. Let's just go take a look."

There was enough lantern light from the hallway to see inside Jane's room. Millicent approached Jane's bed with Sandi in tow.

Sandi peaked down at the sleeping form. Recognizing her, even in the dim light, she whispered excitedly "That's her! She's the one!", happy to know she had been right.

Millicent's mind was spinning. They went back to the common area, and she had Sandi go over the whole story again. So much time passed, that Virgil came to see if there was a problem. She explained what had occurred, and he took Tenley with him back to their home to put her to bed.

Millicent and Sandi continued their discussion, with Millicent explaining Jane's history and diagnosis. But Sandi was adamant, sure about what she'd seen and heard.

"Now, when she called Tenley "Sarah", I admit it was like a whisper, like it was hard for her to say." She mimicked the sound. "But I'm pretty sure that's what she was trying to say. Like I said, I realized later it was probably because she'd heard someone say something about Sarah's

Home, and since Tenley is usually here..." her voice trailed off, speculating.

Millicent was quiet, considering everything she'd learned. Sandi was only an orderly, but was reliable and trustworthy or she wouldn't had left Tenley in her care. And Jane *was* still clutching the cookies, giving more credence to the story.

"Okay," Millicent finally said, with a sigh. "Thank you, Sandi. You did great. I'll take it from here."

Sandi went back to work, while Millicent pondered. After a moment she went to her office and pulled Jane's file to make some notes. When she was done, she went home to get some sleep. She wanted to be good and rested, hoping tomorrow would be an eventful day.

§

She was back at the Home by six a.m. Sleep was out of the question. It was their weekend for church that day, and she hated to say it, but she hoped she missed it. She wanted to be there when Jane woke up, and had no idea what to expect. She thought about sending word to Dr. Wright, and Dr. Martin, but decided to see what transpired upon Jane's waking, first.

She got the staff together and explained the situation. She wanted to make sure that Jane's typical morning routine was executed as closely as possible, so that nothing would be out of the ordinary. In keeping with that course of action, she would observe from the hallway.

The morning progressed as usual. There appeared to be no change in Jane. The cookies rested on the bedside table, unnoticed and seemingly forgotten.

Faith had planned to go feed Jane before church, and then again afterward, for dinner, even though it was her day off, and she would let Benny do the honors for supper, so that she could go to the family supper at her papaws. When she arrived, Millicent gave up her post in the hall outside Jane's room and took a break to fill Faith in on the previous day's events.

Faith's initial reaction was hopeful. She had grown fond of Jane over the past few months, feeding her nearly three times every day. Sure, there was that one incident, but nothing had happened since then. She prayed for Jane daily, in the hopes she would someday come around, but her hopes that today would be that day were dashed by the time Millicent brought her up to this morning. Still, at least there was *some* sign Jane was in there somewhere, trying to get out.

When it was time for Jane to be fed, she donned her smock—not that she needed it but it was routine—and went to Jane's room. Trying not to do anything differently, she watched intently searching for any eye or hand movement from Jane. She saw nothing.

Millicent was baffled. Frustrated, she decided to go on to church with her family, but she couldn't concentrate on anything Caleb preached. Her mind was going over and over what Sandi had told her. Tenley seemed to be the instigating factor. The logical thing to do was to present Tenley to Jane again, in the same manner as the previous two times.

Both Dr. Wright and Dr. Martin were scheduled to come in Monday morning. She would wait until she spoke to them and see if they concurred with her. It would be easier for them to monitor and observe the situation in the common area, where it had transpired each time, without causing any disruption to Jane.

Feeling better at having arrived at a feasible plan, Millicent relaxed just in time for church service to end. Oh well, at least she'd decided what to do next, she reasoned.

She was distracted then, by Chalmer, who was beside himself over his day before. By the time the congregation left for the day, they not only got a good sermon but a complete recount of his experience with the Cas Walker store, Digger O'Dell, and Dolly Parton. Chalmer was the envy of every kid in church that day in Hurricane Holler, and the rest would be soon to follow by school time the next day!

CHAPTER 38

Monday morning, Millicent was at the Home early, again, with her notes ready to go over with the doctors as soon as they arrived. She explained to Tenley that, if the doctors agreed, they were going to do an experiment today, and she would be doing her cookie deliveries after breakfast instead of after dinner. She was sure the other patients wouldn't mind getting their treats earlier than usual.

As she'd hoped, the doctors felt it was the best chance they had, at this point, and everyone aware of what was planned, were on pins and needles awaiting the outcome.

Taking care to do everything as usual, the time had come. Jane had her physical therapy, and then was brought to the common area for breakfast. Nothing out of the ordinary occurred thus far. Millicent and the doctors were seated nearby, where they could easily see any flicker of response from Jane, and any of the other staff that could, were vying to watch from afar.

Finally, Millicent motioned to Sandi, who was asked to stay after her shift to re-enact the cookie delivery since she was the one with Tenley both times before, giving them the go ahead to start.

The second Tenley came into Jane's line of sight, her eyes shifted to focus on her every movement! It was all everyone could do to contain their excitement! Sandi glanced at Millicent to make sure she'd seen Jane's response, and Millicent nodded for her to continue as nonchalantly as possible. They worked the room as usual, making their way to Jane, whose eyes stayed locked on Tenley. Standing in front of Jane now, Tenley held the cookies out to her. Just as before, Jane's right hand slowly turned over in her lap to accept the cookies.

Everyone was amazed. The problem was that they had not discussed what to do next in this situation. Millicent and the doctors conversed as calmly as possible about how to proceed. Any sudden alteration or disruption could set them back. Sandi was watching for direction from Millicent, as Jane and Tenley stared at each other.

With a temporary decision from the doctors to continue as usual, Millicent gave the okay to Sandi to continue around the room with Tenley, as before. As they anticipated now, Jane watched Tenley carry out her task. Again, they frantically discussed the pros and cons of what to do next. One thing was clear. Tenley was the key to getting Jane back. If they pushed too hard it could set them back who knew how much.

Once the deliveries were finished, they told Sandi to keep Tenley occupied in the room somehow, within Jane's vision, until they could arrive at a decision.

While they were brainstorming, keeping their eyes on Jane the whole time, something they hadn't anticipated, happened.

Oppy, noticing Jane in the room, called out to her. "Hi'ya Red!" she yelled with a wave.

Jane blinked a couple of times rapidly, and though her body stayed stationary, her eyes darted around the room, while simultaneously, the hand holding the cookies, clenched, crumbing them to pieces.

Those in the room aware of what was happening were filled with trepidation as they watched this new and unforeseen reaction from Jane. Before they knew it, her eyes lost focus and she was back to her usual blank stare. One thing for sure, the spell was broken.

But Millicent refused to give up. With a quick okay from the doctors, she gathered Tenley, the wagon, more cookies, and marched right up to Jane, hoping to bring her back before she retreated too far.

Unlike before, when Jane was roused just by Tenley's presence in the room, her eyes remained unfocused, not seeing the little girl standing directly in front of her. Millicent glanced questioningly at the doctors for approval to continue. They trusted her judgment and acquiesced.

Millicent bent down to whisper in Tenley's ear, then she watched with bated breath.

Tenley asked Jane, "Don't you want your cookies?"

315

Nothing.

Millicent sighed, but her mind was working overtime. She knelt down to Tenley again.

Tenley made another attempt. "Don't you want your cookies?" but this time she added, "Red?"

The room was silent except for a few patients that were clueless as to what was unfolding. The others watched in disbelief as Jane blinked. Tensions heightened. Jane looked at Tenley, then down to the crumbled cookies in her lap. With her hand and arm trembling with the effort, she reached up to grasp the cookie Tenley was extending.

They had come too far for Millicent to back down now. Without consulting the doctors she took a leap of faith.

"Would you like some milk with your cookies, Red?" she asked, and then held her breath.

As if in slow motion, Jane's eyes moved from Tenley, up to Millicent's face. Millicent's heart was pounding out of her chest. She couldn't hold back the tears when Jane nodded her head twice in answer.

Miracle of miracles! No one could believe it. Someone quickly provided a cup of milk to Millicent, who held the cup to Jane's mouth while she took a drink! The noise level rose in the room momentarily as everyone murmured their surprise, and the doctors quickly waved everyone quiet again.

Millicent reached behind her and carefully pulled a chair up to sit down in, taking her down to Jane's level, careful to keep eye contact with her. Tenley stayed silently in place.

Millicent had so many things to ask Jane. Who are you? Where are you from? What's your name? Is Red your name? Will you talk to me? But reining herself in, she cautioned herself to go easy and not set everything back by being overly excited. She took a deep breath.

"Do you want to eat your cookies, Red?"

When Jane broke eye contact to look at the cookies she had in her hand resting on her lap, Millicent kicked herself for making her look away. She should have held her gaze! But much to her amazement and relief, Jane looked back up and nodded again!

Millicent was beside herself! She brushed the tears away, afraid they would alarm Jane, and asked, "Do you need help?" when Jane made no attempt to eat them.

Jane's head bobbed in answer.

Millicent let out a calming breath, and took Jane's hand that held the treat, carefully assisting her to raise her hand to her mouth. When it reached her lips, she took a bite. When she did, Millicent could swear she saw the triumph in Jane's eyes! She gently let her arm back down, while Jane chewed.

Millicent's mind was racing as she tried think of how to keep Jane's attention locked on her for every precious second that she could, praying that every moment brought Jane that much farther from the void she'd been living in, for who knew how long.

They continued to repeat the process, alternating with sips of milk, until Jane had finished the cookie.

Millicent could see that Tenley was growing weary of standing there, the gravity of this monumental breakthrough, lost on her. Feeling it was crucial that she keep Jane's attention, Millicent brought Tenley into the conversation.

"Red? Do you know who this is?" she asked, pulling Tenley over closer to her side, in front of Jane.

Jane's eyes went to Tenley. Millicent's stomach constricted when she lost Jane's focus again, but she forced herself to stay calm. It's okay, she thought. As long as she's looking at one of us. Much to her relief Jane's eyes met hers again, as she nodded her head once.

"Can you tell me who she is?" Millicent probed gently.

Jane's eyes clouded momentarily, and again Millicent was afraid she'd gone too far, but once more, Jane came back. "Sarah" Jane breathed, barely audible.

Sandi had been right! Jane *had* said Sarah! Millicent was used to thinking on her feet, but she was running out of ideas. Was Sandi also right about why Jane thought Tenley's name was Sarah? She had to be on the right track. Nothing else made sense! Jane saw Tenley handing out the treat every day so it would stand to reason it was her home. She didn't want to correct Jane. She would let her believe what she did, for now, if it kept her with them.

Jane seemed to deflate a bit, beginning to look tired. Millicent chewed her lip, loathing the idea of stopping now, but it had to have been an exhausting morning for Jane. Knowing it was best to let her get some rest, she conceded.

"Are you getting tired, Red?" she asked.

Jane canted her head in agreement.

"Okay, we'll take you to your room for a nap," she told her, getting up to wheel her there herself. On her way, the doctors expressions relayed to her she was doing the right thing. All the way to Jane's room, she prayed that Jane would still be with them after her nap.

In the room, Millicent was able to get Jane into bed with relative ease, though Brenda was standing by, if needed. Millicent assisted Jane to stand and though wobbly, Jane was able to pivot and drop onto the mattress, her legs giving out quickly.

"That was very good, Red," Millicent praised, making sure to use the name she responded to. "You get some rest, and promise me that we'll talk again when you wake up, okay?" she asked, crossing her fingers that the promise worked.

Jane blinked her eyes. Millicent took it as a yes, before Jane's eyes drifted shut.

She instructed Brenda to send for her as soon as Jane awoke.

Millicent rejoined the doctors in the common area. The room was abuzz in the aftermath of the morning. It was phenomenal!

While Jane napped, they discussed all of the corroborating factors. Tenley was at the top of the list. While it was true Jane thought Tenley's name was Sarah, it didn't change the fact that Tenley herself had a positive effect on Jane. *And* it was understandable why she would mistakenly think her name was Sarah. Then, there was the name, "Red". If Oppy hadn't called out to Jane this morning when she had, they may not have gotten to where they were now. The problem was they had already reached a dead end running down that name, or relating it with anyone around there, but it definitely resonated with Jane. They amended Jane's file and made an accordant decision that from that moment on, everyone was to address Jane as Red *only*, and as much as possible. Maybe it was the common thread that would keep her with them, until she was out of danger for good.

Millicent updated the staff with the new instructions and then they all awaited Red's awakening.

CHAPTER 39

Nearly two hours later, just as everyone was becoming concerned with the length of time Red had been asleep, Millicent received word that she was rousing. The poor soul must have been exhausted, Millicent thought.

Both Dr. Wright and Dr. Martin were still there. Wild horses couldn't have dragged them away. During the course of their discussion and then due to the length of Red's nap, their foremost concern was, and must remain, Red's wellbeing. Yes, everyone wanted to power through full speed ahead to finally find out her story, they were only human after all, but being the medical professionals they were, they had to refrain from letting their emotions enter into the equation.

It was unanimous that they proceed exactly as they had in the weeks leading up to today, unless and until, she showed signs of fatigue. If she was alert, and they fervently prayed she would be, they would ask only pertinent questions as to her wants and needs. For the rest of today, there would be no probing into her identity or past. They must be patient and let her recovery take its course.

Millicent was at her bedside within a moment of being notified. Saying a silent prayer, she let out a deep sigh, willing herself to be calm and at ease when Red woke up. She didn't want her anxiety to be written all over her face. She stood by as Red cast away the last vestiges of her slumber and opened her eyes.

While she would usually just lie with a vacant stare, Millicent's knees went weak with relief when Red looked around the room as if trying to place where she was, until she focused on Millicent's smiling face.

"Hi, Red!" Millicent said cheerfully but with reserve, keeping her desire to shout with joy suppressed. "It's so nice to see you again! Would you like to sit up now?" she asked. Millicent could tell that Red was considering her question, which meant she was coherent enough to understand.

A slight nod prompted Millicent to help her sit. "Okay, I'm going to help you. Just hold onto my hand," Millicent took Red's hand, "and I'll slip my other arm behind you, to help." She could feel Red's slight grip on her hand and the tension as she pulled herself up, while Millicent assisted from behind. She was showing an effort to help herself. That was a good sign. Once she was upright, Millicent asked, "Can you swing your legs off the side of the bed on your own?" and waited for Red's response.

Red still had Millicent's hand in her own, and looked down at her legs as if willing them to move, as she tried. After a second of concentration one leg moved about six inches nearer the edge of the bed, but it took a lot of effort. It didn't matter though, as Red clearly considered it a triumph as she looked up to Millicent with her eyes shining and even a glimmer of a smile on her lips!

God love this woman, Millicent thought to herself. She really wants to do this! She waited to see if Red could do more on her own.

With a grimace that showed her determination, Red managed to drag her other leg to meet the first. Then the adrenaline from the small victory must have given her the strength to dig deep and swing both legs together the rest of the way over the side.

Millicent was so excited she forgot herself in the moment and gathered Red in a warm congratulatory hug. Realizing how emotionally vested she was in Red, she pulled back, but she didn't regret the gesture. This woman deserved a hug!

They rested a moment, while Millicent praised her for her amazing feat. "This has been such a big day for you, Red!" she said, remembering to add her name. She'd forgotten in her excitement to say it as much as possible. Somehow, she had a gut feeling that it wasn't going to be all that necessary though. She'd just looked into Red's eyes and seen a strength that she hadn't expected to.

"You nearly slept though dinner! You must be getting hungry!" Millicent said.

It was a statement, but much to Millicent's surprise, Red uttered a breathy, "Yes."

Millicent was overwhelmed with emotion. She dropped down in the bedside chair and looked at Red in wonder. Who *was* this woman? She *must* have a family somewhere? Someone who knew and loved her. But *who?* She vowed she wouldn't give up searching till she had the answers.

Pulling herself together, she asked Red, "Would you rather eat in your room this time?" She thought she may be too tired to go back to the common area, but wanted to let her decide.

Red shook her head, and when Millicent smiled, it reflected in Red's eyes.

"Okay, but you have to try not to overdo it. If you get tired you need to come back and get some rest, agreed?"

"Yes," she answered softly, with an expression that suggested she may have been showing off just a bit with her newfound capabilities.

So, she had a *cheeky* side to her, Millicent chuckled. She liked her already!

"My name is Millicent, and I think you and I are going to be great friends," she predicted, helping her to make the transition from the bed to the wheelchair. On the way to the common area they were met with smiles and greetings from the staff members.

"Hi, Red!" they called out, as they passed. As instructed, they used *her* name, but refrained from overwhelming her with all of their names. They had agreed they would introduce them to her one at a time, as needed, so that she didn't become frustrated trying to remember them all.

Faith was standing by in the common area with Red's dinner, along with the doctors who were waiting to see with their own eyes the remarkable transformation in this patient.

They had made copious notes of their own, while waiting, to share with their peers. They were all pleased to see Red alert and looking at them each in turn, as she was wheeled into the room.

Faith stepped in to feed Red, while Millicent went to apprise the doctors of the particulars of her waking and her current condition, making sure to stay in close proximity for Red's security.

It was a whole new experience for Faith to be able to look Red in the eyes and be able to ask simple questions, like "was she ready for another bite", and have her respond with a nod or shake of her head. While she fed her, she observed the standard issue gown Red wore, and felt a pang of remorse for her having no clothes to call her own. She'd never been an avid fan of sewing, but nevertheless, she decided, on the spot, to sew Red an outfit to have of her own. With Red's new awareness of herself and her surroundings, it would have to make her feel better to have her own clothes, rather than this plain gown.

She had no clue where her idea had come from, but once she had it, she wanted to make it happen as soon as possible. She would start tonight, she decided, happy with the thought.

Red looked at her then, and the edges of her lips turned up in what Faith would swear was a grateful smile.

Faith's heart skipped a beat, and she fed Red another spoonful of her dinner, feeling as though the woman had read her mind. Shaking off the silly feeling, she realized Red was obviously just expressing her gratitude to her for feeding her. Either way, Red sure tugged at her heartstrings.

Though it was a pleasure to feed Red, especially the new *alert* Red, when they were finished Faith decided to ask Millicent if Benny could take her place for supper that evening so she could go home and make the woman a set of clothes.

Millicent thought it was a wonderful idea, and readily agreed.

After Faith left, Millicent went back to sit with Red, not wanting to leave her alone in the fear that she would disappear into the depths of her mind again. When Tenley woke up from her nap, Millicent had her join them with her coloring book and crayons, much to Red's delight.

They kept Red company until Millicent thought she was looking tired and may need to relieve herself, and she suggested they go back to her room. Red glanced at Tenley longingly, but then nodded her head in compliance.

Once more, as she helped Red to lie down, Millicent felt the little tremor of apprehension in her gut that Red would forget the great strides she'd made when she woke back up. However the only alternative would be for her to never go to sleep again which was impossible. She just had to have faith that, come what may, they could and would bring her around again. She had to have her rest. Millicent realized that she was exhausted herself, so Red *had* to be.

Just for extra measure though, Millicent had her promise that they would visit some more when she woke up.

§

It was almost two hours again, before Red stirred from her uneventful slumber, and as promised, Millicent was there when she did. Millicent and the doctors had time to grab a bite to eat, and discuss Red's treatment, going forward. They were eager to see what the status was when Red woke this time, but then they both had to be on their way with practices and other patients of their own to contend with. Millicent assured them she would keep a detailed log of every hour from that moment on, to share with them upon their return, and if there was any major breakthroughs she would notify them immediately. Unless they heard from her, Dr. Wright would return on Wednesday for his regular visit, and Dr. Martin would join him at the Home on Friday.

They left the Home that day with optimistic and expectant hearts. Red was still herself when she awoke!

§

Millicent was running on pure adrenaline, having had barely any sleep since the Friday before, but she couldn't bring herself to leave until Red had retired for the evening. Red had woken with no problems, and the rest of the day was pretty much a repeat of the early afternoon. She was late for supper, having slept so long, but it worked out fine, as Benny had ample time to feed Oppy and see her to her room, before Red was ready to eat.

Afterward, Millicent and Brenda helped Red get bathed and ready for bed for the night. With that done, Millicent checked on the other patients and residents, saying a quick hello to Enos and Jubal, before heading home, and she hoped, to bed to sleep.

§

After supper at the Jenkins' home, Evelyn was recanting the exciting events of the day, regarding the patient

Tommy and Samuel knew as Jane Doe. She took them through the entire day, step by step, up until the time she got off work. "I know she just woke up, but she seems to be the sweetest thing. Millicent has gone above and beyond with her, trying to find out who she is, and where she came from. She's gotten kind of attached to her, I think. But she's not the only one. Faith, believe it or not got off work early today, so that she could go home and sew this lady some clothes of her own! Can you believe that?"

Samuel and Tommy were surprised to hear that. Faith would usually rather wrestle a pole cat than pick up a needle and thread.

"I'm telling you, there's just something about this woman that has gotten into everyone's hearts. Maybe it's just knowing she's all alone in the world. I don't know." Evelyn was lost in her thoughts for a moment, and Samuel stood to refill his cup of coffee, bringing her out of her reverie.

"I'd have gotten that for you," she told him. "It's right behind me."

"I know, but you been a-workin' all day, an' my legs ain't broke," he said.

Chalmer looked up from his homework, and chuckled at what his papaw said.

Evelyn remembered, "You know what the funny thing is? All of this might not have happened today if Oppy hadn't seen Jane this morning, and hollered "Hi, Red".

They all jumped, startled, when they heard Samuel's coffee cup shatter when it hit the floor.

§

328

Ten minutes later, Evelyn was leading Samuel up to Red's door. They crept inside quietly, and peered down at her sleeping figure. In spite of his cane, Samuel faltered.

"What is it? Are you okay?" Evelyn whispered, alarmed, reaching to help steady him.

"Glory be ta God! It's her!" Samuel managed, before sinking into the nearby chair, bewildered.

CHAPTER 40

It seemed that sleep for Millicent was not going to come anytime soon. She was used to dressing at a moment's notice, dealing with emergencies at the Home in the middle of night, and this was no different. Except it wasn't the middle of the night yet, and this regarded Red and Samuel, somehow.

When she got to the Home, the common area was empty except for Samuel and a nurse named Darla, who was checking his blood pressure. He looked pale and shaken. It was unusual to see him in this state. He was still a pretty tough man, in spite of his age. Millicent's mind flashed back to the last time she'd seen him like this. It was the night Sarah had died, and her heart constricted at the painful memory.

Worried about him and Red both, she rushed to his side. "How is he?" she asked the nurse taking his vitals.

"He's okay," she answered. "Just pretty shaken."

Millicent patted Samuel on the arm, and asked him to give her just a moment. She pulled Darla aside and asked what had transpired.

"I'm not entirely sure. All I know is Evelyn and he went to Red's room, and then Evelyn called me to keep watch over him and to send for you, and then she took off to get her husband."

Millicent blinked several times, trying to make sense out of what was going on. "Okay, thank you," she sighed, then verified, "but his pressure is good?"

"Yes, it's a little high, but understandable, since he's clearly upset."

"And Red? Is she alright?"

"She was sleeping peacefully. She had no idea they were even in her room," she affirmed. "Evelyn and I brought him out here, so she wasn't disturbed."

"Good. I'm going to see what I can find out," Millicent told her.

Darla nodded and stood by while Millicent went back to Samuel. She pulled a chair up and sat down beside him, reaching out to squeeze his hand. "How are you doing?" she checked, before questioning him about anything else, even though she couldn't imagine what it would have to do with Red, and was dying to know.

"I reckon I'll be fine, jes a little sh-shook up's all. Wasn't 'spectin' ta see what I did an' cain't seem ta wrap my head 'round it," he admitted, drawing in a ragged breath.

It was the first time Millicent had heard Samuel stutter in a long time. She'd almost forgotten that about him. She knew in the past that it got worse for him when he was upset about something, but he'd miraculously stopped stuttering, shortly after Chalmer came into their lives.

She gave him a moment, then gently asked, "Can you tell me about it?"

"Well, if it's all the same ta ya, I'd k-kindly rather wait till the youngens is here, so's I kin say it all at once't."

"Okay," Millicent placated, squeezing his hand in reassurance. She didn't realize Evelyn was bringing the whole family. What in the *world* did this have to do with Red? she wondered.

The door opened and Faith rushed inside, hand in hand with Adohy. She hurried over to where they sat, concern lining her face. "What is it, Papaw?" she asked, breathless. "Is he okay?" she turned to Millicent before he could answer.

"He's fine," Millicent assured her, adding, "*physically*, anyway, but he's a little worked up about something and wanted to wait till everyone was here before he shared it with us." She looked down at the bundle Faith had in her hand. "What's this?" she asked.

"Oh," Faith said, forgetting she had it. "It's the top and pants I made for Red," she explained, unfolding them to show her.

"You finished them already?!" Millicent asked in disbelief.

"She hasn't stopped working on them since she started," Adohy told them.

Faith blushed. "I just wanted Red to have them to put on in the morning,"she explained.

It was a simple pair of pants and top in a purple seersucker fabric, perfect for the warm days they were having.

Samuel eyed the outfit as Faith held it up, thinking, *She'll really like that. It's her favrit color.*

Faith turned her attention back to Samuel, kneeling beside his seat. "Are you sure you're okay, Papaw?" she asked tenderly.

"I'm fine, sweetheart," he answered, reaching with his free hand to pat her on her shoulder. "Everthin's gonna be jes fine." The shock of what he'd discovered was beginning to wear off, and the over-whelming amazement of the situation was swirling in his head. He was trying to figure out how to say what he had to tell them, when everyone was there.

Virgil came in then, carrying a sleeping Tenley. He was very much concerned for Samuel, but it was his curiosity of what had happened that had gotten the better of him.

Millicent gave Samuel's hand another squeeze before she let go and went to help Virgil with Tenley. They made her comfortable on a couch on the far side of the room, and covered her with a light blanket. Being a sound sleeper, she slept through it all. Millicent envied her of that. She brought Virgil up to date, which didn't take long, as she was still in the dark herself.

Millicent told Darla, the nurse who had tended to Samuel, to go ahead and take a break, that she would take care of him for now, then she and Virgil joined Faith and Adohy with him.

Virgil shook Samuel's hand when he reached him. "Is there anything I can do for you, Samuel?" he asked, his concern evident in his voice.

"Naw, I 'preciate it, but I'm good," Samuel replied sincerely.

Tommy and Evelyn came in then, with Chalmer, who broke away and ran up to Samuel, too young to understand what was going on, but smart enough to know that something was wrong and it had to do with his papaw. "Papaw!" he cried out.

Samuel's face brightened at the sound of Chalmer's voice. "There's my boy!" Samuel said, looking at Chalmer with a smile. "Come 'ere, an' sit on my lap," he said, with a chuckle, pulling Chalmer up.

"What's wrong, Papaw? Are ya sick?" the little boy asked timidly, searching Samuel's face for any sign of illness.

"Naw, son, I ain't sick, jes a lil...well, surprised, I reckon's the word."

"Well, whatcha surprised 'bout? Is that why ya dropped yer coffee cup? Why din'cha come back home?" Chalmer asked, not giving Samuel a chance to answer between questions.

Tommy cut in then. "What's goin on, Papaw?"

"There's somethin' I need ta tell ya, son, but we need ta wait till yer sister's here."

Tommy raked a hand through his hair, both anxious and frustrated, but didn't press the issue. He glanced at the door, watching for Aubry and Horace. They should be there any minute, they'd just had to get Horace Junior, and should have been right behind him and Evelyn.

The nurse, Darla, came out of the kitchen pushing a cart carrying cups, saucers and spoons, with a pot of coffee, a pitcher of milk, with cream and sugar. She'd taken it upon herself to spend her break fixing refreshments for everyone. Millicent was grateful, and thanked her for her thoughtfulness. Coffee was probably the last thing any of them should have, given the time of night and their already jittery nerves, but she sure felt like she could use a cup herself. She began pouring the coffee into cups, and offering them to anyone who wanted one.

Samuel declined, not sure his hands were steady enough to hold the hot liquid, but said, "I wouldn't mind me a sip a-that sweet milk there, though, if'n ya don't mind." He thought it might calm the churning in his stomach.

"Absolutely," Millicent granted. "Would you like some too, Chalmer?" she asked, pouring a bit for Samuel.

"Yes, please," he accepted when his keen eyes spotted a container of Nestle Quick partially hidden behind the coffee pot. "If I kin have chocklit in it," he threw in there casually. He rarely got to be up this late at night, and if he woke up and needed something to drink, it sure wasn't going to be chocolate milk. There was no way he was going to pass that up.

Millicent cast a questioning glance at Evelyn and Tommy before complying.

Tommy gave her a dispirited nod, conceding. What could it possible hurt, and where the heck were Aubry and Horace, he thought, getting antsy to know what was going on.

Aubry bustled in then, a bit disheveled, having dressed and gotten Horace Junior up in such a hurry. Horace was behind her, carrying their son, who was wide awake now.

"I'm sorry! We got here as fast as we could," she said contritely, smoothing down her clothes. "What is it? What's going on?" she asked in the same breath, looking at everyone in the room for explanation.

Millicent had just handed Samuel and Chalmer their milk.

Samuel looked at Chalmer. "Why don'cha take yer milk over ta that table there where ya kin drink it without a spillin it," he suggested, helping Chalmer down off his lap.

Chalmer would have rather stayed where he was, but had a feeling this wasn't a time to argue about it. Instead, he did as his papaw asked.

Samuel took a sip of his milk, then let out a deep sigh. Faith was still sitting on the floor by his side, some of the others were seated, some standing. All of them looking at him earnestly.

He swallowed, and began. "That lady that's been here all this time, that I reckon ever'one called Jane Doe, well til taday anyhow's, cause Oppy seen her an' called her Red? Well, that's cause Oppy knew her from a long time ago, an' that's what some a-us used ta call her. I figgered Oppy was jes confused, cause I jes didn't see how in tarnation it could be, but I came o'er here, and sure enough it's her. It's Red. Thing

337

is, that ain't her real name, that's jes what we called her cause a her head full a hair that looked brown til the sun hit it, then it looked red, like fire. An' I don't rightly know how ta say this, 'cept'n jes ta say it." He paused for a second, then went on. "Tommy, Aubry," he said, singling the two of them out, "that woman in there...God bless her...that's yer mama. It's Rebecca."

CHAPTER 41

Time seemed to stand still as Samuel's words reverberated through everyone's minds. On their individual faces you could almost see the various stages of their thought processes acted out, like scenes in a play. First, the initial confusion, then the pause while mentally replaying what they thought they'd heard, to the dizzying whirlwind of trying to make sense of what their brain had recorded. Some of them didn't make it past this point, sure that they had misunderstood.

One or two of them made it beyond those few, their memories instantly rewinding sixteen years to the horrifying night of the fire, but they were unable to connect what they knew and remembered from that fragmented nightmare to the words that Samuel had just uttered.

One of them, however, hopped, skipped, and jumped through all of that to arrive at the only logical explanation. Disbelief. That person was Tommy.

"What?! No way! What are ya talkin' bout, Papaw? Ya know our mama is dead! If *anybody* should know that, it's you!" he cried out, his words laced with pain. "I don't understand why ya'd say such a thing!"

Tommy's outcry brought Aubry crashing back to the present, and in protest, her legs suddenly refused to hold her. In a daze, she latched onto a nearby chair and slipped down onto it.

Tommy and Aubry's anguish was visceral, but it only added to the pandemonium going on in Faith's head. She had no memory of the woman she'd grown up thinking was her mother, who was in reality her grandmother, and she'd only recently accepted the fact that Sarah was her birth mother. Nor was there any recollection of the fire, or the family home that burned to the ground that night. She'd been only three months old when all that transpired.

She shook her head, trying to unscramble it, to separate the facts from the fiction. The past from the present. She was thankful she was already sitting on the floor, because the room was spinning.

Virgil, Millicent, Horace and Adohy could only watch in silence as the rug was pulled out from under their friends and spouses, unable to do anything to help them. It was as though every second stretched, dwindling time down to a crawl, resulting in a delay in the signal from their brains telling them what to do.

Samuel knew what he'd had to tell them sounded fantastical, he was having a hard time believing it himself. He had no answers to the questions that Tommy asked, or the hundreds that were sure to come. All they could do is unite as a family and start trying to piece the puzzle together. That and thank God for bringing Rebecca back to them.

"Son, I cain't hardly believe it myself, but that don't mean it ain't true. I have no idear where she's been all these years or the hell she's been through, but I'd know yer mama anywhere, and that woman in yonder, is her. Older, an' a little worse for the wear, but it's her," Samuel told him.

Clutching a fistful of his hair in each hand, Tommy paced in a frustrated circle, trying to grasp what his papaw was insisting. Facing them again, he threw his arms down leaving his normally coiffed, thick hair an unruly mess. "Kin I see her?" he asked, not believing the words coming out of his own mouth now. Did this mean he thought it could be true? That his mother was alive?

His request hung in the air for a moment, effectively jump starting Millicent's brain from slow motion to overdrive. While she wanted to grant his request, Jane...Red...*Rebecca* was her patient, and in a very fragile state. She *had* to consider her mental health and best interests, first. She took a deep breath and let out a long sigh, all eyes on her.

"I don't think that's a good idea," she said finally, hurrying to explain when she could see most of them didn't like her answer. "Look, tensions are high right now, and she's not well. She just today showed any sign of improvement, and *anything* or even nothing could set her back. We have no way of knowing that she will wake in the morning and remember the strides she made today. If you were not able to control your emotions...not just you, Tommy, any one of you," she looked at each of them, "it could be emotionally overwhelming to lay eyes on her. That being said, think of what it could do to her if

341

she were to wake and see you peering down at her. It could be catastrophic." She let that sink in before continuing. "We have no idea what she's been through, but it was evidently so horrific that she retreated so far in to the recesses of her mind, that we weren't sure she would ever make it out. We don't know yet if she knows who *she* is, much less any of you. I'm sorry, but until she's had time to heal, we just have to be very careful what she's exposed to."

Faith finally found her voice. "But I've been around her every day since she's been here," she reasoned.

"Yes," Millicent acknowledged, "but you didn't know she was your grandmother at the time, and she obviously wouldn't have recognized you, since you were only a tiny baby the last time she saw you. We were fortunate that we decided not to tell her the names of the staff members, as yours may have certainly triggered something she's not ready to handle yet. You've already formed an emotional bond with her, without even knowing who she was," Millicent reasoned, gesturing to the outfit in Faith's lap.

Faith glanced down at the garments she'd worked so hard on all afternoon, realizing Millicent was right.

Tommy wasn't ready to give up. "I was only seven, and Aubry, four, I doubt she'd recognize either one of us, either," he said, hoping to change Millicent's mind. He just wanted, *needed,* to get even just a glimpse, to see her with his own eyes.

Aubry nodded in agreement with Tommy, her hopes rising, in spite of herself. She understood what Millicent was saying, and knew she was right, but she wanted to see her mother!

"That doesn't change the fact that you know who *she* is now, and that is bound to play into your emotions when you see her for the first time. I'm sorry but we just can't take that risk. You need time to acclimate yourselves to the fact that she's alive, and dig deep to find the patience to wait until she's ready to see you."

"Does this mean I can't continue to feed her now?" Faith asked.

Millicent sighed. "I don't know. I'm going to have to think about it."

The room fell quiet as everyone pondered where to go from there.

Samuel finally broke the silence. "She's right," he conceded. "I coulda caused untold damage rushin' o'er here, an' bargin' in on her. The more important thin' right now is we gotta settle down, an' put our heads tagether an figger out what's best fer her."

Evelyn hung her head, chagrined. She was a nurse. In hindsight, she realized she should have known better.

Millicent noticed and attempted to assuage their guilt. "That's exactly what we need to do, and give her time to heal..." she told everyone. Then addressing Samuel and Evelyn specifically, she said looking at the two of them, "...and fortunately there was no damage done. We just have to proceed with caution." With no disagreement from anyone, Millicent said, "Now I don't know about all of you, but I need a cup of coffee!" She moved over to the cart to pour a cup, when Darla appeared with a fresh pot. Millicent made a mental note to give her a raise.

The others began to move about, getting coffee, giving and/or taking hugs, their minds wandering. They noticed Chalmer had given up the fight, his head on the table, sound asleep, his chocolate milk a thing of the past.

After milling around for a few minutes and getting a boost from the caffeine, their minds started to settle, enabling them to think more clearly. While they sorted things out, questions came to mind that they discussed briefly.

One of which was Benny and his connection to Rebecca. Millicent explained that Benny had been questioned extensively, but they had been unable to ascertain anything of use about his past, or where he'd been before coming to the Home. And that they had to remember that he'd been in a state of panic, much like Rebecca except not to the same extent, suggesting that he'd been subjected to the same or similar atrocities as she had. He had also apparently blocked the memories from his mind in order to survive without fear.

Another question was, if those of them who had not had the opportunity to see Rebecca yet, could do so from afar, if they were careful not to be seen?

Millicent considered this, and came up with a possible solution. She told them, "Depending on Rebecca's state in the morning, if she is willing and able to go outside for a moment, those of you that want to, can observe from afar through a window from my house."

There were nods and murmurs between them, liking her idea.

"*But,*" she cautioned them, "it has to be carefully coordinated so that there is *no* chance Rebecca will be aware of any of it." Turning to Faith, she said, "I think it would be best if you took this opportunity, too, Faith, before I determine whether or not to let you continue feeding her. I have to make sure your emotions are in check, at least for the first time you look at her as your grandmother. That being said, you can decide if you want to wait to give her the outfit you made for her, or let someone else give it her in the morning."

Faith contemplated this. She'd really been looking forward to giving it to her herself, but after wavering for a second, decided it was more important to her that her grandmother had them to put on in the morning, no matter who gave them to her. With that in mind, she asked Millicent, "Will you give them to her for me?"

Millicent smiled. Good girl, she thought. She knew it was a hard, but completely unselfish decision, on Faith's part. "Absolutely," she promised.

They set up the particulars for the morning, and everyone went home for the night, physically, mentally and emotionally exhausted, but thankful to have reached an agreement on at least one of the millions of questions they all had.

CHAPTER 42

Much to Millicent's surprise, she was asleep before her head hit the pillow, the turmoil and coffee no match for her exhaustion. She slept like a rock, but woke early feeling better and clear headed. She went to her office at the Home and wrote a note, then sent it by messenger to Fred at the General Store, filling her in on the news, asking her both for prayers for the family and Rebecca, as well as to make a few quick calls for her, to the doctors and the authorities. She needed to let them know that Rebecca had been identified, and with any luck, rekindle the investigation again to find out where she'd been all these years.

Aubry left Jubal in charge of the class at the school, giving them the option of reading quietly to themselves or drawing until she returned, and as a reward, if everyone complied with no issues, they could possibly earn an early release that day. She didn't tell them that it all depended more on her state of mind after she saw her mother for the first time in sixteen years, rather than how well they followed instructions. She would have canceled school altogether that day, but that would have aroused suspicion and they wanted to keep the news under wrap until they'd had time to figure some things out. Word was bound to travel fast, either way.

Everyone was gathered at Millicent's at the agreed time, emotions running the gamut, and changing by the second. The weather couldn't seem to make its mind up either, mimicking their temperaments; overcast, with a threat of rain one minute, sun shining bright the next. They took their positions at three different windows, Tommy at one, with Evelyn and Samuel looking over his shoulder, giving him space, since they had already seen her.

Adohy and Faith waited in front of another. Faith prepared, already knowing what she would see, but fulfilling Millicent's wishes to make sure she was in command of her ability to look at her grandmother impartially. Adohy was ready to support Faith however she needed.

Aubry and Horace huddled at the third window, Horace Junior asleep, blissfully unaware of the nervous energy permeating the room. Horace was calm, but curious to see Rebecca, his concern reserved for his wife. Aubry was probably the one that was the most conflicted out of them all. She and Tommy were the only two, related by blood, who had not even had a glimpse of Rebecca yet, but at least Tommy had a memory of what their mother looked like from years ago. She couldn't even remember *that*. Any photo's they'd had were destroyed in the fire, and the few she'd seen that Papaw had were old and grainy, nearly impossible to make out how she really looked. And what if Rebecca never recovered? Never recognized any of them? It was so exciting to think she had her mother back, but what if she didn't? What if by some

348

cruel twist of fate she was there in body, but never anything more? It was too much to process.

Virgil waited in the kitchen with Tenley, giving them their privacy, but told them he would be nearby in case they needed anything, even if it was just emotional support. They were like family and he couldn't imagine what they were going through.

There was a knock on the door and he went to answer it. It was Caleb. He explained he'd heard the news when Millicent's note to Fred had been delivered and he came to offer his help and prayers for the family. He'd not known Rebecca, but he was there to offer comfort and solace through the family's loss of Sarah, who had been very dear to him, and he wanted to be there for them now in whatever capacity was needed.

Virgil apologized for the interruption, and then announced Caleb's presence.

Aware they were waiting to see Rebecca for the first time, Caleb quickly relayed his availability to them for friendship, council, prayers or anything else they needed, and he offered a brief prayer asking the Lord to give them strength and peace, then retreated, to let them resume their vantage points.

The moment drew near, and as they waited holding their collective breaths, the sun went behind the clouds again. Rain could end any chance they had of seeing her today. The seconds ticked by and as they watched, the door slowly opened and Millicent wheeled Rebecca outside. The clouds turned out to be a blessing, enabling them to see her clearly, unimpeded by the large cumbersome umbrella they normally used to shield her from the sun.

Tommy gasped audibly, then sucked in a breath. He watched her being pushed along, vague memories rushing to the surface at the sight of his mother's face. She did look older, and she was so thin compared to what he remembered, but he could still see the beauty time couldn't erase. He recalled Papaw saying he would know her face anywhere, and he was right. He'd have recognized her anywhere too. He was unaware that he was crying until he felt the hot tears running down his cheeks. He didn't bother to brush them away, not wanting to close his eyes long enough to wipe them. Instead, he kept his eyes on his mother, drinking in the sight of her, seeing her now as she'd looked in his memories. Her hair full and fiery. She would know them. He knew she would. There was no way she'd make it through hell to come this far and not remember her family.

The second Faith saw Rebecca in the outfit she'd made, she surprised herself by bursting into tears. She thought she was so prepared and could control her emotions, but was proven wrong. It seemed that Millicent knew her better than she knew herself. Thankful for that and the opportunity to get herself in check, she took a closer look. She thought Rebecca looked so pretty in the outfit rather than the plain hospital gown, and thought she detected an air of pride over the pretty clothes, then she realized she was probably imparting her own feelings onto Rebecca. It was sinking in that this woman was her mamaw! She thought back to the connection she'd felt to her almost from the very beginning, and her stomach did a little flip flop. She was going to have to get used to the fact she was her mamaw, yet make sure not to call her that, before it was time. Feeling Adohy's arms around her in a warm comforting embrace, everything seemed to fall into place, and her gut told her that today was just the start of better things to come. She let out a long breath, at peace with the thought.

Aubry's initial reaction to the first glimpse of her mother in over sixteen years, was quite unlike Tommy and Faith's impassioned impulses. Rather she was quite numb, feeling nothing, one way or the other. Then, unexpectedly, a series of images began flashing in her head of scenes long since blocked from her psyche. She saw her mother bending to kiss her goodnight, her mother's beautiful smile as she laughed at something someone said, her mother putting her favorite dessert on the table in front of her, and then an image of herself as a little girl brushing her mother's thick, shiny hair. Her breath hitched in her throat and for a moment, serenity washed over her. Then in an instant, she was gripped by a suffocating fear and her eyes began to burn as the heartwarming scenes distorted and shifted into frightening visions of smoke and terrified screams, a man struggling with her father obviously trying to hurt him, and her mother running back inside the burning house. After that, all she could see was fire, burning and burning, as she recalled the months of being unable to find her voice, her only means of coping in her four year old mind. She cried out then, pulling everyone from their individual moments in time. They all gathered round her as she dropped to her knees, everything finally coming full circle, and wept.

It was several minutes before Aubry was able to pull herself together, having years of repressed terror and tears to purge. Horace helped her to her feet and when she could, she told them what she remembered.

351

Taking a deep, syncopated breath, she confessed, "I remember it." Her face contorted in pain for a second before she forced it back. "I remember the fire. *All* of it," she said, and then the sobs overtook her again. Her husband pulled her to him and wrapped his arms around her, while the others comforted her from behind.

Millicent entered then, having come to see how they were faring after seeing Rebecca, and to relay how Rebecca was this morning. They moved the discussion to the kitchen where Virgil had cake and refreshments waiting for them. They took seats around the table, and Millicent passed out cups of coffee, as each of them shared their feelings. When they were done, Millicent filled them in on Rebecca's condition today.

"First of all, Faith, she was delighted with her new outfit," and Faith felt the tears form again, in spite of herself. "I was thrilled that she was alert when she woke again, and after she had her physical therapy and bath, I gave them to her and told her that they were from someone who wanted her to know that God loved her. She reached out to touch them and she actually said the words, "Thank you"!

That made all of them happy to hear, and they thanked Faith for being so thoughtful.

Samuel told her, "I don't know how ya managed it, but they're her favrit color. Purple."

Faith smiled, wishing she could take the credit by knowing what her grandmother's favorite color had been, but in actuality it had been pure luck. She'd had several pieces of fabric to choose from.

"She really liked them," Millicent said, adding, "And there's more." She had their attention at once. "Obviously things went well during all of this and breakfast, or I wouldn't have brought her outside, but during breakfast she not only *asked* for a cup coffee, but she held the cup herself!"

There were stunned reactions around the table, except for Samuel. He chuckled, and muttered "Atta girl!" not realizing he'd said it out loud till everyone looked at him. Explaining himself, he said, "Red loved her a good cup a-coffee. I'd fergot that til now."

Millicent told them, "Well, I only filled it part full, and made sure it wasn't scalding, and of course made sure she was steady. It took both of her hands, but she drank it on her own. It was quite the accomplishment! She was very proud of herself, and extra careful not to spill it on her new outfit. I swear, she must have practiced last night before she fell asleep."

They all smiled at the thought.

"What's she doing now?" Tommy asked.

"It was a full and exciting morning for her and she tired herself out. She's resting now. And I thought of something else that happened a few days ago, when she first started coming out of the wakeful coma. Sandi told me that Rebecca had thought that Tenley's name was Sarah. We assumed at the time, it was because she'd heard someone say something about Sarah's Home and she assumed that Tenley lived there, hence her name was Sarah. But we've all marveled over how much Tenley resembles what Sarah looked like at that age. I can't help but wonder, in light of what we know now, if Rebecca truly thought Tenley *was* Sarah."

353

Everyone considered this, hoping it could be true, because that would mean she remembered *something* about who she was!

Another knock on the door interrupted their thoughts. The investigators had arrived after receiving the call from Fred, as Millicent had requested. While the family went over the past few days with them, Evelyn slipped out and went to check on the kids at the school. Things had been fine under Jubal's care, and much to the kids delight and per Aubry's instructions, they were allowed to go home early. Evelyn brought Chalmer back to Millicent's with her.

Caleb excused himself, reminding them he was there if they needed him for anything. He needed to get back to the store, but wanted to slip in at the Home to say hello to Oppy. As he entered the door he heard someone holler "Amen!" and looked to see Benny waving to him, Oppy by his side. She looked over and waved, too. It must be one of her good days, he thought to himself, then he chuckled, remembering how Benny had echoed him after a prayer he'd overheard at the Home once before.

He went to them and gave Oppy a kiss on the cheek, greeting Benny with a handshake. He asked Oppy how she was and chatted with her for a moment, then felt the need to explain to Benny what "Amen" meant. He realized that he probably wouldn't understand that it was derived from the Hebrew term for truth, and sometimes rendered as truly or verily, and so opted to explain what it meant when said at the end of the prayer.

"Benny, do you know what the word "Amen" means?" Caleb asked.

Benny considered it a moment, then shook his head. "Thank you?" he guessed.

Though it was wrong, Caleb was impressed his answer. "Close," he said. "When you say it at the end of a prayer, it means that you agree with the content of the prayer. Let's say a prayer right now, and I'll show you." He bowed his head and Benny watched. "Heavenly Father, we thank you for our blessings and for the wonderful care Oppy receives here at Sarah's Home. Thank you for bringing Benny into her life to be her friend. Amen."

"Amen!" Benny echoed.

Caleb had no idea if Benny understood, but it was worth the try. He left feeling good about it.

The investigators left too, armed with their new information, promising to do everything they could to get to the bottom of Rebecca's case.

It was a happy day in Hurricane Holler!

CHAPTER 43

After leaving Millicent's that day, the girl's—wound up like eight day clocks from the emotional morning—spent the rest of the day combining their supplies and sewing more new outfits for Rebecca, and then made supper for everyone. The guy's took to the front porch, speculating on how Rebecca had survived held captive for so long, what she'd endured, her whereabouts for all those years, and worse, after walking the investigators through what they knew that morning, the realization of whose hands she must have been at the mercy of. Then, when Chalmer was down for a nap, they elaborated on what each of them might have done to that person, had Adohy not already sent the piece of scum to his watery grave the night Sarah had died.

Adohy was quiet while they vented, but the fact was, though he was relieved Zeke's death meant he could no longer hurt anyone, he took no comfort in the fact that Zeke had slipped from his grip. Even after what he'd been through at the hands of the man. And though Tommy, Horace and Samuel conveyed that they would have wanted to exact revenge themselves, he was sure it was their emotions talking and was *glad* he spared them carrying the weight of that responsibility. Now, there was the added possibility that Rebecca had been being held captive *inside* at the same place he'd been held *outside*. He'd never stepped foot in that house, but that didn't stop him from wondering if there was something he'd missed, if he should have *known* somehow and tried to help her. The victory of his escape was suddenly crushed under an avalanche of guilt from the possibility that he may have left Rebecca behind with that evil man. If she was there, did Zeke take his anger out on her, after his escape? He couldn't stop the thoughts running through his mind and he felt the need to ask for their forgiveness.

"It hurts my inside if he had her. And it is much greater if I got to my freedom, and she did not," he offered in apology.

His English didn't have to be perfect for them to understand what he was trying to convey. They could read it on his face.

Tommy and Samuel started to speak at the same time.

"We don't—" Tommy began, but stopped, hearing his papaw talking.

"Son, they ain't no need fer ya ta be a-shoulderin' none a-the blame here. They ain't a one a-us that don't know that ya's a victim yerself a-that madman, an' ever' one a-us know that ya'd a-ne'er run off an' left anyone behind, least a-all, a defenseless lady. Truth is, they ain't no tellin' how many a-people ya done saved, now that he's gone. Had it not been fer what ya did, he may a moved 'em agin and we might ne'er a-know'd that she's alive. So ya jes go on ahead an git it outta yer head now, cause this here family's been through anuff grief an' it's high time we started a-countin' our blessin's, startin' with ya an' Rebecca. Faith's happy fer the chance ta git ta know her mamaw, an' she don't need no misplaced bad feelin's takin away from that," Samuel told him in a no nonsense tone he knew not to ignore.

"That's the truth, Adohy," Tommy said. "Ya ain't done nothin' but good here."

Horace nodded his head in agreement. Adohy looked at each one of them in turn and knew they meant what they said. It helped.

They went back to speculating on who the corpse was, that was found when Benny and Rebecca were, and a thought occurred to Tommy that turned his face a pasty white.

"Papaw, what if it's Daddy?"

Samuel looked at him, brow's furrowed. "Whaddya mean, son?"

"Well, Zeke didn't die in the fire like we thought, and now we know Mama didn't. What if Daddy didn't either?"

Samuel's stomach clenched at the possibility. Could Carl have been alive all these years? He just couldn't imagine it. But if Zeke *was* behind all of this and had managed to keep Rebecca captive, could Carl have been a prisoner, too? And if so, why didn't they come home after Zeke died? It brought a whole new mound of questions to the table that they discussed, in addition to who Benny was and what his role in all of it could be. They felt sure he was a victim also, but why? The only one that may ever be able to answer any of these questions was Rebecca.

In closing, Samuel said, "Ain't no need ta worry the girls with all that, til we know more. They got enough ta deal with now."

That evening, Millicent, along with Virgil and Tenley, came to check on them all and deliver the news that Rebecca had done remarkably well the rest of that day and was now in bed for the night. Millicent wanted them to know that she had helped her retire herself, and also to let Faith know that Rebecca verbally asked to make sure that her outfit would be there in the morning and nothing would happen to it overnight. It was the most she had said out loud, to date.

With that news, Faith, Aubry, and Evelyn showed Millicent the two additional outfits they had completed between them that afternoon, similar in style to the first pant set, one in a subtle purple and white plaid, and one in a small floral print with purple iris. They sent them with Millicent for her to give to Rebecca the following morning, and before Millicent left, she told Faith she wanted her to come back to work, but that she was limiting her access to Rebecca to only being in the same room for a few days, before she resumed any meals with her.

Faith was more than fine with this arrangement after to her unexpected reaction that morning, grateful for the opportunity to be in the same room with her, even at a distance.

Everyone went back to their regular duties on Tuesday, the work a welcome distraction to their overtaxed brains. Samuel even found solace in picking the last of the peas, hulling some for canning, and snapping the others. Chalmer had been his helper all summer, but today his mind relished the silence and the thought numbing monotony of his work.

After school, Aubry went to pick up Horace Junior from her mother-in-law, then went to spend the rest of the afternoon with Chalmer and Samuel, until the others arrived. Millicent had promised to bring them another bedtime report on Rebecca, and Faith and Evelyn were able to fill them in on most of her day.

Faith admitted she'd teared up again seeing Rebecca positively glowing in a different one of her new outfits that morning, and she was glad she was across the room where she could hide it, noting that once again, Millicent had made the right decision.

Millicent was personally overseeing Rebecca as a patient, and was extremely happy with the progress she was making. After reporting another exemplary day with Rebecca showing more progress, both physically and verbally, she brought up an idea she had for Halloween, which was the next day.

In years past, Halloween hadn't been a big occasion in Hurricane Holler, as most families didn't have the means to afford candy or costumes. Most of them knew nothing of the history of the pagan holiday, nor the trouble some of the older big city kids got into regarding the "trick" part of trick or treating. In their little community it was known simply as a reason for the kids to masquerade as their favorite cartoon characters or super heroes and get a treat, yet it was rarely celebrated. But with the transistor radio's some of the kids had now announcing the big Halloween displays at the Cas Walker stores, with loads of help from Chalmer, of course, more kids were looking forward to it than ever, and it seemed a shame that they would miss out on the holiday just because of their geography and families finances. Millicent decided the community needed a little celebration, and she could do something about it, but she would need Aubry's help.

She told them that with the help of the kitchen staff who had already volunteered, they would make candy and caramel apples and other goodies, if Aubry would allow the children to make their own masks in school to wear to Sarah's Home the following night to get their treats. They could send an announcement with each child to their parents, asking them to please bring their children to Sarah's Home to get their treats that evening. The adult patients at the home that were willing and able could hand out the treats and the younger patients could participate as well, so everyone could be involved. It was last minute, but Millicent knew they could pull it off.

The next morning she sent one of the employees who'd volunteered to help, with a list to the General Store. On the list was two bushels of apples, the ingredients to candy and caramelize half of them, a large mixed bag of candy and as many boxes of Cracker Jacks and whatever comic books they had in stock. The employee was to drop the comic books off at the school on their way back, to assist the children in the making of their masks in case they didn't yet have a favorite cartoon character or super hero. She doubted some of them had even seen a comic book before.

With that in the works, she went to begin her day with Rebecca. She wasn't getting the painful knots in her stomach with the fear that Rebecca would have transitioned back to the blank stare when she awoke, but since she was aware of the distinct possibility, there were still some nerves to deal with. That, and lots of prayers everytime Rebecca went to sleep. Thankfully this morning was no different than the past three days. Rebecca awoke pleasant and alert, ready to do her physical therapy, get bathed and don yet another new outfit. Then it was on to breakfast and her eagerly awaited cup of coffee.

Much to Millicent's delight, Rebecca asked if she could try to feed herself, and she was happy to give her approval. Rebecca's request brought to mind the words Samuel had used to describe his daughter-in-law, strong and determined. It was no doubt how she'd managed to survive her ordeal, and Millicent hoped it would continue to help expedite her recovery now, so that she could be reunited with her family at long last.

Today they were serving scrambled eggs, bacon, and biscuits. Gravy for the biscuits was available upon request. Millicent was in the process of positioning Rebecca at a table in her wheelchair, but again, Rebecca surprised her.

"Can I...sit in a...chair...at the table?" she asked, haltingly.

After a second to consider it, Millicent told her, "If you feel like you can, then absolutely. If you change your mind at any time, just tell me, and we'll get you back in your wheelchair. Okay?" They had an understanding between them and she was sure that Rebecca would be honest with her.

Millicent locked the wheels on the chair and held her hand out to assist, but remarkably Rebecca waved it away and began to push herself to a standing position. It was slow, but steady, and once she was upright she flashed a triumphant smile at Millicent and only then accepted her hand. It was a sign that, determined though she was, she also realized her limitations. Another victory.

With baby steps she moved herself to the seat at the table, only using Millicent's hand as a precaution, which in the end was unneeded. Her grin of accomplishment said a thousand words. The physical efforts must have worked up her appetite as she ate everything on her plate by herself, then broke the biscuit in two, and asked for some gravy. Adding gravy to the biscuit made it a little more challenging, but she made it without spilling a drop. A refill on her cup of coffee, which she drank black, completed her morning fare.

While she ate, Millicent made small talk, telling her about the holiday and plans for the festivities that evening, when Sandi came in the common area with Tenley. They made their way to their table, and Tenley asked if she could sit with them to make her mask for the Halloween party.

"You sure can! Let me just get Red here back in her wheelchair and comfortable, and I'll help you."

"Can I stay...here...and watch?" Rebecca asked, her eyes on Tenley.

Millicent hesitated only briefly, remembering Rebecca's confusion over Tenley's name. Thinking Tenley's presence might help Rebecca remember the real Sarah, she agreed. "If you would like to, absolutely!" Dismissing Sandi, she said, "We'll help Tenley, Sandi, but you can go help with the candy apples if you want to!"

Sandi left the bag of craft supplies with them and Millicent provided Tenley with several sheets of construction paper to begin with. "Do you know who you want to be?" she asked.

"Cinderella!" Tenley cried out, her lisp barely detectable. It was an animated Walt Disney film that had been out for a few years and as luck would have it, it had been playing at a cinema while they were in Knoxville for Tenley's latest surgery. Millicent and Virgil had taken her to see it after she was released, while they were waiting on Adohy and Faith to meet back up with them from their trip to Gatlinburg. Tenley had been captivated with the story and Cinderella was now her favorite topic.

Millicent noticed the puzzled expression on Rebecca's face, and asked her if she'd heard of Cinderella. When she shook her head, Tenley had the opportunity to tell her all about the film while they worked. Instead of a mask, they worked on a beautiful paper crown, with Millicent suggesting they arrange her hair in a pile on her head like Cinderella, and she would look just like the fairy tale princess!

"Can I wear one of my special fancy dresses, Mama?" Tenley asked.

"Well, what kind of a princess would you be if you didn't wear a fancy dress?" Millicent teased.

When they were finished with the crown, Millicent tried it on Tenley for size, twirling her hair up in a messy bun and slipping the crown around it. Tenley preened and posed, modeling for Rebecca.

"How do I look?" she asked. "Do I look like a princess?"

Smiling at Tenley's antics, Rebecca told her, "Yes you do! You look just like S—" she stopped abruptly and the smile was gone in an instant. Her expression clouded, and she got that faraway look in her eyes.

Millicent pulled the crown off and dropped Tenley's hair, calling out, "Sandi!" over her shoulder, while she went back around the table to Rebecca's side.

Tenley looked on with concern. "Is she okay, Mama?" she asked, as Sandi rushed over to them.

Millicent wasn't sure, and asked Rebecca, "Are you alright, Red?"

She still seemed disoriented but looked up at Millicent. "I think I...want to...lay down...now," she answered, suddenly looking very peaked.

"Of course," Millicent said, helping her back to the wheelchair. This time it took a lot of effort on Millicent's part, as Rebecca's legs were rubbery. Casting a glance to make sure Sandi was to watch Tenley, she wheeled Rebecca back to her room, her stomach flip flopping every step of the way. Did Rebecca remember something? Was she about to say that Tenley looked like Sarah? Back in Rebecca's room, Millicent helped her to bed. She was like a limp noodle, appearing to not have much strength. Or the will to use it. Millicent took a deep breath, praying this wasn't going to be a major setback.

Not pressing the issue, they simply made their usual promise to talk more after she woke, and Millicent let her be, alone with her thoughts and possibly some memories?

She checked back in on her a few minutes later to find her sleeping, presumably peacefully. She tracked down Brenda, and asked her to keep checking on Rebecca until she woke, then went back to see about Tenley.

Tenley was fine, already distracted showing Sandi her crown. With that project finished, the three of them went to work helping with the candy apples and other treats for that evening, until Millicent got word that Rebecca was waking.

Leaving Tenley with Sandi again, she hurried to Rebecca's room to find her awake. She was sitting on the side of her bed speaking to Brenda when Millicent entered. Brenda bowed out quietly with a nod from Millicent.

Watching closely for any signs of anything out of the ordinary, Millicent observed that Rebecca looked better, except maybe still a little weary. "How was your nap, Red?" she asked softly, sitting across from her in the bedside chair.

"Fine," Rebecca answered, not elaborating.

Millicent thought for a moment. She had no way of knowing from Rebecca's answer if there had been any back sliding. Testing her, she asked, "Do you still want to attend the Halloween party tonight?"

Rebecca's face brightened. "Yes...I do," she answered.

A silent sigh escaped Millicent's lips. "Okay!" she said. "But I don't want you to overdo it. I know you're anxious to get your strength back, and you have done an outstanding job so far, but we have to be careful and smart about it. So how about you let someone help you with your dinner in here, so you can relax some more and rest up for this evening?"

A flicker of disappointment reflected in Rebecca's eyes, but after a second she agreed.

"Great! That way you'll be nice and rested and ready for all the excitement! I'm so proud of you!" Millicent told her, reaching over to squeeze her hands gently.

Rebecca answered with a light squeeze back.

"Well, there's still a lot to do to get ready, so why don't we get you settled in this chair, and I'll send Benny in with your dinner, okay?" she asked, standing to assist her.

"Benny?" Rebecca questioned, her brow creased.

Millicent could have kicked herself! How could she be so careless saying Benny's name, of all people! She proceeded without missing a beat though, her heart pounding. "Yes, he's fed you before," she said nonchalantly, holding her breath as she helped Rebecca to the chair. She stood fairly well on her own this time, taking a step, then pivoting to drop into the cushioned seat, but still donning a puzzled expression.

Millicent considered changing her mind and feeding her herself, but was concerned the sudden change in plan would cause Rebecca to question it even more, so she stayed the course. She made sure Rebecca would be okay for a moment, and went to locate Benny.

She found him in the common area, having just finished with Oppy. She approached and asked if he could help her out by feeding Red as well. It seemed a little unfair, as she had a slight advantage of knowing the answer to the question before she voiced it.

He looked around. "Where is she?" he asked, perplexed.

"She's in her room. She needs to get a little rest before the kids come tonight. Are you sure you don't mind?"

"I don't mind! I like Red. She's nice!" he answered with a childlike inflection.

"Thank you, Benny! You know, I think I'm going to have to start giving you an allowance for all the help you are!" she said, meaning every word of it.

"Allowance?" Benny questioned, not understanding the term.

Millicent chuckled. "I'll explain later, okay? Let's get Red's dinner. I'm sure she's hungry by now."

They got a cart and tray with her meal, and when Millicent saw Brenda heading back that way, she asked her to show Benny to Rebecca's room, and to check in on them every few minutes. She didn't expect there to be any problems but felt the need to be overly cautious after her blunder.

There was only one chair in Rebecca's room, so Brenda retrieved an extra chair for Benny to sit in while he fed Rebecca, and once they were situated with everything under control, she went to check on another patient.

Benny fed Rebecca with his usual care, and she ate willingly. He talked about random things as she chewed each bite, while she listened, thoughtfully. When they were done, he wiped her face with a napkin.

She surprised him then, by reaching out to him and laying her hand on his cheek. "I remember you," she said sweetly.

369

CHAPTER 44

Brenda had returned to peek into the room just in time to witness the touching scene between Bennie and Rebecca, and reported it to Millicent at once.

Millicent's heart skipped a beat. "She said she remembered him?!" she repeated, verifying she'd heard Brenda correctly, her eyes wide with incredulity.

"Yes," Brenda confirmed, equally amazed.

"Did she say anything else? Was she afraid?" Millicent fired the questions to Brenda, her mind racing.

"I didn't hear her say anything else, and she wasn't afraid. I could see her face. She said it and was looking at him tenderly."

What did she mean? Millicent wondered. She remembered him? From when?! From when he fed her before, here at the Home? Or from where they came from? Millicent thanked Brenda and rushed once again to Rebecca's room. She

371

found Rebecca and Benny listening to a mixture of static and music on his radio. She swallowed back her disquieted temperament and greeted the two of them with a cheerful hello, scanning Rebecca's face for any fear or trepidation, finding none, much to her relief.

What a day this has been, she thought to herself, forcing her nerves to settle down. She absently dropped down on the side of Rebecca's bed and inquired as to how dinner was.

They both assured her it was fine, then resumed listening to the music. Millicent watched them for a bit, befuddled, then with a sigh, promised to come back and check on them in a little while. She left, taking the cart with the dinner dishes on it with her, for something to lean on.

On her way by, she stopped to look in on the kids at the Home that were also making their masks for trick or treating, making sure everyone had what they needed.

Then, needing a break herself, she went to see how Virgil and the boys were doing getting the yard ready for the party. They had three big wash tubs filled with water so the kids could bob for apples, and things were coming along well. She relayed her day, so far, to Virgil, then after the much needed breath of fresh air, she went back to look in on Rebecca and Benny, once more.

Benny must have left the room and returned at some point because they had moved on to playing Candyland, one of Benny's games he'd apparently gone to collect. Rebecca seemed to be enjoying herself and appeared rested, giving Millicent no indication by her demeanor to what she'd meant earlier when she said she remembered Benny. Millicent inquired as to her personal needs, and she conveyed that she didn't need anything.

Millicent reminded her not to let herself get too tired, keeping the festivities that night in mind and she agreed to send Benny for help if she needed it.

Millicent retreated, considering how much help Benny had been, not only with Rebecca, but with Oppy, too. She began to kick around how he would react to being named an honorary member of the staff, and earning a small salary in exchange for what he did. She knew he helped out for the self-satisfaction, but he was also looking for approval. Having a "job" would have to boost his confidence even more, giving him a feeling of self-worth, and the money part was only fair. Everything he did, freed up a nurse or an orderly's time, allowing them to tend to much more serious matters. By the time she made it to the kitchen to check on the candy apple progress and Tenley, she had made up her mind.

Benny kept Rebecca company in her room all afternoon, justifying Millicent's decision. She would make the announcement tonight. She'd already gone to her office and made a name tag for him. She sent him along to take care of Oppy for supper, sure that Rebecca would need to have some personal time by now. When that was taken care of, she inquired as to how she was feeling.

"Are you tired? You've had a very full day today," Millicent probed.

"No, I'm fine," Rebecca said.

Millicent scrutinized her every action, searching for fatigue or duress. She truly seemed okay. "Do you still feel up to attending the festivities tonight?"

"Oh, yes" Rebecca answered, clearly looking forward to it.

"Okay, the next question is, do you want to have supper in the common area, or in here?"

"Out there, please."

"You got it, but, Red please, it may get a little loud with all the kids, or even overwhelming, and it's nothing to be ashamed of if it becomes too much. So, I'm going to hold you to our promise to let me know if you need to come back to your room at any time, okay?"

"Okay," Rebecca promised.

"Then let's go get this party started," Millicent said, wheeling Rebecca out.

Rebecca fed herself her supper, while Millicent and Faith watched from afar. She did a great job, having no mishaps whatsoever. She'd just finished up, when the kitchen staff began bringing out the trays of candy and caramel apples, and bowls of assorted candy for the patients that had volunteered to pass out to the kids. Rebecca was one of the volunteers, and Millicent was glad she'd thought to include them. They seemed to be looking forward to getting to see all the kids.

Since Rebecca was participating in the common area, Millicent reminded them that either Faith, Evelyn, or Horace would have to accompany Chalmer through the line for his candy apple and treats. The others would need to remain outside where the apple bobbing and other activities were going on.

Then she and Virgil grabbed a bite to eat with Tenley, and barely had time to get Tenley changed and her crown in place before other kids started to arrive.

There were miniature Supermen, Green Hornets, Batmen, and Lone Rangers, as well as a Mickey Mouse or two, Pinocchio, and of course, a few Snow Whites and Wonder Women, but Tenley turned out to be the one and only Cinderella, and she loved it.

Most of the kids were anxious to get their hands on their candy before joining in on the yard games, so they filed through one after the other with their little bags or buckets, collecting their cache of candy from the row of delighted Sarah's Home inhabitant's passing them out.

Evelyn opted to escort Chalmer down the line, and he got a lot of attention, especially from the elderly ladies, when he showed up with the added wardrobe accessory of a cowboy hat, that completed his Lone Ranger ensemble. It was on loan from his Papaw, and way too big for his head, but a towel wrapped around his head helped hold it in place until it was time for apple bobbing. Then it was returned, unblemished, to its rightful owner.

Every single person at the Home was involved in some capacity, whether it was preparation of treats and games, distribution of treats, or participation in eating the treats.

The outdoor games were a big hit, the apple bobbing topping the list. The kids ended up soaked, but they thoroughly enjoyed it, plus it aided in washing the rings off around their mouths from the candy apples without them even realizing it.

Sunset brought the fun to an end, but it was a weeknight after all, with school and work calling for an early start in the morning, and it had been a long day for all of them already. All in all, it was a success and a great release for all the tensions some of them had been under this week.

The patients were all up later than they usually were. On a regular evening most would have already retired to their rooms for the night, if not to bed. Due to that, Faith and Evelyn stayed to help get everyone settled.

Before that happened though, Millicent wanted to make her announcement. "I need everyone's attention for just a moment. First of all, thanks so much to each and every one of you who volunteered and made tonight such a success. You helped make a lot kids and adults alike very happy, and we couldn't have pulled it off in such short notice without you! And there's one more thing. Benny?" she called. "Can you join me here for just a second?"

Benny stood sheepishly, wondering if he'd done something wrong, but joined Millicent as she'd asked.

She could see he was nervous so she hurried to put his mind at ease. Several inches taller than her, she looked up to him, and said, "Benny, you have become an asset to Sarah's Home in many ways, and because of that I felt it was time you were recognized for it! From today forward, I hereby declare you an honorary staff member! And here is your name tag to prove it!" she told him, extending it to him.

Cheers rang out causing Benny to look around the room, then back to Millicent. He glanced at the name tag, and hesitantly reached to accept it.

The room fell silent, and Millicent began to think that maybe she shouldn't have done this, or had at least done it in private, because Benny's expression was bordering on despair.

Sure that she had made a huge mistake, she watched, filled with regret, as his hand slowly reached for the name tag. But he stopped short from taking it from her hand, and his gaze shifted to her face. She cringed when his chin quivered as he asked, "Does this mean I cain't live here no more?"

"Oh, Benny," she cried out, pulling him into a comforting embrace, realization flooding her senses. "This is your home!" she stressed to him urgently. Pulling back to look in his eyes to make sure he understood, she told him, "This is your home! You can live here as long as you want to!" Holding up the name tag, she added, "This just means it's official! This is Benny's home!" she reiterated. She would explain more to him in private, she thought, for now she was just wanting and waiting for him to accept the fact he didn't have to go anywhere.

A few seconds ticked by then Benny startled everyone, Millicent most of all, when he got a big grin on his face and picked her up and spun her around, shouting "Amen! Aammeenn!" Standing her back on her feet, he took the name tag from her hand and tried to stick it to his shirt.

That lightened the mood again, and as Millicent took it to pin it on for him, she waved everyone along who'd been rooted in spot. "Everything's good," she said. "Goodnight everyone!"

377

Nearly everyone had dispersed by the time Benny's name tag was in place, but she still needed to explain to him the rest of what his tag meant. She looked around and saw only Rebecca waiting to be escorted to her room, and Faith, who looked at Millicent questioningly. After a brief hesitation, Millicent relented.

Faith lit up, and hopped a little jig in place before pulling herself together and heading to get Rebecca.

She approached from behind and leaned around Rebecca's shoulder to greet her. "Hi! How are you?" she asked, with a mile wide smile.

Rebecca turned her head to look at her and smiled in return. She remembered her, but hadn't seen her lately. "Where have you been?" she asked.

Faith's heart soared to know she'd noticed her absence. "Oh, I've been around, just doing some different jobs the past few days," she explained. "Did you have fun tonight?"

Rebecca nodded her head. "Yes, but I'm tired now."

"I bet you are! It's been a long day! I'm tired too!" Faith commiserated with her. "We'll get you all fixed up here in just a second, and then you can get all the rest you need!" she said, turning into Rebecca's room. Wheeling her up to her bed, she said, "Why don't I help you out of your top, and we'll slip your gown over your head, and when you stand up you can just step right out of your pants, and collapse on the bed. How does that sound?" she asked.

"That sounds fine," Rebecca answered, her voice beginning to sound tired.

"Okay, raise your arms for me," Faith asked, and Rebecca complied. Faith pulled the top over her head, and slipped the nightgown back down, in two swift moves. "Okay! That wasn't too bad, was it?"

Rebecca shook her head, getting sleepier by the second.

Faith locked the wheel on the wheelchair and stepped to the side of it. "Okay, now let's get you standing and we'll pull your pants down and you can step right out of them. I'll pick them up after your safe in the bed. Here we go, on the count of three...one, two, three." Rebecca did as instructed and was sitting on the side of the bed when Faith let go and bent over to pick up the pants they had just made for her the day before. She was in the process of folding them neatly, when before she knew what was happening, Rebecca's hand shot out and grabbed her arm, the grasp surprising strong.

"Where'd you get that?" Rebecca cried out, her voice ringing with terror.

Faith looked at the arm Rebecca had a white knuckled death grip on. The only thing there was Adohy's mother's bracelet.

CHAPTER 45

The bracelet! The one Zeke stole from Adohy and wore until the night he died! She recognizes it! Faith thought, but didn't know what to do. She understood Rebecca's fear and revulsion. She'd felt it herself when Adohy initially gave it to her, until she realized how much it meant to her husband, being the only thing he had from his parents. But she couldn't explain that to her grandmother yet.

"It's okay," she soothed, trying to think fast. What should she do? "It was a gift from my husband's mother," she explained.

Rebecca's hand was still locked on Faith's arm, but her fearful expression became confused at Faith's words. Her eyes went from Faith's, to the bracelet, and back again, as if contemplating how much merit her explanation had.

Rebecca's eyes narrowed in suspicion. "Your husband?" she questioned.

"Yes," Faith said. "Adohy White Horn Thornton," she added, realizing that Rebecca was wondering if her husband could have been Zeke. She swallowed back an impulse to gag. "He's an Indian, with long black hair," she continued, hoping the description would clear up any doubts.

Millicent happened by then, pausing in the doorway to witness the exchange. It only took a moment to assess the situation, seeing Rebecca holding Faith's arm with the bracelet. They'd forgotten the connection of the bracelet to Zeke! She hurried inside to see how much damage was done.

Putting on a happy front, she entered, asking, "How's it going in here? All ready for bed?"

When neither Faith nor Rebecca responded, Millicent decided to face it head on. "Oh! You're admiring Faith's bracelet! Isn't it pretty?"

"Faith?" Rebecca repeated quietly, her focus shifting back to search Faith's face.

Dammit! Millicent swore. She did it again! She was afraid there was no turning back now, and only hoped that Rebecca was ready and as strong as Samuel recalled. She stepped up close to the two of them, and gently pried Rebecca's hand from Faith's arm. White marks on Faith's flesh marked the grip from Rebecca's fingers.

"Does this bracelet mean anything to you, Red?" Millicent asked softly.

Rebecca tore her gaze from Faith to stare at the bracelet, and they watched as a myriad of emotions wrested her features as her memories fought their way to the surface. They stood by in silence, allowing Rebecca time to process what was happening. A full few minutes passed before she finally broke from her reverie, enlightenment shining in her eyes when she looked back up at them. "Where am I" she asked, resolutely.

Telling her she was at "Sarah's Home" was out of the question and Millicent was hesitant to tell her anything else until she knew what she remembered, so she responded to her a question with a question of her own. "Can you tell me your name first?"

Without hesitation, she answered, "Rebecca. Rebecca Jenkins. And I need to find my family."

An unbidden sob escaped Faith, and too late, she clamped her hands across her mouth.

Rebecca's expression softened with Faith's reaction. "Are you *my* Faith?" she asked, though she already knew the answer.

Faith could only nod, tears coursing down and over her hands keeping her mute, until Rebecca's arms opened wide and she ran into them.

The three of them wept openly until their tears were spent, then Faith pulled back and looked into her grandmother's eyes.

Rebecca asked, "You know who I am?"

Faith nodded, unable to find her voice. It occurred to her then, that it was a blessing Rebecca knew now, before she blurted out the wrong thing. She knew Rebecca was her mamaw, but Rebecca didn't know that Sarah was gone and had revealed the secret before she died.

Millicent interrupted then, before things went too far. She needed to examine Rebecca and determine what she'd remembered on her own before there was anymore outside influence. She also felt that it should be up to the family to determine who told her about Sarah. But one thing was certain, it was going to be devastating news and absolutely no one could tell her before her condition was assessed and they were sure she could handle the tragic news without fear of relapse.

"Rebecca, can you tell me how you're feeling?" Millicent asked.

"Better than I have in a long time, and I wanna see my family," she stated.

"I understand," Millicent said. "But your body and mind has been under a tremendous amount of pressure trying to heal itself. You've only just remembered who you are because you needed time to recuperate and build up your strength."

"My family will help me build up my strength," Rebecca countered.

As if to prove it Faith sat down on the bed beside her, taking Rebecca's hand in hers.

"Yes," Millicent agreed, "of that, I have no doubt. But as your caregiver, there are certain procedures we need to adhere to, to ensure your well-being. It's my professional opinion that we follow protocol as closely as possible."

Rebecca bristled, wanting nothing more than to see her beloved family. It had been...she searched her mind...she had no *idea* how long it had been. She let out a frustrated sigh. "What procedures?" she relented, sounding defeated.

Faith detected the tone, and said, "Millicent has been taking very good care of you, and I promise you, she's only doing what's best."

Rebecca considered what Faith said. Her sincerity and message was hard to miss. She wanted her to do as Millicent asked. How could she disappoint her? "Okay," she said. "What do we do now?"

Millicent and Faith exchanged smiles of encouragement.

"Well, first, when you feel you're strong enough, it's important that we talk about what you remember about the time you were missing."

Rebecca stiffened visibly.

"Only when you're ready," Millicent was quick to tell to her. "You've had an exhausting day, and it's getting late. Tomorrow—"

"No," Rebecca interrupted. "Now. I wanna do it now."

"Oh...well..." Millicent hesitated. She'd planned on calling the doctors in the morning so that they could be present to hear everything for themselves. "You really need to get some rest," she said, stalling.

"I *need* to do it now," Rebecca stressed.

"Okay. Now, it is," Millicent ceded. "If you will, give me just a moment to get ready. I need to get your file and take notes. Faith, on your way out—"

"I want her to stay," Rebecca cut in.

Millicent looked at Faith, silently questioning her wishes.

Faith nodded her head.

"Let me get your file and send word to Virgil and Adohy that we will be late," she said, hurrying out.

When Millicent was gone, Faith gently asked, "Are you sure you want to do this now?"

"Yes, child. I want to do it now, so that I may never speak of it again. But I spoke, asking for you to stay, before I thought about the vile things you'll hear. I fear it will be too much. I think it would be best if you don't hear it."

Faith thought about the bad things she'd been through in her life, including the things Adohy had been through. All of it attributed to Zeke. No. There was nothing that could be said that could be worse than what she'd already lived through. "I think it might surprise you how much I can handle. If my being here will bring you any comfort and support, then I'm not going anywhere."

"Are you sure?" Rebecca asked, not entirely convinced it was a good idea.

"I'm positive," Faith told her, giving her a reassuring hug. "I'm staying," she said with finality.

Millicent rushed to her office to get a pad and the file, and on her way out, her reel to reel recorder she'd used in college caught her eye. It sparked an idea. If Rebecca would allow her to record the session, the doctors could still hear it, word for word, and it would eliminate the need for anyone to question Rebecca over and over. She grabbed it, placing it on her desk, wondering if there was any chance the batteries would still be good. Biting her lip, she pressed the play button to test it. As she'd feared, there was nothing. She searched her mind. Did she have replacement batteries? She ran around her desk pulling open the drawers, hoping to find some. Rapidly losing hope, she opened the final drawer, and under a box of number two pencils she found replacement batteries. Not remembering them at all, she prayed they would work. She swapped the old batteries for the less old, and pushed the play button. They worked! She grabbed the machine, her pad, and the file, and then sent an orderly to relay the message to Virgil and Adohy that they would be late.

The orderly didn't have to go far, as both men were coming in the door to look for their wives, themselves. Wondering what was keeping the two women, they decided to stay there for a while, and Virgil got Tenley settled on a couch so she could go to sleep.

And then they waited.

CHAPTER 46

Rebecca was fine with being recorded, especially if it meant she'd never have to talk about it again. She just wanted to get it all put behind her, and see her family!

Millicent set the recorder up, doing a voice test to make sure it was recording, then got her pad ready to take notes also, just in case they were needed for back up. When she was ready, she gave Rebecca the opportunity once more, to wait until the following day when she was more rested, which she refused. Millicent knew there was no chance that Faith would leave of her own volition, so she didn't bother to ask her if she'd changed her mind.

She pushed record on the machine. "Okay, Rebecca, you won't be interrupted with any questions. It's important that you just relay everything that you can remember. You can begin when you're ready, and if you need to stop at any time, just let me know," Millicent told her.

Faith stayed beside her on the bed, thinking it would be easier for her mamaw if she didn't have to look at her face, and squeezed her hand lightly for reassurance.

While Millicent had been getting everything prepared, Rebecca had that time to think about what she was about to reveal. She had no way of knowing if the family knew who was behind the attack the night of the fire or not. She, her husband Carl, and Sarah were the only one's who would have recognized him, but she wasn't sure if Sarah had gotten a look at him that night. She could only hope that she'd not seen who it was and hadn't had that burden to carry with her all these years, *especially* in addition to the secret the family made a pact never to reveal. Because of that, she realized in order to protect Sarah and Faith, she could not tell them now, the real identity of the devil who was responsible. With that decision, she inhaled deeply, and began.

"I thought the night of the fire was the worst night of my life, but I was wrong," she hesitated, thinking back, then went on. "After making sure the children were safely outside and out of danger, I went back inside the house to get my husband. The fire was spreading quickly and the heat and smoke was almost unbearable. It was hard to see, and harder still, to breathe. When I made it back to them, they were still fighting. Carl wouldn't give up trying to protect his family. I tried to tell him that the kids were outside, safe, that he needed to get out too, but they kept fighting. I don't think he could hear me over the roar of the fire. Then, before I could do anything," she choked back a sob, "he was pushed into the blaze. I tried to get to him, but the man blocked me. I tried my best to get by him, to get to Carl, I fought, scratched and clawed, but he struck me so hard with his fist I fell back and hit my head. I don't remember anything after that, until I woke up I don't know how much later. I was in a room that was empty, except for the mattress on the floor that I was on. My feet and wrists were tied up."

She paused and sucked in a ragged breath. "I was sore, not just from where he'd hit me and where I'd hit my head, but other places. I threw up, realizing what he'd done. Then I screamed. Screamed in anger, screamed for Carl, screamed hoping someone would hear me. I screamed until I lost my voice, but no one ever came. Then I cried. Carl was gone. The only man I'd ever loved, the father of my children, was gone. I grieved for him forever..." her voice trailed off, then she got back to the timeline.

"All I had on was my nightgown, my underpants were gone, and there was only a chamber pot to relieve myself in. I don't know how long it was before he came back, but the first thing he did was have his way with me again. I tried to fight him, but I was still bound, there wasn't much I could do and he forced himself on me. After that, he brought something for me to eat but I refused, and he was fine with that. I don't know if he left completely or just didn't come in the room, but he never responded to me screaming for help. It seemed like days passed. The next time he came into the room, he tried to make me take him in my mouth, but I bit him. Hard. He beat me so bad then, that I thought he was going to kill me. But he didn't quite do it. My eyes were swollen shut, and my lips were busted badly. I couldn't have eaten then, if I'd wanted to. It was a while before he offered food again, but I continued to refuse it, until he realized that I was going to starve. I guess that would have looked like I'd won, to him, so he started forcing whatever slop he could down my throat. He never put *himself* in my mouth again, though." A slight smile formed, recalling her minor victory, then she went on.

"After what must have been a few months, I quit screaming. It became obvious no one could hear me. Everything else remained the same. God hadn't answered any of my prayers for me to be rescued, and after a while I became angry with him. Why was he letting this happen? Why had he let Carl be killed? I couldn't understand it. We were good people. We didn't deserve this. My children didn't deserve to lose their parents. Our family had been through enough. My only solace was knowing the children had Samuel to look after them. Then I began to fear I was going to get pregnant with that evil man's spawn. In spite of my anger, I prayed and prayed for God to not let it happen. For some reason, he answered that prayer and because of that, I never lost my faith. I continued to pray that he would bring me back to my family." She took another deep breath, and continued.

"He always stunk, and his breath was putrid. He seemed to always have the same clothes on. Then one day, he had a bracelet on his wrist that looked just like the one Faith has. It was there from that day forward. Nothing else changed, and I eventually stopped fighting him. One, because it didn't do any good. Two, because I think it excited him even more. So I quit. But I had realized during the time my eyes were swollen shut, that when he came to me I could block out what was happening and visualize some other place and time, and before I knew it, it would be over. So after I healed, during those times I began to squeeze my eyes shut and go away in my mind. After a while I started to forget to come back. What did I have to come back to?"

She paused, trying to remember what came next. "I don't remember being moved, I only remember one day hearing a voice. It was a different voice than I'd heard for so long. When I opened my eyes he was there. Benny. I had no idea how long he'd been there, or how he got there. I soon realized that he must not have been there very long because he was clean shaven, and after only a week or so, a beard started to form. He was very sweet, but clearly afraid of the man. It became his job to feed me. It was dark in the room where I was. There was a window, but something was covering it from the outside. My hands and feet were still tied, but I could move around and use the chamber pot when I needed, so I knew I could stand for a while, at least. I tried to get Benny to untie me and help us get outside, but he kept saying we weren't allowed to go outside or we would get in big trouble. Since it was his job to feed me, I thought if I refused to eat, he would be more afraid of getting into trouble over that and he would try to help us escape when I promised, if we did, he wouldn't get in trouble ever again. I don't know if it would have eventually worked or not, because when the man came back and found out I hadn't been eating, he beat poor Benny, right in front of me, to within an inch of his life. Benny started crying for his mama, and the man told him "*She's* yer mama now, an *I'm* yer new daddy an' ya better damn well do whut I tell ya!" He pulled back like he was going to hit Benny again, but Benny started promising he would do what he was told. I felt so bad, I never asked Benny to help us escape again, and if I got near the window, he would panic and pull me away. If I refused to eat, he would force me. It was hopeless. I went away in my head and stayed away longer and longer each time. The next vague memory I have, is of some men that I'd never seen before, looking at me. I went away again. Then I

393

thought I saw Sarah. But I know now, that was your daughter," she said, looking at Millicent.

"For some reason, after it all started coming back to me, I remembered Benny when he was feeding me today. He looked just like the first time I saw him. He's a good boy. I hope we never have to see that man again." She paused again, then said, "That's it, that's all I remember. I see Faith is all grown up now, and she said she's married." She looked at Faith, and smiled, then back to Millicent. "Can you tell me now how long I've been gone?"

Millicent didn't think it could hurt anything. "Sixteen years," she answered.

Rebecca looked thoughtful. She must have assumed it was about that long, from seeing Faith.

Millicent realized then, she hadn't written a word on her pad, and reached to turn off the recorder. Even of it hadn't recorded everything, it wouldn't matter. She didn't think she'd ever forget a word of what she'd heard.

CHAPTER 47

Faith was speechless. What she'd just heard that her mamaw had endured at the hands of that monster, sickened her. When her swirling thoughts came full circle with the realization that the monster was her father, it couldn't have hurt any worse than if he'd punched her in the gut himself. She had to swallow back the bile that rose in her throat to keep from throwing up. Was the nightmare that was this man ever going to end? Yes, he was dead now, but he just kept coming back.

She had to keep her emotions under control for her mamaw's sake. She'd almost lost it when her grandmother remarked about being worried of getting pregnant with the evil man's spawn. Is that how she would see her when she found out the men were one and the same? As evil spawn of his? She shuddered. In time, Faith supposed, her mamaw would come to find out who the person was that had done this to her, but for now they had to be very careful what they said to her, lest something slip out that shouldn't, like Sarah's death at the hands of the same monster. It was going to be traumatic enough for her to hear about Sarah, and much more so when she knows who did it.

She hoped the doctors and Millicent would know how to handle her finding out about all of that. Right now she wanted to do whatever she could to make her comfortable. She tried to wipe the tears away with her free hand nonchalantly, giving her mamaw's hand a squeeze with her other.

"I'm sorry you had to hear that, Faith," Rebecca told her.

"No, don't you worry none about that. I'm a big girl. *I'm* sorry you had to go *through* it. The important thing is that you're here now, and you were strong enough to get through it and come back to us!" she said, wrapping her arms around Rebecca.

"Can I get you anything?" Millicent asked her softly.

"I think I'd really just like to get some rest now," Rebecca answered, sounding deflated. Then as if to pump herself up again, she added, "I'm hoping to have a big day tomorrow!"

"Of course," Millicent said. "Either of us are just a minute away if you need *anything*. Even if it's only a hand to hold."

"That's right, M—" Faith started to call her mamaw and caught herself. "—my house is just next door." My gosh, she thought. That was close. I have *got* to be more careful!

They got Rebecca tucked in for the night and left the room, each of them wondering briefly who could possibly be more exhausted, before they clearly realized...Rebecca. She definitely had to be the most exhausted.

They found their spouses waiting patiently in the common area, Tenley sound asleep on one of the couches. Millicent was thankful she could sleep through anything. Especially with all the disruptions lately.

Virgil and Adohy stood when they entered, both concerned over what had transpired. Faith took the opportunity to release all the tension, and promptly broke into tears, rushing into Adohy's embrace.

Virgil shot a questioning glance at Millicent. She seemed on the verge of tears, too. Millicent just shook her head and sighed, dropping into an extra seat at the table. While Faith purged all her pent up emotions, Millicent explained to Virgil, "Rebecca remembered who she is...and she just told us what she'd been through."

Compassion washed over Virgil's face. He sat down beside Millicent and took her hand in both of his. "Are you okay, Honey?" he asked, already knowing she wasn't, but not sure what else he could do.

"I'm fine," Millicent fibbed. "Clearly better than Faith and Rebecca," she added, glancing at Faith with concern.

Virgil looked that way, too. His heart hurt for his daughter-in-law. She'd been through so much in her short life. He hoped that all the bad was behind them now, and that with Rebecca back, there could be a fresh start, with happiness and joy for a long time to come.

"What about Rebecca?" Virgil asked. "Is she alright?"

"She's putting up a strong front, at least. Samuel was right about her. She's pretty tough. I think that's probably the only reason she made it through the ordeal. I just hope now that she's remembered everything it's not too overwhelming for her overnight. We'll see in the morning, I guess."

By this time Faith had cried herself out, and pulled back to look up at Adohy, sheepishly. She rarely cried but she'd been making up for it lately.

"Hey! Hey!" Adohy said softly, putting the palms of his hands on each side of her face. "Don't look like that. It's okay to cry!" he said to comfort her.

She swallowed back the tears and tried to smile.

Adohy pulled out a chair, and gestured for her to sit down, then took the seat beside her, never taking his hand off of her. She was his world, and if she hurt, he hurt.

Millicent reached across the table and grasped Faith's hand, giving it a squeeze. She couldn't imagine the toll it had to have taken on Faith to hear what she'd just heard. Everyone was silent for a moment, giving Faith time to regroup. Millicent wasn't sure if she would want to talk more about it tonight while they were together, or wait and talk to Adohy in private, later. After a moment Faith started to relay what her grandmother told them. Millicent was quiet and let her talk, knowing that talking about it would be cathartic.

There were more tears before she was done, but by the end she seemed to have come to grips with it, and had moved on to her concern for when Rebecca found out who Zeke was and that he'd killed Sarah.

Millicent was concerned with that as well. That was why she'd already made her mind up to call in the two doctors in the morning before anything else was revealed. She knew she'd have to get an early start, because Rebecca was already adamant about seeing her family, and Millicent fully understood that. But she simply had to look out for Rebecca's best interests first.

~~§~~

The next morning, Faith and Adohy brought everyone together at Samuel's before Tommy and Horace went out to the fields, and gave them the news from the prior night. They were amazed that Rebecca had made so much progress so quickly, but were thrilled.

Faith told them she could recap what Rebecca had said about her ordeal, or since the session had been recorded and they had Rebecca's permission, they could listen to *it* if they wanted to, but they opted not to. So, once again, she went over the years of Rebecca's captivity.

Each of them could see the discomfort on Adohy's face as Faith spoke, and each had their own perception of his discomfort.

Some felt that it was hard for him to hear what someone had been through by the same man who'd held him captive.

Some thought that he was feeling guilty again for not knowing that Rebecca was being held, and for escaping without her.

399

Some were sure it was the pain he knew that Faith was feeling, hearing what her grandmother had been through knowing it was her father that had done it.

Collectively, they were all right.

When Faith was done, you could read their faces like they had read Adohy's. Some were appalled. Some were angry. Some were sad. As the story swirled in their heads, their faces traded emotions.

She summed the previous night up by telling them that Millicent was calling the doctors in first thing to evaluate Rebecca, and depending on the outcome of that, they should be able to see her. But since they had Sarah's death to consider, they may limit who she got to see, and how soon she got to see them. Either way, the obvious choice to be first, was Samuel. And it would more than likely rest on his shoulders to be the one to give Rebecca the devastating news.

Evelyn really wanted to go to Sarah's Home to lend moral support to Tommy, but since Aubry needed someone to tend to the school, she volunteered. As it turned out, Millicent had already asked Jubal to keep class in Aubry's stead.

So the entire family, with the exception of Chalmer, awaited the doctor's assessment at Sarah's Home.

~~§~~

After many cups of coffee, cracked knuckles, and several hundred paces, the doctors and Millicent emerged from the hallway into the common area where everyone was gathered.

The family held their breath as they watched them approach.

Dr. Wright spoke first. "She is amazingly resilient. She checked out well, and is determined to see her family today!" he announced.

Sighs of relief, smiles and excitement made the rounds.

"I understand that there is some news that she is not aware of." He had all of their attention again.

They nodded solemnly, listening for further instruction.

"I think it would be best if you, Samuel, as head of the family, and the family member she is most familiar with, go in to see her first and use your judgment as to how and when to break this news gently to her. I think that she is strong enough to survive the news mentally, however it is still going to be devastating, emotionally. Depending on how she handles that, it will determine how soon the rest of you can go see her. Obviously, seeing each and every one of you should bring her some comfort."

Samuel nodded, contemplating how he was going to tell her about Sarah, but he'd already figured it was going to rest on his shoulders to break it to her. He looked up when the doctor spoke again.

"That being said, congratulations on getting her back!" Dr Wright said.

Both doctors received hugs, handshakes, and sincere thank you' from the family.

Afterward, Samuel asked, "When kin I go an see er?"

"She's waiting for you now!" Millicent said, excited for the whole family.

Samuel turned and made eye contact with each one of the family, either in an effort to draw strength from them, or for them to say a prayer for him and Rebecca, they weren't sure, but they were all praying, either way.

~~§~~

Samuel couldn't remember the way to Rebecca's room, so Millicent led the way. When they were near, she pointed out the doorway, gave him a hug of encouragement, and left him alone.

He hesitated for a moment gathering his thoughts, then took a deep breath, and stepped into the doorway.

Rebecca was seated in the stuffed chair, and looked up. They looked at each other for a few seconds, before smiles spread across both their faces.

"Samuel!" she said, standing slowly.

He walked to her as quickly as he could with his cane, and they embraced. "I cain't tell ya how good it is ta see ya, girl!" he said, his voice cracking.

Tears were streaming down her face when she leaned back and looked at his face. "You're a sight for sore eyes yourself!" she told him, and pulled him close again.

Samuel couldn't help but notice the difference in her body since the last time he'd hugged even though it was years ago. She'd been strong and solid, firm from the hard work she did daily. Now she was smaller and there were no muscles, just frailty. But he could see in her eyes the inner strength she had. She'd be back. He knew she would. He just wished he didn't have to knock her back down first.

She let go and looked past his shoulder. "Where are they? The kids?" she asked, anxiously. She looked back into his eyes then and knew something was amiss. "What is it Samuel? What's wrong?"

"Why don't we sit a spell. They's somethin' I gotta tell ya," he admitted, his voice somber. He gently urged her to sit, and took a seat across from her, while she looked at him expectantly, trying to read his face.

"Faith told us about what ya done been through these years, 'cept'n ya din't say who a-done it ta ya. But we done figgered out it was Zeke—"

"I couldn't tell anyone. I had to protect Sarah and Faith," she interrupted.

"But see, we done knowed Zeke wadn't dead. He come back. And Faith knows he was her father."

"What?!" Rebecca exclaimed. "But *he* didn't know he was her father! How did she find out? No one was supposed to know, to protect Sarah! Samuel, you promised to keep Sarah's secret! How is she? She must be so ashamed! Where is she? I need to see her!" Rebecca cried, starting to stand to go find her daughter.

"Now, hold on 'ere jes a minute," Samuel said, stopping her.

She sat back down, wringing her hands with worry. "I *need* to see her, Samuel!" she pleaded.

"Rebecca, the thing is, honey, ya *cain't* see her. She ain't here," he said softly.

Rebecca didn't say anything right away, she sat looking into Samuel's eyes. When she finally spoke, she said, "You said that so clearly. You didn't stutter once." There was no emotion in her voice, no excitement with his overcoming his disability, no mention of *what* he'd said. Only *how* he'd said it. She just uttered two simple statements about Samuel, nothing about Sarah.

Samuel didn't remark. He could see that she understood what he was trying to say. He just waited, giving her time to process what she didn't want to hear, what her brain didn't want to accept. He hoped he was right, believing she was strong enough to handle it. They sat looking at each other until a tear ran down her cheek.

Then he slid off the chair onto his knees in front of her and wrapped his arms around her. She began to sob, softly at first, then it seemed all of her grief from the past sixteen years came pouring out all at once. She cried and cried, and he cried right along with her, feeling her pain all over again.

He held her long after they both stopped crying, then had to use his cane to get back into the seat, his knees numb.

Once they were seated across from each other again, she squared her shoulders and said, "Tell me what happened."

He started from the time Millicent and Virgil realized they had an unknown guest, and continued from there, stopping at times to answer questions, or to cry, and finished at the point they were now. Neither of them had any idea how much time had elapsed.

They were silent for a while, spent. Rebecca contemplating all that had transpired.

"My precious Sarah," she grieved.

"Ya'd a-been a-proud of 'er. She had yer strength, yer fire. She stepped right up an' took care of all a-us, an' them youngun's like they was all 'er own. Sewed, cooked, cleaned, started the school. She'd a-give ya a run fer yer money on her cornbread, now, I tell ya!" he said with a chuckle, reminiscing.

Rebecca smiled. That sounded like her girl. In a bit, she asked, "So, I'm three times a mamaw, now?" He knew she was trying to think about something happy.

"Yep, they's all a-waitin' out yonder ta see ya, well, 'ceptin Chalmer. He's at school 'cause he's a whole visit in hisself," he joked. "I'll bring 'em in, one atta time. We'll start with Tommy," he said, standing to go get him.

CHAPTER 48

Samuel was taken aback to realize that over two hours had passed while he was with Rebecca. He took a moment to give the doctors and Millicent a brief synopsis of everything, and accepted Millicent's offer to bring them some coffee. Then he asked Tommy if he was ready to go see his mother.

Tommy had been chomping at the bit, anxious to see her, then worried what was taking so long, then anxious again. Now that the time was here, his knees felt weak and his legs refused to move.

Evelyn gave him a hug and a kiss, then a gentle nudge to get him moving. He didn't ask any questions going back, having heard what Samuel had relayed to the doctors.

He paused at the doorway, and peaked around the corner, unsure of what to expect. But when he saw her sitting there, all the years faded away and he was seven years old again. "Mama!" he cried out and rushed to her.

Samuel hesitated at the door, thinking he should give them some privacy and time to catch up, but Tommy let his mother go long enough to look back over his shoulder and say, "Get in here, Papaw!" and hugged his mother again.

He pulled back and Rebecca took his face in her hands. "My Tommy! So handsome! Stand up and let me get a look at you!"

Tommy stood up, puffing up his chest a bit, flexing the muscles in his arms, a wide grin on his face as she looked him over.

"So strong! Just like your daddy!" she told him, reaching out to take his hand.

Tommy motioned for Samuel to sit in the empty chair, and he knelt beside his mother, keeping her hand in his. They talked about how much they had missed each other, and how glad they were that she was back, and he told her a little about Evelyn and Chalmer, then he went to get Aubry, knowing how much she wanted to see her mother, too.

Sandi, the orderly, took the opportunity to wheel in a cart with coffee and Samuel poured them each a cup. Rebecca had just taken a sip and sat her cup back down, when Aubry stepped in the door.

"Mama?" she questioned, then immediately started crying. But she didn't move until Rebecca held her arms out to her. Even then the steps were faltering, as if she was afraid her mother would disappear if she made any sudden movements. When she reached Rebecca, she dropped to her knees and fell into her embrace.

Rebecca held and rocked her, letting her release all of her emotions. Aubry finally pulled back wiping her eyes, with a chuckle. "I'm sorry," she said. "I swore I wasn't going to cry!"

Rebecca pulled her close again, saying, "It's okay, my beautiful Aubry! We can cry all we want to today!"

"Good!" Aubry laughed, wiping her eyes again.

"Let me see your pretty face," Rebecca requested.

"It's probably not so pretty right now!" Aubry joked.

"You are gorgeous!" her mother told her. "Don't you ever forget that!"

"She's purty inside *an'* out," Samuel added. "Ya shore got ya some fine younguns, Rebecca."

"I've *always* known that, Samuel!" Rebecca agreed. "And I hear I have me a new little grandbaby!" she said to Aubry, brushing a tendril of Aubry's hair back from her face.

Aubry beamed! "You sure do! I can't wait for you to see him!"

They talked for a while until Millicent stuck her head in the door and asked if they were hungry, suggesting they go to the common area and have dinner together as a family, and Rebecca could meet everyone else that was waiting.

They agreed and Rebecca took another sip of her coffee before they made their way out to see the rest of the family. She insisted on walking with one arm linked through Samuel's, and one through Aubry's.

Faith ran up to hug her first. "Are you okay, Mamaw?" she asked, happy not to have to worry about saying the wrong thing now.

"I'm fine, my sweet girl, happy to see every one of you!" she answered, reaching out to take Adohy's hand. She pulled him to her, her face a portrait of seriousness now. "I am so sorry, Adohy, for what you went through. I promise I did not know you were there, and that I couldn't do anything to save you. And I will never be able to thank you enough for trying to save my Sarah, and for taking care of Faith. You will always have a place in my heart," she said, kissing him on his cheek, then hugging him.

When they were through, Aubry was standing by, her face lit up, presenting Horace and Horace Junior.

"Oh my goodness! Let me get a look at this big boy!" Rebecca sang out.

Aubry ushered them closer.

Horace couldn't contain himself. "His names Horace Junior, an' he's six months old now, cute lil feller, ain't he, an' he sleeps all night most a-the time, 'cept fer a while back, he wouldn't a-go ta sleep fer nuthin', 'cept fer when he was at school with Aubry, then he'd sleep with all them youngens makin all kind a racket, but ya get eem at home an' at bed time an' he's wide awake, thought we wuz ne'er gone get ta sleep agin, but he finely got it straightened out, an' he sleeps good now, an' he's already startin' ta eat fruit an' stuff that Aubry mashes up, an' his favrit is peaches, he prolly gets that from me cause I really like me some peach cobbler, or blackberry cobbler, that's good too, but Aubry ain't gave him none a-them yet cause a-the seeds, but I bet he'd like 'em too, 'cause

410

a-me, an' he's been a-rollin over already an' he's already tryin' a-talk, he's been a-tryin' ta tell me how purty he thinks his mama is, and she is, yeah, he's gonna be a talker, don't rightly know where he got that from, maybe from his mama, she likes ta talk—" Horace stopped and looked around when everyone busted out laughing.

"Come here and give me a hug!" Rebecca told him, still laughing. Then she kissed Horace Junior's head. "I need to sit down, now!" she chuckled.

A seat was pulled out and she sat down just as their meals were brought out. "Before we eat, I want to give my beautiful daughter-in-law a hug!" Rebecca told them.

Evelyn had stayed in the back ground, letting the family say hello, and she smiled that Rebecca remembered her. They shared a warm embrace.

"So beautiful!" Rebecca told her. "I know if Tommy picked you, that you are just as beautiful inside too! And you've proven it, by giving that little boy I haven't met yet, a home and a family of his own! Thank you for taking care of my family!"

"It's been my pleasure," Evelyn told her. "They all mean everything to me!"

"Then *you* mean everything to *me*!" Rebecca promised.

When everyone was seated, Samuel said a blessing, and when he was done and said "Amen", they heard from across the room, "AMEN! Aaaamen!"

It was Benny wheeling Oppy in for her dinner.

411

"Red!" Oppy yelled, waving to Rebecca.

Rebecca's face lit up. "Oppy! How are you?" she asked, when Benny rolled her up.

"Oh, fair to middlin', I reckon," Oppy answered. "Where's Carl got off to?" she asked, looking around. It was apparently one of Oppy's good days, but Rebecca was caught a little off guard.

Her face clouded for the briefest of moments, then she said, "Off shootin' the breeze with your other half, I imagine."

"Yer probly right! That sounds like 'em, don't it?" Oppy said.

The family spread apart and made room for Benny and Oppy to join them, and they enjoyed their meal together.

Millicent and the doctors took the opportunity to eat as well, happy to observe how well Rebecca was doing, from afar.

~~§~~

After they ate, Rebecca felt strong enough to hold Horace Junior, and while she did the family told her all about Millicent, Virgil, and Tenley, and how it was Millicent's idea to build the Home to help people in need, and to do it in Sarah's honor.

"I knew there was something special about her," Rebecca said, thoughtfully, sending a smile across the room to Millicent.

Acknowledging her, Millicent came to ask if they needed anything.

"Yes," Rebecca answered. "I need to thank you—"

Millicent started shaking her head, but Rebecca continued—"thank you for taking care of me, thank you for being my daughter's best friend, thank you for looking after my family, and thank you for building this Home and helping those who need it, in my daughter's name."

"There's no need to thank me. I am so happy I was in a position to honor Sarah this way. It has been a blessing to me, more than you know. I miss her every single day, but this may have never come about had it not been for Sarah, and her dear friendship to me."

"Well, thank you from the bottom of my heart, and I look forward to seeing Tenley again and meeting Virgil."

"That is going to happen very soon! In the meantime, I have some news I think will make you very happy. I'm not sure if you've been told how close to home you actually are, yet?" she asked, glancing around to everyone, as they shook their heads.

"It ain't had a chance ta come up, yet," Samuel admitted.

"The doctors and I have discussed this and I've come to let you all know that we feel there's no reason that Rebecca can't go home!"

Surprise and elation circulated among them.

"Now, I realize that it's short notice so—"

"No," Evelyn interjected, "Her room will be ready by the time she can get there, whenever she's ready!"

"How far away is it?" Rebecca asked, not sure if it would be too far to go today, after all the excitement.

They all pointed out the window. "See that house over there?" they said, in unison.

She looked and couldn't believe she hadn't noticed the house before. It was a little ways away, but not so far that she didn't recognize it. A peacefulness washed over her.

She smiled, and said, "Let's go home!"

CHAPTER 49

The afternoon turned into an impromptu family reunion, of sorts. Tenley joined them after they had dinner, then shortly after that, Virgil came to be introduced to Rebecca. While they visited, Evelyn and Faith slipped off to get the spare bedroom that had been Sarah's, ready for Rebecca. They were sure she would feel close to Sarah in that room, and draw some comfort.

The room hadn't been touched since Sarah's death, and they carefully packed up her things to sort out, at a later date. Other than that, there wasn't much to do, except sweep and dust, and put clean linens on the bed.

When they were finished, it was nearly time for school to let out, so they went to see how the children were doing. The room was quiet as the kids worked on their assignment. Jubal, it seemed, was a natural. The kids not only obeyed him, but looked up to him, like an older brother. And he enjoyed it. It made him feel good to know there was something he was good at, like his brother, Enos.

Evelyn and Faith collected Chalmer, and headed back to the Home. Now it was Chalmer's turn to meet Rebecca.

Chalmer was so happy to get out of school early he didn't care what the reason was, and Evelyn and Faith were so wrapped up in making sure everything was ready for Rebecca, they didn't think to tell him why. It wasn't until they were almost there and he realized where they were going, that he said anything.

"Did I do somethin' wrong?" he asked, interrupting them mid-sentence.

"What?" Evelyn asked. The look on his face just about tore her heart out. "What do you mean, Chalmer?"

"Are ya takin' me back?" he asked, his chin quivering. He knew it wasn't Halloween anymore, and no one told him about any party. And where was his papaw? And his daddy? They must have decided that they didn't want him anymore, like all the rest of them.

"Oh my gosh, Chalmer!" Evelyn exclaimed, kneeling down to him. "NO!" she pulled him to her. "I'm so sorry! We would *never* give you back! You are *our* son, now! You are a part of this family for ever and ever!" She held him back and looked into his eyes. "Do you understand me? We would never give you up!"

He nodded his head, but his bottom lip was still telling the tale.

"Honey, Daddy and Papaw are at Sarah's Home waiting for us, because we have a surprise for you!"

He stood a little straighter, and his eyes brightened. "A surprise?" he asked.

"Yes, there's someone there we want you to meet! Your family just got a little bigger!" she said excitedly, trying to boost his spirits.

"I'm a-getting' a brother?!" he squealed.

Evelyn looked up at Faith who laughed out loud. "Sorry," she said. "I couldn't help it."

Evelyn turned back to Chalmer. "No, it's not a brother," she answered. "*Or* a sister," she added quickly. "But it's someone I think you are *really going to like!*"

"Well, what are we a-waitin' on?" he said, his previous worries forgotten. He ran up ahead of them the rest of the way.

By the time they got back, the doctors had left their best wishes and bid the family farewell.

At the Home, he ran inside to his Papaw, and Evelyn told Tommy what had just happened.

The remorse on Tommy's face was palpable. "We gotta fix that. He cain't go a-worryin' all the time that we'd jes give 'em back anytime he messes up," he told her, looking at Chalmer with pain in his eyes.

"I know, I think I made it clear but it would be good for him to hear it from you and Samuel, too."

"We will," he said to Evelyn. Then he called to Chalmer, "Hey, Chalmer! Come here, son, they's someone I wantcha ta meet."

Chalmer left his papaw's side and ran to Tommy, taking his hand. They approached Rebecca.

"Chalmer, this here is yer Mamaw! And Mamaw, this here is *our son,* Chalmer," he made the introductions, putting the emphasis on the two words for Chalmer's benefit.

"My, oh my, would you look at this big boy!" Rebecca said. "Can you give your mamaw a hug?"

Chalmer obliged, but his brow was furrowed, deep in thought.

When they leaned back out of the hug, Chalmer scrunched his face up and asked, "Yer my papaw's wife?"

Tommy jumped into the conversation. "No, she ain't Papaw's wife. She's my momma, an' that means she's yer mamaw!"

Chalmer's brows were still knit in concentration. "So, how'd ya get ta be my mamaw, if'n ya ain't a-married to my papaw?"

"Because I'm your daddy's mother, and your daddy's daddy is in heaven, and Samuel is your daddy's grandfather, and *your* great grandfather, but you both call Samuel, Papaw, instead of great papaw. Does that make sense?" Rebecca asked.

"Yep. Why din't daddy jes say that?" Chalmer asked, like it would have been much simpler.

"I..." Tommy started, then looked around exasperated.

Everyone laughed.

"Anyways, it's 'yes ma'am' to yer mamaw, not 'yep'," Tommy reminded Chalmer.

"Oh, yeah!" Chalmer said. "Yes ma'am," he told Rebecca. "So, where ya been?"

"Outta the mouths of babes," Samuel interjected. "She's jes been away, but she's back fer good, now. That's all that matters."

That was good enough for Chalmer. He asked her, "So ya live here, now?"

"Well, I do, but do you think it would be okay if I came and lived with you?"

Chalmer's eyes widened and his brows raised. He turned to look up at his Daddy and then to Evelyn, and they both nodded. He looked back at Rebecca, and said, "Ya got yerself a deal!"

At that point, a woman came in the front door. She was accompanied by two officers. Millicent saw them, and while the Jenkins' family were busy celebrating, she went to see what they needed.

The officers asked if there was somewhere they could speak in private. Millicent quickly ushered them to her office, so not to disturb anyone else in the common area.

In her office, the woman took a seat when Millicent offered, and the two officers remained standing behind her.

"How can I help you?" Millicent asked, as she went behind her desk and took her own seat. She observed the woman. She was slight of build, and her clothes were clean but obviously well worn. She appeared to be in her late fifties, but that depended greatly on the kind of life she'd had.

"I think my boy may be here," the woman stated.

"Okay," Millicent said, wondering which of the boys she could be referring to. "What's your boy's name?"

CHAPTER 50

The Jenkins' family were still gathered in the common area, not wanting to go without thanking Millicent, and saying goodbye.

She was pale when she came back in the room, and clearly unsettled. Both heartsick and relieved to see the family still there, she'd known in her heart they wouldn't have left without telling her. On one hand, she was glad they would hear this news now, on the other, she'd hoped they would have some time to get settled without anymore disruptions. But it was what it was, and there was nothing she could do about it.

She'd come out to try to prepare them, lighten the blow somehow, before the officers and woman broke the news to them. She didn't know where to begin.

"There she is! We a wondered where ya'd got off ta," Samuel said, chuckling, when he spotted her.

Virgil noted Millicent's pallor, and asked, "What is it, Honey? Are you okay?"

"I'm fine," she said with a smile that didn't quite make it to her eyes. "But, I'm afraid there's some news that everyone needs to hear. I'm sorry, I know the timing isn't good, but it's out of my control." Her apology *did* reach her eyes, and she instantly had everyone's attention.

She looked back and nodded, and the officers and woman emerged from the hall, where they'd been waiting.

Instinctively, Adohy stiffened, and Faith reached over to squeeze his arm, her heart pounding in her throat, too.

A chair scraped back. "Mama?"

The woman rushed over to the table and wrapped her arms around her son.

Curious, confused glances made their way around the table, as the officers approached. But they stopped before reaching them, and stood by.

The woman pulled back and looked into her sons face. "I've missed you so! Are you okay? Have they taken good care of you?" she asked, searching for any signs of abuse.

He nodded his head.

Millicent began to explain. "There's some news that's just been brought to my attention, and as it pertains to all of you, I wanted you to hear it firsthand," she said, nodding to the woman to give her the floor.

The woman turned her attention to them. There was genuine remorse on her face. "I'm so sorry ta interrupt yer day. Mrs. Thornton here, told me that ya'd all jes got back together this very day, and it grieves me ta ruin it in any way. But they's somthin' that needs ta be set right, an' that's what I'm here a-aimin' ta do now."

Trying the meet each of their eyes individually, silently imploring them to be patient and understand, she went on. "Seems like forever and ago, I had me a son. He was a sweet lil baby. Hardly a-ever cried, 'lessin' his daddy, who was mean as a snake, would pinch eem, jes ta get eem a-cryin' so'd he could yell at eem ta shut up, or at me ta shut eem up. I tried my best ta keep eem quiet an' away so's he wouldn'a get pestered an' all, but tweren't no use. 'Fore too long he's a walkin' an' a-getting' tripped jes outta pure meanness. I'd a taken eem an' run away if I coulda, but I din't have no where's ta go. I din't have no kinfolk around, they wudn't no families nearby, ner someplace he couldn'a found us. They wadn't no place like this no place 'round then," she looked at Millicent and a few at the table, hoping they understood, then went on.

"So, 'fore long, my boy started a-actin' jes like his daddy. They wadn't nuthin I could do ner say, he got meaner by the day. An' I tried, Lord knows I tried, not ta get pregnant agin, but it happened. When my first boy was five years old, I had me anuther 'un. I tole his daddy he was sick, jes ta keep 'em away from eem, but after a while, they know'd it wudn't true, and they a-both started in on eem. He was such a sweet boy, din't have a mean bone in his body. An' that jes set his daddy off. Couldn'a hardly make this one cry, no matter what he a-done ta eem. An' that made it worse. When my boy was older, if he smiled at somethin', it'd jes set his daddy off. Time went by an' nuthin changed. I tried ta find somewheres ta go but ever'time I got a dollar or two hid, he'd find it tearin' everthin' apart. An' that's what happened that last time. His daddy went ta hittin eem, an' then when he was on the ground, he went ta kickin' eem. I was screamin at eem ta stop, I tried ta knock eem off a eem with the broom, an' that was when he finely turned his attention on me. He beat me til I blacked out."

One look at Adohy revealed the story had hit close to home, and you could visibly see the pain on his face. Rebecca and Faith had tears running down their cheeks at the horrifying story.

The woman went on. "When I woke up, my boy was hurt bad," she looked at her son with remorse in her eyes. "He was differnt after that. He din't smile so easily no more, din't laugh. I knew I had ta save eem, so I set out ta figger a way ta get eem away from ere. Then 'fore I could, he jes up an' disappeared. I jes knew his daddy'd done gone an' kilt eem, but what din't make no sense was his daddy kep accusin' *me* a hidin eem sumwheres."

"We went a while, both a-thinkin the other'n done somethin to eem, til he went ta beatin on me agin. He wouldn'a let up. I knew he was gonna kill me this time, an' I started to look forward ta the end, but then I jes couldn't. I couldn'a let eem, not a-knowin' where my boy was, so 'fore I realized it I stuck eem with the kitchen knife, an' run. I run til I couldn't run no more. I had nothin' but the clothes on my back. I run in the woods as far as I could ever day, til I came ta a town. Then I went ta a crick, washed myself n my clothes, an' went house ta house till I got me a housekeepin' job, with room an' board an a lil bit a-spendin money. I had ta get me some clothes, but other'n that, I stayed as close ta the house as I could. I couldn'a take a chance on eem a-findin' me. But I jes kep a worryin' 'bout why he kep accusin' me a-doin' somethin' to my boy, like he hadn'a-done nuthin'. It was eatin' me alive, so even though he'd learn where I was, I finely went ta the police ta see if they could find my boy for me."

She paused and took a breath. "I finely got me some answers, but they wadn't what I was hopin' fer. Ya see, it turned out that when I stuck his daddy that day, he died. I din't have no idear. They say the lan'lord came ta the house one day an' found eem. So they'd been a-lookin' fer me already. I told 'em 'bout what happened, an' they took me to see if a body they had was my boy. It was. But not this'n. It was the other'n that turnt out even meaner'n his daddy, like the devil hisself. The one that caused ever'body so much grief, that hurt yer family so much. It was Zeke. He cain't ne'er hurt y'all, ner no one else no more. An' I thank the good Lord above fer savin' my sweet Benny."

There was silence around the table as everyone tried to absorb and sort out what they'd just been told. It explained why the officers were standing by. All eyes shifted to Benny, when his mother wrapped her arms around him again.

It was a tender scene. They'd both been through so much. To say it was a relief for all of them to have Zeke's death confirmed would have been an understatement, but they were still reeling from the story. Adohy and Rebecca were the most affected by it, having been at the same hands themselves.

Faith turned her attention to them, guilt threatening to overcome her. She tried to put it out of her mind, but it was very hard to deal with the fact that it was her father behind all of this pain. Yes, he had been a victim, too, in his youth, but that didn't excuse what he'd done as an adult. Lots of people had been abused as children and still turned out to be a good person. Look at Adohy. And Benny. Then it struck her.

Benny was her uncle!

CHAPTER 51

Before allowing Irene Kufner to speak to the Jenkins family, or even her own son, Millicent got the full story from her, as well as from the officers. She then relayed to Mrs. Kufner what Zeke had since done to the Jenkins', including his harassment of Faith, Sarah's death, Rebecca's captivity and abuse, and Benny's abduction, captivity, and abuse.

Mrs. Kufner was very apologetic and told them she'd been aware of the rape of Sarah all those years ago, due to the authorities looking for her son afterward, and she'd heard about the fire and presumed deaths of the three of them. However, she was not aware that Faith was born as a result of the rape, and she'd only just learned that her son had been alive until his death this last year.

The officers went on to explain that depending on what they learned from the witnesses today, that Mrs. Kufner could possibly be held and charged with the murder of her husband, unless it was determined to be self-defense.

427

Millicent questioned how the body recovered from the scene, where Rebecca and Benny had been found, could be Zeke when he had presumably died after the scuffle with Adohy on the night of Sarah's death, when he fell off the bluff.

The officers reminded her that his body had never been recovered from the scene, and revealed that during their investigation, they had questioned a man that had admitted to giving an unidentified man a ride that night, who not only fit Zeke's physical description, but also appeared to be severely injured, and wet. But he had dropped the unidentified man off in what appeared to be a rural area with no homesteads, and they were unable to follow the trail further. The lead went cold. However, with Mrs. Kufner's identification, made possible only by her knowledge of the location and description of several broken teeth her son had acquired due to the abuse of his father, they found in his case file that his body was recovered in close proximity to where the potential witness had admitted to dropping the unidentified man off that night, last year.

Millicent told the officers that she had no firsthand knowledge of the abuse from either Mr. Kufner, or his son, Zeke, but she *had* witnessed, firsthand, the severe trauma that several of her close friends, including her own adopted son, had been subjected to, and *they could* testify that it was at the hands of Zeke Kufner. Even Sarah had told them who'd been responsible for her injuries before she'd died. She also confirmed the disability that Benny carried, to this day, was consistent with Mrs. Kufner's description of a brain injury due to trauma. She admitted that while it was possible that he could confirm his and his mothers abuse from Mr. Kufner, that unless his testimony made the difference between his mother's freedom or being charged with murder, she had to highly advise against it for the best interest of his mental health.

During this discussion, an idea came to her regarding Mrs. Kufner. Whether she acted on it depended greatly on what transpired between her, Benny, and the Jenkins', after Mrs. Kufner talked to them, as well as what the officers determined, as far as charging her or not.

After Mrs. Kufner told the Jenkins her story, the first person to react was Rebecca. She stood slowly, made her way carefully around the table, holding on to the backs of the seats on the way, and approached Mrs. Kufner.

Everyone watched silently.

Mrs. Kufner stood firm, but her face was washed in uncertainty, and the apprehension in her eyes increased with every step closer Rebecca took. She swallowed hard when Rebecca stood face to face, expecting and ready for the worst. Though she tried brace herself, she visibly flinched when Rebecca raised her arms, but she blinked in confusion when Rebecca's arms encircled her in an embrace.

Though the others hadn't completely formed an opinion of Mrs. Kufner yet, they were all leaning toward how Rebecca obviously felt, and her actions drove their feelings home for them.

Benny cemented it, "Amen! Aaammmeennn!"

His mother and Rebecca pulled him into the hug, too.

With the blessing of the Jenkins family, Millicent offered Mrs. Kufner a job with the housekeeping staff of Sarah's Home, including room and board, so she could be near Benny. It also provided her with a permanent address, to help with the officer's decision. They discussed the case with all of those present, and left Mrs. Kufner at the Home saying they were going to recommend that all charges be dropped and the case closed.

The Jenkins family ended up having supper at Sarah's Home with the Thornton's, Benny and his mother, and Oppy. It was comfortable, like they'd all been together for years.

Afterward, the women began to talk about household things, cooking, canning, sewing, and the conversation automatically turned to Sarah since she played such an important role, being the one to teach them they way their mother and mamaw had done things. Even Evelyn and Millicent had pleasant memories to share. They stopped abruptly, realizing that the conversation had to be uncomfortable for Irene.

"Please don't stop a-talkin' 'bout her on my behalf. Ya got ever' right ta talk about her, an' it keeps her close in yer hearts. I am sincerely sorry that she's not here no more, and ya missed all those years with her," Irene said, directing the last part of her apology to Rebecca.

They attempted to interrupt to tell her an apology wasn't necessary, but she asked if they would please let her say her piece, and they obliged.

"I would gladly give my life to trade places with her if'n I could. But I cain't. I kin see how much she was loved around here, she must a-been a beautiful soul, an' it ain't fair. I will beg God ever'day ta fergive me fer being partly responsible fer all the grief that was brought down on yer family, at the hands a-my flesh an' blood. But if'n it don't make ya too upset fer me ta be here, I would very much love ta get ta know her through each and ever'one of y'all, an' I'll do ever'thin' in my power ta make sure her memory lives on. I wouldn'a blame none a-ya if'n ya ne'er wanta lay eyes on me agin. An' I'll take my leave from here if'n it'll ease yore pain atall."

Rebecca assured Irene that she held no malice toward her, and all of the girls agreed. They knew she'd played no part in what Zeke had done. They explained to her that she'd asked for their forgiveness, and it was granted. She was part of their family now, including Benny, and that was all that mattered. And if it didn't make her too uncomfortable, they would love to tell her about Sarah.

Some tears and hugs were shared, and they began reminiscing again.

It warmed Rebecca's heart to know they all loved Sarah so much.

While the women were bonding, the men talked about work. Tommy and Horace had been clearing a new area to get ready for spring planting, but were having issues with a few tree stumps. They had been hoping to remedy the situation on their own, but the stumps had proven to be more stubborn than they were, so they took the opportunity to discuss it with Samuel and Virgil. After telling the older and wiser men the problem, Tommy asked, "We's a-thinkin' 'bout takin' the truck up yonder an' a-usin it ta pull the stump. Think it'll work?"

"Naw," Samuel said. "That dog ain't gonna hunt. Jes get it stuck and prolly tear the transmission outta it."

Virgil offered,"Why don't I come over in the morning with the tractor and pull them out? Won't take but a minute, and save y'all a bunch of work."

Tommy looked for Samuel's okay, before accepting.

"That's mighty nice a-ya, Virgil. If it ain't much trouble, I'm shore it help the boys out a lot," Samuel answered for Tommy.

"No trouble at all! Helps me justify buying it, to Millicent!" Virgil laughed.

Chalmer and Tenley had been coloring and playing with each other most of the afternoon, paying no attention to all the talk among the adults. Everyone noticed though, how Chalmer—normally rambunctious—handled Tenley with care, tending to her every need. That started whispers that Dolly *may just* have a problem on her hands.

~~§~~

Rebecca and Irene got settled into their new homes with ease. Rebecca got stronger daily, and began helping with the household chores, a little at a time. Irene was a blessing in disguise, showing Millicent's housekeeping staff a few tricks of her own and she kept them hopping. She and Benny were closer than ever.

A community get together was planned as a church social on Sunday, a week and a half after Irene came to Sarah's Home.

Unfortunately, there was inclement weather, so the social was moved indoors at Sarah's Home. Between the common area and large covered porch, there was plenty of room to accommodate everyone. It was *better* really, Millicent thought, because it allowed others from the Home that couldn't make it to the church, to join in as well.

In true neighborly Appalachian style, everyone pitched in, doing their part. The men helped set up extra folding tables and chairs everywhere there was room, and the women started putting out their covered dishes, and getting the tables set with plates and utensils.

Every person in the community came to church to give thanks and to the social to visit. Those who had known Rebecca were thrilled to have her back, and wanted to welcome her face to face.

Caleb said blessing, and everyone filled their plates and found a place to settle down to eat.

The spread of food was something to behold. The dessert table was overflowing. It looked like the only thing missing was homemade ice cream, but it was a bit cold and rainy for that. Faith had to hold onto Adohy to keep him away from it till after dinner. He still had a weakness for every kind of pie he could get his hands on.

Rebecca was awestruck with Faith and Adohy. She knew deep love. She'd had it herself. But there was something between the two of them that she couldn't identify or explain. It lit up a room.

Her heart was full, as she glanced around the room at her family and friends.

In just a week and a half, she'd come to love Horace and he'd finally got to the point he could talk to her without needing a speedometer. She could tell that he was warming up to her, too. She had especially fallen for her little grandson, Horace Junior. She'd had the pleasure of meeting Horace's parents earlier in the week, and they were there today seated at the same table with them. They seemed like fine people, who had raised a good boy, and she was sure they'd become close friends. Aubry had chosen the perfect man for herself, and had a beautiful family and lovely home. It was another feather in Sarah's hat for raising the children as she had, with Samuel's help of course.

Rebecca wasn't blind to the fact that her family had survived and thrived, greatly due to him. She'd loved him and her mother-in-law as much as she'd loved her own parents. They were good, honest, God loving people. When she looked at Samuel she saw an older version of his son, Carl.

She could see both Samuel and Carl, in Tommy. He couldn't have asked for better role models. And Rebecca thought Evelyn and her Aunt Millicent must have been gifts from God. She couldn't have hand picked a better wife for Tommy, or best friend in Millicent, for Sarah.

And Chalmer. He was just a huge blessing wrapped up in a little boy's body. He brought the family so much laughter and joy. Although, he seemed a little at odds today. He kept looking toward the door, and peering out the windows, as though he was expecting someone else, but she wasn't sure who it could be. Everyone they knew was there in the room with them. She made a mental note to find out what was going on, when they finished eating.

She spotted Jubal and Enos at the next table. She'd only met them the week before, but had learned about their plight before they'd come to Sarah's Home and their transformation with the love and care of Virgil and Millicent. The two of them were certainly special people, and they'd done so much, not only for their community but for others like Jubal and Enos. There was Chalmer. And Tenley.

Oh, little Tenley. She looked so much like Sarah did at that age, it sometimes hurt. But more often it brought special memories to her of her own precious daughter at the same age.

Rebecca heard Oppy laugh somewhere and found her seated at another table, surrounded by Caleb and his wife, Fred. She was thankful the Lord had brought Oppy and Caleb together, for her to love and care for him. Oppy was another really deserving woman that Rebecca was grateful to know. Caleb had obviously been good for her. And though she didn't know Fred well yet, she seemed to be the perfect fit for Caleb, and Rebecca noticed that Fred was positively glowing.

Seated at the table with Oppy, Caleb and Fred, was Benny and his mother. They'd had so much grief and heartache in their life. She prayed that it was all behind them now, and they would have happy, healthy lives filled with love here at Sarah's Home. She owed her life to Benny. Had it not been for him forcing her to eat, she'd have died in that shack with Zeke. She shuddered.

People were beginning to mill around now, their bellies full, but still gravitating toward the desserts. She could hear the instruments being tuned by the musicians, ready to have a good old fashioned hoe down.

She noticed Chalmer looked out the front door, peering in both directions, before turning back inside, looking solemn.

Rebecca mentioned it to Samuel, and he called Chalmer to them.

"Wha'cha a-looking fer, son?" he asked, concerned.

"Ah, it ain't nothin'," he said forlornly, kicking the toe of his shoe at an invisible rock.

"Well, why don'cha share it, an' let us be the judge a-that. You don't ever know. We jes might have a' answer," Samuel coaxed.

Chalmer sighed deeply, not at all sure sharing would help. But then, figuring it couldn't hurt, he relented. "It's jes, I been a teachin' Happy stuff all week, ever since last week when I hear'd y'all a-talkin. An' taday was the test ta see if'n he'd learnt any of it. But I don't reckon he did," he sighed again, looking over his shoulder toward the door.

Samuel and Rebecca exchanged a questioning glance.

"What were ya trying ta teach Happy, Chalmer?" Rebecca asked.

"See Mamaw, I din't want Happy ta be one a-them dogs that don't hunt, like Papaw said the other day. So I been a-teachin' him ta hunt." He hung his head. "I left a trail all the way here, but I reckon—"

A bark echoed around the room. Chalmer stopped mid-sentence. He slowly looked up. Another bark resounded. Chalmer's eyes lit up and got big as silver dollars. A smile spread across his face, before he dared to turn and look. When he did, he saw Happy standing outside the screen door, wagging his tail. He cast a grin toward Samuel and Rebecca and ran out the door to be covered in Happy puppy kisses.

Samuel and Rebecca chuckled at the two of them playing.

"So much fer him not payin' no attention ta us the other day, when we was all here a-talkin'," Samuel commented.

"I know," Rebecca said. "He's probably gonna outsmart all of us one day. He's special, that one."

"That he is," Samuel agreed. "That he is."

Desserts were sampled and shared. Music played. People danced. There was love all around, that day in Hurricane Holler.

Some people say that it was Sarah that brought everyone home.

"Amen, aammeennnn!" Benny could be heard shouting somewhere in the distance.

ACKNOWLEDGMENTS

It's impossible to say who had the most impact on helping to make this book a reality, from the people who requested it, to the people who did whatever they could to allow me time to write it, to those who read it chapter by chapter urging me for more, to those who proof read, those who offered advice for anything from recapping the first book to this sequel, to suggestions on the cover. I am going to try to thank everyone for their help, though they are in no particular order.

Ann Edwards ~ Mom, you are the most voracious reader in the family...so that would be reason enough alone for me to value your opinion on the merit of the storyline, but in addition to that I know that you are always honest with me no matter what. Plus you read enough to know what is good and what isn't, what's been done and what hasn't. Your opinion means the world to me! I can't thank you enough! I love you!

Vic Edwards ~ Dad, even from Heaven you were a huge inspiration and help in writing this book! I so wish you were here to see and read them yourself. I miss you more than you could ever know, and thank you and Mom from the bottom of my heart for all that you sacrificed personally to see that your family was taken care of, and raised with love, morals, and most of all, God. I love you!

Rodney, my dear husband, it absolutely thrills me to see your reactions and facial expressions when I read back to you what I've written in each sitting. It's a huge gauge in deciding if what I've written is good enough to continue on, or if it needs work! I can't begin to list everything you handle so that I can write uninterrupted! You are my hero! I love you!

Maresa Pezzulo ~ In spite of your grueling schedule with work, home, shuttling kids to and from the rink and everywhere else, you manage to find time to proof read, edit, and advise each chapter as it's written. You too, tell me how you see it and your opinion means so much! You catch things that I've looked at over and over and not caught! I wait with bated breath for your feedback, and truly value your help and opinion!! Thank you! I love you dearly!

Kimberley Pierce ~ One of my biggest fans, cheerleader, and kindred spirit! It's crazy how much alike we are! You are also a huge part of my writing process! You are my sounding board, and I truly value your insight and suggestions. No matter what's on your plate you have time for me and help me more than you realize! Thanks so much for everything you do to help me and promote my books! You are an incredible writer in your own rite! Thanks so much and love you bunches!

Anjelica Lewis ~ Wow! You tell me like it is! No holds barred! I can't thank you enough for that, even though it's scary sometimes! Lol! When I'm being hardheaded, you don't stop until I see your point of view! I can't imagine not having your input not only with my books, but spiritually! Thank you for being an incredible friend, and I love you to the moon and back! Thanks so much!

Bobbye Edwards & Carolyn Oglesby ~ My two favorite aunts! Thank you very much for being two of my biggest fans and supporters! Knowing how much you love and recommend my books warms my heart and is so encouraging! I love you both with all my heart! Thank you!

Cathy New Trumball ~ You are a very bright light for so many people that have the good fortune to know you! I have NEVER seen you without a smile on your face and a song in your heart, not to mention, all the good cheer that you spread to your friends and family! You have been so uplifting and positive with me during my roller coaster book writing journey. Knowing that you love the books I've written so far, and recommend them to everyone you know is truly a blessing to me! Love ya, beautiful soul!

Amanda Hook ~ You have to be the leader of the pack as far as promoting both my books, especially "Things He Hadn't Told Her"! I love that you got an autographed copy for your mother! I can't tell how much it means to me to see that you have recommended one of them when ever some asks in a book group! It is the very best form of advertising possible! Thanks so much!

The rest of my friends and family ~ I have countless others to thank for believing in me, and encouraging me to continue writing, for promoting my books, and just being there for me in general. If your name is not listed individually please know that it does not mean my gratitude for you is in any way diminished! Thank you all so much!

OTHER BOOKS BY VICKY WHEDBEE

- Things He Hadn't Told Her ~
  https://www.amazon.com/dp/B01M0JJNLP

- Sarah's Song ~
  https://www.amazon.com/dp/B072BMPSYR

Can I Ask A Favor?

Thank you so much for reading Sarah's Home! If you enjoyed this book, I would really appreciate it if you would post a short review. I do read all the reviews personally, so that I can continue to take my readers interests into consideration with what I write!

If you'd like to leave a review, then please visit the site where you purchased this copy. You can also leave reviews on my Facebook page ~ Vicky Whedbee. Please "LIKE" my page while you are there to see updates, or special deals on new books! I welcome contact from my readers! You can also follow me on Twitter! Another easy way to contact me is to visit my website!

https://www.facebook.com/vickywhedbeeauthor/

https://twitter.com/vicky_whedbee

https://crwvao.wixsite.com/vickywhedbee

Word of mouth is priceless! A sincere Thank You in advance for your support!

Made in the USA
Coppell, TX
10 April 2020